THE FIRST MOUNTAIN MAN
PREACHER'S
FRENZY

THE FIRST MOUNTAIN MAN
PREACHER'S FRENZY

WILLIAM W. JOHNSTONE

with J. A. Johnstone

PINNACLE BOOKS
Kensington Publishing Corp.
www.kensingtonbooks.com

PINNACLE BOOKS are published by

Kensington Publishing Corp.
119 West 40th Street
New York, NY 10018

PUBLISHER'S NOTE
Following the death of William W. Johnstone, the Johnstone family is working with a carefully selected writer to organize and complete Mr. Johnstone's outlines and many unfinished manuscripts to create additional novels in all of his series like The Last Gunfighter, Mountain Man, and Eagles, among others. This novel was inspired by Mr. Johnstone's superb storytelling.

All Kensington titles, imprints, and distributed lines are available at special quantity discounts for bulk purchases for sales promotions, premiums, fund-raising, educational, or institutional use. Special book excerpts or customized printings can also be created to fit specific needs. For details, write or phone the office of the Kensington sales manager: Kensington Publishing Corp., 119 West 40th Street, New York, NY 10018, attn: Sales Department; phone 1-800-221-2647.

PINNACLE BOOKS, the Pinnacle logo, and the WWJ steer head logo are Reg. U.S. Pat. & TM Off.

ISBN-13: 978-0-7860-4414-6
ISBN-10: 0-7860-4414-4

First printing: January 2020

10 9 8 7 6 5 4 3 2 1

Printed in the United States of America

Electronic edition:

ISBN-13: 978-0-7860-4415-3
ISBN-10: 0-7860-4415-2

THE JENSEN FAMILY
FIRST FAMILY OF THE AMERICAN FRONTIER

Smoke Jensen—*The Mountain Man*
The youngest of three children and orphaned as a young boy, Smoke Jensen is considered one of the fastest draws in the West. His quest to tame the lawless West has become the stuff of legend. Smoke owns the Sugarloaf Ranch in Colorado. Married to Sally Jensen, father to Denise ("Denny") and Louis.

Preacher—*The First Mountain Man*
Though not a blood relative, grizzled frontiersman Preacher became a father figure to the young Smoke Jensen, teaching him how to survive in the brutal, often deadly Rocky Mountains. Fought the battles that forged his destiny. Armed with a long gun, Preacher is as fierce as the land itself.

Matt Jensen—*The Last Mountain Man*
Orphaned but taken in by Smoke Jensen, Matt Jensen has become like a younger brother to Smoke and even took the Jensen name. And like Smoke, Matt has carved out his destiny on the American frontier. He lives by the gun and surrenders to no man.

Luke Jensen—*Bounty Hunter*
Mountain Man Smoke Jensen's long-lost brother Luke Jensen is scarred by war and a dead shot—the

right qualities to be a bounty hunter. And he's cunning, and fierce enough, to bring down the deadliest outlaws of his day.

Ace Jensen and Chance Jensen—*Those Jensen Boys!*
Smoke Jensen's long-lost nephews, Ace and Chance, are a pair of young-gun twins as reckless and wild as the frontier itself . . . Their father is Luke Jensen, thought killed in the Civil War. Their uncle Smoke Jensen is one of the fiercest gunfighters the West has ever known. It's no surprise that the inseparable Ace and Chance Jensen have a knack for taking risks— even if they have to blast their way out of them.

CHAPTER 1

The alligator lunged at Preacher, massive jaws wide open and sharp teeth ready to clamp down on him with flesh-rending ferocity and bone-crushing power. The mountain man dived out of the way and then flung himself back across the muddy ground, slipping and sliding a little on the bayou bank. The gator writhed after him, its tail thrashing wildly as it pursued him. Preacher had to leap straight up to avoid the next savage attack.

He turned in midair so he faced the same direction when he came down on top of the gator.

Preacher clamped his knees around the deadly reptile's barrel-shaped torso and yanked his hunting knife from the sheath at his waist. As the alligator curled its head around toward him, trying to reach him with those deadly teeth, Preacher leaned forward and rammed the blade into the creature's right eye as hard as he could.

The gator spasmed, thrashing so hard that it almost threw Preacher off. Even in the beast's death throes, those massive jaws continued snapping, so Preacher figured the safest place for him was still on top. He hung on, hugging that wet, scaly hide as he ripped the blade free and struck again and again.

The gator rolled over onto him. Preacher's ribs groaned from the weight. Then abruptly the burden lifted and Preacher found himself on top again—but only long enough for him to grab a breath and replace the air that had been forced out of his lungs.

The gator rolled onto him again and both of them tumbled off the mossy bank into the bayou. Water splashed high around them and flooded into Preacher's mouth, nose, and eyes. He gagged and spat out the stinky, slimy stuff.

A few yards away, the gator continued to flail and send water flying into the air with its futile struggles. Death had claimed the creature already, Preacher's knife having pierced its prehistoric reptilian brain, but that message hadn't caught up with the alligator's body.

Where one of the blasted critters lurked, there could be another—or more—Preacher reminded himself. Not to mention cottonmouth moccasins and who knew what other dangerous things. Best to get out of the bayou as quickly as he could.

As he pulled himself out of the water, a foot in a high-topped black boot stomped down right in front of him, squishing water out of the muddy ground. Preacher stopped and raised his head so his eyes could follow the whipcord-clad leg up to the burly torso of a man pointing a flintlock pistol at his face. From Preacher's angle, the barrel of that pistol looked about as big around as the mouth of a cannon, with the hammer already pulled back and cocked, ready to fire.

"You never should've come into the swamp, mountain man," the fellow said.

Preacher thought about the gator and everything else he had run into in this blasted muck and knew the man spoke the truth.

Preacher made his home in the mountains, and he never should have left.

St. Louis, three weeks earlier

"There she be," Preacher said as he reined Horse to a halt atop a brush-dotted hill with a view down toward the settlement sprawled beside the Mississippi River.

"I know," Charlie Todd said as he brought his horse to a stop, as well. "I've been here before, remember? Aaron and I outfitted here before we headed west."

Even after all this time, Charlie's voice still had a little catch in it when he said his friend's name. They had been close, and Charlie hadn't forgotten— would never forget—the terrible way Aaron Buckley had died.

"I know how you feel, but you're doin' all you can for him," Preacher said. "Takin' his share of the money from those pelts back to his family is more 'n a lot of fellas would do." He jerked a thumb over his shoulder to indicate the four packhorses on lead ropes trailing behind them. Those animals carried bundles of beaver pelts that Preacher and Charlie planned to sell in St. Louis.

Charlie and Aaron came from the same town back in Virginia, and the two young men had headed west together, looking to make their fortune in the fur-trapping business—and have some adventures along the way, to be honest about it.

They had found adventure, all right—more than they had bargained for since teaming up with the rugged mountain man known as Preacher.

"You're sure about not comin' back out here?" Preacher went on as he and Charlie sat on horseback, looking down at St. Louis in the distance. A faint haze of smoke from all the chimneys hung over the settlement, a sure sign of so-called civilization.

Charlie sighed and nodded. "I'm sure, Preacher. I've had enough of the frontier. You're cut out for it, but I'm not."

Preacher regarded his young companion for a moment. Charlie's time in the mountains had toughened him, honing away the soft pudginess, turning his fair skin bronze, giving his features a harder, more seasoned cast than they'd had when Preacher first met him.

But at the same time, Preacher knew the truth of what Charlie said. The young man had survived the wilderness and all its dangers, and he could be justly proud of that fact, but the time had come for him to go home.

"All right," Preacher said. "Let's go sell these furs."

He nudged the rangy gray stallion called Horse into motion and started down the trail made by thousands of saddle mounts and pack animals as fur trappers set out for and returned from the distant mountains. Ahead of them, the big, wolflike cur known only as Dog bounded on down the gentle slope, on the lookout for a rabbit or some other prey in the clumps of brush.

Suddenly, he stopped and stood stiff-legged, the hair on the back of his neck and along his backbone standing up a little.

Preacher heard the low growl that came from the cur's throat and reacted instantly. "Dog, hunt!" he yelled. "Split up, Charlie!"

He jerked Horse to the left even as he shouted the commands. From the corner of his eye, he saw Charlie veer swiftly to the right. Charlie had spent enough time with Preacher to know that he needed to follow the mountain man's orders immediately, without hesitating or even thinking about them.

At the same time, Dog leaped forward, low to the ground. As a rifle boomed from the brush, the ball kicked up dirt well behind the big cur. He disappeared into the growth, his thick fur making him heedless of any branches that might catch and claw at him.

Preacher guided Horse with his knees as he yanked two loaded and primed flintlock pistols from behind the broad belt at his waist. He saw a muzzle flash from the brush close at hand, followed instantly by the roar of a shot and a spurt of powder smoke. A low hum sounded in his ear as the ball passed close.

Thumbing back the hammer of his left-hand pistol, he pointed it and pulled the trigger. The weapon, double-shotted with an extra-heavy charge of powder, bucked hard in Preacher's hand, but his great strength controlled the recoil. The balls ripped through the brush, rewarding the mountain man with a cry of pain.

Somebody else screamed over where the brush thrashed around, and Preacher figured Dog had introduced himself to that ambusher. He threw a glance toward Charlie, still mounted and with his rifle at his shoulder. Preacher fired into the brush in the other direction.

Movement caught Preacher's eye as another man to his left stood up and fired an old-fashioned blunderbuss at him. Preacher had plenty of time to duck, and as he did, he turned in the saddle to bring his right-hand pistol to bear. Smoke and flame billowed from its muzzle, and the ambusher flew backward as if slapped by a giant hand. Preacher knew both balls had slammed into the man's chest.

The first man he'd shot wasn't out of the fight after all, he discovered a second later. The would-be killer burst out of the brush, shrieking in rage. Crimson coated the left side of his face from a wound that had laid his cheek open to the bone. One of the balls from Preacher's pistol had ripped along there, and it should have been enough to leave the man whimpering in pain on the ground.

Instead, he used the agony to fuel his anger. He had a tomahawk in each hand and whipped them around as he rushed toward Preacher and Horse.

The stallion trumpeted shrilly. Horse would have reared up to fight back with slashing hooves, but Preacher didn't want his trail partner to get hurt. He kicked his feet free of the stirrups, swung his right leg over Horse's back, and dropped to the ground to meet the assault. He barely had time to let the empty pistols fall to the ground and yank out his knife and his own tomahawk.

The wounded ambusher's arms moved in a whirlwind of motion as he slashed at Preacher, but the mountain man's reflexes were up to the task of avoiding the strokes. He darted and weaved, blocked some of the blows and ducked others, and then he closed in to launch an attack of his own.

The knife in his hand flicked out and sliced through the inside of the man's upper left arm. The blade cut deep, severing muscles and nerves, and the tomahawk in the ambusher's hand dropped from suddenly useless fingers.

The man swung the right-hand tomahawk, coming close enough to knock the broad-brimmed brown hat off the mountain man's head. That was the high-water mark of his attack, though. It had left him open to a sweeping stroke of the tomahawk in Preacher's left hand. The weapon smashed into the side of the man's head with the crunch of bone. His knees buckled, and Preacher stepped back to let him topple forward onto his ruined face.

Seeing no sign of anyone else about to attack him, Preacher turned to see about Charlie. The young man had drawn his pistol, and as Preacher watched, Charlie lifted the weapon and fired it.

Then he exclaimed, "Blast it!"

"He get away?" Preacher called with a dry tone in his voice.

Charlie turned in the saddle to look at him. "Yes, he made it to a horse and rode off. Shouldn't we go after him?"

"Not sure it'd be worth the bother. You did for one of the varmints, didn't you?"

"I think so—"

"Better be sure," Preacher warned him. "Nothin' more dangerous than a man you think is dead—but ain't."

With a wide-eyed look of alarm on his face, Charlie hurriedly dismounted and drew his other pistol as he stalked into the brush. By the time he came back a minute later, Preacher had already started reloading his pistols.

"The other one on this side is dead, all right," Charlie reported. He swallowed hard. "I, uh, shot him in the head. I aimed for his chest, but I guess the shot went a little high."

"Got the job done, though, I expect." Preacher tucked the ready pistols behind his belt again as Dog emerged from the brush with blood on his muzzle. Preacher nodded toward the cur and added, "So did Dog."

"Why did they ambush us?"

"Those pelts," Preacher said as he leaned his head toward the packhorses, which stood stolidly nearby, still attached by their lead ropes to Horse. "Some fellas think it's a good idea to lurk out here on the trail and wait for somebody to come along with a load of furs they're plannin' to sell in town. This ain't the first time I've been jumped by varmints like that."

"Highwaymen," Charlie said.

"Well . . . this trail ain't exactly a highway, but I reckon it's the same idea."

"What about . . . those men?"

"The carcasses?" Preacher swung up onto Horse's back. "I don't feel like buryin' 'em. Do you?"

"Not really," Charlie replied. "I can't say as I do."

The two men rode on toward St. Louis as, overhead, buzzards began to wheel slowly through the sky.

CHAPTER 2

They delivered their pelts to one of the still-operating fur companies and got a good price for them, but the deal was not as lucrative as those Preacher had gotten in previous years. The man who ran this branch of the company had known Preacher for a long time, and he gave the mountain man the best price he could.

As they left the business, Preacher commented, "I hate to think about it, but I can see a time comin'—and it ain't too long from now—when fellas won't be able to make a livin' as free trappers anymore, Charlie. The demand for furs ain't what it used to be even a few years ago, and all the companies want to hire a man to work for wages when he goes out trappin'." Preacher shook his head regretfully at the very idea. "When that happens, I reckon I'll have to look for a new line of work. I've hired on to do a particular job now and then, like goin' west with a bunch of pilgrims who needed somebody to guide and look after 'em, but I don't intend to collect wages regular-like."

"Nearly everyone in the world works for wages of one sort or another, Preacher," Charlie pointed out.

"Yeah, but I ain't nearly everyone in the world," the mountain man said. He weighed the pouch of gold coins in his hand, then opened the drawstring and took out a few of them. He held out the rest to Charlie and said, "Here. I've got as much as I need."

Charlie stared at him and didn't take the money. "We agreed to equal shares," he said. "You were already generous enough to set aside that much for Aaron's family."

"I've got plenty to pay for a couple of days here in St. Louis and then to outfit me for a trip back to the mountains. I plan on goin' back to that Crow camp and winterin' there with Hawk and Butterfly and our friends." Preacher smiled. "Any more gold would just weigh me down, son."

Charlie still hesitated, but after a moment he reached out and took the pouch from Preacher. "Thank you. I'm going to pass along Aaron's share of the extra money to his family."

"I expected you would. You're an honorable young fella, Charlie."

"You don't know how much it means to me that you think so," Charlie said, his voice thick with emotion.

With their newly acquired funds, they went to a restaurant to have a couple of thick steaks with all the trimmings. Charlie had already put aside the share of the profits he intended to deliver to Aaron Buckley's parents back in Virginia. He and Preacher had agreed that it would be a full third, even though Aaron had been killed before some of the pelts were taken, and now Charlie had the extra coins from Preacher's share to divide, as well.

Money was scant recompense for the loss of a son, as Charlie put it, but he couldn't do anything else. The past couldn't be changed.

They ate at Trammell's, a decent restaurant that

didn't go in for the sort of frills and finery that rich folks liked but served good, solid food at a decent price. The pretty, buxom waitress remembered Preacher from past visits, flirted shamelessly with him, and brought them cups of strong black coffee while they waited for their steaks, potatoes, and biscuits.

"That girl likes you," Charlie said when the waitress had gone.

"Molly?" Preacher grinned and shook his head. "Naw, she just likes to josh around with me. It don't mean nothin'. If I ever tried to take her up on any of the stuff she hints around about, she'd prob'ly run screamin' into the night."

"I wouldn't be so sure about that." Charlie sipped his coffee, leaned forward in his chair, and lowered his voice as he went on. "Now, look at that girl over there. The one sitting by herself in the corner."

Without being too obvious, Preacher looked. An attractive young brunette sat at the other table, well dressed but seeming to lack something of the decorum that a respectable lady ought to have. Of course, a respectable lady wouldn't be sitting by herself in a public accommodation, either. She would be with her father or her husband or, at the very least, her brother.

"Do you think she might like to join us, since she's alone?" Charlie went on.

"She's nice-lookin', all right," Preacher said, "but maybe not the sort of gal you should be takin' an interest in, Charlie."

"Why in the world not?"

"You said it yourself. She's alone."

Charlie stared at him for a second, then said, "Surely you don't think that means anything. I never took you for the sort to be judgmental about another person."

"I ain't judgin' nobody," Preacher said. "Just tryin' to look out for you, that's all."

"And you know how much I appreciate that. We're not in the wilderness now, though. I think I can take care of myself in a situation such as this." With that, Charlie pushed his chair back and stood up to walk toward the girl's table.

Preacher watched as Charlie spoke to her. He couldn't make out any of the words, but he saw the look of surprise on the young woman's face as if she hadn't expected anyone to talk to her.

Then she smiled, and her already pretty face became even lovelier.

"Well, if she's fishin', she just set the hook," Preacher muttered to himself.

Lucy Tarleton introduced herself after Charlie took her arm and escorted her back to the table he shared with Preacher. The mountain man saw now that she had a small beauty mark on her right cheek, not far from the corner of her mouth. It just made her more attractive.

"I'm pleased to meet you, Miss Tarleton," Preacher said with his natural chivalry.

"Oh, please, call me Lucy," she said brightly. "I don't believe in standing on a lot of formality."

Preacher had long since rejected any sort of formality for himself, but it bothered him to hear a young woman say such a thing. Ladies ought to consider proper behavior important, more so than hairy-legged ol' mountain men did. He knew that his friend Audie, who had been a college professor before giving up that life to become a fur trapper, would call him a *hypocritter*, or some word like that, but he couldn't help feeling that way.

Lucy had plenty of charm to go with her looks, though. Preacher had to give her credit for that. And to hear her tell it, her being out and about alone didn't mean anything scandalous.

"I'm traveling with my aunt," she explained, "and we have lodging at the hotel in the next block. She gets tired so easily, you know, and she decided she preferred to just go on to bed instead of getting something to eat. The hotel doesn't have a dining room, but the clerk told me this was the closest restaurant and a respectable place, so . . . here I am."

"Here you are," Charlie said. "And I'm glad you decided to come."

"Well, a girl has to eat. I'm just so thankful that you approached me, Mr. Todd, so I would have some company."

"Good fortune has smiled on both of us, I'd say."

"Indeed it has! And Mr. Preacher, too, of course."

"Just Preacher," the mountain man said. "No *mister* needed or wanted."

"How did you come by such an unusual name? It's not *actually* your name, is it?"

Preacher shook his head. "No, but folks have been calling me that for so long I sort of disremember what my real moniker is."

That comment stretched the truth considerably. His ma had named him Arthur, as he knew quite well. But he didn't feel like explaining that or how he had come to be called Preacher.

When he resisted telling the story, Charlie said, "Let me. I've heard it plenty of times."

Preacher sighed and waved for him to go ahead.

"When Preacher first began trapping in the mountains as a young man, he clashed with the Blackfoot Indians so often and so successfully that they came to regard him as one of their greatest enemies," Charlie began.

Lucy shivered a little. "Just the very idea of dealing with those bloodthirsty savages terrifies me."

"You can find plenty of good folks out there among the tribes," Preacher said. That included his own son, the young Absaroka warrior Hawk That Soars, who now lived with a band of Crow hundreds of miles from here. Preacher missed the boy, who had fought at his side in numerous adventures after their first meeting when Hawk was nearly grown.

"But not the Blackfeet," Charlie said. He had his own compelling reasons to hate them. "And one time when they captured Preacher, they decided to burn him at the stake."

Lucy shuddered again. "Obviously, they didn't. But what a horrible fate to be faced with."

"I wasn't lookin' forward to it," Preacher said dryly.

"Earlier, when he'd been right here in St. Louis, he had seen a man preaching the gospel on the street. So he began imitating that man. The Blackfeet hadn't gagged him, so even though they tied him to a tree, he started preaching and kept it up the rest of that day and all through the night, never stopping even though he was exhausted and his mouth and throat were as dry as the desert."

Lucy frowned across the table at Preacher and asked, "What did you believe you would accomplish by that? Did you hope for divine intervention?"

"I was hopin' them Blackfeet would think I was touched in the head," Preacher said.

Charlie nodded. "You see, the Indians won't harm a man they believe to be insane. They think it will bring down all sorts of bad luck on them. So even though they had Preacher in their power—a mortal enemy who has gone on to be a thorn in their sides for many years—they felt they had no choice but to let him go." The young man sat back. "So they did. And when other mountain men heard what had happened, they started calling him Preacher. The name stuck and that's what he's been known as ever since."

"What a thrilling tale," Lucy said with a breathless note in her voice.

"Didn't seem too thrillin' at the time," Preacher said. "More like scared and desperate."

"Well, I'm glad you survived."

"So am I," Charlie said. "Preacher has saved my life on numerous occasions."

"The two of you are partners in the fur-trapping business?"

"That's right. We just got back to St. Louis today with a season's worth of pelts."

"What do you do with them?" Lucy asked with a curious frown.

"Sell them, of course. That's where beaver hats and beaver robes come from."

The girl laughed. "That *does* make perfect sense. I just never really thought about where such things come from. Have you already sold those . . . pelts, did you call them?"

"That's right. Yes, we sold them to one of the fur companies that has an office and warehouse here. We received a pretty penny for them, too."

Preacher wouldn't have gone so far as to say that, but he supposed Charlie exaggerated in an attempt to impress the girl. Young fellas had been doing that since the beginning of time.

"Well, I've learned a lot today, and enjoyed your company, as well." Lucy drank the last of the coffee in her cup. "But I really should be getting back to the hotel so I can check on my aunt."

"I thought you said she'd gone to bed."

"She has, but the old dear might wake up and need something. She knew I was coming over here for dinner, but she might worry if she knew I wasn't back yet."

"I hoped we could continue our conversation—" Charlie began.

She gave him a dazzling smile and said, "Perhaps we shall. Are you going to be in town for a few days?"

Charlie glanced at Preacher and said, "We hadn't really made any plans yet." He didn't mention that he'd been figuring on heading back to Virginia as soon as possible.

He might have changed those plans some, though, after meeting Lucy Tarleton, Preacher mused.

"Good. I'm sure we'll run into each other again." Her brown eyes twinkled. "Say . . . for dinner here tomorrow?"

"We'll be here," Charlie responded without hesitation. "Won't we, Preacher?"

"Sure," the mountain man said. Let Charlie enjoy himself and end his Western adventures with a pleasant experience, he thought—although he didn't believe for a second that Lucy Tarleton wanted any sort of serious friendship with the young man.

But maybe he'd been wrong about the sort of girl she was, after all.

CHAPTER 3

If Preacher's true home lay in the mountains, then the tavern called Red Mike's served as his home away from home. He spent more time there than anywhere else whenever he visited St. Louis. He considered the burly, redheaded Irishman who ran the place to be a friend—even though Mike allowed all sorts in the tavern, including, in the past, a number of folks who had wanted Preacher dead.

Preacher didn't mind that. He had never figured he needed someone else to look after him and keep him out of danger. If he'd felt like that, he never would have set off for the mountains as a youngster, leaving behind his family's farm back east without any regrets.

Charlie Todd hadn't been to Red Mike's when he and Aaron Buckley were in St. Louis before. He hadn't even heard of the place at that time. He seemed to be having a good time on his first visit as he sat at a table with Preacher and drank a big, foaming mug of beer. Having supper with Lucy Tarleton had cheered him up considerably and made him forget about his gloomy mood earlier in the day.

As Preacher had explained, despite Red Mike's not being a fancy place, a fella could have a good time there.

"There's nearly always some music of an evenin', folks playin' fiddles and banjos, and if there's any Mexicans around, some gee-tars, and sometimes one of 'em will sing a lively tune. Most of the servin' gals Mike's got workin' for him don't mind dancin' a bit with the customers, either."

Some of those serving wenches didn't mind providing a different sort of female companionship, too, especially if coins changed hands. Earlier in the day, Preacher had had half a mind to see if he could arrange something of that sort for Charlie, but he didn't know how the youngster would take to the idea, especially now that he'd met Lucy and seemed smitten with her. He might see cavorting with some other gal as being disloyal.

Some of Preacher's friends among the other fur trappers in the tavern came over to say hello and catch up on the latest news among their scattered but tight-knit community. One of them, Jed Bannerman, surprised Preacher by saying that he intended to give up trapping and go back to his home in Tennessee.

"You've been in the mountains for years, Jed. What made you up and decide to call it quits?"

Bannerman, a hulking man with shaggy blond hair and a drooping mustache, shook his head. "Nothin', really," he said. "No one thing, that is. Just a feelin' that the time's come. It ain't like it used to be. The mountains are gettin' plumb crowded. Why, you might see a white man one day, and then see another 'un a week later! I recollect when I could spend a whole season out there and never set eyes on anybody that wasn't Crow or Shoshone or such."

Preacher nodded solemnly. "I know. It's changed, sure enough. But that's the way life is, and there's nothing we can do to stop it."

"No, I s'pose not. But if I'm gonna be surrounded by folks, I might as well go home and see some of my family while they're still alive."

Preacher raised his beer mug and nodded. "Good luck to you, then."

After Bannerman finished his beer and left the tavern, Charlie said to Preacher, "I think I might sit in on that poker game going on over in the corner."

Preacher cocked a bushy eyebrow and asked, "You know how to play poker?"

"Of course. Aaron and I used to play all the time back home with some of our friends."

"For what?"

"Money, of course." Charlie sounded vaguely offended that Preacher would ask such a question.

"All right. But just remember you plan on takin' Aaron's share back to his family, not to mention needin' some of your own share to get back to Virginia. You don't want to go broke."

"Of course. Anyway, I can't lose much, because I already hid most of the money back in the hotel room, just to be sure nothing would happen to it."

When Preacher was in St. Louis, he always stayed at Patterson's Livery Stable, where the proprietor, another old friend, looked after Horse and Dog and was happy to let the mountain man sleep in the hayloft. Even having a barn roof over his head made him feel too hemmed in at times. A hotel room, with its ceiling and walls and curtains on the windows and rugs on the floor, was enough to give him the galloping fantods, although he figured he would get used to it if he had to stay in such a place permanently.

Nothing beat the open sky with its canopy of stars at night, though. Preacher slept better out on the wild trails than anywhere else.

However, he understood why Charlie didn't feel that way. Charlie had had enough of the frontier. He had taken a room at a small inn not far from the waterfront. A boardinghouse would have been cheaper, but he wasn't planning on staying in St. Louis long enough for that.

"Besides, I can take care of myself," Charlie went on.

Preacher could have pointed out that on numerous occasions, that simply hadn't been true. But his young friend likely would have been insulted by that, so he kept his mouth shut.

He studied the men playing cards in the corner, though, as Charlie downed the rest of his beer, stood up, and moved in that direction.

Four men sat at the table. Two of them, judging by their buckskins and broad-brimmed hats, were frontiersmen, probably fur trappers. Another, going by his rough work clothes, was a riverman, laboring either on the docks or on one of the riverboats that plied the waters of the broad Mississippi.

The fourth man wore a frock coat over a vest and a white shirt and a string tie. The garb marked him as a professional gambler. One or two of that sort usually hung around Red Mike's. Probably, some were honest. Preacher felt an instinctive distrust and dislike for them, anyway.

Charlie waited until they finished with the hand they were playing. The frock-coated gambler was the one who raked in the pot, Preacher noted.

Then Charlie asked, "Mind if I sit in for a spell, gents?"

"I have no objection, my young friend," the gambler replied, "as long as you can pay the freight."

"I can," Charlie said.

The two fur trappers nodded, and the riverman muttered something, obviously agreeing because Charlie pulled back the empty chair at the table and sat down. The gambler had the deal, so he shuffled, cut, and began passing out the cards.

One of Red Mike's gals brought over another mug of beer and set it on the table in front of Preacher. He hadn't had to ask for it. They saw to his needs. He said, "Thank you, darlin'," then added, "Hold on a minute."

"You need something else, Preacher?" The tone of her voice and the bold gaze in her eyes made it plain she wouldn't mind providing whatever he wanted.

She seemed a little disappointed when he said, "You know any of those fellas playin' poker over there?"

"Besides your friend, you mean?"

"Yeah."

She cocked her auburn-haired head a little to the side. "I don't know the two trappers. They're new in these parts. The riverman's name is Dooley or something like that. He's a keelboater. We see him in here sometimes, even though most of the keelboat men do their drinking elsewhere. The fancy-dressed one is Edmund Cornelius. He's been coming around for the past couple of weeks."

"Honest gambler, is he?"

The girl shrugged. "There haven't been any shoot-ings or stabbings over the games he's in. That's all I can tell you, Preacher."

He nodded. The girl lingered, rested a hand on his buckskin-clad shoulder, and went on. "You're sure there's nothing else I can do for you?"

"You know I'm probably old enough to be your pa, don't you?"

"But you *ain't* my pa, are you?"

He grinned. "Not as far as I know. Might be best not to take the chance, though."

She laughed, shook her head, and went back to the bar. Preacher resumed watching the poker game.

The keelboatman won the next hand, but Charlie folded early and didn't lose much. The gambler took the next two pots, but again, Charlie played cautiously and lost only a small amount, as far as Preacher could tell. Then he won a hand and recouped most of what he'd lost so far.

Play went on like that for a while, with Charlie losing more than he won but winning often enough to keep him from going too far in the hole. Preacher watched the gambler, Edmund Cornelius, most of the time but also, now and then, studied how the other three men played. He didn't see any signs of cheating, which was his main worry.

After an hour, the keelboatman threw in his cards for the last time, said, "That's it for me, boys," and stood up. He didn't seem upset, just done for the evening. He left the tavern, and while Cornelius, who had won the last hand, shuffled the cards, Preacher got to his feet and ambled over to the table.

"See you've got an empty chair," he said. "Anybody mind if I fill it for a spell?"

"You're welcome to join us, friend, as far as I'm concerned," Cornelius said. "That is, if you have the money."

"I ain't broke." Preacher looked at the other two men, who nodded their agreement with his request to join the game.

One of the trappers said, "Didn't I see the two of you fellas sittin' together a while ago?" He nodded from Preacher to Charlie.

"That's right. We're partners. Been out in the high lonesome trappin'." The mountain man extended a hand. "They call me Preacher."

The man who had spoken grunted in surprise, but he clasped Preacher's hand. "Heard tell of you, plenty of times. I'm Hank Kanigher. This here's Bill Bridwell."

"And I'm Edmund Cornelius," the gambler introduced himself after Preacher shook and howdied with Bridwell, too. Cornelius took Preacher's hand in a firm grip, unlike the limp, cold, dead fish handshake many gamblers had. Evidently he had done some actual work at some point in his life.

If he had any idea of the real reason why Preacher had joined the game, he gave no sign of it. The mountain man wanted to get a closer look at the other players. He didn't intend for anybody to cheat Charlie and get away with it.

Charlie seemed to have a suspicion of Preacher's true motive, judging by the frown on his face. Like most young men, he resented being looked after, even though sometimes he clearly needed it. But he didn't say anything as play got underway again.

The other men talked quite a bit, though. The game itself, the money won or lost and the excitement of wagering, wasn't the only appeal of poker. The companionship meant a great deal, too. Kanigher and Bridwell talked some about their experiences while trapping in the Rockies, but having heard of Preacher, who had become something of a legend in that part of the country, they wanted to hear about his exploits.

"Is it true," Bridwell asked, "that you used to slip into Injun camps and cut the throats of some of them red devils whilst they slept, so the bloodthirsty varmints never woke up?"

Kanigher put in, "They had it comin', if you ask me."

"Only the Blackfeet," Preacher said as he looked at the cards Cornelius had just dealt him. "I've tangled with warriors from many another tribe, now and then, but they were honorable fightin' men, and even though we might be tryin' to kill each other, I never stopped respectin' 'em. The Blackfeet, though . . ." He tossed a coin into the pot. "I spose there must be a good one here and there, but if there is, I never run into him."

Charlie said, "They call Preacher Ghost Killer, because of what you just brought up, Hank—the way he can get in and out of their camps without ever being seen."

Cornelius chuckled. "You sound like quite a formidable adversary, Preacher. I'll take care to always stay on your good side."

"My friend and I were really lucky when we ran into Preacher, all right," Charlie said.

"You've got another partner?" Bridwell asked.

A solemn expression came over Charlie's face. "I

did. My friend Aaron. But . . . he didn't make it out of the mountains."

"I'm sorry to hear that," Cornelius said. "I guess you're not infallible, eh, Preacher?"

"Nobody is," the mountain man said, his voice hardening.

"Oh, I meant no offense. From what I hear, that wilderness out there is a dangerous place." The gambler looked around the table. "To be honest, I'm a bit surprised that *any* of you make it out of there alive. But I suppose the risks are worth it, eh? You get to live as you choose, then come back here and reap the rewards when you sell the furs you harvest."

"That's right," Charlie said. "We already sold our pelts and collected a tidy sum for them, didn't we, Preacher?"

"They didn't bring as much as they once did," Preacher said. He frowned at Charlie, hoping the boy would understand that how much they'd been paid for the furs wasn't anybody else's business. He'd already boasted a little to Lucy Tarleton, and now he repeated that exaggeration with these strangers.

"Well, it seemed like a lot to me," Charlie went on heedlessly. "I'm going to take Aaron's share back to his family. It's the right thing to do."

"Indeed," Cornelius agreed. "Very commendable of you. Now, gentlemen, what's the bet going to be?"

The game went on, the subject of the money Preacher and Charlie had gotten for the furs seemingly forgotten.

Preacher hoped that actually was the case.

CHAPTER 4

Early the next morning, Preacher showed up at the inn where Charlie had a room, having arranged to meet the young man there for breakfast. A bleary-eyed Charlie walked out of the building to join Preacher and head for a nearby café.

"I think I drank too much beer last night," Charlie said as he took his hat off and ran his fingers through sleep-tousled hair. "After all those months in the mountains without any, I suppose I'm not used to it."

"You'll feel better once you get a few cups of coffee in you," Preacher told him. "Are you startin' back home today? You know I figure on you takin' one of the packhorses with you for your supplies."

"I'm, ah, not leaving St. Louis just yet. I thought I might stay around here for a while."

Preacher frowned. "It's a long ride back to Virginia. Probably be best if you didn't wait too long."

"That's true, but I don't think a short delay will hurt anything." Charlie laughed. "You almost sound like you're eager to get rid of me, Preacher."

"Nope. But I'll be headin' back to the mountains

before long myself, to spend the winter there, and I'd like to see you safely on your way first."

Charlie said, "Why don't you come with me? I could introduce you to my family, instead of just telling them all about you. And you could help me tell Aaron's family about what happened to him."

Although he had made that suggestion before, Preacher didn't intend to take him up on it.

"I appreciate the invite, but St. Louis is plenty of civilization for me. Too much, really." Preacher paused, then asked, "Are you lingerin' here because of that gal you met yesterday evenin'?"

"You mean Miss Tarleton?"

"She's the only gal you actually know in these parts, ain't she?"

Charlie cleared his throat, and when Preacher looked over at him, he saw the blush on the young man's face.

"We did tell Lucy that we'd meet her for dinner at Trammell's again today, and I thought I'd go back to Red Mike's to play cards with Edmund Cornelius this evening."

"I ain't so sure that's a good idea."

Charlie looked sharply at him. "What's wrong with Lucy? I think she's a very nice young lady."

"I wouldn't know about that. She seems pleasant enough, I reckon. I meant about sittin' in on that game with Cornelius."

"You played cards with him."

"I did," Preacher said, "but mostly so's I could keep a closer eye on him and make sure he didn't try to cheat you."

Charlie's eyes widened. "What in the world made you think he'd do that?"

"The fella *is* a professional gambler."

"Well, he didn't cheat me," Charlie insisted.

"You came out on the losin' end of the game last night, didn't you?"

"Yes, but I only lost a couple of dollars, total. That's not much, considering how long we played. And *you* won a few dollars, as I recall. Did you see any sign that Edmund might be cheating?"

"No, I didn't," Preacher admitted. "There's just somethin' about the fella that makes me not trust him."

"Don't worry. I'll be careful."

Maybe Charlie was right, Preacher mused. Maybe he had no reason to be so suspicious. His instincts had kept him alive this long, though, so he tended to trust them. And Charlie, bless his heart, was maybe a mite *too* trusting.

Young fellas had to make their own mistakes and learn from them. With luck, such mistakes wouldn't prove to be fatal.

The sun slanting in through a gap in the curtains over the window made Edmund Cornelius groan as it struck his eyes. For that very reason, he never liked having a hotel room on the east side of a building. Waking up before noon always seemed downright depressing to him. For that very reason, among others, he followed a profession in which he could sleep during the day and go about his business at night.

Not today, though. Today he and his partner would accomplish their current goal while the sun loomed high overhead. At its zenith, in fact, if all went according to plan.

Cornelius groaned again and rolled over. That brought him face-to-face with the young woman still sleeping next to him. Cornelius reached out with a long-fingered hand made for dealing cards and moved aside a wing of thick brown hair that had fallen in front of her face.

"Wake up, Lucy," he said.

Lucy Tarleton stirred, made some distinctly unladylike noises, and then opened her eyes. She winced at the brightness in the room. "Edmund, why are you bothering me at the crack of dawn?"

"It's long past dawn, my dear. In fact, judging by the light I'd say it's the middle of the morning. We have to get up so we can prepare for this day's work."

She stifled a yawn and asked, "How difficult can it be? That fat fool doesn't know we're working together. He doesn't even have any idea that we know each other."

Cornelius sat up, partially dislodging the sheet draped over Lucy's exquisite, unclad form. The sight of her bare, creamy skin distracted him quite a bit, but he forced his mind back onto more important things. "We need to pack. I want all our bags ready to be taken down and loaded on the *Majestic* before noon. She casts off at twelve-thirty."

"I know. We'll have plenty of time." Lucy sat up and stretched, distracting Cornelius even more. "He's supposed to meet me at the restaurant at noon. I'm certain he'll wait there for at least half an hour before he figures out that I'm not coming. And even then, he won't want to admit it, even to himself. He'll wait around longer, hoping that he's wrong."

"You seem very sure of that."

"I should be." She smiled as she lifted her arms and ran her fingers through her hair. "I know men."

"Yes, I suppose you know them very well," Cornelius said. "You should, by now. We've been working together for a year, and I'm hardly your first partner in crime, am I?"

She glared at him and snapped, "It's not a crime when you're taking money away from someone that foolish. Can you believe he actually *told* me he planned to hide that pouch full of gold coins in his hotel room? He thinks it will be safer there! He deserves to lose them."

"Where was the mountain man when Charlie told you this?" Cornelius wanted to know. He didn't trust anyone, certainly not the men they targeted to rob.

"He'd stepped out to visit the privy. I think Charlie was trying to impress me with his intelligence while Preacher was gone."

A worried frown creased the gambler's forehead as he said, "Perhaps we should wait until Preacher has left St. Louis. From the things I've heard about him, he's a bad man to have as an enemy. A *very* bad man."

Lucy threw back the sheet the rest of the way, swung her legs out of bed, and stood up. The morning light made a figure of golden beauty out of her, almost like a statue come to life, lovely enough to take any man's breath away.

"I'm not worried about Preacher," she said. "If we wait too long, Charlie might decide to leave town first, and then where would we be?"

"You could make him linger, though, couldn't you?"

"I can make him do whatever I want," Lucy purred. "But it's not necessary. Just be at his hotel a little before noon and search his room. It won't take you long to find the money, I'm sure. There are only so many hiding places. I'll meet you at the riverboat and we'll be miles down the Mississippi toward New Orleans before Charlie ever knows what's happened. He'll never find us, and neither will Preacher."

"Don't underestimate that mountain man," Cornelius said.

Lucy laughed. "Preacher may be a force to be reckoned with in the mountains, but we're going to New Orleans. An uneducated lout like him would never stand a chance there!"

CHAPTER 5

After breakfast, Preacher and Charlie went to Higginbotham's Mercantile, where Preacher usually picked up the supplies he needed for his trips to the mountains. He visited with the proprietor for a while before giving the man the list of the goods he wanted to purchase. Since Preacher didn't know for sure when he would leave town, they reached an agreement that the supplies would be packed up and stored there until the time came for him to collect them.

As they left the store, Charlie said, "You know everybody in St. Louis, don't you?"

"No, not hardly," Preacher replied. "But I've been goin' to the mountains for quite a spell and doin' business with folks here for that long, too. It makes sense I've gotten to know some of 'em pretty well."

They walked around the sprawling settlement for a while. As they strolled along the riverfront, Charlie paused to look at a side-wheeler tied up at one of the wharves. The large, impressive boat had the name *Majestic* lettered across its stern. Workers loaded cargo on it in anticipation of its obviously imminent departure.

"Have you ever ridden on one of those, Preacher?" Charlie asked the mountain man.

"Yep, several times. Went up the Missouri on one of 'em a few years back. Ran into all kinds of trouble, too."

Charlie chuckled. "Somehow, that doesn't surprise me. Have you ever gone anywhere you *didn't* run into trouble?"

"I'm sure I have." With a frown, Preacher went on. "Got to admit, though, right now I can't think of where it might've been."

As they continued walking around St. Louis, Charlie talked about Lucy Tarleton. Clearly, the girl had made a big impression on him.

"She's very devoted to her aunt, you know," Charlie said. "They travel together frequently."

"How come?"

Charlie frowned. "You mean, why is she devoted to her aunt?"

"No, I mean how do they come to do all that travelin'?"

"Well, I"—Charlie's frown deepened—"I don't know. She never really explained that part. I suppose they just enjoy traveling. Some people do. You should understand that, since you're always on the move yourself."

"Yeah, I'm a fiddle-footed sort," Preacher admitted. "Don't see that very often in ladies, though."

"I'll ask her when we meet for dinner later at the restaurant," Charlie said. "That is, if I can come up with a way to do so without seeming to pry too much. I mean, it's really not any of our business, is it?"

"Reckon not." Preacher waited a few moments, then asked, "Where are they from?"

"Lucy and her aunt?" Charlie sounded a little irritated now, rather than puzzled. "She never said. I didn't demand answers to such questions, though. We simply had a pleasant conversation, and the subjects you're addressing now never came up." Charlie paused, then said, "You still think there's something suspicious about her, don't you?"

"I'm just sayin' it's a good idea to be careful, especially when you're dealin' with somebody you don't know much about."

"Aaron and I didn't know *anything* about you when we met you," Charlie pointed out.

"And maybe you'd have been better off if you hadn't run into me," Preacher said.

Without hesitation, Charlie shook his head. "No, I don't believe that. Even with the way everything worked out, I'm richer for having known you, Preacher, and Aaron was, too. He said as much to me more than once." His voice caught a little. "I . . . I don't think he would have traded the time we spent in the mountains for anything."

"Well . . . I hope that's true. Come on. Let's amble toward Trammell's. It'll be gettin' close to dinner time when we get there."

At the restaurant, a waitress showed them to a table and brought them cups of coffee while they waited. When they sat down, the midday crowd hadn't arrived yet, but as time passed, more and more people came into the place.

Not Lucy Tarleton, though.

Charlie's forehead creased in a frown again. "I

hope everything is all right. I expected her to be here by now."

"Maybe her aunt ain't feelin' well," Preacher suggested.

"Assuming she even *has* an aunt. That's what you're thinking, isn't it? That she lied to us? To me?"

"Well, we ain't met the old lady," Preacher pointed out, "but that don't mean she ain't real. I'm just sayin' there's all sorts of things that could've happened to delay Miss Tarleton."

"I suppose you're right," Charlie said grudgingly. As the time continued to pass with no sign of Lucy, though, his distress grew.

Finally, after taking out his pocket watch and checking it, he said, "I'm going to the hotel to make sure she's all right."

"All right," Preacher said as he started to get to his feet. "I don't reckon that would hurt anything."

Charlie waved him back into his chair. "If you don't mind, I'd rather you stay here. That way, if I miss her and she *does* show up, you can tell her where I am and that I'll be back shortly."

Preacher sat back and shrugged. "If that's what you want me to do."

"It is. Thank you, Preacher."

"Nothin' to thank me for. I ain't doin' nothin' except sittin' here drinkin' coffee."

Charlie hurried out of the restaurant. The waitress came over and asked Preacher, "Is anything wrong?"

"Nope. My friend'll be back." Preacher paused, then added, "He's just young and maybe thinks a mite too much."

The hotel where Lucy Tarleton and her mysterious aunt had a room was just in the next block, Preacher reminded himself. He didn't figure Charlie could get into any trouble in broad daylight, in the middle of St. Louis.

Charlie stared across the counter at the hotel clerk. "What do you mean, there's no Miss Tarleton staying here?"

The clerk apparently couldn't resist the temptation to smirk, as hotel clerks tended to do. He said, "I'm sorry, sir," without sounding as if he meant it, then added, "Perhaps you got the young lady's name wrong."

"No, it's Miss Lucy Tarleton, I'm sure of it. She's staying here with her aunt."

The clerk raised an eyebrow and asked, "And the aunt's name?"

"I . . . I don't know," Charlie had to admit. "Miss Tarleton never mentioned it."

"Well, then, I don't see how I can help you."

The man's smugly superior tone made Charlie want to lunge across the desk, grab his shirtfront, and hold a knife to his throat. See if he felt like smirking and sneering then! Charlie had fought white renegades and Blackfoot warriors and survived all those adventures with Preacher. No blasted hotel clerk could look down his nose at him and get away with it!

But Charlie didn't do that, because worry and confusion over Lucy occupied his mind instead. Had she lied to him? Had Preacher been right to be suspicious of her? As much as he admired the mountain man, Charlie had to admit he hoped Preacher had been wrong in this case.

He muttered his thanks and walked out of the hotel, seeming to feel the clerk's arrogant gaze on his back. When he reached the street, he started to turn back toward Trammell's, but then he stopped short. He remembered how he had told Lucy about hiding the money from the furs in his room.

He didn't want to consider even the possibility that she might be a thief, but *something* was wrong, no doubt about that. There might be many excuses for Lucy being late to arrive at the restaurant, but not for her lying to him about where she was staying. He wanted to find out the truth before he saw Preacher again. Maybe he could regain some respect in the mountain man's eyes if he got to the bottom of this.

With that thought in mind, he turned his steps toward the inn where he had spent the night. If Lucy really was after his money, maybe he could catch her there. And if she wasn't, he could at least get the pouch of coins and make sure it was safe.

Within a block, he was running.

CHAPTER 6

The inn, a narrow, one-story building, had no real amenities such as a bar or dining room, just a desk up front and rooms where the guests stayed lining either side of a long hallway. Charlie had a room on the right side of the corridor, almost all the way in the back.

A slatternly older woman sat in a rocking chair behind the desk, a big orange tomcat in her lap.

Charlie asked her, "Has a young woman been here? Brown hair, very attractive?"

"Lookin' for you, you mean?" The woman laughed. "Nobody like that. Could've come in the back, though, I reckon."

A back door opened into an alley behind the place, Charlie recalled. People could come and go that way without being seen. He supposed some people preferred that arrangement.

He turned and hurried along the hall, ignoring the questions the old woman called after him. At one point, she screeched indignantly, "This is a decent place, you know!"

Charlie had begun to doubt that. He also thought that he had been a fool to leave his money here. He'd been trying to be safe, and instead he had done one of the worst things he could possibly do.

But maybe he still had a chance to make things right.

He saw the closed door of his room as he approached and thought for a second that all his wild imaginings had been just that—crazy thoughts with no basis to them. But then he heard a noise inside, not a loud crash, but still the sound of something falling over.

Charlie grasped the door knob, twisted it, and threw the door open. With his heart pounding, he stepped into the room and said, "Lucy, I can't believe—"

He stopped short as he saw that Lucy Tarleton hadn't broken into his room, after all.

Edmund Cornelius stood there instead, and in his left hand, the gambler held the leather pouch containing Charlie's money.

A bitter curse ripped from Cornelius's throat. He glanced toward the single small window, looking for a way out, perhaps, then said, "Lucy was so sure you wouldn't come back here this soon, blast her!"

For a second, Charlie's spirits had soared at the sight of Cornelius, even though he knew the gambler meant to steal all his money. He had enjoyed the card game the night before, but he felt no real affection for the man. For that precious instant, Lucy had been blameless again in his mind.

Then it had all come crashing down once more because of the man's startled exclamation, even worse because it meant that Cornelius and Lucy had been working together all along. They had moved in on him like a pair of wolves stalking and then attacking a helpless sheep.

That described him pretty well, he thought.

Rage and humiliation roared up inside him like a flooding river. He took a step toward Cornelius.

The gambler held up his right hand, palm out, and said, "Hold on there, boy. You don't want to do this. It's only money. You can earn more."

"You . . . you . . . She *tricked* me!"

Cornelius laughed. "You think you're the only man who's ever been tricked by a woman? It's what they do! They tell you what you want to hear until they get what they want, then they snatch it all out from under you! You're not too young to learn that. You'll be better off in the long run if you do."

Charlie stuck out his hand and said, "Give me that. It's mine."

Cornelius appeared to be a well-built man, as far as Charlie could tell, but he had been in numerous desperate fights during his time in the mountains. He had killed men. He could handle one gambler—

Cornelius lunged at him, snake-quick, as the man's empty hand darted under his coat and came out holding a dagger. Charlie felt the blade's bite in his mid-section, also like a snake, and reeled back. Cornelius crowded in and struck again.

Charlie gasped in pain as the cold steel invaded his body. He flailed out at the gambler but couldn't seem to put any real strength behind the blows. Cornelius stabbed him yet again. Charlie's knees buckled.

As he fell, Cornelius kicked him in the face. The brutal attack knocked Charlie onto his back. The hot, wet, terrible pain in his middle swelled enormously until it threatened to swallow him whole. It hurt so bad he hadn't really noticed that much when Cornelius kicked him.

Something moved between him and the light from the window. Charlie forced his eyes to focus and saw Cornelius leaning over him. The knife moved toward Charlie's throat, as if the gambler intended to slash it and end his life. But then Cornelius stopped and chuckled.

"No need," he said. "You'll bleed to death soon. And in the time you have left, you can think about what a fool you are, boy. That's what she called you, you know—a fat fool." He straightened, bounced the pouch of coins on the palm of the hand not holding the knife. "Feels like not quite as much as I'd hoped, but it should be plenty to get us to New Orleans."

Cornelius wiped the blade on Charlie's coat, then sheathed it under his coat and moved to the door. He opened it, looked back, and said, "Good-bye, Charlie."

Then he stepped out and closed the door behind him, leaving Charlie lying there on the floor in the dingy rented room, bleeding his life out as the light faded more and more.

As Preacher sat in the restaurant and sipped his coffee, his instincts told him that Lucy Tarleton would not show up. He couldn't have said why he felt so sure about that, but he didn't doubt it for a second.

Charlie would be upset with him if he left, though, so he stayed there for a while, until his gut began to insist something bad had happened. Preacher didn't make a habit of sitting around brooding. He stood up, dropped a coin on the table to pay for the coffee, and stalked out of the restaurant.

It took him only a minute to walk to the next block and find the hotel where Lucy and her aunt had a room. When he went inside and asked the clerk about them, however, the man scowled.

"Why do people keep coming in and asking about a woman who doesn't exist, as far as I know?"

"What do you mean by that?" Preacher asked.

"You're the second fellow to inquire about someone named Miss Tarleton. If she's real, she must be telling lies about where she's staying, because she's not here." The man's lips curled. "Perhaps she's the sort of woman who doesn't want a man to know where to find her once their business is concluded."

Even though Preacher had harbored similar suspicions about Lucy, he didn't like hearing this oily varmint saying the same thing. In a hard voice, he said, "Who else asked about her? A stocky young fella with a short brown beard?"

"That's right," the clerk admitted. "Is he a friend of yours?"

Preacher ignored that question and asked another of his own. "You told him Miss Tarleton ain't here?"

"What else could I tell him? It's the truth. No one by that name has ever stayed here, as far as I recall."

"Where'd he go?"

The clerk's narrow shoulders rose and fell. "I have no idea."

"Did you see which way he turned when he left here?"

The man considered, then said, "Toward the river, I believe."

The inn where Charlie had a room lay in that direction, Preacher thought. The youngster might have headed over there once he found out that Lucy had lied to him. He would want to make sure the money he'd left there hadn't been stolen.

Without saying anything else to the clerk, Preacher stalked out of the hotel. His long legs carried him toward the inn, and when he got there, he said to the old woman at the desk, "Where's Charlie Todd's room?"

"Fifth door on the right," she told him.

"You know if he's here?"

"He came in about twenty minutes ago. Ain't seen nor heard anything from him since, so I reckon he still is. 'Less 'n he went out the back."

Charlie must have come here directly from the hotel, Preacher thought as he strode along the dim corridor. When he came to the fifth door, he banged a fist on it and called, "Charlie! Are you in there?"

No answer came, but Preacher frowned as he thought he heard something from the other side of the panel. He leaned closer to the door and turned his head, trying to catch the sound.

A faint rasping noise came to his ear. For a couple of seconds, he couldn't tell what it was, then he stiffened as he realized he was listening to the harsh sound of someone struggling to breathe.

He flung the door open with his left hand while his right closed around the butt of one of the pistols stuck behind his belt. He didn't pull the gun, but he could bring it into play quickly enough if he needed to.

No threat lurked in the room, however.

Only a crumpled body lying on the floor in a pool of blood.

Charlie.

CHAPTER 7

At first glance, Preacher thought anybody who had lost that much blood ought to be dead. Charlie's chest still rose and fell, though, and Preacher had been able to hear his harsh breathing all the way out in the hall.

He dropped to his knees beside the young man. From the looks of the bloodstains on Charlie's clothes, somebody had stabbed him three times. Preacher knew his young friend hadn't been shot. Pistol balls would have ripped through Charlie's shirt in a different manner, and the old crone up at the desk would have heard the gunfire and probably run screeching into the street.

Preacher slid his left hand under Charlie's head and propped it up a little. In response, Charlie's eyelids fluttered for a few seconds and then stayed open. He seemed to have trouble focusing his gaze, though.

"Wh-who . . ." he asked in a weak voice barely above a whisper.

"It's Preacher, Charlie. Preacher. You hang on. You're hurt bad, but you're gonna be all right."

Charlie's eyes finally swung toward the mountain man and locked in on him. "P-Preacher?"

"That's right. Who done this to you, Charlie?" Preacher's voice took on the hardness of flint as he went on. "Was it that gal?"

"L-Lucy . . . No . . . not . . . Lucy . . ."

That answer surprised Preacher a little. But hurt as bad as Charlie appeared to be, maybe he couldn't think straight. Lucy might still be to blame for what had happened.

"Cornelius . . ." Charlie rasped.

Preacher leaned closer to him. "Edmund Cornelius, the gambler? He's the one who stabbed you?"

"And stole the m-money."

Preacher bit back a curse. His instincts had warned him about Cornelius, too. But how had Cornelius known about the pouch of gold coins hidden in this room? Charlie had told only Lucy Tarleton—

As if Charlie had read his mind, the young man forced out, "He and . . . Lucy . . . working together . . ."

"I'll find 'em," Preacher vowed. He could digest what Charlie had just told him about Lucy and Cornelius being partners later. Right now, getting some help for the young man mattered more than anything else.

Charlie lifted a hand, though, clutched feebly on the sleeve of Preacher's buckskin shirt. "Nuh . . . nuh . . . New Orleans! That's where . . . they're g-going . . ."

His hand fell away from Preacher's arm and his head sagged back. Preacher thought he had died, but the raspy sound of Charlie's breathing continued. As gently as possible, Preacher lowered Charlie's head to the floor.

He stood up, went to the door, and shouted down the hall to the old woman, "Hey! Fetch a doctor!"

"What?" she called back in a querulous voice.

"A doctor, blast it! Now!"

"All right, all right," the woman said. She shuffled out, carrying her cat with her.

Preacher turned back to Charlie. The mountain man's thoughts whirled in his head. Charlie's life mattered more than anything else at the moment, but fires of anger already burned inside Preacher. Lucy Tarleton and Edmund Cornelius had been working together all along, according to Charlie, and Cornelius had stabbed him. But to Preacher's way of thinking, if Lucy had been in on it, she deserved some of the blame, too.

Preacher didn't forget about the money, either. Even though he had handed over most of his share to Charlie, it had started out belonging to him, and he felt like he had been robbed, too. That rubbed Preacher the wrong way and called for revenge, just as the attack on Charlie did.

Charlie had said that Cornelius and Lucy were going to New Orleans. Preacher didn't know how Charlie had found that out, but he believed his young friend.

The best way to get from St. Louis to New Orleans involved boarding one of the riverboats that traveled up and down the Mississippi. He and Charlie had seen one of those boats being loaded this very morning, and it seemed likely that Cornelius and Lucy intended to take it downriver to the Crescent City. Preacher had no idea when it would depart from St. Louis. It might have already done so.

He fought off the urge to race down to the waterfront immediately and see if he could find the two people responsible for what had happened to Charlie. He couldn't leave the young man here, badly wounded and on the brink of death. He went to a knee again and looked down into Charlie's unconscious face.

"I'll get 'em, Charlie," he promised. "They won't get away with this. I swear it."

A hurried footstep in the doorway made Preacher look around. A scruffy-looking man in a frock coat and a beaver hat came into the room carrying a black bag in one hand, marking him as a doctor.

"Let me in there, sir," he said. "Mrs. Malone came to fetch me but didn't know what was wrong. Was this man stabbed?"

"Looks like it to me," Preacher replied as he stood up. "And he's lost a heap of blood."

"Indeed he has." The doctor knelt beside Charlie.

Preacher thought he smelled rum on the man, but that might not be a bad thing. Liquor calmed the nerves in some men, and a doctor needed a steady hand.

The medico moved Charlie's clothes aside to study the wounds. "Cut some pieces off that sheet," he told Preacher. "I'm going to need bandages, and that's handier than getting them from my office."

Preacher took out his knife, pulled the sheet off the bed, and started cutting it up.

From the doorway, the old woman objected. "You're gonna have to pay for that!"

"Shut up," Preacher told her. He found a coin and tossed it to her.

She caught it with a deftness belying her age and apparent feebleness. After biting the coin to make sure of its authenticity, she grinned down at the cat tucked under her arm and said, "Ooh. We'll eat tonight."

Preacher watched the doctor working on Charlie, stanching the flow of blood from the wounds. "You reckon he's gonna live, Doc?"

"By all rights, he should be dead already, so I'd say your guess is as good as mine, my friend."

"Well, do your best to keep him alive."

"I certainly intend to," the doctor responded crisply. "That's my job, after all."

After a few more minutes, Preacher asked, "Have you got a place where you can take him?"

"If he survives, you mean? Yes, I operate a small private hospital. I can have him taken there once I've stabilized him. These wounds need to be cleaned and stitched up, and I can do a better job of it there."

Preacher took another coin from his pocket, this time a double eagle, and laid it on the small table beside the bed. "Do whatever you need to," he told the doctor. "Where's that hospital of yours? I got to get down to the river, but I'll be back in a spell."

"What's so important at the river?" the doctor asked without looking up from his work.

"Couple of folks who took somethin' that don't belong to 'em," Preacher answered flatly. "And I figure on havin' a word with 'em about it."

Preacher trotted up to the wharf where he and Charlie had seen the riverboat being loaded that morning. He came to a stop and stared at the empty stretch of water for a long moment, then turned to a burly, roughly dressed man nearby.

"What happened to the boat that was tied up here?"

"You mean the *Majestic*?" The man shrugged. "She cast off a little while ago. By now she's a few miles downriver, steamin' toward N'Orleans."

"Blast it!" Preacher grated.

"Missed your boat, eh?" The man laughed. "She left

behind schedule, got held up for a spell by some problem with the engine. So you almost got lucky, mister. Too bad it didn't take a little longer."

Preacher glared down the broad, slow-moving stream and asked, "Were you here when the boat left?"

"Yeah, me and the other boys didn't finish loadin' the cargo until the last minute. No reason to get in a hurry, you know, since she wasn't goin' anywhere until they got the engine workin' right."

"Did you happen to see a man and a woman get on board, maybe half an hour ago?"

"Saw a lot of folks get on board, mister. The *Majestic*, she carries plenty of passengers."

"This fella would be dressed like a gambler, and the woman with him was young and pretty, with dark hair."

The man frowned and rubbed his chin as he appeared to think about the question. Then he said, "That ain't much to go on. Could fit a lot of different folks. But I do seem to recall maybe seein' a couple like that—"

The pause seemed like a ploy to get Preacher to slip him a coin, but then, evidently demonstrating that the man really had been thinking about it, he laid a thick finger against his right cheek and went on. "The gal had a mark right around here. Not a big one, mind you, but I remember seein' it. Mighty pretty girl."

"That's her, all right," Preacher said. Mighty pretty, sure, but a viper lurked underneath that beauty.

Emotions warred within him. The dockworker had said that the riverboat left only a short time earlier. If Preacher fetched Horse from the stable right now, he might be able to ride along the river and catch up with the boat. Maybe even get ahead of it so he could be waiting for Cornelius and Lucy at the next town downriver.

But that would mean leaving St. Louis without knowing Charlie's condition or even whether the young man still lived. He didn't like the idea of doing that.

"How often do boats go downriver to New Orleans?" he asked.

"Nearly every day. Sometimes more 'n one in a day. Happens the next one is leavin' tomorrow mornin', I believe. The *Powhatan*."

The man pointed at a compact stern-wheeler tied up at one of the wharves farther upriver.

Preacher made up his mind. If he waited until the next morning to go after Edmund Cornelius and Lucy Tarleton, they would have too big a lead for him to catch up before they reached New Orleans. But they wouldn't be expecting any pursuit. As far as Cornelius knew, Charlie had died within minutes of him leaving the inn. The gambler wouldn't have expected anyone wounded that badly to survive for long. That meant they wouldn't be trying to cover their trail.

He would find them in New Orleans, Preacher thought as he turned away from the river. By the next morning when the *Powhatan* cast off, he would have a better idea whether or not Charlie was going to make it, whether he would be avenging his young friend's murder or just delivering justice for the attack on him and the theft of that money.

Yeah, he would catch up to those two varmints in New Orleans, he told himself—and then they would pay for what they'd done.

CHAPTER 8

"I'm sorry, Preacher," Charlie said, his voice husky with weariness and strain. "I should have . . . listened to what you . . . tried to tell me."

Preacher stood beside the bed where Charlie rested. Through the sheet, he awkwardly patted the young man on the shoulder and said, "Don't you worry about that. You didn't have any way of knowin' Cornelius and that Tarleton gal were plottin' against you."

"You knew, though."

"I had a hunch. It could've been wrong."

But it hadn't been. Cornelius and Lucy had turned out as bad as Preacher suspected they might, and the fact that Charlie hadn't died because of them could only be considered a miracle. That was Dr. Hennessey's medical opinion.

"He lost enough blood to choke a horse," the doctor had told Preacher a short time earlier, while they'd talked in Hennessey's examining room. "But by pure luck, the knife seems to have missed all the vital organs. So, since the blood loss didn't kill him outright—" Hennessey shrugged. "He seems to have a surprisingly strong constitution, so he stands at least a chance of surviving. It'll be a long recovery, and he'll still be in considerable danger while he's recuperating . . . but perhaps he'll live."

"See to it that he does," Preacher had said.

Hennessey had told him he could go in and visit with Charlie, but only for a few moments.

Charlie seemed determined to take up that time with apologies. "You lost all that money because of me—"

"I didn't lose a thing," Preacher said. "I'd already given it to you, remember?"

"But you didn't mean . . . for those two to have it."

"I'll make sure they don't get away with it."

"If I could . . . ask one more thing of you . . ."

"Sure," Preacher told him. "Go ahead."

"Don't . . . don't hurt Lucy. I don't care . . . what happens to Cornelius . . . but I don't want her harmed."

Preacher's jaw tightened. To tell the truth, he hadn't figured out yet what he would do about Lucy Tarleton when he caught up to the two of them. He hoped Edmund Cornelius would put up a fight so he'd be justified in blowing a hole through the varmint or carving his gizzard out with a knife, but he didn't make a habit of hurting women. He supposed he could turn her over to the law, for whatever that was worth.

"She won't come to any harm at my hands," Preacher told Charlie.

"Thanks . . . Know it's foolish of me . . . to feel that way . . . but . . . 'preciate . . ."

Charlie's eyes drooped closed as his voice trailed off. The young man's midsection, bulky with bandages under the sheet, rose and fell in time with his chest. Charlie had just drifted off to sleep.

Preacher left the room quietly and found Dr. Hennessey in the medico's office. "Charlie's restin'."

"Good," Hennessey said with a nod. "Best thing for him right now."

"Listen, Doc, I want you to take care of him, but I don't have the money to pay you right now."

Preacher had already done some figuring. He would need all the money he had left in order to arrange for Horse and Dog to be cared for at the livery stable and to buy his own passage to New Orleans on the riverboat *Powhatan*. He wouldn't be able to pay Higginbotham, but the storekeeper could return all those supplies to his stock and wouldn't lose anything.

Hennessey opened a drawer in his desk and took out a jug and a couple of cups. "I swore an oath to heal the sick," he said as he poured rum into the cups. He pushed one across to Preacher and went on. "I'll look after young Mr. Todd, don't worry. You're going after the man who attacked him, aren't you?"

"I sure am."

"Then you can settle up with me when you get back." Hennessey lifted his cup. "In the meantime, we'll drink to the young man recovering his health."

"Can't argue with that." Preacher clinked his cup against the doctor's, swallowed a healthy slug of the fiery liquor, then added, "And to the two varmints who did that to him gettin' what's comin' to 'em."

Preacher walked onto the dock the next morning half an hour before the riverboat was supposed to cast off. He had visited the company's office the previous afternoon after leaving Dr. Hennessey's place and bought a ticket for the journey downriver to New Orleans. When the clerk asked him if he wanted a return ticket as well, Preacher hadn't hesitated.

"That's right," he'd said. "I plan on comin' back." But not until he had dealt with Cornelius and Lucy and recovered as much of that stolen money as he could.

Preacher paused at the bottom of the plank walk that led from the wharf to the riverboat's deck. He had his possibles bag slung over his shoulder and his rifle in his left hand.

One of the deckhands saw him and said, "Hold on there, Daniel Boone. Where do you think you're going?"

"New Orleans," Preacher said. "I got a ticket."

The man came down the plank and held out his hand. "Let me see."

Preacher didn't care for the man's attitude, but he didn't want any trouble that might slow down his pursuit of Cornelius and Lucy. He took the ticket out of his pocket and handed it over. The crewman, as tall as Preacher and a little heavier, took it and looked at it, then grunted and handed it back.

"Reckon you've got a right to be here," he said, "but don't cause any trouble."

"Why do you reckon I'd do that?" Preacher wanted to know.

"I know what you trappers are like. You go out there to the mountains and live with the Indians and the wild animals, and after a while, you're just as un-tamed as they are."

Preacher grinned. "Sounds like you're payin' me a

compliment, mister, whether that was your intention or not."

"Just behave yourself," the man said, pointing a warning finger. "Start any trouble and I'll be happy to toss you off this boat, even if we're in the middle of the river." He gave Preacher an ugly grin. "Hope you can swim."

The brawny crewman moved on. Preacher walked along the deck toward the bow. He hadn't been able to book a cabin for this trip; they were already all spoken for. He had paid for deck space instead and would share it not only with cargo but also with other passengers who couldn't afford cabins or had tried to book them too late, like Preacher.

Men, women, children, dogs, and even a few crates of chickens already crowded the forward deck. Preacher supposed he ought to be happy he didn't see any mules or cows. He found himself a place to sit on a crate—a solid one filled with cargo of some kind, not chickens—and rested the rifle's butt on the deck at his feet.

He hadn't been there even a minute when two kids sidled up in front of him, a boy about eight and a girl a few years younger.

The boy, with red hair sticking out from under his hat and freckles covering his face, said, "You're a mountain man, ain't you?"

"That's right, son," Preacher said. "You know about mountain men?"

"Sure. You fight Injuns."

"Well, that ain't all I do, but I've been in a few scrapes like that, I reckon."

"How many Injuns have you killed?"

Preacher frowned. For one thing, he didn't have

any idea how many Indian warriors he had killed in battle over the years. He didn't keep track of such things. But quite a few, no doubt about that. He didn't think he should be discussing that subject with some nosy kid, though.

"You young'uns best run on back to your ma," he said.

"Our ma's dead," the little girl piped up.

"Yeah, she got the fever and died," the boy added. "We're goin' back down to Memphis where we come from, to live with our grandma and grandpa. Can I hold your rifle?"

"No," Preacher said, trying not to growl at the youngster. He didn't know how long it would take to get to Memphis—the whole trip to New Orleans took take five or six days, according to what the clerk in the riverboat company office told him—but if he had these two kids hanging around him the whole way, it would seem even longer.

CHAPTER 9

The youngsters got bored pretty quickly and wandered off, which Preacher considered a good thing. If you had to have kids, he thought, best to wait until they were nearly full-grown to meet them, the way he had with Hawk That Soars.

Some people got sick on boats, but not Preacher, especially not on a stream as placid as the Mississippi was at that time of year. The *Powhatan* chugged steadily downriver, the paddle wheel at the back of the boat throwing a glittering spray of water high in the air around it as the miles fell behind. The only excitement came whenever a riffle appeared, signifying the presence of a sandbar or some other sort of snag, but each time that happened, the *Powhatan*'s pilot steered expertly around the obstacle.

The deck passengers could buy sandwiches and fruit from a boy who came around with a box of them. Preacher made do with an apple at midday. He had to be careful with the little money he had left, so that he could eat during the trip and also have something left for whatever he needed to buy once he reached

New Orleans. He had plenty of powder and shot, but a man couldn't eat ammunition.

Of course, after he retrieved that stolen money from Edmund Cornelius and Lucy Tarleton, he wouldn't have to worry about that, he reminded himself.

The riverboat put in to shore frequently, not only to take on cargo and passengers at the settlements it came to, but also to take on wood for the firebox down in the engine room. Because of those stops, the vessel didn't cover a great deal of distance during the day.

Boats sometimes traveled at night, but that meant running a risk because snags couldn't always be seen in the dark. Most captains weren't willing to take a chance on ripping out their boat's hull. Too many of them had wound up on the bottom of the river because of that.

When evening came, the *Powhatan* tied up at one of the towns on the river's eastern bank. Preacher didn't know the name of the place. During the day, he had seen numerous other boats on the river, ranging from stern-wheelers and side-wheelers churning northward to flatboats and keelboats heading in both directions. This stretch of the Mississippi was probably the busiest waterway in the country. So Preacher wasn't surprised that several keelboats had tied up at the settlement, too.

It also came as no surprise that several taverns operated near the riverfront. Preacher heard raucous music coming from at least one of them. Fiddles and squeezeboxes put out sprightly tunes that floated through the evening air over the water.

Passengers were free to go ashore and spend the

evening in town however they wished, as long as they were back on board the next morning when the *Powhatan* cast off. After a day spent in the open on the deck, Preacher thought a mug of beer might go down nicely. He slung his bag over his shoulder, picked up his rifle, and headed for the gangplank that had been put in place between the deck and the wharf extending into the river.

One of the crewmen—not the man who had given Preacher a hard time when he first boarded the boat in St. Louis—was standing near the gangplank. Preacher asked him, "What do they call this place, anyway?"

"The settlement, you mean? It's Carver's Junction."

Preacher nodded toward the buildings and asked, "Are any of those taverns over yonder the sort that a mild-mannered fella like me oughta steer clear of?"

"You mean where there's liable to be trouble?" the young crewman said. "I'd stay away from Rancid Dave's."

"Rancid Dave?" Preacher repeated with a chuckle. "They really call him that?"

"Just get downwind of him. You'll know why! But yeah, that's the roughest place in Carver's Junction, I'd say."

"I'll remember that," Preacher said solemnly as he started down the gangplank. "Much obliged, son."

As he walked along the riverfront street in the twilight, he asked the first local he encountered which of the taverns belonged to Rancid Dave.

The man raised his eyebrows and answered, "You don't want to go there, mister. People make bets on how many killings there'll be in the alley behind the place each night."

"I'll chance it," Preacher said. "I've been known to be pretty good at takin' care of myself."

The local sighed and said, "Well, if you're sure . . . That's it there, the third building along." He indicated a squat, windowless structure that appeared to be cobbled together from logs, stone, and mud.

"Much obliged," Preacher said with a nod, then ambled on toward his destination.

Rancid Dave's smelled pretty bad when he opened the door made of thick, rough-hewn planks, and stepped inside, but no worse than many other frontier taverns Preacher had visited. Pipe smoke, along with the dank odor of the dirt floor, mixed with a combined stench of spilled liquor, human waste, and unwashed flesh to thicken the air.

Several lanterns and candles scattered around the single room lit the place with a dim glow quickly swallowed up by shadows in the corners. A low mutter of conversation came from customers seated on crude stools around tables made from barrels. The bar to Preacher's right consisted of planks laid across more barrels. Jugs of whiskey, probably distilled right out back, sat on a shelf behind the bar that also held a couple of lanterns, one at each end.

A short man, who looked almost as wide as he was tall, stood behind the bar. A black, tangled beard hung down over his chest and compensated for the lack of hair on top of his head. He wore a grimy apron over a homespun shirt with sleeves rolled up to leave thick, hairy forearms bare. When he grinned at Preacher, the lanternlight glinted off a gold tooth in the front of his mouth, next to an empty spot where another tooth hadn't been replaced. He waved a hand with sausagelike fingers at the mountain man and boomed, "Come on in, stranger. Welcome to Dave's. You off that riverboat *Powhatan*?"

Preacher supposed the man didn't refer to himself as *Rancid Dave*. Could be he had grown so accustomed to his own stench that he didn't even smell it anymore. Preacher did, though, from all the way across the room.

He braved the smell anyway and approached the bar. "Yeah, I'm headed for New Orleans.

"What can I get you?"

Preacher glanced at the men on either side of him, both of whom nursed drinks in tin cups. "You have any beer?" he asked.

Dave shook his head solemnly. "I do, but you wouldn't want it. Skunk fell in the barrel and drowned, and I ain't got around to fishin' it out yet."

Preacher noted that the man didn't say he intended to dump that beer, just fish out the dead skunk. "What else you got?"

"Whiskey!" Dave rested his hands on the plank bar. "Best in these parts."

Preacher nodded. "I'll give it a try."

Dave got a jug off the shelf and a cup from under the bar. He pulled the jug's cork with his teeth and splashed clear liquid into the cup, then set it in front of Preacher.

"Be a nickel," Dave said around the cork clenched between his teeth.

Preacher laid the coin on the bar and picked up the cup. He eyed the contents warily, wondering if it might be better to throw the drink back quickly. Dave hadn't mentioned any dead animals floating in the barrel where he cooked up this stuff, but Preacher didn't think such a possibility was beyond the pale.

He risked a sip, then frowned and took another. Then he looked up at the proprietor and said, "Dave, this here is some of the best, smoothest-sippin' whiskey I've ever tasted."

The gold tooth glinted again as Dave grinned. "Told ya! Drink up and I'll pour you another."

Sometimes you found a flower growing out of a dung heap, Preacher reflected. This whiskey reminded him of that, and he supposed it was the reason men chose to drink here despite the absolute squalidness of the place and its reputation for violence. Preacher swallowed the rest of the potent liquid in his cup, then after Dave filled it again, he turned to look around the tavern as he drank at a more leisurely pace.

Men sat at all the tables and filled most of the places at the bar. A group of roughly dressed fellows crowded around a large round table in a rear corner, talking and laughing loudly. Their clothes marked them as rivermen. All of Dave's customers looked like rivermen, Preacher noted, except for a few who probably farmed in the area or maybe worked as woodcutters. Folks probably did a booming business supplying wood for the fireboxes of the riverboats traveling up and down the Mississippi.

One of the men sitting at the big table in the back glanced up, spotted Preacher looking in their direction, and abruptly heaved to his feet. Thick slabs of muscle on his arms and shoulders stretched the homespun fabric of his shirt. He had a flat-topped beaver hat canted at a rakish angle on his head, which as far as Preacher could see, was as bald as Rancid Dave's. Unlike Dave, though, this man didn't sport a beard.

He had a number of tattoos on his arms and peeking out through the drawstring at the throat of his shirt, as well. As the man left the table and swaggered toward the bar, the mountain man saw more tattoos curling up his neck onto the back of his head. Preacher had seen tattoos like that in the past, usually on men who had spent a lot of time on the high seas, sailing off to exotic islands. He had never felt the urge to do that himself, but he could understand how some men would give in to such wanderlust. He had done the same thing, only in a different direction, to the mountains instead of the sea.

This man came up to Preacher and demanded, "What are you supposed to be?"

"Don't reckon I get your drift," Preacher drawled.

"You're wearin' buckskins like a blasted Injun. Even carryin' a tomahawk like one of them savages. Are you white or red?"

"I've knowed plenty of fine red men, but I happen to be white, nearabouts as I can tell," Preacher said.

"I'll bet you cozy up to those squaws, though, don't you?" The man poked a blunt finger against Preacher's chest. "Injuns ain't nothin' more than animals, and any man who'd crawl into their robes with 'em is an animal his own self!"

Dave leaned on the bar and said, "Hold on there, Abner. I don't want no trouble in here."

The man called Abner snorted, giving Preacher a good whiff of the whiskey on his breath. "Shoot, there ain't been a drop of blood spilled since the boys and me got here. That's plumb peaceful for this place!"

"Maybe I'd like for it to stay that way." Dave reached under the bar and picked up a bungstarter. He laid it on the bar to emphasize his point.

Abner didn't take the hint. Maybe he was too drunk for that, or just too belligerent. "You're warnin' the wrong man, Dave. I ain't the one lookin' for trouble. It's this varmint, comin' in here lookin' like a Injun! It's gettin' so decent men can't get a drink in peace!"

"Don't push it, friend," Preacher advised. He started to turn away. He had places to go and things to do, and he didn't need the distraction of a brawl. He tossed back the rest of the whiskey in his cup and placed the empty on the bar, then reached in his pocket to get out another nickel and pay for the second drink.

"Never mind, mister," Dave said. "That one's on me." He hoped Preacher would leave and trouble could be forestalled that way.

Abner yelled, "You'll buy a drink for this Injun-lover but not for me? Well, you can just go to Hades, Dave! And as for you, mister—"

"Don't say it," Preacher warned, tight-jawed with anger.

Abner ignored those cautionary words, probably because his companions had gotten up and were moving toward the bar, as well. He didn't want to back down in front of them. Instead, he let the curses spill out of his mouth, vile epithets directed at Preacher, who *still* would have let it go as he started to walk out of the tavern.

Abner grabbed him, and Preacher didn't allow any man to lay hands on him like that. As Abner's hand closed on his shoulder, Preacher pivoted, brought his right elbow back sharply, and rammed it hard into Abner's solar plexus, making hot air and more raw whiskey fumes gust out of the man's mouth.

CHAPTER 10

The blow drove Abner back against the bar, nearly overturning the barrels. Dave yelled a protest and lashed out with the bungstarter at Abner's head, but the man had recovered his balance already and leaped at Preacher, causing the bungstarter to miss by an inch or two. Abner probably never knew how close he came to getting brained by it.

He swung a roundhouse right of his own. Preacher ducked under it as he dropped his rifle so he would have both hands free. Balling them into fists, he stepped closer and hooked a left and then a right into Abner's belly, with about the same effect as punching a wall.

Abner threw a wild left that clipped Preacher on the side of the head, knocking the mountain man toward the tables. Preacher slapped a hand down on one of them to catch himself, but he was off-balance for a second, just long enough for Abner to rampage in and get both arms around his waist in a bear hug. He grunted with the effort as he lifted Preacher from the floor and tried to squeeze the guts out of him.

Despite his rangy build, the mountain man was no lightweight.

Preacher grimaced at the incredible force of his opponent's arms as they closed around him like a vise. He kicked at Abner's shins, but the man ignored the blows. Preacher felt his ribs groaning as Abner increased the pressure. Shouts filled the tavern as Abner's friends called encouragement to him. Battles like this were probably a regular occurrence at Rancid Dave's.

The shouting seemed to recede, even though Preacher knew it had to be as loud as ever. The light seemed even dimmer, too. He was on the verge of passing out, he realized. If he didn't act quickly, he would not only lose the fight, but more than likely, Abner would crush his ribs so they splintered and pierced his lungs, causing him to drown in his own blood.

His arms still free, Preacher cupped his hands and slammed them against Abner's ears. He could tell that bothered the big brute a little, but not enough to make Abner's grip weaken. Preacher clapped his hands on Abner's face and dug at the man's eyes with his thumbs. Dirty fighting like that bothered him a little, but when it came down to a man's survival, no tactic was too dirty to use.

Abner roared in pain and jerked his head back. Preacher leaned his torso backward, lowered his head, and butted it into Abner's face. Staggered, Abner stumbled back against the bar again, where Dave had the bungstarter poised to strike another blow.

Again, sheer luck saved Abner from getting his head stove in. He sagged to one side, so the bungstarter hit the back of his left shoulder. That was enough to loosen his grip at last. Preacher chopped the side of his hand into Abner's throat and that finished the job of breaking him free. As Abner gagged, Preacher writhed out of his grasp.

As soon as his feet hit the dirt floor, the mountain man braced himself and launched a right that crashed into Abner's jaw and jerked his head to the side. The beaver hat flew off, revealing that the tattoos climbed all the way to the top of his shaven head.

Not giving him a chance to recover, Preacher swung a hard left that jolted Abner's head back the other way, then followed with another right. It landed on Abner's nose and caused blood to spurt hotly across Preacher's knuckles.

Abner seemed surprised to be knocked back on his heels. Given his size and brute strength, it probably didn't happen often. But he didn't intend to give in. He shook his head, slinging drops of crimson from his bloody nose, then bellowed like a bull and charged at Preacher, moving with surprising swiftness for a man of his size.

Preacher tried to get out of the way, but Abner snagged him with a wide-flung arm. Abner's rush had turned into a flying tackle, and he and Preacher went down, landing hard on one of the tables. The men who had been drinking there had scattered frantically when they saw Abner and Preacher coming in their direction.

The table's legs splintered and collapsed under the weight suddenly crashing down on them. Preacher and Abner sprawled amidst the debris. Having Abner land mostly on top of him knocked the wind out of

Preacher's lungs, so he gasped for air as he tried to struggle out from under.

Abner grabbed one of the broken chair legs and raised it high over his head, then brought it sweeping down. The blow would have cracked Preacher's skull like an eggshell if it had landed. He saw it coming and jerked his head to the side just in time. The makeshift club slammed down right beside his ear. Abner lifted it and tried again. Preacher rolled his head the other way to avoid the second blow.

The mountain man flung his leg up, hooked it in front of Abner's throat, and pried him off. Freed of the weight as Abner toppled to the side, Preacher scrambled the other direction, got his hands and knees underneath him, and surged to his feet. His chest heaved, his heart slugged in his chest, and his pulse hammered wildly inside his head. But his blood was up and he was eager to continue the fight.

So was Abner. He came up throwing punches and waded in. Preacher met him head-on and gave as good as he got. The two men stood toe to toe in the center of the tavern and pounded away at each other, both of them absorbing tremendous amounts of punishment.

Preacher finally sensed that the tide of battle was turning in his direction. Abner wasn't quite as steady on his feet as he had been, and even though he still landed many of his punches, they lacked as much power as they had possessed when the fight began. Preacher put aside his own aches and pains and weariness and bored in. He snapped a series of left jabs into Abner's face, blacking the man's eyes, splitting his lips, and making the blood flow even more copiously from his nose. Abner's eyes began to glaze over.

As if sensing that their champion had begun to fade, several of the men who had been sitting at the table with Abner let out angry yells and started forward, obviously intending to gang up on Preacher. He would take them all on if he had to, the mountain man thought, and with the fires of rage fueling him, he wasn't sure but what he could beat them.

However, Abner saw what was happening, too, and he stepped back long enough to wave an arm at his friends and shout, "No! Stay outta this! It's between him and me!"

Yelling like that seemed to exhaust him even more, but he pulled himself up, squared his shoulders, and beckoned to Preacher with a bruised and bloody hand.

"Come on, Injun-lover," he taunted as he swayed back and forth. "Come and get me."

"You're just about out on your feet," Preacher told him. "Best call this off while you still can."

"I'm not . . . callin' anything off!" Abner charged again.

Preacher was ready for him. He would have stepped aside from the charge and delivered the finishing stroke—if he hadn't stepped on one of those broken table legs at just the wrong moment. The table leg rolled under his foot and threw him off-balance. He couldn't get out of the way in time, and Abner's shoulder rammed into his chest. The collision knocked them apart. They went spinning away from each other, lost their footing, and tumbled onto the dirt floor again.

Preacher struggled to get up. A few yards away, so did Abner. Preacher wasn't sure that either of them would be able to make it to their feet again. But the sound of double hammers being cocked rendered their efforts moot.

Rancid Dave pointed a shotgun over the bar at them. "That's it!" he bellowed. "Fight's over!" He added a few colorful curses for emphasis. "No more, either of you. You hear me?"

Abner struggled to get out, "You . . . you can go to—"

He didn't finish the sentence. The shotgun barrels had turned menacingly toward him.

"I've heard enough outta you, Abner Rowland. Your friends can pick you up and get you outta here, right now!"

"Blast it, Dave—" one of the other men began.

"You want some o' this buckshot, Hooper?" Dave roared.

"No, no, take it easy," the man called Hooper responded. He motioned to his companions, and several of them hurried forward and lifted Abner to his feet.

Once he was standing—none too steadily—Abner pawed the air in Preacher's direction and demanded, "Wha' about him? He was fightin', too. You . . . you kickin' him out?"

"He didn't start it," Dave said coldly. "Now move. The whole lot of you."

The men half carried Abner out of the tavern. He made them stop at the door so he could look back over his shoulder, glare at Preacher, and say, "This ain't over, mister."

The mountain man climbed wearily to his feet and said, "It is as far as I'm concerned." He started looking around for his hat, which had gone flying off during the fracas. His pistols had remained tucked behind his belt, which was something of a surprise considering how rough and tumble the fight had been.

Abner spat a few more curses, then let his companions lead him on out of the tavern.

"I hope you ain't expectin' me to pay for all this damage," Preacher told Dave. "I can't afford it."

The gold tooth glinted as Dave grinned. "Reckon I should've thought of that 'fore I chased Rowland and his men out, shouldn't I? But no, I ain't gonna make you pay up, mister. The table that got busted up ain't worth much. Anyway, you was just defendin' yourself. Rowland started that whole ruckus because he wanted an excuse to pound on somebody. He's done it before. He's a sorry son of a gun that way." The tavernkeeper chuckled. "Too bad for him he picked the wrong fella this time."

Dave carefully lowered the hammers on the scatter-gun, replaced it under the bar, and picked up the jug to fill Preacher's cup again. "No charge for this one, neither. That was the best fight I seen in a long time. Worth the price of a drink, for dang sure."

"Obliged to you," Preacher said. He sipped the whiskey, wincing a little as the fiery stuff stung his bruised and cut lips. Well, that was good for them, he told himself. Whiskey had medicinal value, after all. "Those fellas were rivermen?" he went on.

"Yeah, keelboaters," Dave said. "Abner Rowland don't own the boat, but he's the captain of that crew. Likes to brag that they're the toughest bunch on the Mississipp'. And to be honest, he ain't far wrong." A frown creased Dave's forehead. "When you head back to the riverboat you came off of, you might better keep a sharp eye peeled in the shadows. I ain't sayin' they'd try to jump you in the dark . . . but I ain't sayin' they wouldn't, either."

"I tend to be a mite careful," Preacher said. He touched the butt of one of his pistols.

"I believe it. What do they call you, anyway?"

"Preacher."

Dave's eyes widened at that. He let out a surprised whistle. "I've heard of you. Rowland may not know it, but I reckon he's lucky to still be alive! Still, you watch out for him. He's mean as a snake and twice as twisty."

And it was still a long way to New Orleans, Preacher thought.

CHAPTER 11

Before leaving Rancid Dave's, Preacher checked both pistols and his rifle to make sure they were in good working order. He slipped his knife in and out of its sheath and repositioned his tomahawk slightly, making it easier to reach. If anybody tried to ambush him, he would be ready.

Nothing happened as he returned to the docks and went aboard the *Powhatan*. Either Abner Rowland had given up on the idea of revenge—or he had decided to wait and try for it at a better time. He could have heard Preacher say that he was a passenger on the stern-wheeler. If Rowland's keelboat was headed downstream, too, he could afford to take some time to plot his vengeance.

Or it could be that Rowland's parting threat was nothing but bluster, an attempt at saving face in front of his men. Preacher didn't really care one way or the other. Abner Rowland didn't scare him, and he always tried to be careful, anyway.

He found himself a place to curl up on the riverboat's deck. The snores from the other deck passengers didn't bother him, and he soon drifted off to sleep, though a part of his brain remained on hair-trigger alertness.

He woke up in the morning with the freckle-faced boy and his little sister standing beside him, staring at him. Preacher took his hand away from the pistol he had automatically reached for when he realized some-one was hovering over him.

"You scamps shouldn't ought to sneak up on a fella that way," he growled as he sat up.

"We didn't sneak up on you, mister," the boy said. "We were standin' out here in the open where any-body could see us."

"Yeah, but not somebody sleepin'." Preacher stretched. "Anyway, what do you want?"

"We're fixin' to leave. Thought you might want to be awake for it. Anyways, the cap'n is gonna blow the steam whistle any time now, and that would've woke you up."

"It'll be loud and scary," the little girl said.

Preacher managed to smile at her. "Well, don't you worry, honey. You ain't got nothin' to be scared of."

"There's always something to be scared of," she said solemnly. "Sometimes you just don't know what it is."

Preacher grunted. The little girl had a grim way of looking at things, but he really couldn't argue with what she said, either.

And the boy's comment proved to be true, too, when mere moments later the boat's whistle let out a shrill, earsplitting blast that would have jolted Preacher out of his slumber in a pretty surprising and unpleasant manner. The *Powhatan*'s paddle wheel began to revolve, slowly at first and then faster and faster as it backed away from the dock and turned out into the great river's current.

Preacher kept an eye out for Abner Rowland on the keelboats they passed during the day but never spotted the burly, tattooed man. The same situation held true over the next couple of days as the *Powhatan* steamed downriver. The kids hung around with him quite a bit but proved not to be too annoying, although they asked a lot of questions. The little boy, who told Preacher his name was Jonas, seemed to be pretty smart. The little girl was called Sara Beth. She had a rag doll she carried around with her, and she paid more attention to it than she did to Preacher, which the mountain man didn't mind.

Most of his thoughts centered on Edmund Cornelius and Lucy Tarleton. Preacher had been on the river four days and knew they probably had reached New Orleans on the *Majestic* already. If anything had happened to delay the other riverboat, the *Powhatan* would have caught up with it. One thing about traveling down the Mississippi, a steamboat couldn't just veer off in another direction and disappear. The boats could go only north or south.

Preacher's quarry had a small lead on him, less than twenty-four hours. But twenty-four hours in New Orleans wasn't the same thing as that amount of time on the frontier. A person could find a lot more places to hide in a big city.

But wherever those two hid, Preacher would root them out. He never doubted it and struggled to contain his eagerness to get there and begin the search for justice and vengeance.

The New Orleans waterfront sounded like a madhouse. All the shouting in different languages, from the crews of boats from all over the world, might as well have been the raving of lunatics, Edmund Cornelius thought as he led Lucy Tarleton down the gangplank from the *Majestic.* The docks were crowded, and so were the streets.

"It's exciting, isn't it?" Lucy said with a breathless note in her voice as she looked around. "All these people, I mean."

"Lots of easy marks, I imagine," Cornelius replied.

"Oh, that's not what I meant at all! I'm talking about how colorful and . . . and exotic everything is. And everyone."

Cornelius wasn't sure he would have called this area along the river colorful and exotic. The air stank of dead fish, rotting vegetation, and too many people. Many of the buildings were constructed of unpainted lumber that had warped and faded in the constant humidity. The sturdier stone buildings still had a patina of age overlaying them. Founded a hundred and twenty years earlier, New Orleans was an old town, squatting on the Mississippi delta like a fat, evil, ancient toad.

And yet Cornelius felt the excitement in the air, too, just as Lucy did. This was a place of infinite possibilities, especially for anyone possessing as few scruples as the two of them had.

When they paused on the dock, Lucy hugged his arm and asked, "What are we going to do first?"

"Find a place to stay, I suppose," Cornelius answered.

"A *nice* place. We have money. I don't see any reason we shouldn't enjoy it."

She wouldn't see any reason for that, Cornelius thought, because she never got her own hands dirty obtaining that money. When there was real work to be done—like dealing with that foolish young trapper back in St. Louis—Lucy was always nowhere to be found. Cornelius handled the chores that involved blood and violence and death.

But she *did* have her own talents, he reminded himself wryly, and she was good enough at them to make the things he did for her worthwhile. He said, "I knew that's what you would want, so I already spoke to one of the stewards on board and made arrangements to have our bags delivered to the St. Charles Hotel and a room rented for us. The man assured me that it's the best place in town, and it's very near the French Quarter."

Lucy squeezed his arm again. "I've heard so much about the French Quarter. I can't wait to see it for myself."

"Soon, my dear, soon."

They strolled arm in arm along the street. One of the locals gave them directions to the St. Charles Hotel, which was an impressive four-story building with Greek columns along the front and a towering dome on the roof like the one Cornelius had heard adorned the capitol building in Washington City. Lucy peered up at it with awe and admiration on her pretty face.

"This is where we're going to stay, Edmund?"

"It is," he assured her. "Nothing is too good for you."

"You're so wonderful. Let's go inside." A sultry smile curved her lips. "I want to show you just how wonderful I think you are."

Cornelius hoped the hotel had their room ready for them.

* * *

That evening, they ate dinner in the hotel's luxurious dining room, then went downstairs to the ornately furnished, octagonal barroom in the basement. That seemed an odd place for a bar, but Cornelius had to admit it was something to see as he escorted Lucy past a statue of George Washington and down broad marble steps. A large crowd was on hand, the men all dressed in fine suits, the ladies wearing expensive gowns in a wide variety of colors and styles, many of them cut low in front so that the upper half moons of their bosoms were on provocative display.

None of those ladies were quite so sensuous and lovely as his own companion, though, Cornelius thought as he glanced over at Lucy, exquisite in a dark green gown that bared her creamy shoulders. A necklace he had bought her rested in the hollow of her throat, and earrings dangled from her lobes. She had piled her thick, dark hair high on her head in an elaborate arrangement of curls. The sight of her would take any man's breath away. It certainly did where Cornelius was concerned.

They shouldn't have dined together, and they should have entered the hotel's bar separately. Normally, that's what they would have done, so it wouldn't be obvious they were together and Lucy could search for a suitable target for their schemes.

But for now, they had agreed to put that aside. As Lucy had pointed out, they had money. They weren't desperate for funds the way they sometimes found themselves. They could afford to put aside their normal activities for a while.

A white-coated waiter showed them to a table next to a potted palm and took Cornelius's order to bring them a bottle of brandy. When it arrived, the waiter poured the liquor into snifters, and Cornelius lifted his to toast Lucy with, "To you, my dear . . . the loveliest woman in all New Orleans."

"Oh, you exaggerate, Edmund," she scolded him, but he could tell she enjoyed the compliment. "I mean, just look around you. This room is filled with beautiful women, and it's only one bar in one hotel. There must be many others."

"None to compare to you," Cornelius murmured.

They drank their brandy and looked around the room.

Only a few minutes had gone by when Lucy said quietly, "Edmund, look at that old gentleman in a white suit at the bar. The one with the white hair and goatee."

Cornelius saw the man she described, standing next to the bar talking to several other men. "What about him?" the gambler asked.

"Look at the stickpin he's wearing in his cravat. That's a diamond in it, and a valuable one, too."

Cornelius frowned. Lucy had a fine eye for gemstones, so he didn't doubt what she said. "You're right, I'm sure, but what of it?"

Lucy's eyes gleamed as she said, "We could take that pin from him, along with everything else he has."

For a moment, Cornelius didn't say anything. Then he reminded her, "Lucy, we said we weren't going to do anything like that for a while, that we would just enjoy the money we have."

"We have it *now*," she said, a sharp edge entering her voice. "But in time it will run out, Edmund. It always does. You know that."

"And when it does, we'll find some other source of funds. That always happens, as well."

"But if we had more money, we could stop worrying about it for even longer," she said.

He couldn't dispute the logic of her argument.

Her tongue darted out for a second and licked her lips eagerly. "Think about what it would be like to be really rich."

She painted a pretty picture of it, and the sight of her—breasts rising and falling in the low-cut gown as she began to breathe a little quicker—was a very pretty picture as well. A picture too pretty to argue with.

"All right, my dear," Cornelius said. "Should I just sit back and watch?"

"Of course." She stood up and went to work.

CHAPTER 12

Balthazar Crowe sat in a high-backed rattan chair in an alcove at one side of the St. Charles Hotel's basement barroom, partially screened by one of the potted palms scattered around the big room. He stretched his long legs in front of him and crossed them casually at the ankles. From time to time he lifted a snifter of cognac from the small, marble-inlaid table beside him and sipped from it. His dark brown eyes never left the white-goateed man standing at the bar. His job was to keep an eye on Colonel Augustus Osborne, and Crowe was very good at his job.

A massive, shaven-headed man with skin the same shade as café au lait, his excellently tailored suit made it less noticeable just how big he really was. Thinking that Crowe had to be a slave, a rich man had wanted to buy him a few years earlier, offering Crowe's employer a good price for him. The man had regretted that temerity. Balthazar Crowe was a free man, had been since birth. And he worked for one of the most powerful individuals in New Orleans—if not *the* most powerful.

Crowe's nonchalant attitude disappeared as a very attractive young woman approached Colonel Osborne. She didn't appear to be a threat, but she was a stranger and Crowe never fully trusted strangers. Ready to stand up and let his long legs carry him quickly to the colonel's side in case of danger, Crowe continued watching as the young woman spoke animatedly to Osborne with a friendly smile on her face.

The big man's smooth brow gradually furrowed as the conversation continued. The old colonel threw back his head and laughed at something the young woman said, and then she reacted the same way when he responded. The two of them seemed to be having the time of their lives. Then the young woman rested the fingertips of her left hand on the right sleeve of Osborne's white coat. The touch lasted only a second but carried an undeniably seductive air.

Balthazar Crowe had seen enough. He stood up, rising to his towering height, and set the snifter of cognac on the table. Without seeming to hurry, he moved into the crowd and headed toward the bar. People got out of his way, not because of his expression, which was emotionless, or his dark skin, but simply because the sheer size of him intimidated most folks. Crowe counted on that.

He stepped up behind the young woman, being careful not to touch her. He was a free man, had been born a free man, but even so, the sight of a black man putting his hand on a white woman invited trouble, and Crowe never hunted trouble.

He said quietly, in a voice so deep it sounded as if it came from the bottom of a well, "I think it would be better if you moved along now, miss."

Colonel Osborne glared over the woman's shoulder at him, pooched his lips out in annoyance, and said, "See here, Mr. Crowe, I believe I have the right to speak with anyone I want to, do I not?"

"You do, sir," Crowe replied. "But you know my job tonight is to look out for your best interests, and I don't believe this young lady has them at heart."

The young woman had turned her head to look at him when he first spoke, and her eyes widened at the sight of him. Anger replaced awe, though, as she began, "Why, I never—"

"Please, miss, don't make a scene," Crowe said. Then he stiffened, mentally berating himself for allowing someone to get behind him, as he felt something sharp prick his back.

A man's voice said, "You make a move, boy, and I'll put this knife right in your heart."

Like everyone else in the room, Edmund Cornelius had seen the big black man emerge from the alcove and approach Lucy and the old-timer. He didn't look particularly threatening other than his size, but that was enough to alarm Cornelius. He had never seen a black man dressed in such a fancy suit and acting like he belonged around white folks. Having grown up in New York, Cornelius had encountered a few free blacks, but none such as this.

The man didn't look or act threatening. He hadn't touched Lucy. If he had, Cornelius might have sunk the dagger in his back without even saying anything. But his size was ominous enough by itself. Cornelius wasn't going to have him bothering Lucy.

The black man spoke up in a rumbling voice. "This isn't necessary. I mean no harm."

"Then why are you harassing this lady?"

The white-suited old man said, "Please, sir, don't concern yourself with this. Mr. Crowe here would never harm your lady friend. I can vouch for that."

Cornelius frowned as he looked past the black man's bulky form. "He's your slave? Your servant, sir?"

"No, no," the old man said hastily. "He's not a slave, and he doesn't work for me. His employer is M'sieu LeCarde."

Cornelius had never heard that name before and didn't really care who Crowe worked for.

The old man went on. "Allow me to introduce myself, sir. I am Colonel Augustus Osborne, with an *e.* Of the Jefferson Parish Osbornes."

Lucy said, "This is my friend, Mr. Edmund Cornelius."

Now that he had gone over and stuck his knife in Crowe's back because he thought she might be in danger, there was no longer any point in pretending that they didn't know each other. Lucy was smart enough to have realized that right away, so the only thing to do was manipulate the situation to their advantage.

"It's an honor to make your acquaintance, sir," Osborne said. He moved a hand in a languid, eloquent gesture. "Now, would you mind removing that pistol or knife or whatever it is you have stuck in Mr. Crowe's back?"

Cornelius hesitated for a moment longer, then took the dagger away from the black man and slipped it back into the sheath under his coat. The man stepped to the side. His head swiveled on his thick neck so he could look at Cornelius. Despite the impassive expression on his face, his eyes smoldered with anger.

Cornelius didn't care. He didn't intend to apologize, not to Crowe at any rate. However, he turned to Osborne, tipped his head forward slightly, and said, "I regret any unpleasantness, Colonel. It wasn't my intention to cause a scene. I simply reacted to what I perceived as a possible threat to Miss Tarleton."

Intentional or not, he *had* caused a scene, judging by the silence that had fallen over the big room and the weight of the eyes he felt as people directed their gazes toward him. That scrutiny eased as it became obvious that violence wasn't about to erupt.

Osborne said, "You can go on back to your seat, Mr. Crowe. I assure you, I'm in no danger from either Miss Tarleton or Mr. Cornelius." He smiled at Lucy. "Isn't that right, my dear?"

She returned the smile and said, "Why, of course, Colonel. Why would anyone ever want to harm an old sweetheart such as yourself?"

"There have been plenty of men in the past who might believe they had reason to hold a grudge against me," Osborne replied with a smile that was half-smirk, half-leer, "especially those with beautiful wives. But I fear those days are long past me now."

"Oh, I wouldn't be so sure about that. I'll wager you're still a charming devil with the ladies."

Osborne laughed. "I can but try, my dear. I can but try."

Crowe said in his deep voice, "If you need me, Colonel . . ."

He seemed content to let that trail off as he started

to turn away, but Cornelius stopped him by saying, "Just a moment. I believe there's an apology owed here. An apology to the lady."

Crowe gave him a hard stare, and for a few long seconds, their eyes dueled. Then the black man's brawny shoulders rose and fell in a shrug almost too minuscule to be seen. He turned to Lucy, inclined his head a fraction of an inch, and said, "My sincere apologies, miss, if I was too protective of Colonel Osborne. I meant no offense."

"Of course," Lucy acknowledged coolly.

When Crowe turned away, Cornelius let him go.

Colonel Osborne said, "Perhaps you would allow me to buy you a drink in a feeble attempt to make up for this little contretemps, Mr. Cornelius."

"Most kind of you, sir. I accept."

Lucy said, "I can think of something even better." She turned to Cornelius. "The colonel was telling me about a quaint little place in the French Quarter, and perhaps you and I could pay it a visit, Edmund."

Osborne lifted a hand and said, "You speak of the Catamount's Den, Miss Tarleton? It's a very exclusive club. One must have an invitation or at the very least be accompanied by one of its regular patrons."

"And *you* are one of those regular patrons, aren't you, Colonel? You were speaking of taking me there just a short time ago."

Osborne's eyes flicked toward Cornelius, and the man's thoughts were plain to see on his weathered old face. He had planned to take Lucy to this so-called Catamount's Den when he was unaware that she already had a male companion. Now the situation had changed.

But Cornelius saw acceptance of that come into the old man's eyes.

Osborne said, "Of course. I'd be delighted to show both of you around the French Quarter, and our first stop will be the Catamount's Den. I should make you aware, though, that it's owned by M'sieu Simon LeCarde, Mr. Crowe's employer."

"This M'sieu LeCarde must set a great deal of store by you, sir, if he has one of his men look out for you," Cornelius said.

"Yes, he does, he does. I suppose I'm a valued customer to him. Very well, it's settled, then. We'll have a drink here, and then we'll all go on over to Bourbon Street and pay a visit to M'sieu LeCarde's establishment."

"Thank you so much, Colonel." Lucy linked her arm with the old man's and laughed. "Why, being escorted by two such handsome gentlemen and treated to the legendary nightlife of the district, I'll feel like the belle of the French Quarter."

"Please," Osborne said, "call me Augustus."

"Of course . . . Augustus. I believe this is going to be a very memorable and entertaining evening!"

And with any luck, Cornelius thought, a lucrative evening as well.

CHAPTER 13

From the looks of it, the building that housed the Catamount's Den had been a private residence at one time. Moss coated the stone walls of its two stories. A balcony with a wrought iron railing in the Spanish style ran along the front of the second floor. Like much of the architecture in New Orleans, the French style could be seen in the basic structure, but with such Spanish touches overlaying it. And as with so many buildings in the town, the Catamount's Den had an air of antiquity about it.

As the carriage pulled up in front of the place, Colonel Osborne said, "Rumor has it that this building was owned originally by Jean and Pierre Lafitte, but if you walk down almost any street in New Orleans, you'll find someplace that people claim the Lafitte brothers owned. They're some of our most famous citizens, you know."

"Pirates, weren't they?" Edmund Cornelius asked.

Osborne laughed. "Of course, even though they fought on the side of the Americans in the last war against the British. Why, it's said that Jean Lafitte met with General Jackson himself and helped him plan the Battle of New Orleans." With a note of pride in his voice, the old man added, "I was there myself for that battle. Served as a captain under the general's command. Old Hickory, himself. This country will never see another commander as able. I can't speak quite as well of the job he did as president, mind you. The military mind and temperament are not always well suited for politics. But I'm proud to have served under him. What a day that was. What a day. We caught the bloody British . . ."

Cornelius and Lucy sat and listened tolerantly as the colonel rambled, lost in his memories of the famous battle, even though Osborne's carriage had come to a halt.

After a couple of minutes, the giant black man named Crowe, who was riding on top with the driver, leaned over and called through the carriage window, "We're here, Colonel."

"So we are, so we are. Give me a hand, would you, Mr. Crowe?"

Light on his feet despite his size, Crowe dropped to the ground from the driver's seat and opened the carriage door. He helped Osborne climb out of the vehicle and would have assisted Cornelius, but the gambler pretended not to see the gesture. Cornelius turned back quickly to make sure he helped Lucy out of the carriage, not Crowe.

A painted sign hung from a beam extending out over the front door. It had a picture of a snarling mountain lion on it, as well as the words THE CATAMOUNT'S DEN.

Lucy looked at the sign and asked, "How in the world did the place get its name?"

"Speaking of pirates . . ." Osborne laughed. "Years

ago, one of the fiercest brigands to roam the seas in this part of the world was a man called Catamount Jack LeCarde. A Frenchman he was, by birth, although like most who took to the high seas he came to consider himself a citizen of the world. He never seized as much treasure as the Lafitte brothers did, but he did well for himself. Very well. He had one son, a lad named Simon, and when old Catamount Jack passed on—he actually died at a ripe old age, of natural causes, something rather unheard of for a man in his profession—Simon took the money he inherited and started this place. The boy, so it's said, lacked the seagoing abilities of his sire and preferred dry land, but he's no less the pirate for all that!"

That started Osborne laughing so hard he almost choked.

After a moment, Crowe rumbled, "We should go on in, Colonel."

"Yes, yes, by all means. Lead the way, Mr. Crowe."

Thick wooden beams, banded together with iron straps, formed the arched front door. Considerable force would be required to batter it down, if anyone should ever be foolish enough to attempt it. Crowe worked an iron latch, gripped an iron bar fastened to the door with huge nails, and swung it open.

Inside was a small, dim foyer where a man sat on a stool with a short-barreled shotgun across his lap. He was a dwarf, with short, stunted legs that didn't reach the floor, topped by a stocky, broad-shouldered torso. He glared at Crowe and said, "You should have used the special knock, Balthazar. I was ready to greet you with a double load of buckshot."

"But you did not, Long Sam," Crowe said, "so no harm was done."

"'Tis lucky for you my reflexes are so exceptionally sharp."

"I've said as much myself, on more than one occasion."

Cornelius could tell that the two men were friends, despite the scolding tone of the guard's voice. Crowe ushered them past the guard and into a long, smoky, low-ceilinged room. Candles burned on makeshift chandeliers fashioned out of wagon wheels. The bar stretched along the right side of the room. To the left a number of tables crowded into the space, with booths divided by thick partitions along the left wall.

Cornelius's heartbeat kicked up to a higher pace when he spotted a card game going on at one of the tables.

Osborne, despite seeming rather addled by age at times, remained sharp enough to catch Cornelius's look. "Perhaps you'd like to play a few hands later?"

"I've always enjoyed cards," Cornelius admitted.

"Drinks first. Mr. Crowe, a bottle of cognac, if you would."

"Right away, Colonel," Crowe said.

Osborne ushered Cornelius and Lucy to a booth in a corner that had a curtain which could be pulled across the opening to provide some privacy. Cornelius didn't bother wondering what sorts of acts might have taken place behind that curtain in the past.

All he cared about was what was going to happen tonight.

"When do we get to meet this Simon LeCarde?" Lucy asked. "I'd like to hear about being the son of a notorious pirate."

They had been sitting in the booth for a while, Lucy and Cornelius on one side, the colonel on the other, and the level in the bottle of cognac Balthazar Crowe had brought them had gone down considerably.

Cornelius had been careful about how much he actually drank, but he could tell that Lucy had a warm, comfortable glow about her. Colonel Osborne was drunk, to put it bluntly, but hadn't yet reached the falling-down stage.

Osborne poured more cognac into his glass and said, "I suspect that's not possible. To be honest with you, Simon is something of a mystery. I've never met the lad, myself. Everyone knows of him, but no one spends time with him."

"Well, that's odd," Cornelius said. "If no one ever meets him, how do you know he even exists?"

Osborne waved a hand. "Look around you! How else could this place even be here?"

Lucy giggled. "Perhaps that black giant really owns it. Or that little man at the door. Or maybe they're partners!"

She and Osborne laughed about that, while Cornelius thought about it. He didn't actually believe that Balthazar Crowe and the dwarf called Long Sam owned this place, but the fact that no one ever seemed to meet Simon LeCarde—according to the colonel—was definitely odd. Something fishy there, Cornelius decided. But it was none of his business, and he wasn't going to spend a lot of time pondering it.

Osborne tossed back the rest of the cognac in his glass and set it on the table. "Let's go see about sitting in on that game," he said to Cornelius. He reached across the table, took hold of Lucy's hand, and brought it to his lips. "You can wait for us here, if you don't mind, my dear. I'm sure we won't be gone long. We won't be able to bear being away from you for an extended period of time. Isn't that right, Edmund?"

Lucy didn't give Cornelius a chance to answer. She pouted and said, "What if I want to come with you and watch the game?"

"Not a good idea," Osborne said, shaking his head. "I know those men playing. Scoundrels and degenerates, every one. Why, if they saw you, they might suggest something as scandalous as making you the stakes of a bet!"

"Oh, my, that *is* scandalous! And a bit intriguing, to be honest."

The colonel leered at her. "Oh, ho! Quite the little minx, aren't you?"

Cornelius managed not to roll his eyes. "Lucy, stay here. I'm eager to get to those cards, Colonel, if you'll put in a good word for me with the other players."

"Of course, my boy, of course. Come along." Osborne waggled his bushy white eyebrows a couple of times at Lucy, but he got up, walked over to the other table with Cornelius, and introduced him to the men sitting around the table.

All of them appeared to be wealthy planters like Osborne, with the exception of one man, Saul Drake, who was a professional gambler.

Cornelius had no trouble spotting one of his own breed, and he was sure Drake recognized him as the same sort. He could tell that Drake wasn't happy about him sitting in on the game, either, but the man couldn't very well object. Cornelius wondered if Drake had been fleecing the other players.

"Welcome to the game, gentlemen," Drake said.

He held the deck of cards, having won the previous hand. "We're playing straight poker."

Cornelius nodded. The game had become extremely popular during the past decade and had replaced whist as the game of choice in places such as this. He enjoyed it more—and the stakes had a tendency to be higher, which meant bigger winnings. All to the good.

Drake dealt the cards. The other men had been drinking heavily like Osborne, and Cornelius soon knew that Drake completely controlled the pace of the game and the outcome of the hands. He didn't win consistently—that honor rotated among the other players—but whenever the pot grew to a certain size, those hands inevitably went to Drake. The other men won often enough that they didn't get angry or suspect anything, but the pots they pulled in were meager.

Smiling, Cornelius set out to put a stop to that.

He didn't try to win himself, though. He directed as many hands as he could to Colonel Osborne, whose already high spirits grew even more celebratory as he racked up triumphs.

Drake knew what Cornelius was doing, of course. Cornelius didn't really try to hide it from the other gambler whenever he fed winning cards to the colonel. He smiled coolly when he saw Drake's beefy face glowing even redder with anger.

Osborne chortled, reached to pull in a pot he'd just won, and said, "I can't believe how my luck is running tonight!"

Finally Drake's patience snapped. "I can't believe it, either, Colonel. In fact, I *don't* believe it."

"Eh?" Osborne looked up from the pile of coins and currency he had in front of him. Even drunk as he was, his voice took on a sharp edge as he said, "What do you mean by that, Mr. Drake?"

"I mean it's very strange how you and this *gentleman*"—his tone was insulting as he nodded toward Cornelius—"joined the game at the same time and yet you seem to be having all the luck."

Osborne sniffed. "Happens that way sometimes, doesn't it? They refer to it as the luck of the draw for a reason, my friend."

Drake slowly shook his head. "I don't think luck has a thing to do with it."

Osborne's eyes widened. In a voice shaking with outrage, he said, "Why . . . why, you scoundrel! Are you accusing me of cheating?"

"Not you, maybe, because you're too drunk to know any better. But your so-called friend there. He's making sure that you win. He and that trollop you came in with are probably trying to ingratiate themselves with you so they can fleece you."

Osborne cursed and started to get to his feet. "How dare you insult the lady! I demand—"

Drake bolted to his feet, bringing up a derringer from below the table, which stopped the colonel from making his demand.

CHAPTER 14

Colonel Osborne wasn't Drake's intended target. The derringer's twin over-and-under barrels lifted toward Cornelius, who darted a hand underneath his coat as life and death hung in the balance, a matter of a shaved fraction of a second.

Cornelius's arm flicked out, and the dagger flashed from his fingers. At the short distance, he put no spin on it but threw it straight and true, with the strength developed by long hours of practice. The needle-sharp tip struck Drake's coat, sliced neatly through it and the shirt underneath, and drove through skin and muscle to his heart.

Dying, Drake lurched forward over the table. His finger clenched on the derringer's triggers and fired both barrels. The small slugs struck the table, scattered cards and coins, and sent splinters flying, but neither penetrated all the way through the thick wood. The derringer slipped from his suddenly nerveless fingers and thudded onto the table. With his other hand, he pawed futilely at the dagger's handle for a second and then collapsed, folding up in the middle and pitching facedown on the table.

The shots had silenced the hubbub inside the Catamount's Den. The other customers turned to stare toward the table where death had interrupted the poker game. Long Sam rushed in from the foyer, brandishing the shotgun, the fierce look on his face indicating his readiness to blast someone.

Balthazar Crowe had been standing at the bar, talking to the bartender, when the trouble broke out. He hadn't had time to do more than look around before it was all over. He strode forward, saying, "Hold your fire, Long Sam. The trouble is over." He looked at Cornelius. "Isn't it?"

"As far as I'm concerned, it is," Cornelius replied coolly. "I was simply defending myself, and if the threat is finished—"

"Drake accused me of cheating!" Colonel Osborne said as he stood up. "Well, he accused Cornelius here of helping me win . . . as if I needed anyone's help for that!" Osborne frowned down at the corpse lying in the table. "Scoundrel got what he had coming to him, if you ask me."

Lucy had stood up as well and went over to Cornelius. She put a hand on his arm and asked, "Are you all right, Edmund?"

"Fine," the gambler replied. "Those shots didn't hit me. It was a near thing, though." He looked around at the other men at the table, who were pale from the shock of being so close to what had just happened. "Are all of you gentlemen unharmed?"

One man swallowed hard and said, "I-I believe we're fine."

"I think this game is over now," Crowe said. "Gentlemen, gather up the money you have coming, then there will be drinks on the house waiting at the bar for you."

None of the other players argued with that judgment. They were happy to gather the money—the part that Drake hadn't bled on, anyway—and depart for the bar and the promised free drink.

However, Colonel Osborne said, "That hardly seems fair to me, Mr. Crowe. Drake was the one who caused the trouble, after all. He made that reprehensible accusation, and then he reached for a gun."

Crowe leveled a hard stare at Cornelius. "He accused you of cheating. Were you?"

Cornelius slipped a cigar from his vest pocket. He didn't have any way of lighting it at the moment, but he didn't let that stop him from taking his time putting the cigar into his mouth. He didn't like being interrogated by a black man, but Balthazar Crowe seemed to be a figure of some importance despite his skin color.

Finally Cornelius decided how he wanted to play this affair. "Yes," he said around the cigar.

Crowe arched an eyebrow. "You admit you were cheating?"

"Yes . . . but only because Drake was cheating, too. He made sure that he won all the big pots himself while letting the others have enough dribs and drabs to keep them satisfied. He just wasn't good enough at it to fool me." Cornelius shrugged. "So I figured turnabout was fair play. I started nudging the big pots toward Colonel Osborne."

The old man stared at him and asked, "You mean I wasn't winning on my own, sir?"

"Not all the time, Colonel. Although you played

skillfully enough that Drake was afraid of you and had to resort to trickery to beat you. I just counteracted that trickery."

Drake wasn't alive to contradict the flattery, which stretched the truth to a considerable degree.

Osborne swallowed it completely, nodding slowly and murmuring, "I see, I see." He drew in a deep breath. "It seems I owe you a great debt, Mr. Cornelius."

Cornelius made a dismissive gesture. "I'm just happy I was on hand to assist."

Lucy said, "That's the kind of man Edmund is, Colonel. You can see why we're such good friends."

"Friends?" Osborne raised an eyebrow. "I was under the impression that the two of you are considerably more than friends."

"Oh, no," Lucy said. "Isn't that right, Edmund?"

"She's like the dear sister I never had," Cornelius said without a second's hesitation.

Balthazar Crowe looked like he wanted to scoff at that, but all he said was, "I have to ask the two of you to come back to the office with me."

Instantly, Cornelius was wary. "Why?" He glanced at the body of Saul Drake. The dead man still lay on the table with Cornelius's dagger underneath him. Cornelius wasn't unarmed—he had a razor in his pocket that he could open with a flick of his wrist. Expert in its use as a weapon, he would have felt better about things if he'd had the dagger. Not for the first time in his life, he thought it was too bad he'd never cared for firearms.

"There are things I need to discuss with you," Crowe said. "I mean you no harm."

"You can take Mr. Crowe's word for that," Colonel Osborne said. "He's a very honest man, even though that's an unusual quality to come across in the, ah, likes of him."

The colonel probably owned slaves, which meant he had to be very impressed with Crowe to have said such a thing.

Osborne went on. "I'll accompany you to the office, if that will make you feel better about things."

Lucy said, "Having you around will certainly make me feel better, Colonel."

Osborne seemed to have sobered up some but still preened at Lucy's words. He looked at the giant black man and said, "Is that all right with you, Mr. Crowe?"

Crowe's expression indicated that he *didn't* like the colonel's suggestion but felt that he couldn't refuse. "Of course, Colonel." He nodded toward Drake's corpse and said to the dwarf, "Have the men take care of that, Long Sam," then held out a hand and ushered them all toward a curtain of beads in the back of the room.

Cornelius still wished he had his dagger, but he touched the closed razor in his pocket to assure himself it was still there. He would recover the dagger later—assuming the meeting with Crowe went satisfactorily.

Behind the curtain was a short hallway lit by a single candle in a holder sitting on a shelf. Crowe picked up the candle, opened a door at the corridor's far end, and stepped back to allow the others to enter before him.

A gleaming hardwood table dominated the room, which had a heavily curtained window on one side. Ornately carved and decorated armchairs flanked the table. Crowe placed the candleholder in the center and nodded toward the chairs. "Please, have a seat."

The three of them sat down. A definite note of excitement was in Colonel Osborne's voice as he asked, "Are we about to meet M'sieu Simon LeCarde himself?"

"No, M'sieu LeCarde sees visitors only very rarely."

"Oh." Osborne sounded disappointed. "What do you want with us, then?"

"Actually, I only wanted to speak with Mr. Cornelius, since he was the one who violated the rule."

"Rule?" Cornelius repeated sharply. "What rule?"

"The one made by M'sieu LeCarde."

Cornelius snorted. A sense of danger lurked in the room, but he was angry, too, and didn't try to hide it. "Is it a rule in this town that a man cannot defend himself?"

Crowe leaned forward and placed his hands on the table, the fingers curled under so his weight rested on his knuckles. "Saul Drake was officially under M'sieu LeCarde's protection. That means he was not to be harmed."

"So I was supposed to sit there and let him shoot me?" Cornelius got to his feet. "This is mad, and I see no reason to continue. Come on, Lucy, we're leaving."

Crowe straightened and held up a hand. Tension filled the air in the room. Cornelius didn't know if he could fight his way out past this behemoth, but he would give it his best attempt. He would inflict some damage, anyway. Crowe wouldn't come out of the clash unscathed. Cornelius slid a hand in his pocket and closed it around the razor.

"Wait, please," Crowe said. "There's no need for trouble. You misunderstand me, Mr. Cornelius."

"Maybe you'd better speak plain, then."

"Very well. Saul Drake was arrogant and careless. While he was here in this place, he was supposed to play a clean game. You caught him cheating because you, too, are a professional. But in time, someone else would have tumbled to what he was doing. Perhaps even someone more highly valued to M'sieu LeCarde than Drake himself, and he would have been dealt with then."

The way Balthazar Crowe said *dealt with* would send chills down the back of most people. Cornelius felt a tiny shiver himself.

"So, even though what you did was a transgression against M'sieu LeCarde, you simply made the day of Saul Drake's reckoning arrive sooner than it would have otherwise. That makes the situation somewhat different from what it might have been . . . and leads me to make a proposition."

Lucy looked surprised, but Cornelius managed to keep a similar expression off his face. Bargaining with a man like Crowe was abhorrent, but the gambler said, "I'm listening."

"To speak plainly, Simon LeCarde controls most of the criminal activity in New Orleans. Those who wish to engage in such activities, such as Saul Drake, do so only with M'sieu LeCarde's permission and under his protection, as I said. This arrangement proves beneficial to everyone involved."

"And I assume LeCarde gets his cut as well."

"All of life can be reduced to a business transaction of some sort. Nothing happens in this world without it being a benefit . . . or a loss . . . for someone. If

M'sieu LeCarde makes profit possible, then a share of it should be his. This is only fair."

"But what does it have to do with me?" Cornelius asked.

Crowe grunted. "You and Miss Tarleton have come here to New Orleans with the intention of fleecing someone." He held up a hand again as Cornelius opened his mouth. "Don't waste your breath protesting, Mr. Cornelius. You know I speak the truth."

Colonel Osborne stared at Lucy, "Is that right, my dear? Have you come to rob me?"

"Why, Colonel, I never—"

"Perhaps not you, particularly, Colonel," Crowe broke in. "They're new in town. They probably had no real target in mind. They were just looking around for one when they saw you at the St. Charles."

Tight-jawed, Cornelius asked, "What in blazes is it you want, Crowe?"

"I'm offering you the chance to take Saul Drake's place in the greater scheme of things," Crowe said. "Feel free to cheat men at cards or bilk them in whatever scheme you might concoct. But you don't do it here"—he tapped a finger on the table—"in the Catamount's Den, and you don't go after certain individuals, including Colonel Osborne. I'll provide you with the names of those who are to be left alone. Other than that"—Crowe spread his hands—"New Orleans is your oyster, Mr. Cornelius. Do with it what you will, and you will be protected . . . as long as you deliver twenty percent of your earnings here, to me, every week."

"That's outrageous!"

Crowe shrugged. "It seems only fair to M'sieu LeCarde. Your only other choice is to operate on your own, and I assure you, that is a dangerous choice. For example, agree with my proposal, and the law will never trouble you over Saul Drake's death. Be so foolish as to refuse, and there will be witnesses to swear that you killed Drake with no provocation in an act of wanton murder."

"But that's not true!" Lucy said.

"Truth is what enough people say it is."

She turned her head to look at Cornelius. "Edmund, can he really do what he says?"

"I don't doubt it," Cornelius replied. To Crowe, he went on. "You have the authority to make this deal?"

"I do."

Osborne said, "I'd believe him, my boy. Balthazar Crowe is M'sieu LeCarde's right-hand man. Everybody knows that."

"Right-hand boy, you mean," Cornelius said.

Crowe breathed a little harder, but that was the only sign of anger he displayed. He simply stood there with his level gaze fixed on Cornelius as he said, "What is your decision?"

Cornelius hesitated only a moment longer before he said, "Tell your M'sieu LeCarde that we agree to the arrangement and will abide by his rules."

The colonel blew out an obviously relieved breath.

"I believe it will be a lucrative arrangement for all concerned," Crowe said.

"I hope so."

It wasn't just the money, though, Cornelius reflected. He didn't think it was possible that mountain man would ever be able to track them from St. Louis, but if somehow that happened, Preacher would find a lot more trouble waiting for him in New Orleans than he bargained for.

CHAPTER 15

The *Powhatan* docked in New Orleans in the late afternoon. Preacher hadn't been there for quite a few years.

His very first visit to the Crescent City had been in 1814, when, after making his first trip down the Mississippi River, he'd wound up joining the army under General Andrew Jackson, an unofficial enlistment in the force of volunteers and regular army that had been formed to oppose the British troops advancing on the city.

Early in January of 1815, they had all come together in a bloody clash several miles southeast, and for the first time, Preacher experienced full-scale battle involving thousands of men, all desperate to survive and win the day for their side.

The American forces had emerged victorious, suffering only a small fraction of the losses inflicted on the British. Later, they had found out that a treaty had already been signed to end the war, so the battle never should have taken place. Nobody in New Orleans knew that at the time, however—and nobody really cared, either. It had been quite a fight.

New Orleans had been a big city even then, and it had grown larger since the last time Preacher set foot there. The air along the riverfront held the familiar odors of rotting fish and vegetation and mud. Smoke from hundreds of chimneys thickened the atmosphere as well, along with the smell of human flesh and waste.

As Preacher paused at the foot of the gangplank, someone bumped heavily into him from behind. He looked around and saw the deckhand from the *Powhatan* who had given him trouble the day he boarded the riverboat in St. Louis.

"Better keep moving," the man said. "I know a half-savage like you is probably amazed by all the buildings, but civilized folks have things to do and you're in the way."

"I don't know what you've got against me, mister, but I'm gettin' a mite tired of listenin' to you yap."

The man's face turned red and his shoulders bunched as he balled his hands into fists. "The cap'n don't like members of the crew fightin' with passengers, but you ain't a passenger on the *Powhatan* anymore." With that rasped comment, he swung a punch at Preacher's head.

The mountain man swayed aside from it and jabbed the barrel of the rifle in his left hand into the deckhand's stomach. When the man gasped in pain and surprise and leaned forward, Preacher whipped his right fist around and crashed it into the deckhand's jaw. His head slewed to the side, his eyes rolled up in their sockets, and his knees buckled.

Preacher stepped back to let him collapse on the dock. He would have turned to walk away, but the sound of clapping surprised him and made him look up. The young crewman he had also talked to during the trip stood on the *Powhatan*'s deck with several other members of the crew, and they all were applauding.

The young crewman called, "Some of us have been wanting to do that for a long time, mister, but Shugart would have killed us. Maybe that knocked some of the meanness out of him."

"Maybe," Preacher said, "but I wouldn't count on it." He lifted a hand in farewell and moved off along the dock, heading for the row of buildings on the other side of the riverfront street. Asking a few questions of folks he ran into helped him find the office of the fellow who ran the docks.

A clerk sat at a desk in the outer office, and Preacher asked him, "How do I find out whether a particular riverboat got here all right?"

"I can help you with that," the young man said. "What's the name of the vessel?"

"The *Majestic.*"

The clerk opened a large book and ran a finger down a column of names with dates and other notations beside them. After a moment, he said, "Yes, here she is. She docked yesterday afternoon and will depart again for St. Louis and Louisville tomorrow morning."

"You happen to have a list of all the folks who got off of her?"

"The disembarking passengers, you mean?" The clerk frowned and shook his head. "I'm afraid not. We don't keep records of such things, only the vessels themselves and the cargo they carry."

Preacher nodded. He'd expected that answer. Lucy

Tarleton and Edmund Cornelius could have gotten off the riverboat at any of the stops along the way between St. Louis and New Orleans. Preacher had no way of knowing that they hadn't.

But according to what Charlie Todd told him, Cornelius had claimed that he and Lucy were headed for New Orleans, so Preacher had no choice but to assume they had traveled all the way on the *Majestic.*

They'd had almost twenty-four hours to lose themselves in the sprawling city. Most people would have assumed that finding them was impossible.

But that just took a heap of mule-headed stubbornness, and Preacher had plenty of that.

"I'm obliged to you," he told the clerk, then thought for a second.

Lucy and Cornelius had the money they had taken from Charlie, which meant they were flush with cash. Since Cornelius was a gambler, and probably a crooked one, at that, he could have won even more during the trip downriver. Likely, they would be staying in a nice place.

Preacher turned back to the clerk. "What's the best hotel in New Orleans?"

"The St. Charles," the clerk answered. He hesitated a second, then went on. "But they, ah, probably won't be disposed to have a guest such as yourself, sir. I mean no offense, but . . ."

"Fellas in buckskins don't check in there very often, is that what you mean?" Preacher grinned. "I don't intend to pitch my tent there, son. I just got a few questions I need answers to."

"Oh. Well, I hope you get them."

"Where do I find that St. Charles Hotel?"

The clerk gave him directions. Preacher thanked the young man and left, joining the throngs on the streets of New Orleans again. Looking around, he saw more people than he'd seen in a month of Sundays, and he didn't like the feeling of being surrounded. He recalled a trip he had made to Philadelphia several years earlier. That had been even worse, but New Orleans was the most crowded place he had visited since then.

With his frontiersman's instinct for direction, he had no trouble finding the hotel. He stopped in front of the massive building and looked up at it. Not in awe—Preacher had seen too many spectacular things in his life to be in awe of much of anything—but it was an impressive structure, no denying that. After a moment, he climbed the stairs, went across the columned portico, and strode into the hotel lobby.

A quick look around didn't reveal anybody else dressed in buckskins and carrying a flintlock rifle. The men all wore suits and top hats and the women were in elegant traveling outfits. but Preacher didn't let that stop him or even slow him down as he headed across the marble floor toward the desk.

A clerk in a fancy waistcoat, frilly shirt, and striped trousers saw him coming and backed off a step, eyes widening for a second before he glanced around hurriedly as if looking for help.

"Take it easy, son," Preacher told him as he came up to the desk. "I ain't lookin' for trouble. But I *am* lookin' for a couple of folks I know. A man and a woman, name of Mr. Edmund Cornelius and Miss Lucy Tarleton. Could you tell me if they're maybe stayin' here?"

"No, sir, I-I can't. We d-don't give out information like that."

"They're friends of mine—" Preacher began, although that statement was about as far from the truth as anybody could get.

"It doesn't matter. We have a strict policy of protecting our guests' privacy."

Preacher could tell this young man was afraid of him. New Orleans had its share of rough characters, but probably not many of them ventured into the St. Charles Hotel. He knew he looked fresh from the frontier, ready to spit, whittle, cut, and shoot. The mountain man thought about setting his rifle on the counter—that would probably spook the young clerk even more—but he felt a mite sorry for the lad.

He said, "I reckon I understand, son. Can I ask a favor of you?"

"Of . . . of course, sir."

"If Mr. Cornelius and Miss Tarleton *are* stayin' here, I'd sure appreciate it if you didn't mention to 'em that somebody came around lookin' for 'em. Think you could do that?"

The clerk swallowed. "Of course. Discretion is . . . is always our policy here at the St. Charles."

"I'm much obliged to you." Preacher was fairly confident the clerk would do as he'd asked.

The young fellow seemed afraid that Preacher would come back and hunt him down if he didn't do as the mountain man asked.

Preacher turned away and started toward the door. The expensively dressed guests in the lobby gave him a wide berth, as if they feared that getting too close to him might contaminate them. Might get a little frontier dirt on 'em, Preacher thought wryly.

He left the hotel and paused on the street outside to look around. He would need a place to stay, and it would have to be somewhere a lot less extravagant and expensive than the St. Charles. Until he recovered the money stolen by Cornelius and Lucy, he couldn't afford to be wasteful.

There had to be a livery stable somewhere in these parts with a proprietor who would let him sleep in the hayloft, he thought. He was about to go look for one when a voice said behind him, "Sir, I heard what you were asking in there."

Preacher turned his head and saw an older man with graying, reddish hair standing there. He was dressed in a brown suit and beaver hat and looked solidly respectable and successful, but without the fancy airs that so many people in this town seemed to put on. In fact, something about him struck Preacher as being familiar, as if he had seen the man before but didn't really know him.

"Have we met?" he asked.

The man smiled and shook his head. "Not really. My name is Andrew Fletcher. I used to own a general store in St. Louis, but I don't believe you ever bought any supplies there. You *are* the man called Preacher, aren't you?"

"That's right," Preacher admitted. "How come you know me if we didn't do business together?"

Fletcher chuckled. "Everybody in St. Louis has heard of the legendary Preacher, just as twenty years ago, everyone knew John Colter and Jim Bridger. You were pointed out to me on the street more than once by friends who work in the fur business." He stuck out his hand. "It's an honor to meet you."

Preacher shook hands with the man and asked, "You don't live in St. Louis no more?"

"No, I moved down here to be nearer my daughter and her family. I'm getting older, you know, ready to slow down and enjoy the time I have left."

Preacher couldn't really grasp that. Slowing down didn't seem to him the best way to enjoy life. He figured life needed to be lived full-blast, the way he always had. But each fella had his own way of going about things, he supposed.

"At any rate," Fletcher continued, "I was on my way through the lobby, intending to have a drink in the bar downstairs, when I heard you asking about a man named Cornelius."

"And a young woman named Lucy Tarleton," Preacher said.

"Well, the man I'm thinking about had a young woman with him, but I don't believe I ever heard her name spoken. This was in a tavern called the Catamount's Den. It has a rather unsavory reputation, but I venture there occasionally. A man still needs his diversions, you understand."

"Sure," Preacher said, wishing Fletcher would get to the point, whatever it was.

"The man I saw there, the one I heard called Cornelius, was dressed like a gambler. A medium-sized fellow, brown hair, a mustache . . . and the woman with him had dark brown hair and was very beautiful."

Preacher's pulse kicked up a notch. That sure sounded like the pair he sought. He nodded to Fletcher and said, "Go on."

"They were with a plantation owner named Osborne, an older man. The woman was playing up to him, I'd say."

Yep, that was Lucy. Preacher didn't doubt it a bit. The two of them had found themselves a new target.

"I'm acquainted with Osborne a bit," Fletcher went on. "Enough that I wouldn't want to see him taken advantage of. Do you mind if I ask you what your interest is in this fellow Cornelius . . . and the woman?"

Preacher studied the former businessman. Trusting his instincts, he decided that Fletcher was honest and wasn't up to any tricks.

"They robbed and hurt a friend of mine," Preacher said bluntly. "I intend to see that they pay for it."

Fletcher nodded. "I thought it might be something like that. And that's why I decided to tell you that I'd seen them in the Catamount's Den. I don't know if you can find them there or not, but it's a place to start looking, anyway."

"I'm obliged to you for the help," Preacher said.

"One more thing. If you would, please don't let on who told you where to look for them. There might be . . . repercussions."

"From who?" Preacher asked with a frown. "It ain't like there's a real catamount there, is it?"

"No," Fletcher said, "but what lurks in *that* den might be even worse."

CHAPTER 16

After thanking Andrew Fletcher for his help, Preacher asked one more favor, and the man gave him directions to a nearby livery stable and blacksmith shop run by a man named Jean Paul Dufresne.

"You don't appear to have a horse with you, though," Fletcher commented with a slightly puzzled frown. "Why do you need a livery stable?"

Preacher grinned and said cryptically, "Horses ain't the only critters that can bed down in a good stable."

"I suppose not," Fletcher replied, still clearly not understanding. But he shook hands with the mountain man again and wished him luck in the quest that had brought him to New Orleans.

Preacher found the livery stable and adjoining blacksmith shop and followed the sound of a hammer ringing on an anvil into the smoky, low-ceilinged shop. The man doing the pounding was medium height, with very broad shoulders and muscular arms. He wore a canvas apron and a long-sleeved shirt to protect his arms from flying sparks. Dark eyes in a rugged face under close-cropped, curly black hair turned toward Preacher as the mountain man walked into the shop.

"Help you with something, m'sieu?" the man asked as he paused in hammering out the glowing-hot horseshoe he was working on.

"You'd be Jean Paul Dufresne? Own the livery stable next door?"

"*Oui.* To both questions."

"I'm lookin' for a place to stay," Preacher said.

Dufresne frowned. "Perhaps I am missing something, but you do not appear to have four legs, m'sieu."

"You've got a hayloft, don't you? Well, I've slept in plenty of them."

"Ah," the blacksmith said as understanding dawned on him. "You search for someplace inexpensive to stay while you are in New Orleans."

"That's right. I can pay the same amount you'd charge for a horse." Preacher chuckled. "And you won't even have to provide any grain."

Dufresne laughed and said, "Very well. This is the first time anyone has suggested such an unusual arrangement, but I see no reason not to agree. You know, of course, that you may be sharing the straw with other . . . guests, shall we say? Nonpaying ones."

"Bugs and vermin, sure. I won't bother them if they don't bother me."

"And Matilde," Dufresne said. "She may wish to curl up with you."

Preacher raised an eyebrow.

"Be careful of her claws," the blacksmith went on. "They are very sharp, and she can be rather capricious in their use."

"You *are* talkin' about a cat, ain't you?" Preacher said.

"*Mais oui,* of course! What else?" Laughter boomed out from Dufresne's barrel chest.

Preacher paid the blacksmith for several nights' lodging, then asked, "What do you know about a place called the Catamount's Den?"

A scowl replaced the affable expression on Dufresne's face. "From what I hear, it can be a dangerous place. I have never been there, myself. I have a good wife and child and no need for such vice. But everyone in New Orleans knows the Catamount's Den is run by a man named Simon LeCarde. A very bad man, who has much to do with the crime in this city."

"The boss of all the wrongdoin', eh?"

Dufresne's brawny shoulders rose and fell. "Perhaps not all. But most, certainly. From what I hear, LeCarde extends his protection to many of the criminals who infest New Orleans, in return for part of their ill-gotten gains. It is a scandal, but—" He shrugged again. "This town is not known as a law-abiding community. The authorities, such as they are, can be as crooked as the criminals. I, myself, have been approached more than once by those who would offer me 'protection' in return for a regular payment."

"You don't go along with that, do you?" Preacher asked.

Dufresne lifted the heavy hammer he held and said, "I have my own means of protection, m'sieu, and it works very well."

"I'll just bet it does." Preacher felt an instinctive liking for this burly blacksmith and hoped that Dufresne's defiance of the local criminal underworld wouldn't bring harm to the man and his family someday.

Dufresne went back to hammering on the horseshoe while Preacher went into the livery stable, climbed the ladder to the hayloft, and left his rifle and warbag there. The long-barreled flintlock wasn't really suitable for any trouble he might encounter in the Crescent City. He had his brace of pistols, his knife, and his tomahawk, and those weapons all did the job just fine for close work.

Even without the rifle, they drew plenty of stares. Evidently, folks in New Orleans weren't accustomed to seeing a fellow go around so openly armed. They preferred derringers that would fit in a pocket and knives that could be hidden up a man's sleeve—or inside a garter belt, for those ladies who liked to carry some cold steel from time to time.

Dusk was settling over the city by the time Preacher walked into the French Quarter in search of the Catamount's Den. He strolled down Bourbon Street, taking in the jostling crowds around him, habitually keeping a wary eye out for anyone who might want to do him harm, even though as far as he knew, he didn't have any enemies in New Orleans other than Edmund Cornelius and Lucy Tarleton.

The narrow, cobblestoned street ran between buildings that seemed to lean in toward each other with their balconies railed by ornate wrought-iron scrollwork. That gave the area an intimate atmosphere, but the close quarters seemed oppressive to a man such as Preacher, who spent most of each year in wide-open spaces where he might go a week or more without laying eyes on another human being and could see for miles in every direction. Spending all his time in a place like the French Quarter would be like being in prison, he thought.

Andrew Fletcher had told him how to find the Catamount's Den. Having no trouble locating it,

Preacher paused outside to admire the artwork on the sign hanging over the arched, iron-banded door. Having seen more than his share of mountain lions in his time, he thought whoever had painted this one had done a pretty good job of capturing the creature's sleek ferocity.

Men went in and out of the place, some dressed in finery, others in rough work clothes. Evidently the Catamount's Den catered to all kinds. Preacher supposed the tavern was the sort of place where it didn't matter who you were or where you came from, as long as you had money. From what Jean Paul Dufresne had told him, profit was the only thing Simon LeCarde really cared about.

One thing he noticed was that many of the people who went in rapped first on the door in a certain pattern—three knocks, then a pause, three more, another pause, and a final three. After that, they opened the door and went inside.

Preacher stepped up to the door and repeated that pattern, then pulled it open and stepped inside, only to be greeted by the twin barrels of a shotgun swinging up to point at him. He controlled the impulse to duck, jerk one of the pistols from behind his belt, and shoot the man with the scattergun.

At first glance he thought the person pointing the shotgun at him was a child. The fellow was perched on a high stool and his legs didn't come close to hitting the floor. Then he realized the guardian of this particular den was a dwarf, brawny enough from the waist up that he didn't have any trouble handling the weapon, although it appeared the barrels had been sawed off somewhat to make it easier for him.

"Just stand right there and let me take a look at you," the dwarf ordered. "I don't know you."

"That don't surprise me none, seein' as I've never been here before," Preacher said. "How about puttin' down that scattergun? Them things make me a mite nervous."

"Yeah, well, I'd be nervous if I *wasn't* pointing it at you." The dwarf frowned. "Who are you? How'd you know the special knock? Somebody tell you about it?"

Preacher couldn't help laughing. "Shoot, I just stood out yonder on Bourbon Street and watched for a few minutes until I figured out what folks were doin' as they came in here. It didn't take a whole lot of ponderin' on my part."

"Well, I suppose that's true," the guard admitted with obvious reluctance. "What do you want here?"

"The same thing everybody else who comes here does, I reckon. Something to drink, maybe some good company. A game of cards, a friendly, good-lookin' gal—"

"The Catamount's Den can offer you all those things. What's your name?"

"Art," Preacher replied, falling back on his seldom-used real name. If Cornelius and Lucy had fallen in with this Simon LeCarde, it was possible they might have mentioned his name as someone who could be looking for them.

They could have described him as well, he realized. But maybe he wasn't the only one in New Orleans wearing buckskins and armed for bear, although he hadn't noticed anybody else who fit that description.

"Are you a stranger in town, Art?" the dwarf went on.

"That's right. Just got here today, in fact."

"Who told you about the Catamount's Den?"

"I just heard talk about it," Preacher replied vaguely, honoring Andrew Fletcher's request to keep his name out of it. "Never got introduced to the fellas who mentioned it."

The dwarf appeared to think about it for a moment, then he finally lowered the shotgun. "All right," he said as he jerked his head toward the other side of the foyer. "Go on in. Just remember . . . no trouble while you're inside. Any problems, you take 'em outside."

"Fair enough," Preacher said. He strolled on into the tavern, glad the guardian hadn't demanded that he turn over his weapons. Preacher never would have done that, even if it meant taking that shotgun away from the fella and starting a ruckus.

With his hat brim pulled low to partially shield his face, he paused just inside the room to look around. At first glance, he didn't see Edmund Cornelius or Lucy Tarleton, but that didn't mean they weren't there. The room was smoky and dimly lit, with shadowy corners that were all but impossible to see into.

After a moment, Preacher headed for the bar.

He hadn't gotten there when a harsh voice ripped out a curse and a hard hand fell heavily on his shoulder. Whoever had grabbed him jerked him around, and Preacher had only a second to see the knobby-knuckled fist flashing toward his face.

CHAPTER 17

The punch came at him too swiftly for him to avoid it entirely, but he managed to dip his head to the side so the fist struck him a glancing blow just above the left ear. His hat flew off. So much for trying to keep his features obscured.

But the goal of not drawing attention to himself had evaporated as soon as he came under attack. Everybody in the place turned to look as Preacher's assailant roared another curse and waded in with arms swinging.

The man's identity didn't surprise Preacher. He recognized the big deckhand from the riverboat who had clashed with him on the dock that afternoon, soon after the *Powhatan*'s arrival in New Orleans.

Shugart, that was the man's name, Preacher recalled as he blocked a second punch and stepped aside from another.

He couldn't avoid all the blows, however. A big fist crashed against his sternum and knocked him back a step. An instant later, Shugart's other first sank into Preacher's belly and drove most of the air out of his body.

Preacher planted his feet, ducked his head, and let another punch skid off his skull. Braced and ready now, he snapped a left into Shugart's face and landed it cleanly on the man's mouth. The blow rocked Shugart's head back, and Preacher followed it with a right that smashed into the deckhand's jaw and staggered him.

Preacher had forgotten all about the dwarf's admonition regarding fighting inside the Catamount's Den, but even if he'd remembered, it wouldn't have made any difference. He had never been the sort to just stand there and take it when somebody jumped him. He always fought back and always would.

Crowding in on Shugart, Preacher threw another left and right combination that rocked the man's head back and forth and knocked him back on his heels. He was too strong and angry to continue giving ground, though. His head was hard as a rock, too, as Preacher had discovered. Shugart bellowed again like a maddened bull and threw himself at Preacher, wrapping his arms around the mountain man and forcing him off his feet.

They slammed down on the thick-planked floor with enough impact that it seemed like it ought to shake the building. The sturdy old structure took it just fine, though. Better than Preacher did, because aches and pains were already shooting through his body. He had the consolation, though, of knowing that Shugart was probably in worse shape. The man's lips were swollen and bleeding, and a big bruise had started to form on his jaw.

Those bloody lips pulled back from Shugart's teeth in a snarling grimace. He grappled with Preacher and tried to ram a knee into his groin. Preacher twisted away from it, so the blow struck him on the hip. He closed a hand on Shugart's thick throat and arched up from the floor, bucking and rolling.

Shugart wound up lying on his back. Preacher hammered his other fist against the man's cheek, hitting him three times in very close succession. Shugart started to go limp, as if he were on the verge of passing out or giving up, but then a fresh resolve seemed to grip him. He tangled both hands in the front of Preacher's buckskin shirt and heaved.

Loading and unloading cargo had given Shugart plenty of strength. Preacher flew through the air and crashed into the legs of a table, knocking it over and spilling a bucket of beer. One of the men who'd been sitting there yelled and kicked at Preacher. Another man grabbed him and punched him, evidently not liking the idea of kicking a man while he was down.

In a matter of moments, the tavern descended into chaos as the customers wound up fighting with each other. It was a full-fledged brawl, and Preacher nearly got stomped on several times as he fought to get back to his feet.

He and Shugart made it upright at the same time. They surged together and slugged wildly for a long moment, dishing out punishment. Each of them took plenty of it, before they grappled again. It was a no-holds-barred fight and had been from the first. Men such as Preacher and Shugart didn't know any other form of combat. They gouged and kicked, and if Preacher could have gotten his teeth into one of Shugart's ears, he would have ripped it right off the varmint's head.

The battle reminded Preacher of his fight with Abner Rowland in Red Mike's a week or so previously.

Shugart wasn't as strong or as canny as Rowland, though, and he had to start giving ground again. Preacher pressed him, and Shugart responded with a wild, looping punch that fatigue slowed down enough that Preacher had no trouble ducking under it.

As soon as the big fist had missed by half a foot, Preacher stepped in and hooked a left and right into Shugart's ribs, staggering him again. Shugart's arms dropped in pain and weariness. Preacher hit him in the face with a left that opened Shugart's stance and put him in perfect position for the uppercut Preacher lifted from his knees. The perfectly timed and aimed blow landed with such devastating impact that Shugart actually rose in the air a couple of inches before crashing down on his back, out cold.

Preacher stood there with his chest heaving as he caught his breath. Around him, more violence ebbed and flowed as the brawl continued. One man picked up a chair and ran at him, yelling. Preacher bent over, caught hold of the man around the waist, and heaved him up and over. The man's angry shout became a terrified screech as he flew through the air, dropped the chair he'd been brandishing as a weapon, and landed with tooth-rattling, bone-jarring force on the bar. Momentum carried him on over, and he disappeared behind the bar.

Preacher felt pretty sure he didn't know anyone except Shugart—unless Cornelius and Lucy were around—but that hadn't stopped the man with the chair from rushing him, and he knew it wouldn't stop some of the others who were caught up in a battle frenzy, as well. He set his feet, balled his fists, and looked around, ready to defend himself again.

That proved to be unnecessary. A black man every

bit as towering and massive as his Crow Indian friend Big Thunder plowed through the struggling crowd. He caught men by their shirt collars and flung them left and right. Others he pounded on top of the head as if they were nails and he was a human hammer trying to drive them into the floor. A few of the brawlers tried to fight back, but the black man made short work of them, flicking them away like brushing off gnats.

He left a trail of sprawled men behind him, some of them moaning, some out cold. The rest of the battlers lowered their fists and backed off apprehensively. None of them wanted to experience the behemoth's wrath, and Preacher couldn't blame them for that.

The man came to a stop in the center of the room. He wore a fine black suit, a white, frilly shirt, and a ribbon tie and didn't look like any slave Preacher had ever seen in St. Louis.

He didn't hold with slavery. There hadn't been any slaves around where he had grown up. Some Indian tribes made slaves out of captives they took from other tribes, so he had witnessed instances of that, and he saw black slaves from time to time in St. Louis. He had assumed that any blacks he encountered in New Orleans would also be slaves.

Not this fellow, though, that was plain. He bellowed, "Enough!" with the authority of a free man.

The dwarf Preacher had seen at the entrance was inside the main room, too, still holding that shotgun. He used a chair to scramble up onto the bar and stood there swinging the double-barreled weapon from side to side as he shouted, "The next man who throws a punch gets a load of buckshot!"

Preacher figured that was an empty threat. As

crowded as the room was, firing that shotgun would prove fatal for more than one man. But the dwarf had sort of a wild-eyed, loco look about him that said he might not draw the line at such wholesale slaughter, and that was enough to make everybody careful not to set him off.

The dwarf blustered several obscenities, then demanded, "Who started this?"

At least half a dozen fingers pointed at Preacher.

"That's a blasted lie," the mountain man snapped. "I hadn't no more 'n walked into the place when that fella"—he jerked a hand toward Shugart's senseless form—"grabbed me and threw a punch at me."

"Why would he do that?" the black man asked in a deep, rumbling voice.

"He don't like me because we had some trouble down at the docks earlier. Right after both of us got off the riverboat that brought us to New Orleans."

"You followed him here tonight?" the dwarf asked.

"Shoot, no! I didn't care if I ever saw him again. I came in for a drink and to pass the time, and he just happened to be here."

And a stroke of mighty bad luck *that* had been, Preacher reflected. Even if Cornelius and Lucy weren't here—and he still hadn't spotted them in the tavern— most likely they would learn about this ruckus and would hear that a mountain man had been at the center of it. If anybody described him to them, they would know he had followed them from St. Louis. Probably they had been concerned about that possibility all along.

"Whether you were defending yourself or not, you were in the middle of this trouble," the black man said. "That means you're no longer welcome in the Catamount's Den."

"That ain't hardly fair," Preacher said. "A man's got a right to defend hisself."

The dwarf pointed the shotgun at him again. "Shut your mouth! Balthazar has spoke. You get outta here, mister."

Preacher nodded toward Shugart and asked, "What about him?"

"We'll toss him out back and let him wake up on his own." The dwarf cocked his head to the side. "Are you thinkin' about finding him and cutting his throat before he comes to?"

Preacher grimaced. "I ain't the sort to do a thing like that," he said disgustedly.

"No," the black man said, "I can see that you aren't. But you still have to leave."

Preacher didn't see any point in making the disastrous outing even worse. And he was pretty doggoned sure that nobody would be willing to answer his questions about Cornelius and Lucy. He had made a mistake by visiting the Catamount's Den, he realized. He should have waited somewhere outside, hidden from sight, and watched for his quarry to come or go. The problem was, such skulking around went directly against Preacher's nature. He was built to tackle problems head-on, even if that wasn't always the wisest course of action.

"All right," he said as he picked up his hat and slapped it against his thigh to get rid of the sawdust clinging to it. "But I don't like it."

"No one said you have to like it," the black man told him. "You just have to get out."

Preacher put on his hat and left the tavern, feeling

frustrated by the turn of events things had taken. At least nobody jumped him on his way back to Jean Paul Dufresne's livery stable. The way his luck was running, he ought to be thankful for that, anyway, he told himself.

He ran into the blacksmith and stable owner right outside the place. Dufresne appeared to be leaving for the day. He had removed the canvas apron he wore while working at the anvil.

"I left some bread and cheese wrapped up for you in the blacksmith shop," Dufresne said.

"Feedin' me wasn't part of our deal," Preacher reminded him.

The blacksmith shrugged. "My wife was here earlier and said she would not see a man go hungry. She believes you must be quite poor, or else you would not sleep in a hayloft."

Preacher grinned. "I ain't broke, but I ain't exactly flush, either. Tell your missus I'm mighty obliged to her."

"There is part of a bottle of wine in there, too." Dufresne shrugged. "My contribution."

"Then I'm obliged to you as well."

"Good night, *mon ami.*"

"That means friend, don't it?"

"*Oui.*"

"Good night," Preacher said. The kindness Dufresne and his wife had displayed made the mountain man feel a little better about his trip to New Orleans, even though he had a hunch his search for Cornelius and Lucy might have already hit a dead end.

He went into the blacksmith shop and found that Dufresne had left a candle burning in a brass holder. Spotting the cloth-wrapped bundle and the bottle on the anvil, he picked them up, tucked the bottle under his arm, and then took the candle with him as well, to light his way into the livery stable.

He froze as he turned toward the doorway. A huge, menacing figure filled it, blocking his path.

CHAPTER 18

The flickering candlelight threw stark, shifting shadows over the looming figure as the man took another step into the livery barn.

"Hold it right there, mister," Preacher told him.

The towering black man looked even taller now because he wore a top hat. He smiled at Preacher and said, "What if I do not *hold it*, as you say? You will attack me with a loaf of bread? That's what you have in that bundle, isn't it? Or do you think you can drop it and pull one of those pistols before I reach you?"

"You'll be bettin' a lot if you figure I can't do that," Preacher pointed out. "Your life, to be exact. As a matter of fact, I *am* pretty handy with these here pistols." He shrugged. "But if you want to find out for yourself, I reckon you can go ahead."

The man shook his head, and a low, gravelly sound came from him. Preached needed a second to recognize it as laughter.

"I did not come here with the intent that either of us should die," the black man said.

"Then why *are* you here?" Preacher asked. "If you

plan on makin' me pay for the damages in that tavern brawl, you're outta luck. I ain't got the money for that."

The black man waved a hamlike hand in a dismissive gesture. "That fight and those damages mean nothing in the larger scheme of things. My name is Balthazar Crowe, and my employer sent me here to extend an invitation."

"What sort of invitation?" Preacher asked as his eyes narrowed warily.

"To dine with Simon LeCarde."

The answer surprised Preacher. He couldn't see any reason the boss of New Orleans' criminal underworld should want to have dinner with him. "I've got my supper right here." Preacher hefted the bundle of bread and cheese.

"I can promise you, the fare upstairs at the Catamount's Den will be much better," Balthazar Crowe said.

"Upstairs, eh? I reckon that's where this fella LeCarde lives?"

Crowe inclined his head in agreement.

"I've got a sneakin' suspicion this is a trap of some sort."

"You have my assurance that it is not," Crowe said. "Ask anyone in New Orleans. They will tell you that my word is my bond."

"Maybe so, but I don't hardly know a soul here, so why would I trust 'em?"

A look of annoyed impatience appeared on Crowe's face. "I was sent to bring you back with me. Will you accompany me peacefully, or . . ." He left the rest of it unsaid.

Preacher turned and placed the candleholder back on the anvil, set the bread and cheese beside it. "All right. I reckon if you want to tangle—" He stopped short.

He didn't like Crowe's arrogance. The man's high-handed attitude was almost enough to make Preacher want to fight him. On the other hand, Crowe might be unwittingly offering him a path right to the destination he sought. If everything he'd heard about Simon LeCarde was true, the man either knew where Edmund Cornelius and Lucy Tarleton were—or would know how to find them.

Preacher heaved a sigh. "I reckon it ain't worth a tussle." He didn't want to appear to be giving in too easily, though, so he added, "I still don't like the idea of somebody bein' sent to fetch me."

"A black man, you mean."

Preacher shook his head. "I don't give a mule's hind end what color you are, mister. I just don't like fellas who figure they can tell me where to go or what to do. Never have."

"In that, you and I are alike . . . to a certain extent."

"You got a boss who gives you orders, though. I don't."

"Everyone has someone to whom they have to answer, sooner or later, in this world or the next." The massive shoulders rose and fell, and then Crowe gestured toward the stable's open doors. "Shall we go?"

"Just a minute." Preacher picked up the bottle of wine, pulled the cork with his teeth, spat it into his hand, and then took a long drink. As he pushed the cork back in, he said, "Now I'm ready. Let's go meet this Monsieur LeCarde of yours."

Preacher and Crowe walked through the still-crowded streets, but people got out of Crowe's way, so the throng of pedestrians wasn't any problem.

As they walked, Preacher asked, "How'd you know where to find me?"

"Simon LeCarde knows how to find almost anyone in New Orleans," Crowe answered cryptically.

"You make him sound like some sort of magician." Preacher thought about rumors he had heard concerning this city. "He ain't one of them voodoo fellas, is he?"

Crowe laughed. "Voodoo—*voudon*, as it is properly known—is a superstition. Whether or not it has any real power depends largely on whether you *believe* that it does. Rest assured, Simon LeCarde does not traffic in superstition."

"All right." Preacher didn't press Crowe for a more forthcoming answer, but he thought about it and wondered if LeCarde had had someone follow him when he left the Catamount's Den. That made the most sense. He wondered, as well, if the mysterious Simon LeCarde had been watching that brawl from somewhere. Maybe he had caught LeCarde's eye for some reason. Preacher figured he'd get to the bottom of it sooner or later, but mostly he wanted to use the unexpected development to help him find Edmund Cornelius and Lucy Tarleton.

It took the two men only a few minutes to reach the Catamount's Den. Crowe didn't head for the front door when they got there, however, leading Preacher into a shadow-clogged alley alongside the building.

Preacher put a hand on a pistol butt and said, "Remember what I told you about this feelin' like a trap to me?"

Crowe laughed. "I assure you, it is not. My orders were to bring you in the back way, that's all. If you don't trust me, go ahead and draw that gun. I won't try to stop you. You must put it away, however, when you meet Simon LeCarde."

"Just don't try anything," Preacher warned.

Not much light penetrated back there, but Crowe clearly knew where he was going. He opened a door, and lamplight spilled into the alley. He motioned for Preacher to precede him, but the mountain man shook his head.

"You go first."

Amusement tinged Crowe's voice again as the massive man said, "But of course." He went inside, the light casting a huge shadow behind him as he entered.

Preacher followed, still ready to pull out that pistol and fire if he needed to. He nodded toward the narrow flight of stairs that led up to the second floor and told Crowe, "Go ahead."

The black man's shoulders almost brushed the sides of the stairwell as he climbed. Preacher gave him a little room as he went up the stairs, just in case Crowe tried to turn around and dive back down at him.

But Preacher had started to believe that Crowe had told the truth about it not being a trap. If Crowe actually wanted to try any tricks, he could have done it already.

They reached a landing at the top of the stairs. To the right, a hall ran toward the front of the building.

Crowe turned to the closed door on the left and rapped on it, called, "It's Balthazar Crowe. I have the frontiersman with me."

Preacher didn't hear any response from inside, but Crowe reached down, twisted the ornate glass knob, and opened the door. He stepped aside, but once again, Preacher shook his head and gestured toward the opening, indicating that Crowe should go first. Once again, the huge black man looked vaguely amused as he entered the room.

Preacher stepped in after him and glanced around the large room. From the looks of it, it functioned as a combination dining and sitting room, with woven rugs on the floor, a gleaming, rectangular hardwood table with several matching chairs at the ends, a pair of armchairs next to a small fireplace, and two lushly upholstered divans. Thick curtains covered two windows in the rear wall.

The table was set for two, one at each end, with fine china plates, crystal wineglasses, and sparkling silver utensils. In between were several platters of food, including a roast bird of some kind, probably a chicken, Preacher decided. Too small to be a turkey.

Preacher quickly noted all those details, but the real object of his search was the presence of enemies. He didn't see any. Indeed, he and Crowe were the only ones in the room. But to the right, on the opposite side of the room from the fireplace, another door stood partially open.

Crowe closed the door they had come in and turned toward the other one. Evidently speaking to someone on the other side of that panel, he said, "Allow me to present—" He paused and looked around at Preacher. "I just realized that I don't know your name."

"They call me Preacher," the mountain man said.

"Preacher? That's all? Surely you have another name."

"Preacher will do."

Crowe shrugged. "Very well. Allow me to present Preacher."

Preacher's breath hissed between his teeth as his host stepped through the door from the adjoining room. The most beautiful woman he had seen in quite some time smiled at him and said, "Welcome, Preacher, to the Catamount's Den. I am Simone LeCarde."

CHAPTER 19

Preacher tried not to stare at the woman, but that wasn't easy. She had the sort of looks that would draw and hold just about any man's gaze.

Hair as black as midnight piled high on her head in an elaborate arrangement of curls. The face beneath that swept-up hair had a slightly exotic cast to it. The dark eyes went well with the faintly olive skin, as did the tiny beauty mark near the left corner of her red-lipped mouth. She wore a dark burgundy gown cut low in front to reveal the swells of her breasts. A wide collar stood up to frame her face even more effectively. The dress concealed but also accentuated the rest of her ample curves. She was somewhere between the ages of twenty-five and thirty, Preacher estimated, although he knew that judging a woman's true age often posed even more challenges than following a cold, faint path through the wilderness.

She was waiting for him to say something, he realized, so he said, "I reckon you must be Simon's sister."

She laughed and said, "I think you know better than that, Mister . . . Preacher, was it?"

"Just Preacher. No *mister*. And how in blazes

would I know if this LeCarde fella has a sister? Lots of folks do."

"That's true enough, I suppose," she said as she came toward him. "But just to be clear, there is no Simon LeCarde. Only me. Simon is . . . a useful illusion."

From behind him, Crowe said softly, "You should consider yourself fortunate. The number of people who know the truth of what was just revealed to you can be counted on one hand."

"That's true," Simone LeCarde said as she rested her right hand on the back of the chair at the other end of the table.

An elegant, long-fingered hand with nails painted to match the dress she wore, Preacher noted, as well as rings on a couple of the fingers.

"Balthazar here, our stalwart compatriot Long Sam, Francis Bennington, the man who keeps my accounts for me . . . and now you."

"I reckon the question is, why me?" Preacher said.

Crowe rumbled, "When fortune smiles on a man, he is wise not to question it."

"No, I can see why Preacher would be puzzled," Simone said. "Why don't we have a seat, and I'll explain everything."

She might be waiting for him to hustle to the other end of the table and hold her chair for her, Preacher realized. Normally, he treated women with a sort of rough chivalry and probably would have done just that in other circumstances, but he didn't trust her, felt that something was fishy about this whole deal, and stayed where he was.

Crowe strode past him and performed the task

instead, pulling the chair out from the table and sliding it under Simone when she sat down.

Preacher took the seat at the other end. He didn't see any reason to be completely rude, so he removed his hat and set it on the table beside him.

Crowe picked up the bottle of wine that sat on the table and filled both their glasses. Then he put food on their plates and served them before withdrawing to stand at the side of the room. With anyone else, Preacher suspected, Crowe wouldn't accept being treated like a servant, but he seemed not to mind serving Simone LeCarde.

"Please," she said, "we'll eat, and then we'll talk."

"Well . . . it's true I ain't had supper yet." Preacher glanced at Crowe. "Was about to, but then I got interrupted."

Preacher dug in. The chicken was roasted perfectly, and the potatoes were equally tasty. He was no expert on wine, but what was in his glass was good, too.

Simone ate with a healthy appetite, which Preacher liked. Women who picked at their food always annoyed him. He had found that women who liked to eat enjoyed other pleasures as well and generally were more honest, too.

Honest might not be a very good description of Simone LeCarde, he reminded himself. If the rumors about the fictitious "Simon" were true, with her taking the place of an imaginary male, that could well be the biggest criminal in the city sitting at the other end of the table from him.

"This was mighty good grub," he commented when he finished the food on the plate in front of him.

"Thank you. I prepared it myself."

"Really? Somehow you don't strike me as the sort of gal who'd do much cookin'."

Simone cocked her head to the side. "And why is that? Am I not feminine enough?"

"You're plenty feminine," Preacher told her. "I just figured you had your plate full with other things . . . like runnin' most of the crime here in New Orleans."

She laughed and said, "You've been listening to rumors about me, haven't you? Or rather, about Simon. You can't believe everything you hear, Preacher."

"Are you sayin' you *don't* have any crooked dealin's or offer protection to lawbreakers who can pay your price?"

She sipped her wine and regarded him coolly over the rim of her crystal wineglass. "You sound like a man who's looking for someone."

"Didn't say that. I'm just curious what I'm doin' here."

"Very well." Simone placed her glass back on the table. "The time has come for blunt talk. Does it bother you when a woman speaks plainly, Preacher?"

"Not one little bit," the mountain man replied.

"Good, because I prefer to speak my mind. I saw the fight that took place earlier."

"I already told Mr. Crowe that I can't pay for the damages."

Simone waved a hand dismissively and managed to make the gesture look elegant. "I don't care about the damages. A few broken tables and chairs are nothing. I'm more interested in the man right in the thick of the violence."

"That fella Shugart started it."

"I know. I'm familiar with Shugart. He's a bully and a braggart, and he's caused trouble here before. I've instructed Long Sam that he's no longer welcome at the Catamount's Den."

"Long Sam bein' the little fella with the shotgun who sits at the door," Preacher guessed.

"That's right. Don't underestimate him because of his size."

Preacher shook his head. "I wouldn't hardly do that. I've got a friend who's a lot like him, and Audie's just about the smartest, toughest fella I know."

"At any rate," Simone continued, "this wasn't the first fight Shugart started . . . but it *was* the first one he lost. It caught my interest when someone was able to defeat an animal like him."

"I didn't see you in there watchin' the ruckus."

"I'm only seen when I want to be, like now. And that doesn't happen very often."

Crowe spoke up. "It *never* happens. You have no idea what an honor it is for you to even be here, Preacher."

"Forgive Balthazar," Simone said. "He's quite devoted to me, just as he was to my father."

"Catamount Jack," Preacher said. "I've heard about *him*, too." He looked at Crowe. "Were you part of his pirate crew?"

The cool, slightly mocking smile on Simone's face disappeared instantly. She held up a hand to stop whatever reply Crowe was about to make.

"Balthazar sailed with my father," she said, "and so did Long Sam. But none of them were pirates. They were privateers, operating under letters of marque during the war against the British in 1812. That's not the same thing at all."

Preacher shook his head. "I wouldn't know. I've spent most of my life on dry land, if you don't count riverboats and canoes and rafts and such. Never been on the high seas and don't know a thing about it other than what I've heard."

"Well, you can take my word for it, then," Simone snapped. "My father was not a pirate."

"All right. I didn't mean no offense."

Simone smiled again. "Forgive me. I didn't mean to lose my temper. I'm just a bit sensitive on the subject of my father, that's all." She reached for her wine, took another sip, and went on. "Now, as I started to say, you caught my interest, Preacher, and I wanted to know more about you. That's why I had Long Sam follow you back to the place where you're staying and then asked Balthazar to bring you here for supper with me. I'd like to know more about you."

"There ain't much to tell," Preacher said. "I'm a fur trapper, most of the time. Now and then I sign on to guide a wagon train or some such. I've spent most of my time in the Rockies for the past twenty years or more."

"You must have seen some spectacular sights."

"The scenery's pretty impressive," Preacher admitted.

"And survived a great many dangers, too."

"My share of 'em, that's for sure. Includin' run-ins with a few mountain lions, like the one painted on your sign outside."

"That was Long Sam's work. He has surprising talents."

"I'm sure he does. If you don't mind *me* askin' a question . . ."

"Please, go ahead," Simone replied with another of those languid, elegant gestures.

"If your pa was a seagoin' man, how'd he wind up

bein' called Catamount Jack? You don't run into too many of those critters out on the ocean, I expect."

"He didn't spend his entire life at sea," she explained. "In fact, when he was a young man, he lived in the mountains in Tennessee. They had big cats there, and when he was little more than a child, he was attacked by one of them. All he had to defend himself with was a knife. But he killed that beast and survived it trying to maul him, even though he was badly hurt."

"Sounds like a tough fella, all right."

Simone nodded. "He was. After that, people started calling him Catamount Jack, instead of plain Jack LeCarde, and the name stuck." She paused. "The same way some incident must have make people start calling you Preacher. I can't imagine that your mother gave you that name."

"Well, the truth is, she didn't. But that's what folks have been callin' me for a whole heap of years, so I've gotten used to it. Don't know that I'd answer to anything else."

"That's what I'll call you, then." Simone studied him intently across the table for a long moment, then she picked up her wineglass and said, "Here's to the success of our continued association."

Preacher frowned. "What association is that?"

"I've made up my mind," Simone said. "I want you to go to work for me."

CHAPTER 20

Preacher reached for his wineglass and took a sip to conceal his surprise and give him a second to think, although he had a feeling Simone was canny enough she might know what he was doing. As he set the glass back on the table, he said, "I don't see what I'd do for you. I don't know a blasted thing about runnin' a tavern."

"You know the fur business, though. You said yourself that you've been trapping for many years. I've been thinking about trying to establish some new enterprises. Perhaps expand into another city . . ."

"Like St. Louis?" Preacher suggested. He shook his head. "I can tell you right now, that wouldn't be a smart thing to do."

"And why not?" she asked. "I should make it clear that I'm not necessarily talking about anything, well, illegal. I thought perhaps investing in the fur business would be a shrewd idea. But I would need someone on hand to make sure that everything was done properly."

"Yeah, it might have been a good idea . . . ten or fifteen years ago. But these days . . . The way it looks to me, the fur business will be just about dried up and blowed away in another few years. People don't wear beaver hats the way they used to. From what I hear, the rich folks are startin' to favor silk top hats, and they're the only ones who have the money to buy such foofaraws. I know the last load of pelts I sold, I didn't get near as much for it as I used to."

And that money had been stolen by Edmund Cornelius and Lucy Tarleton, he thought—two people who might be under Simone's protection even now. Preacher warned himself to tread carefully here. He didn't want to tip her off to his real goal too soon.

Simone frowned as she looked across the table at him. "You really believe things are that bad where the fur business is concerned?"

"I can only go by what I see," Preacher replied with a shrug. "There ain't as many fellas trappin' as there used to be. There's fewer of 'em at the big rendezvous every year. And they're makin' less money at it. That ain't somethin' I'd want to jump into with both feet."

"And yet you're still spending most of your time in the mountains, trapping," Simone pointed out.

Preacher grinned. "I don't hardly know how to do anything else. Anyway, I'm gettin' too long in the tooth to change my ways now. Reckon I'll stay with it as long as there's any money to be made at all. As long as I can pay for the supplies for another trip, that's all I really need."

"I have to say, this discussion hasn't gone the way I hoped it would," Simone said as she sat back and shook her head. "I was looking forward to trying something new and having you represent my interests, Preacher, but if you're right in your assessment, I doubt the effort would be worthwhile."

"I'm just tellin' you the truth, the way I see it."

"I appreciate that." She smiled. "At least you got a good meal out of the invitation."

Balthazar Crowe said, "And discovered a secret he need not have known."

"I think we can trust Preacher not to reveal anything that he shouldn't." Simone raised an eyebrow at him. "Can't we?"

"Sure," the mountain man agreed. "New Orleans ain't my city. It don't matter that much to me what goes on here."

His natural tendency toward honesty and straight talk had led him to approach this the wrong way, he realized now. He should have played along with Simone's plan so that he could stay closer to her and maybe pick up the trail of Edmund Cornelius and Lucy Tarleton. It didn't matter whether her idea of moving in on the fur trade was a good one or not, and he didn't believe for a second her claim that she wanted to get involved with it legally. She was his only lead to the thieves who had stolen his and Charlie's money and nearly killed the young man. Probably he had just talked her out of having anything more to do with him.

He was just in the habit of being too blasted honest, he told himself. Now Simone might send him on his way, and he wouldn't be any closer to finding his quarry.

She eased that worry by saying, "Balthazar, you can go on back downstairs now."

"Long Sam can handle anything that comes up down there," Crowe said, frowning.

"And I can handle anything up here," Simone responded with a sharp edge in her voice.

Preacher could tell that Crowe didn't like it at all,

but the big man was accustomed to doing whatever Simone LeCarde told him to do.

After a moment during which their gazes briefly dueled, he bowed slightly and murmured, "Whatever you wish, of course, mademoiselle."

"Don't worry, I'll summon you if I have need of you," she told him.

With obvious reluctance, Crowe left the room. Preacher supposed another flight of stairs led down to the tavern itself, in addition to the one that opened onto the alley.

Simone stood up and went along the table toward Preacher, taking her glass and the bottle of wine with her. She poured wine in each of their glasses, then leaned a hip against the table as she looked down at the mountain man. She held out her glass, and he clinked his against it.

"Even though my plans didn't work out, I'm still glad I had Balthazar bring you here tonight," she said. "I was curious about the sort of man who could defeat Shugart. Not many would ever even challenge a brute such as that to start with."

"I didn't exactly challenge him," Preacher pointed out. "Just stood up for myself when he tried to run roughshod over me."

"And you don't allow that from anyone, do you?"

"No, ma'am, I don't."

She cocked an eyebrow again. "What if it's a woman you're up against?"

Preacher shook his head slowly. "I don't fight with women." He remembered the Blackfoot woman called Winter Wind, who considered herself a warrior and had made it her business to try to kill Preacher and Hawk That Soars—and had almost succeeded. "Well, not usually, anyway."

Simone drank more of her wine, then set the glass on the table and leaned closer to Preacher. "Maybe we can think of some other way we could work together, if you don't think the fur business is a good idea."

"You mean here in New Orleans?"

"This *is* my home," she said, her voice not much more than a whisper now. "I don't intend to leave it."

She was close enough that it was obvious what she intended. Preacher didn't pull away. Simone was a beautiful woman, and even though she was a criminal, at least according to everything he had heard, he found himself powerfully attracted to her. She leaned in more and kissed him.

Her lips were warm and soft and tasted as sweet as they looked. The kiss was not a hard, passionate one, but it packed enough rising heat and urgency to bring Preacher to his feet when Simone pulled away and stepped back.

His arms went around her and brought her body against his. In the back of his mind, the thought that this might be a trick or a trap of some sort lingered, but he felt confident in his ability to take care of himself. He lowered his head and his mouth found hers again. Her arms went around his neck and tightened.

Preacher wasn't really sure how much time had passed when Simone broke the kiss again and suggested, "Why don't we go sit over there on the divan?"

"Sounds like a good idea," Preacher said. "You want your wine?"

She shook her head. "I don't need it."

She came into his arms again as soon as they were

sitting down. When she leaned back, Preacher went with her. For a time, the two of them were lost in the sensuousness of this shared experience.

He remembered an old trapper telling him, when he was a young man, that it was never smart for a fella to get involved with a woman who had more troubles than he did. If everything he'd heard about Simone LeCarde was true, then running a criminal empire certainly qualified.

But there were times—and this was one of them, Preacher realized—when he just didn't give a hang about following somebody else's advice, no matter how good it was.

As they sat on the divan with Simone in Preacher's arms, leaning against his shoulder, she said, "My father was a wonderful man, but there's no denying the fact that he was disappointed when I was born."

"Why in blazes would he feel like that?"

"Because he was hoping for a boy, of course. A son to carry on in his footsteps, to someday take over as the captain of the *Calypso*."

"That was his ship?"

"Yes. A beautiful little fore-and-aft-rigged sloop, as fast as anything on the water, he claimed."

"I'm a dry land sort of fella," Preacher reminded her. "I don't know much about ships."

"Well, the *Calypso* could outrun just about any pursuit. And it carried enough guns to put up a good fight, if running wasn't going to work. Catamount Jack harried the British from one end of the Caribbean to the other during the war. He disrupted their shipping lanes between the islands and England and kept a lot of cargoes meant for the army from arriving. I like to think he contributed a great deal toward winning the war."

"I'm sure he did," Preacher said. "Did he teach you all about sailin'?"

"Yes, and how to scramble up the rigging and handle a sword and a pistol, as well. As I said, he wanted a boy . . ."

"So he raised you like one."

"He tried," Simone said with a faint note of bitterness in her voice. "Unfortunately, I let him down. I took to sailing and fighting quite well, but never well enough to replace the son he'd hoped for. I wasn't going to take over for him as a buccaneer, and he knew it. So now I follow in his footsteps in other ways."

"I thought you said he wasn't a pirate."

She sighed. "I'd like to believe that he wasn't . . . but I'm not a child anymore, blind to what was really going on. Yes, he was a privateer during the war, fighting for his country in the best way he knew how, but afterward . . . well, he continued targeting British shipping, and Spanish and French and Portuguese, too. He dreamed that someday he would rule an empire stretching from Panama to Bermuda. The largest empire of pirates ever known, bigger than Teach or Flint or Morgan ever achieved." Slowly, Simone shook her head. "That dream died with him. He knew I'd never be able to fulfill it. So instead, I do what I can. I have the Catamount's Den and other enterprises here in New Orleans, as well as a number of ships operating in the Gulf of Mexico and the Caribbean, including the *Calypso*. It's under the command now of one of my partners, a man named Jabez Sampson."

She fell silent, and after a few moments, Preacher said, "I'm glad you're comfortable talkin' to me, but why are you tellin' me all this?"

"I meant what I said earlier about expanding my operations. Natchez is the next logical spot, and St. Louis after that. But I need a good man helping me. A man tough enough to take on any challenge." She turned her head to look up at him. "As soon as I saw you during that battle tonight, Preacher, I knew you were that man. I felt it in my bones . . . and I trust my instincts."

"So do I," Preacher said. Those instincts were telling him that if he played along with Simone LeCarde for the time being, that was his best chance of finding Edmund Cornelius and Lucy Tarleton and recovering some of the money they had stolen.

Of course, that would mean pretending to be a criminal. That went against the grain for Preacher, who was as honest as the day was long and always had been. But it wouldn't be for long, he told himself. Once he found Cornelius and Lucy and dealt with them, he would be on his way back to St. Louis and Simone could stay in New Orleans, dreaming of empire and hoping to live up to what she believed her father would want of her—whether that was truly the case or not.

"Well?" she said, breaking into his reverie. "Are we going to work together or not?"

Preacher nodded and said, "We are."

CHAPTER 21

Simone insisted that Preacher shouldn't have to sleep in the hayloft at Jean Paul Dufresne's livery stable. There was a perfectly good room above the carriage house behind the Catamount's Den. Balthazar Crowe and Long Sam also had their quarters there, she explained.

"I reckon I can go along with that," Preacher said as they sat at the table later and finished off the bottle of wine. "My possibles bag and rifle are at the stable, though, so I should go and fetch them."

"Long Sam can do that for you."

Preacher shook his head. "I'll tend to my own gear."

He saw a flicker of annoyance in Simone's dark green eyes. She didn't like having one of her suggestions questioned, he thought, even something as minor as this. But the reaction lasted only for a second, and then she smiled.

"Of course. Whatever you like, Preacher. I know you said you don't allow anyone to run roughshod over you. That should include me as well, or else I'll lose my respect for you."

"Not much chance of that happenin'. You runnin' roughshod over me, I mean."

Her lips tightened. "Just don't get the idea you can defy me simply for the sake of defying me."

"We're workin' together," Preacher said, even though he had no idea what she actually wanted him to do. "No point in us squabblin'."

"I couldn't agree more."

Preacher left the tavern a short time later after saying good night to Simone and agreeing to have breakfast with her the next morning. He took the same narrow staircase down to the alley door, and as he descended, he heard the raucous noises still coming from the main room. Things probably wouldn't slow down in the Catamount's Den until after midnight.

Bourbon Street was less crowded than earlier in the evening, although more people were still out and about than Preacher was used to seeing at that hour, even in St. Louis. His long legs carried him quickly along the street and out of the French Quarter to the livery stable and adjoining blacksmith shop.

He had blown out the candle before leaving with Balthazar Crowe, so the place was in darkness when he entered. Preacher had moved around in the stable enough when he was there earlier that he was able to find where he had left his bag and rifle, despite the lack of light. He picked them up and turned back toward the entrance, then stopped short. His keen eyes saw movement silhouetted against the faint glow that came from lights farther along the street.

"Kill him!" a harsh voice growled, followed by a rush of footsteps.

Preacher dropped the possibles bag. He knew his rifle wouldn't do him any good in the close quarters, so he let it fall to the hard-packed dirt at his feet, too. He had recognized the voice uttering the curt, guttural command. It belonged to the riverboatman named Shugart, who must have returned to the *Majestic* to get some help from his friends after the fight with Preacher at the tavern. They had watched the Catamount's Den until he came out and then followed him.

Preacher had no doubt that they intended to stomp him into the ground, so not knowing exactly how many opponents he faced and that his life was at stake, he did the only sensible thing.

He yanked the pistols from behind his belt, thumbed back the hammers as he thrust the weapons toward the men rushing at him, and pulled the triggers.

The double boom was deafening in the low-ceilinged room. A tongue of flame almost a foot long licked out from the muzzle of each gun. The bright orange flash lit up the inside of the livery stable like a bolt of particularly garish lightning.

In that split second of illumination, Preacher saw four men charging him—Shugart and three companions almost as brawny and ugly. The men should have thought twice before agreeing to help Shugart get his vengeance on the mountain man. Two of them ran right into the heavy lead balls from Preacher's pistols. The impact of those balls slamming into their chests at close range pitched them backward as if they'd been flicked off their feet by a giant hand.

With the pistols empty, Preacher cast them aside and reached for his knife and tomahawk. His incredibly sharp hearing saved his life. Despite the commotion of the attack, his ears picked up the metallic sound of a pistol being cocked. He dived forward as the gun went off. Sparks flying from the barrel landed on the back of his neck and stung for a second. He rolled over on the ground and came up lunging with the knife in his right hand.

He felt the blade go into something soft, then come to a stop as the hilt jarred against the attacker's belly. With almost a foot of razor-sharp steel buried in his guts, the luckless man groaned. Preacher ripped the knife from side to side and then yanked it free. He felt the hot spill of guts over his hand and pushed the dying man away.

That left just one of the attackers. Preacher heard something whipping through the air toward him, probably a club, and ducked again. The man gave a grunt of effort as the blow missed. Preacher lashed out into the darkness with the tomahawk in his left hand and felt it strike something. The attacker cursed, and his voice was enough to identify him as Shugart. He had brought three of his friends to their deaths, but he was still alive and fighting.

Shugart bulled forward and rammed into Preacher, knocking him backward. The two men's feet tangled, and Preacher lost his balance. When he went down, Shugart fell on top of him, driving the air out of Preacher's lungs.

Gasping and half-stunned, Preacher realized crashing to the ground had jolted the knife and the tomahawk out of his hands. He knew he wouldn't be able to find them in the dark.

With no time to just lie there and try to recover, Preacher forced his muscles to work and shot both hands upward. Something cracked against his left arm and made pain shoot all the way up to his shoulder. Pure luck had allowed him to block another blow from the club Shugart was using to try to bash his brains out.

Preacher's other hand landed on Shugart's face. He clenched his fingers and tried to dig them into Shugart's eyes. Roaring in anger, the riverboatman wrenched his head back, away from Preacher's clawing fingers, but that allowed Preacher's hand to slip under Shugart's chin and close around his neck. Preacher's grip was like iron as he clamped down on his enemy's throat.

He bucked up from the floor, the muscles in his arm and shoulders bunching as he heaved Shugart to the side. Over the pounding of the pulse inside his skull, Preacher heard a clatter and figured Shugart had lost his club. That was it bouncing away as the men rolled over and over.

A great commotion filled the livery barn. The pistol shots and the smell of blood had combined to spook the horses. They whinnied shrilly and kicked at the walls of their stalls. Chaos ruled, and Preacher and Shugart battled in the middle of it, smashing punches blindly at each other.

Preacher landed a solid blow and knocked Shugart away from him. That gave him a chance to surge to his feet and stand there for a second with his chest heaving as he dragged in great gulps of air. That harsh breathing just gave Shugart something to aim at, he realized as he heard rapid footsteps pounding toward him again. Preacher wheeled to the side and reached out to tackle his opponent. Grappling fiercely, they reeled across the room, slammed into the wall between the livery stable and the blacksmith shop, rebounded from it, and then lurched back and forth as they continued to struggle.

Something hard rammed painfully into Preacher's hip. He grimaced in the darkness and tried to fend off Shugart with one hand while he reached down with the other to feel around and find out what he had run into. He was a little surprised to discover it was the anvil in the blacksmith shop. He and Shugart had stumbled through the open door between the adjoining businesses while they were fighting.

Shugart rammed a knee into Preacher's belly. Preacher was lucky it hadn't landed in his groin, which might well have disabled him enough for the man to finish him off. As it was, he doubled over as once again the breath was knocked out of him. He had barely recovered from the other times that happened.

The worst part, though, was that Shugart took advantage of the opportunity to clamp both hands around Preacher's neck. The tables were turned, and Shugart began squeezing the life out of the mountain man, bending him backward over the anvil. The anvil's edge cut painfully into Preacher's back, but that was nothing compared to the terrible pressure on his throat and the crimson haze that began to drop down over his eyes like a curtain.

Preacher had been in plenty of tight spots in his life, had been a hair's-breadth away from death many times. Whenever that happened, the will to survive welled up inside him with overwhelming force. As Shugart choked him, he felt around on the broad wooden pedestal on which the anvil sat and after an interminably long moment closed his fingers around the handle of the blacksmith's hammer.

Guided by instinct, he brought the hammer up and struck swiftly and savagely. He could tell by the impact and the crunch of bone as the hammer smashed into Shugart's head that the fight was over. Shugart grunted and then let out a long sigh as his hands fell away from Preacher's throat and he slumped forward, his suddenly dead weight threatening to keep the mountain man pinned to the anvil.

Grimacing in revulsion, Preacher shoved the corpse off himself and heard it thud on the ground. He pushed himself up, leaned on the anvil with one hand as once again he tried to catch his breath. He kept the hammer in his other hand, ready to strike if he needed to. He didn't hear any other enemies moving around inside the stable or the blacksmith shop, though, just the skittish horses in their stalls.

A grim smile touched Preacher's rugged face in the darkness. He would have to come back in the morning and apologize to Jean Paul Dufresne. The blacksmith was in for an unpleasant surprise when he found four dead men scattered around the place and a hammer smeared with blood and brains lying on the anvil!

CHAPTER 22

It took a rare woman to look as good at breakfast as she had the previous evening, but Simone LeCarde certainly fit that description, Preacher thought as Balthazar Crowe ushered him into the sitting room on the second floor of the Catamount's Den.

Simone wore her hair down this morning, curving in two soft, raven-dark wings around her lovely face. A cloth belt cinched the dressing gown she wore tightly around her waist, but the gown hung open enough at the top to reveal the upper part of the intriguing valley between her breasts.

She spread some marmalade on a beignet, took a delicate bite, then set the pastry down on a saucer and picked up the cup of coffee beside it. After taking a sip, she said, "Please, Preacher, sit down and join me."

"Don't mind if I do," the mountain man said. "I don't want to seem ungrateful for the invitation, but do you have anything to eat besides them fancy little things? Like maybe a steak?"

Simone laughed softly. "I think that can be arranged." She looked at Crowe. "You'll see to it?"

"Of course, mam'selle," he replied with a slight bow.

"Oh, and maybe some black coffee," Preacher added as Crowe started past the table to leave the room.

"You don't care for café au lait?" Simone asked with a smile.

Preacher grinned back across the table at her. "I like my coffee strong enough to get up and walk around on its own hind legs."

That brought another laugh from Simone. She said to Crowe, "See to that, too, Balthazar."

Crowe nodded a little curtly and left the room.

"That fella don't like me much," Preacher commented when Crowe was gone.

"Balthazar is very protective of me. He and Long Sam promised my father that they would look after me and make certain no harm ever overtook me."

"How are they succeedin' so far?"

"Quite well, don't you think? You can see the results for yourself."

"That's true," Preacher said, nodding slowly. "You appear to be doin' just fine."

Simone moved the tray of beignets closer to him. "Are you sure you don't want to try one?"

"Too sweet for me," Preacher replied as he shook his head.

"I imagine where you spend most of your time, there are very few sweets."

"That's true. In the mountains, most of what a fella eats is pretty simple fare. You might come across some sweet berries now and then, but most of 'em are pretty tart."

"Like life itself," Simone suggested.

Preacher shrugged.

She ate the rest of the pastry on the saucer in front

of her, then said, "I suppose you're wondering just what it is I want you to do for me."

"The thought crossed my mind."

"I have a warehouse where goods are stored," Simone said.

Stolen goods, more than likely, Preacher thought, but he kept that to himself.

"I believe the man in charge of that warehouse has been cheating me," she went on. "A shipment of goods will be leaving there today, to be loaded on a riverboat and sent north to St. Louis. I have a list of those goods, prepared for me by Francis Bennington. I'd like for you to go down there and keep track of everything that's loaded on the wagons at the warehouse and transported to the docks."

"Seems to me like Crowe or the little fella could handle that job just as well for you."

Simone shook her head. "Everyone in New Orleans knows that Balthazar and Long Sam work for me. But by being discreet about your visit to me last night, we've made it possible for you to represent my interests without anyone knowing about it."

"You fixed it so's I can spy for you, is what you mean."

She inclined her head slightly to acknowledge his statement. "If you want to call it that. I'll tell you how to find the warehouse, and you can locate a good spot to keep an eye on it. You won't be able to tell what's in the crates being carried out, but you can keep track of how many there are. We'll start with that."

It sounded like busywork to Preacher, and he suspected she was just testing him, seeing if he could follow orders. He didn't care for that. Even worse, he didn't see how this job would put him a bit closer to finding Edmund Cornelius and Lucy Tarleton.

If he refused to go along with what she wanted, though, he might lose the ground he had gained. So he nodded and said, "I reckon I can do that. Anything in particular I need to watch out for?"

"No, just count the crates as they're being loaded, that's all."

Balthazar Crowe's entry with a platter containing a thick, juicy-looking steak and a pile of fried potatoes allowed Preacher not to say anything else at the moment. Crowe also carried a cup and saucer with tendrils of steam curling upward from the cup. His massive hands cradled the fine china with surprising deftness. As he set the meal in front of the mountain man, he said, "I wasn't sure how you preferred your steak, but I thought rare was quite likely. If you'd like, I can take it back down and have it cooked more."

"It don't look like it's wigglin' around on the plate, so I reckon it'll be fine. I'm obliged to you."

Crowe just grunted and stepped back from the table.

The food was good, the coffee just the way Preacher liked it. When he was finished, Simone handed him a sheet of foolscap on which someone had used pen and ink to inscribe a long list of goods.

"Can you read?" she asked him.

"Fair to middlin'." The question didn't offend him, since many of his fellow trappers—indeed, a significant percentage of the population at large—couldn't make heads or tails out of letters scrawled on paper. However, many of the men who headed west to the mountains were actually well-educated and highly literate, including Preacher's friend Audie.

"This is an inventory of the cargo going out today. As you can see"—Simone pointed to a figure at the bottom of the paper—"there should be fifty-eight crates taken from the warehouse, loaded on wagons, and taken to the docks to be loaded on the riverboat *Powhatan*."

"*Powhatan*, eh?"

"Yes. I hope the boat's captain was able to hire some men this morning, or else he'll be shorthanded on the trip back up the Mississippi."

"Is that so?" Preacher said.

"I have . . . sources, shall we say . . . in the local constabulary, and they inform me that Adolph Shugart and three of his friends who were also members of the *Powhatan*'s crew were killed last night not far from here. Their bodies were found at the blacksmith shop and livery stable where you had planned to spend the night."

"Good thing I got outta there before all the trouble broke out, then," Preacher said.

"Yes, very fortunate indeed," Simone said with a wry smile that told Preacher she had figured out what had occurred at Dufresne's place.

"What do you reckon happened to them?"

"The authorities thought at first it was likely they'd tried to break in and rob the place, perhaps steal the horses stabled there, and the owner, one Jean Paul Dufresne, stopped them. But Dufresne's wife insists that he was at home with her and their child all night." She spread her slender-fingered hands. "So it's something of a mystery, one that it's doubtful the constables will ever solve."

"Well, I can't say that I'd lose much sleep over whatever happened to that varmint Shugart, and anybody who'd throw in with him was likely the same no-good sort."

"Undoubtedly," Simone agreed. "Such things happen frequently in New Orleans. The authorities know it's best just to move on and forget about them."

Preacher was certain she knew he was responsible for the deaths of the four men who had attacked him—and she didn't care, either. As she said, such violence was common in New Orleans.

After she told him where to find the warehouse, he left the cargo inventory with her, since he wasn't expected to check it, and departed to perform the task for her. If he carried it out successfully, he would gain that much more of her trust, he told himself— but even so, the whole thing still went against the grain for him. He was built for straight-ahead action, not subterfuge.

The warehouse was a huge brick structure that had a moldering, ancient look about it, like every other building in New Orleans more than six months old. Preacher found an alcove in an alley diagonally across the street from it where he could keep an eye on the big double doors. The thick shadows where he stood ought to be enough to keep anybody from noticing him, he thought.

He watched the place for maybe half an hour before several wagons pulled by teams of four mules apiece rolled up. A fat man with his shirtsleeves rolled up over muscular forearms came out of the warehouse and greeted the drivers. Then he turned and waved a hand at someone in the warehouse.

A moment later, black men in tattered shirts and trousers began carrying crates out of the warehouse and placing them in the wagon beds. A couple of

lean white men with pistols stuck behind their belts
emerged from the warehouse as well and watched,
eagle-eyed, as the cargo was brought out and loaded.
Preacher figured the black fellas were slaves, the two
gun-toters were their overseers, and the fat man was
the warehouse manager Simone suspected of cheating her.

The workers moved slowly enough that Preacher
had no trouble keeping count of how many crates
they loaded. When they were finished, they had
placed fifty-eight crates in the wagons, just as Simone
had said they were supposed to. When the vehicles
had rolled away over the cobblestone streets, Preacher
left the alley and headed for the docks himself, just to
make sure the cargo made it onto the *Powhatan* safely.
Simone hadn't asked him to do that, but he supposed
he might as well.

A different group of workers, some white, some
black, took over when the wagons reached the docks.
Preacher watched them carry the crates on board the
riverboat and stack them on the deck. He counted
them again and got the same total, fifty-eight. Grum-
bling to himself because it seemed to him like he had
just wasted the morning, he walked back to the French
Quarter and into the Catamount's Den. The stool
where Long Sam usually sat was empty.

At that time of day, the tavern was open for business but not doing much, which explained why it
wasn't necessary for Long Sam and his shotgun to
guard the door. A couple of men leaned on the bar.
Only one table was occupied, that by Balthazar Crowe
and Long Sam.

"Any trouble?" Crowe asked as Preacher walked up
to the table.

"Not a bit. And the count—"

Crowe held up a hand to stop him. "You do not report to me. You report to M'sieu LeCarde."

Preacher took note of how Crowe referred to Simone. He had a hunch the fiction of "Simon LeCarde" being male was always used except in that second floor sitting room. That was a good idea, if Simone wanted to keep her true identity a secret.

Crowe went on. "Long Sam, will you inform M'sieu LeCarde that Preacher has returned?"

"Sure." The dwarf got up and headed for the stairs at the back of the room.

Preacher thought Crowe might ask him to sit down with him, but that invitation wasn't forthcoming. Crowe had a cup of coffee in front of him and sipped from it as Preacher stood there waiting for Long Sam to return.

"I went on down to the docks," Preacher said. "Watched 'em load the cargo."

"None of my business," Crowe replied distractedly.

Preacher narrowed his eyes. "You don't like me bein' here, do you?"

"It's none of my business," Crowe said again, but Preacher thought he didn't sound the least bit sincere.

He was glad when Long Sam clattered back down the staircase a few moments later, ending the awkward conversation.

"Come on," Long Sam said as he motioned for Preacher to follow him up the stairs.

Balthazar Crowe swallowed the rest of the coffee in his cup and stood up to go along behind Preacher. Clearly, Crowe didn't want Preacher to be alone up there with Simone. It was probably a good thing Crowe and Long Sam were as protective of their mistress as they were, but at the same time, Preacher thought it pretty likely that Simone could take care of herself. She had mentioned that her pirate father had taught her how to use a pistol and a saber, and she'd claimed to be pretty good with them. Preacher had a hunch she was telling the truth about that. Maybe he would have a chance to find out someday, he thought as he started up the narrow staircase after Long Sam.

He hadn't entered Simone's living quarters from that direction. They wound up in the same hall he had been in the night before, with the door that led to the alley stairs at its far end. The door to Simone's sitting room stood open. Long Sam reached it first but stood aside to let Preacher precede him into the room.

Preacher didn't argue. He stepped into the sitting room, expecting to see Simone on one of the divans or maybe in an armchair over by the fireplace.

Instead she stood beside the table, with her hair still down but pulled back from her face and fastened with a clip behind her head. She wore a dark blue gown with white lace at the sleeves and throat.

She wasn't alone, either. Two other people stood to the side, and Preacher stopped short at the sight of them, recognizing them instantly. He had come to New Orleans to find Edmund Cornelius and Lucy Tarleton, but he hadn't expected to run into them in Simone LeCarde's sitting room above the Catamount's Den.

Still, somehow, he wasn't surprised.

Just as the feeling of a pistol's barrel being pressed into his back didn't surprise him, either, or the rumbling growl of Balthazar Crowe.

"Go on in, mountain man. Mademoiselle has a few things to say to you."

CHAPTER 23

Knowing that Crowe would be happy for an excuse to pull the trigger on that pistol, Preacher didn't try anything. Long Sam hadn't had the shotgun with him when they came up the stairs, but Preacher was willing to bet the dwarf was armed, too.

"Yes, please come in, Preacher," Simone said. Her voice was tight, and anger blazed like green fire in her eyes.

Preacher sauntered on into the sitting room. The door closed behind him. He stopped and hooked his thumbs in his belt, near the butts of his pistols. He didn't reach for the weapons, though. He was confident he could get the pistols out and put a ball in Edmund Cornelius before Crowe or Long Sam could stop him, but while that would avenge the attack on Charlie Todd, it wouldn't accomplish anything else except to get him killed.

Best to wait and find out what Simone had in mind, he told himself.

"Looks like you ain't keepin' who you really are such a big secret anymore," he drawled. "These varmints make three people you've let in on it just recentlike. That doubles the number, don't it?"

Taunting her like that probably wasn't a good idea, either, but he was angry, as well. Had she been playing him for a fool all along?

"You're right," she said, "and that's one very good reason I'm upset with you, Preacher. You've forced me into doing something I don't normally do. When I found out you'd been lying to me, I wanted to find out the truth, and talking directly to Mr. Cornelius and Miss Tarleton seemed to be the most efficient way of doing that."

"You can see for yourself that he's not denying it, Mademoiselle LeCarde," Lucy said with a strident note in her voice. "He followed us to New Orleans to kill us! He's no better than those red savages he associates with in the mountains!"

"Be quiet," Simone snapped. "I told you I'd get to the bottom of this, and I will." She turned her attention back to Preacher. "These two claim you tried to rob and murder them in St. Louis, and that you followed them down here to finish the job. Is there any truth to that?"

Preacher threw back his head and laughed, despite the seriousness of the situation. It was an honest reaction. The brazenness of the two crooks amused him.

"More like the other way around," he said. "They're the thieves. The gal played up to a young friend of mine and found out he had the money from sellin' a season's worth o' pelts hidden in his hotel room. The gambler went there to steal it, but my friend came in and caught him and got a knife in the belly for his trouble."

"That's a lie—" Cornelius began, but Simone held up a hand to stop him.

"Let Preacher finish," she said.

"That's most of the story," the mountain man said. "That young pard of mine didn't die. That surprises you, don't it, Cornelius? You figured he'd bleed to death, lyin' there on the floor of that hotel room, but he was too stubborn to give up. He hung on until I found him, and he told me you'd said you were comin' down here to New Orleans. I didn't make it to the docks in time to stop you from leavin', but I promised Charlie I'd find you and settle the score for him."

"By murdering us," Lucy said with a quaver in her voice.

"I never killed nobody who didn't have it comin'," Preacher said curtly. "And even then, I always gave 'em a fair break. Charlie was alive when I left St. Louis, and I hope he still is. Give me back that money you stole from him—"

"And you'll call it square?" Cornelius suggested.

Preacher's eyes narrowed as he looked at the gambler. "He was alive, but that wasn't no fault of yours. You did your best to kill him. We'll still have to settle that between us, you and me." He shrugged. "I reckon the gal's just as much at fault, but I don't make war on women. Mostly."

Cornelius turned to Simone and said, "He's lying, Mademoiselle LeCarde. There's not a bit of truth in that insane story he just told you."

Simone regarded him coolly. "On the contrary, my instincts tell me that Preacher *is* telling the truth. We all know perfectly well that the two of you had your eyes on Colonel Osborne and intended to swindle him, if not worse, before we came to an agreement that you'd leave him alone. I imagine you targeted Preacher's young friend in St. Louis in much the same fashion."

Cornelius and Lucy looked uncomfortable but didn't dispute the charge.

Simone turned back to Preacher and went on. "All I can assume is that somehow you discovered a connection between this place and these two and came here last night looking for them. It was pure happenstance that brawl erupted and you caught *my* attention. Is that true?"

"I sure didn't plan it that way," Preacher answered honestly. "And I was plenty surprised at the way things turned out."

"But you tried to turn the situation to your advantage anyway," Simone said with an accusatory note in her voice. "You intended to use me."

"I intended to keep the promise I made to my friend Charlie." Preacher glanced at Cornelius and Lucy. "I still do."

He looked at Simone again, and for a long moment the two of them stood there, their gazes locked, before her lips formed a taut line.

She said, "That's the problem. I feel no great sympathy for Mr. Cornelius and Miss Tarleton, but I made a bargain with them and they haven't broken it, so I can't, either. My word has to remain good, or I soon won't be able to continue in business in New Orleans. Everyone knows that Simon LeCarde honors his arrangements."

"They just don't know who Simon LeCarde really is," Preacher said.

"That doesn't matter!" She was breathing harder, as that blazing anger warred in her eyes with some other emotion—regret, perhaps. She turned and pointed a finger at Cornelius and Lucy. Simone's expression was so fierce that Lucy shrank against the gambler in apprehension. "If either of you ever so much as breathe a whisper of what you've found out—"

"You don't have to worry, mademoiselle," Cornelius said quickly as he held up a placating hand. "You have our solemn word that your secret is safe with us. We want to continue under your protection. That's why we came to Mr. Crowe after I spotted Preacher leaving here last night. I knew he might have filled your head with lies about us."

Coldly, Simone said, "I told you, I don't care about who's telling the truth and who isn't. The only important thing is that I have to honor the bargain we made. Preacher will not hurt you."

"How can you be sure of that?" Lucy asked. "He could lie to you, promise to forget about coming after us—"

"I wouldn't do that," Preacher broke in. "Lyin' don't come natural-like to me . . . the way it does to some people."

Lucy flushed at those scathing words.

"I'm afraid his word wouldn't be sufficient, in any case," Simone went on. "But I give you *my* word that I'll handle this matter." She sighed. "The two of you can go on about your own business now, however sordid it may be. You're still welcome at the Catamount's Den, but I say again . . . your lives depend entirely upon your discretion."

"Thank you, Mademoiselle LeCarde," Cornelius said. "I knew we'd done the right thing by aligning ourselves with you."

"Perhaps you can return the favor someday."

"Anything you ask, mademoiselle," Cornelius assured her eagerly.

The oily varmint made Preacher's gorge rise. He would have liked to lunge across the room and split the gambler's skull with his tomahawk. That would have been mighty satisfying.

He figured Balthazar Crowe would shoot him down if he did it, though.

Simone waved a hand in a dismissive gesture and said, "Long Sam, get them out of here."

"A pleasure, mam'selle," the dwarf said, distaste evident in his tone.

"I'd advise you not to do anything else to bring yourselves to my attention, at least in the near future," she added to the crooked pair.

"Of course," Cornelius murmured. He took hold of Lucy's arm and steered her out of the sitting room. Both of them looked glad to be leaving as they followed Long Sam from the room.

"Balthazar, you stay here," Simone ordered. She stepped away from the table and went closer to Preacher. "I really did have high hopes for our association. Our . . . friendship, if you will. Otherwise I never would have revealed my secret to you. But you didn't really care about me. All you wanted was to find those two thieves, wasn't it?"

"That's why I came to New Orleans," Preacher said. He wasn't going to lie to her, try to weasel his way out of this predicament with honeyed words. But he wasn't lying when he added, "I was mighty glad the two of us seemed to be gettin' along so well, though."

Her lips tightened again. "If you had found Cornelius and the woman first . . . ?"

"I would've dealt with 'em. Wouldn't have been no need to bring you into it."

"And then you would have gone back to St. Louis." Simone's voice was flat, accusatory.

"I would've had to see how Charlie's doin'. And he needs money to get back to Virginia, where he comes from. After that . . ." Preacher shrugged. "Reckon I'd have headed for the mountains again."

"To spend the winter with some . . . some Indian squaw?"

Preacher didn't say anything.

"You and I could have worked well together," Simone said after a moment. "It's a shame your ulterior motive has ruined all that."

"I'm sorry if I hurt your feelin's. That wasn't part of the plan."

"My feelings aren't hurt!" She laughed, but Preacher could tell the sound wasn't genuine. She might be a ruthless criminal, but she felt like a woman scorned, whether she wanted to admit it or not. "I'm fine. Just annoyed that now I have to deal with this problem."

"And how do you figure on doin' that?" Preacher's muscles were tense, ready to move. He didn't believe she would order Balthazar Crowe to shoot him in the back, right in the middle of her sitting room, but if her eyes flicked toward the big man, Preacher was prepared to act fast. Turning, drawing his pistols, and firing before Crowe could get a shot off would be difficult, but maybe not impossible.

"I'm not going to have you killed. There are other ways to handle this."

"I told you, I ain't gonna promise to leave town and not bother those two thieves—"

"You don't have to promise," Simone said, "but you *will* be leaving New Orleans."

Preacher suddenly knew she had made up her mind what she was going to do before Crowe and Long Sam even took him up there. She had to side with Cornelius and Lucy. Her reputation depended on it.

But maybe she really did feel something for him. Maybe what he had sensed between them the previous night hadn't all been false, on either side. She didn't want to just have him killed outright, but she had to do *something*—

Those thoughts flashed through his mind in a fraction of a second. Simone hadn't given any signal to Crowe as far as Preacher could see, but he knew he needed to act anyway. He had started to whirl around when he felt a sharp sting on the side of his neck. Preacher reached up automatically, felt the tiny, feathered dart stuck in his flesh.

"A little something from the islands where my father used to sail," Simone said. "A trick he picked up from the natives and taught to Balthazar."

Preacher reached for his pistols, but his muscles didn't seem to obey his brain's commands, and his movements were incredibly slow. Crowe's rapid footsteps were slow and echoing in Preacher's ears. The room felt hollow, and so did he. He finally managed to turn around, just in time to see Crowe's enormous fist looming larger and larger as it came toward his face.

Preacher felt the impact of that fist, but he wasn't aware of hitting the floor. He was already out cold when that happened.

CHAPTER 24

Water sloshed in Preacher's face, filling his nose and mouth and making him sputter as he jerked his head up to get away from it. He got a bit of relief, but then the world shifted under him and the water washed over his head again. In addition to almost drowning him, the vile, oily, scummy taste of it gagged him and made his stomach wrench in protest. When he got his head above the surface, he spewed out what he had just swallowed.

He tried to paw at his eyes and wipe the nasty stuff out of them, too, but he couldn't raise either hand. As awareness and understanding began to seep back into his brain, he realized that his arms were pulled back painfully and his wrists were lashed together behind his back. He attempted to kick his feet and found that his ankles were bound, as well.

He forced his eyes open and blinked them rapidly. After a few moments, his vision cleared, but he couldn't see much. Thick shadows wrapped around him in the gloomy darkness. Here and there a thin shaft of brilliant sunlight slanted through the gloom. The light came in through cracks between the boards that formed his prison, wherever that might be.

Gradually, as he twisted around and worked his way into a sitting position with his back braced against a slimy surface behind him, Preacher's brain began to work again. He heard creaking and slapping sounds, and the water-covered surface on which he had been lying constantly tilted back and forth beneath him. The water was only a few inches deep, he saw as his eyes adjusted more to the poor light, but he had almost drowned in it anyway.

He was in the hold of a ship, and based on what he was experiencing, it had to be at sea.

It wasn't Preacher's first time on a seagoing vessel, but his experience in such matters was very limited. Luckily, he had a strong stomach, or he might already be heaving his guts out. It could still come to that, he thought.

He shook his head to get his wet hair out of his eyes. If he had more trouble headed in his direction, as seemed likely, he wanted to be able to see it coming.

As he sat there breathing hard, he thought about the dire situation and how he had come to be in it. The last thing he remembered before waking up with that bilgewater in his face was being in Simone LeCarde's sitting room on the upstairs floor of the Catamount's Den. Simone had honored her deal to protect Edmund Cornelius and Lucy Tarleton by getting rid of Preacher. She had claimed that she wasn't going to kill him, and clearly, she hadn't.

But he was willing to bet he was no longer in New Orleans, just as she had said would be the case.

The questions were, what ship was he on—and where was it bound?

He listened and heard footsteps and voices overhead. Shadows occasionally blocked the shafts of sunlight coming through the cracks. The ship's crew was at work as the wind took the vessel wherever it was going.

Time passed interminably. Preacher began to wonder if his captors had forgotten he was down there. Maybe they were just giving him a chance to drown and would come into the hold later to retrieve his body and pitch it into the ocean.

A little while after that grim thought went through his mind, blinding light suddenly spilled around him. Someone had lifted a hatch in the deck. A ladder was lowered into the hold and booted feet and thick legs clad in canvas trousers descended the rungs. Preacher squinted against the glare and watched as the man reached the bottom of the ladder and turned toward him.

The man had a thick torso and prominent gut under a short blue jacket. A black cap was pushed back on a thatch of curly, graying brown hair. Beard stubble grizzled his beefy face. He leered at Preacher, revealing square yellow teeth.

"You're awake, are ye?" the man rasped. "When the African brought ye on board, ye seemed half dead from whatever foul concoction he'd stuck you with. I wasn't sure if ye'd even wake up. Not that ol' Balthazar would've cared if you didn't. That boy don't like you, son."

Preacher found his voice, but it wasn't easy. His mouth and throat were so dry and his tongue felt swollen to twice its normal size. He sounded rusty to himself as he said, "I know that. I ain't sure how he managed to stick me with that dart, though."

The visitor waved a hand with fingers like short, stubby sausages. "Oh, he has a little wooden tube he uses to blow them darts. Them Africans all know how to do that, and so do them Indians out in the Caribees. A lot of them devils are half African, at least, you know."

Preacher shook his head. "I don't know a thing about that."

The man laughed and said, "I reckon ye wouldn't. From what I been told, you're one of them frontiersman. Ye know about the mountains and the red Injuns and grizzle bears and the like, ain't that right?"

"I've fought a griz or two in my time."

"I wouldn't mind seein' something like that. Bet it's a pretty good show. No grizzle bears where you're goin', though."

"And where's that?" Preacher asked.

"You'll find out when the time comes. Until then, there ain't no need to worry about it." The man put his hands on his hips. "You know who I am?"

"No earthly idea."

"Name's Sampson. Jabez Sampson. I'm the master of this ship, the cap'n of—"

"The *Calypso*," Preacher interrupted, remembering the story Simone had told him about her father's ship.

Sampson looked a little surprised. "Aye. The finest, fastest sloop in gulf waters."

"That would make you a pirate."

Sampson frowned and drew back, clearly offended by that statement. "This is a trading vessel," he declared, "and I be an honest trader, just like ol' Catamount Jack afore me."

Preacher just grunted. Sampson could tell himself whatever lies he wanted to, but Preacher didn't believe any honest man would work for Simone LeCarde.

After a moment, he asked, "So what am I doin' here? Are you supposed to murder me and drop me over the side?"

"Nobody said nothin' about murder. Might as well go ahead and tell ye, I suppose. Accordin' to the African, Monsieur LeCarde wants ye taken to his sugar plantation on the island of San Patricio. You'll work as a member of me crew on the way there, and once we reach the island, you'll work on the plantation. It'll be a hard life, lad, devil if it won't be, but better than dyin', eh?"

Preacher wasn't so sure about that. Being condemned to spend the rest of his days on some godforsaken sugar plantation on an isolated island, with no way off . . . sounded like pure torture to him, who had always lived his life roaming free.

"I don't reckon I've got any choice in the matter?"

"Well . . . I suppose ye could always jump overboard. No one'll try to stop ye. But then you'd have to swim miles and miles through shark-infested waters to reach land again. If ye believe you're up to that task . . ." Sampson shrugged.

The captain was right, Preacher thought. He was trapped as effectively as if he'd been locked away in a prison cell. There was no point in fighting because there was nowhere to go.

He had seldom experienced despair in his life. Hardly ever, in fact. And he didn't give in to it now. Resolve stiffened inside him. Surrendering to fate wasn't in his nature. Biding his time, waiting for the right moment to strike back—that he could do.

"I reckon I've got just one question," he said.

"What's that, son?"

"You think I could get somethin' to drink? This mouth o' mine tastes and feels like somethin' curled up and died in it."

Sampson's face split in a grin as he brayed, "Haw, haw! Now you're talkin', son! I'll have some of the lads cut you loose and bring you up to the deck. Things may not look very good to ye right now, but I guarantee they'll look a wee bit better after a couple of swallows of rum!" He turned and went up the ladder with a catlike grace that belied his bulky build.

Preacher leaned back against the hull and waited.

Only a couple of minutes passed before heavy footsteps sounded above his head and then more legs appeared coming down the ladder. The first man to reach the bottom turned toward Preacher and grinned, revealing blackened stubs of teeth. He was lean to the point of gauntness with lank hair the color of straw. He had a knife tucked behind the length of rope tied around his scrawny waist that served as a belt.

The second man was a lot bigger and more muscular. His feet were bare, his long legs clad in tight canvas trousers, and he wore only a brown vest above the waist, no shirt. As he came farther down the ladder, Preacher spotted the tattoos on the back of his neck and stiffened. The tattoos climbed under the flat-topped beaver hat perched on a head that appeared to be bald except for the ink.

The man reached the bottom of the ladder and turned toward Preacher. A grin stretched across his ugly face. Abner Rowland, the keelboater Preacher had battled to a draw in Rancid Dave's tavern, said, "Remember me?" and added a vile obscenity. "When I saw who it was that big darkie was bringin' on board, I couldn't believe my luck!"

CHAPTER 25

"What're you doin' here, Rowland?" Preacher asked. The dryness of his mouth and throat made his voice a croak, which annoyed him.

"I got tired of that blasted river. No real challenge to it. I used to be a seafarin' man, so when we got to New Orleans this last time, I went lookin' for a berth on a *real* ship. Never figured we'd wind up sailin' on the same one!"

"Cap'n said we was to cut him loose and get him up on deck," the other man reminded Rowland. He reached for the knife at his waist. "We better get to it."

Rowland stuck out a brawny arm and held it across the man's chest to bar his way. He held out his other hand and said, "Gimme that knife."

The man frowned. "What're you gonna do with it?"

"Follow orders, of course." The evil smirk on Rowland's face seemed to say something else, however.

"I dunno . . ."

"Give me the blasted knife, Finch," Rowland snapped.

The sailor called Finch still hesitated, but only for a couple of seconds. Then he shrugged his narrow shoulders and pulled the knife from the rope belt and slapped the handle in Rowland's outstretched palm.

Preacher drew his knees up. With his hands tied behind his back, he couldn't put up much of a fight but rather than just sit there and meekly allow Abner Rowland to cut his throat, Preacher planned to kick the varmint where it would do the most good. He'd make Rowland work at killing him.

As Rowland approached, though, he said, "Take it easy, Preacher. I'm not gonna do anything except what Cap'n Sampson told us to do. But I could. I could carve you from gizzard to gullet if I wanted to."

"You could try," Preacher said.

Rowland snorted, then turned and handed the knife back to Finch. "You go cut him loose. I might scare him to death, gettin' that close to him with a knife, and the cap'n might be upset."

Finch looked nervous as he approached the mountain man and said, "Don't try anything, now. I'll cut your feet loose first and then your hands, all right?"

"Just get it done," Preacher growled. "I'm gettin' a mite cramped up, sittin' here in this dirty water."

The knife sawed quickly through the cords around Preacher's ankles. He leaned forward to allow Finch to cut the ones around his wrists. He could have taken the knife away from the skinny sailor then and killed Finch, and there was a good chance he could have disposed of Rowland, too.

But then what would he do? Kill Sampson and the rest of the *Calypso*'s crew? That seemed pretty unlikely. Even if he managed to carry out such a slaughter against overwhelming odds, could he sail the ship back to New Orleans? That was an even more far-fetched idea.

He had to give Simone credit. If she wanted to get rid of him without actually killing him, this was a pretty effective way of doing so.

"All right. Get up," Rowland ordered when Preacher's hands and feet were free and Finch had backed off out of reach.

Leaning against the hull, Preacher pushed himself up. His legs, arms, and hands were mostly numb. He flexed his fingers to get the blood flowing again. A fierce sensation of pins and needles went through his extremities, but he didn't show any signs of discomfort on his rugged face.

"You look strong enough to me to climb that ladder by yourself," Rowland said. "Get moving."

Slowly, Preacher went up the ladder into the hold below the surface deck, then climbed another ladder into the sunshine, glad to be out of the damp, gloomy bilge even though the brightness half blinded him.

Blinking, he stepped out onto the deck and looked around. Simone had said that the *Calypso* was a sloop, he recalled, but he didn't know exactly what that meant. What he saw was a ship with a single mast rising from the deck about a third of the way along from the front to the back. The *bow* and the *stern*? Was that what they were called? Preacher knew what port and starboard meant, but beyond that, he was pretty much lost when it came to nautical terms.

The *Calypso* had three smaller, triangular sails rigged before the mast, and two larger ones behind it. All of them bulged with the wind that filled them. The vessel was about sixty feet long, Preacher guessed, and had a cabin at the rear with a short set of steps leading down a few feet into it. Half a dozen small cannon were lined up along each side, their barrels thrust through gaps designed for that purpose. He also saw openings along the sides that he took to be oarlocks, but they didn't have any oars in them at the moment.

Men were aloft in the rigging, doing things with the sails and lines that made no sense to him. Others scurried around the deck. He didn't know how many were aboard—several dozen, at least. Captain Jabez Sampson stood on the deck that formed the ceiling of the cabin at the rear of the ship. A crewman was beside him, his arm draped casually over the long handle of the steering tiller that extended behind the *Calypso.*

A strong, steady wind carried the sloop along at what seemed like a fast clip.

Preacher turned his head to look from side to side, then slowly came around in a circle. Nothing but blue water and blue sky, as far as the eye could see in every direction. His heart began to pound a little harder. He didn't like being out there . . . on the ocean. He didn't like it one little bit.

At the moment, however, he couldn't do a blasted thing about it.

Over the popping of the sails and the whoosh of water past the ship's bow, he heard someone calling his name and turned to see Jabez Sampson motioning to him from that raised deck at the rear. Preacher looked at Rowland and Finch, who had followed him up out of the ship's bowels. Rowland jerked his head to indicate that Preacher should join Sampson back there.

A very narrow set of steps went up at the side of that deck. Preacher warily eyed the water beside and below him as he climbed those steps. If the ship pitched at just the wrong moment and he went over the side, would they bother fishing him out? Or would they just sail away and leave him there?

He reached the upper deck without mishap and joined Sampson and the man at the tiller.

Sampson extended a silver flask to him and said, "I promised ye a couple of swigs of rum. Here ye go. Don't get carried away."

Preacher took the flask and lifted it to his mouth. The rich, fiery bite of the rum had an immediate bracing effect on him. The second swallow kindled a welcome fire in his belly.

Then Sampson held out his hand. "I'll have it back."

Preacher surrendered the flask and wiped the back of his hand across his mouth. He asked, "What now?"

"Now you get to work," Sampson answered with a grin. "You've never crewed on a sailin' ship, have ye?"

"Nope."

"We'll start with somethin' simple, then." Sampson pointed forward. "See those fellows on their knees up yonder, t'other side of the mast? They're holystonin' the deck. You can help 'em."

"I don't know what that is."

"You'll learn." Sampson made a shooing motion. "Go along with ye, then. Ol' Bramble's in charge. He'll tell ye what to do."

Preacher spent a couple of seconds wondering how hard it would be to kill Sampson, knock out the man at the tiller, and turn this blasted ship around. Of course, he'd probably wind up sinking them, he thought, assuming Abner Rowland or another member of the crew didn't just shoot him.

Without saying anything, Preacher turned and carefully went down the steps to the main deck and started forward. As he passed Rowland, the tattooed man smirked at him. Preacher did his best to ignore him.

Bramble turned out to be a wiry, elderly sailor with a tangled white beard that had given him the nickname. He handed Preacher a rectangular chunk of some sort of porous rock and said, "This here's holystone. Get down on your knees like them boys there and go to scrubbin'. That's the only way to keep these decks clean."

Preacher grumbled to himself as he followed the order. Four men were lined up on their knees, bent forward to rub the stones over the planks that formed the deck. Another man stood nearby holding a bucket of water, which he sloshed over the area from time to time to wash away whatever the men had scraped up.

Preacher joined the line at the end of it, next to a young man with bright red hair and an abundance of freckles. "Howdy," the mountain man said under his breath.

"Save your energy for the work," the young sailor advised, equally quietly. "Bramble may look like somebody's kindly old grandpa, but you don't want to get on his bad side."

"Why not?"

The youngster just shook his head and continued scrubbing at the deck with the holystone. Preacher followed his example.

The work didn't *look* that hard, but Preacher soon found his knees and back aching. The rough stone irritated his hands. Whenever the sailor with the bucket washed down the deck, some of the water inevitably splashed up in his face. Maybe this chore actually needed to be done, he didn't know about that, but it became obvious to him that being assigned to it was something of a punishment, too.

His clothes were already wet from being down in the bilge, and they didn't dry because water kept being flung in his general direction. That added to the misery, as did the sun, which beat down without pity on the men working on deck.

After a while, Preacher had had enough of it. He stood up and tossed the holystone onto the deck at his feet. Beside him, the freckle-faced sailor drew in his breath with a frightened hiss and whispered, "What are you doing?"

"You there!" Bramble barked immediately as he leveled a gnarled finger at Preacher. "Pick that up and get back to work."

"I ain't no sailor," Preacher said, "but that deck looks plenty clean to me. I don't mind workin' for my keep, but there's got to be jobs that make more sense than this."

"Your betters will decide what you're to do!" Bramble stomped up to him, beard bristling in outrage. "Now pick up that stone and get back down on your knees, blast your eyes!"

Slowly, Preacher shook his head. "I don't cotton to bein' on my knees."

The confrontation caught the attention of most of the men on deck. They stopped whatever they were doing and turned to look at Preacher and Bramble. Preacher's back was turned toward the spot where Sampson stood, but he had a hunch that was the captain's gaze he felt boring into his back.

Bramble was a head shorter, but he squinted up fiercely at the mountain man and said, "A touch of the lash'll knock some of that starch outta you, boy."

"I ain't a boy, and I won't be whipped."

Bramble snorted. "We'll just see about that. Cap'n!"

Preacher heard a footstep behind him.

"What's going on here, Bramble?" Jabez Sampson asked.

"This new feller don't want to work. Says he's too good for holystonin' and won't get on his knees. Won't be whipped, neither, he says."

Sampson strolled around so Preacher could see him from the corner of his eye. The captain wasn't alone. Abner Rowland and two more burly sailors were with him.

"A ship's crew has to have discipline, mister," Sampson said to Preacher. "Sailors have to take orders, or the whole system breaks down. Ye understand that, don't ye?"

Preacher just stared stonily at him.

After a moment, Sampson sighed and said, "All right, if that's the way it's to be. String him up to the mast. Bosun, fetch the cat-o'-nine-tails from my cabin."

"I'd be happy to, Cap'n," Rowland said. "And I'd be happy to use it on this man, too."

"How many lashes do you think?" Sampson asked. "Five?"

"More like a dozen," Rowland said.

The casual way they were discussing whipping him made anger boil up inside Preacher. He was unarmed. His head still ached from whatever drug had been on that dart, and his muscles and reflexes weren't at their peak. He was outnumbered fifty to one.

But despite all that, if they laid hands on him, he would fight. He would make them kill him before they subjected him to the indignity of stringing him up and whipping him.

His hands clenched into fists as the sailors who were with Sampson and Rowland began to close in on him.

That was when one of the sailors up in the rigging cupped his hands around his mouth and shouted, *"Sail ho!"*

CHAPTER 26

Everyone immediately forgot the confrontation with Preacher and craned their necks to gaze up into the rigging and see which way the sailor was pointing. He hung on with his left hand and leveled his right at an angle, ahead and to starboard.

Preacher was as curious as anybody else. He peered in that direction, narrowing his eyes as he tried to spot the sails on the other ship. He didn't see a blasted thing—

No, wait, there it was! A tiny triangle of white on the horizon, miles away. Preacher had no trouble estimating distances in the mountains or on the prairie, but out in the middle of the seemingly endless sweep of blue water, he had no real idea how far away the other ship might be.

Sampson reached into the pocket of his jacket and brought out a brass telescope, which he extended and lifted to his right eye. Squinting through the lens, he studied the distant ship for a long moment, then announced, "'Tis a merchantman, boys. British, I think, but that doesn't really matter, now does it?" He lowered the spyglass and bellowed at the man at the tiller, "Take us to starboard, Florey!"

"We're goin' after her, Cap'n?" Rowland asked.

"Aye!"

Rowland gestured toward the mountain man and said, "We were supposed to take him to San Patricio."

"And we will, lad," Sampson assured him. "But there be nothin' wrong with makin' a wee detour first, especially if 'tis a profitable one!"

The man at the tiller hauled on it and sent the ship angling to the right. Rowland shouted more orders to the men in the rigging, who adjusted the sails accordingly. The process was incomprehensible to Preacher, but he couldn't help but admire the skill with which the sailors worked and the way they scrambled around up there like monkeys.

"What about those lashes Preacher was supposed to get?" Rowland asked.

"A prize is more important than a whippin'," the captain snapped. "And there'll be time for all that later, after we've dealt with that beauty up yonder."

That was never going to happen, Preacher thought. They weren't going to whip him.

Rowland didn't seem to like the answer, either. He glared and said, "Discipline on board—"

"Is my responsibility, Mr. Rowland," Sampson broke in, and his jovial tone turned ominous. "See to the guns. You claimed to be good with them."

"I am," Rowland said. With a last scowl at Preacher, he turned to the cannon and began calling out orders to the crew members who would be manning them.

Sampson regarded Preacher and frowned in thought. "You're a frontiersman, aye?"

"That's right."

"Then ye must be a hunter, and a good shot with a rifle."

"Fair to middlin'," Preacher said, although that was a vast underrating of his skill.

Sampson lifted a finger and said, "I'm goin' to do a bold thing. I'm goin' to give ye a rifle and a powder horn and a pouch of shot. You'll be up there with me, and ye will pick off the targets I tell ye. Can ye do that?"

Preacher's jaw tightened. Sampson was asking him to murder innocent sailors on that merchant ship. He was never going to do that, no matter what happened to him.

But he saw a narrow opening and took it by saying, "I can."

He didn't promise that he actually *would*, though.

"Good! Now, don't get any ideas about turnin' that weapon on me. I'll have a man right there with us, holdin' a pistol aimed at your head. If that rifle so much as starts to turn any direction except where I tell ye to point it, he'll put a ball through your brain. I told the African when he brought ye aboard that I'd try to keep ye alive so's ye could go to the sugar plantation on San Patricio, but I made no promises."

Preacher gave a curt nod and then gestured toward the sea surrounding them. "Like you said . . . out here, where could I go?"

A bustle of frantic activity filled the ship during the next few minutes. The gun crews prepared the cannon for firing. The sailors who'd been aloft climbed down out of the rigging, except for one man who perched in the crow's nest at the top of the mast. He had a mouth trumpet so he could call down information to the captain during the battle, if there was one. Long oars were brought out and fastened in the oarlocks, to help with fast maneuvering if it became necessary.

Preacher went back up on the rear deck with Sampson. A man brought him rifle, powder, and shot, as the captain had said. As Preacher looked over the weapon, he saw that it wasn't as fine as his own long-barreled flintlock, but at least it appeared to be in good working order. His own rifle, pistols, knife, and tomahawk were probably somewhere back in New Orleans, and he wondered if he would ever see them again.

At least Dog and Horse were safe and well cared for at the livery stable in St. Louis. Preacher had an understanding with the man who ran the place. If he left his trail partners there and hadn't returned in a year's time, Patterson would be free to sell Horse as long as he was confident the stallion was going to someone who would be a good owner. Dog would remain there and live out his life at the stable, since Patterson was fond of the big cur.

Preacher wasn't going to even consider the possibility of not being reunited with his friends, though. For now, he needed to concentrate on the challenges directly ahead of him.

"You plan on chasin' that other ship down?" he asked Sampson.

"Aye. The *Calypso* is faster than any merchantman, have ye no doubts of that."

"I don't know enough about boats to have doubts one way or the other."

Sampson threw back his head and laughed. "Ah, ye landlubbers never fail to amuse me. We all *came* from the sea, lad. Bein' out here on the bonnie blue foam is the most natural thing in the world for a human bein'."

"Maybe so, but that don't make me like it any better."

"How's your belly holdin' up?"

"I ain't sick, if that's what you mean," Preacher said.

Sampson slapped him on the back. "Ye've got your sea legs already! We'll make a sailor outta you!"

Preacher seriously doubted that. For one thing, he didn't intend to be on this blasted boat for that long.

Slowly but surely, the *Calypso* cut into the lead the other vessel had. When they were closer, Sampson studied the ship through the spyglass again and said with some satisfaction, "She's flyin' the Union Jack, just like I thought. 'Tis a British ship, and I never tire of makin' those scoundrels uncomfortable. I fought 'em durin' the war, ye know. The one about twenty-five years ago."

"So did I," Preacher said.

Sampson looked at him with new interest. "Is that true, now?"

"I was with Andy Jackson at the Battle of New Orleans."

"Ye must've been but a lad at the time. I did all my fightin' on this very ship, with ol' Catamount Jack in command then. A finer man there never was. Never could really understand how he could give up the sea like he did and move back onto the land. 'Twas the young'un he had with that Cajun woman, I reckon. He didn't want the boy bein' raised up while he was away at sea all the time."

So Sampson didn't know that "Simon" LeCarde was really Simone. By using Balthazar Crowe and Long

Sam as go-betweens, she had kept her true identity a secret from nearly all of her associates. There was no real reason for that secrecy, other than wanting to live up to what her father's dream had been for his off-spring, Preacher mused. The past had a powerful grip on most folks and steered them in their day-to-day lives and in the big decisions they had to make, whether they ever realized that or not. He had never dwelled overmuch on it himself, but he had realized a long time ago that he wasn't exactly the normal sort of fellow.

Preacher began to make out more details about the ship they were pursuing. He didn't know what type it was, but it had three masts instead of one and a lot more sails. Even so, it was moving considerably slower than the *Calypso*, and he supposed that had to do with the vessel's weight. More sails didn't necessarily equal more speed.

Even though he wasn't happy about his situation, he couldn't help but take some interest in what was going on. He asked Sampson, "Do they know we're chasin' 'em?"

"Oh, aye. They keep a watch for other ships, just like we do. I reckon they laid eyes on us about the same time we did on them, mayhap even sooner. But there be nothin' they can do about it, 'less'n they figure out how to sprout a giant pair o' wings!" The captain's wit evidently struck him as hilarious as he bellowed with laughter and slapped his thigh.

"It don't seem like they're even tryin' to get away," Preacher commented.

"They're tryin', all right, but they know they can't outrun us."

The man at the tiller spoke up for the first time.

"So they'll wait until we get close enough and then try to blow us out of the water."

"To do that, they'd have to be better shots than any Englisher ever born!" Sampson made a disgusted sound and shook his head. "And Preacher's gonna help us, too." He pointed and said to the mountain man, "See those guns in the stern?"

They were close enough to the other ship for Preacher's keen eyes to spot the twin muzzles of a pair of cannon mounted at the back end of the ship. "I see 'em," he told Sampson.

"As soon as we're close enough, I want ye to start pickin' off the lads who try to man those culverins. They can't shoot at us if they've got rifle balls in their guts!" Sampson found that funny as well.

Preacher took a deep breath and let it out slowly. He looked to his right. One of the sailors stood there, as Sampson had promised, with a loaded pistol in his hand. Sampson had made it plain that if Preacher didn't follow orders, he'd be shot.

"I'd better get to loadin' this rifle, then," he said.

"Aye, ye do that."

By the time Preacher had the rifle ready, the *Calypso* had closed to within a few hundred yards of the British merchantman. Suddenly, smoke and fire belched from the two cannon at the other vessel's stern. The man at the tiller leaned hard on it, and the sloop veered left. The two cannonballs splashed into the water well to the right.

"How close do we need to get before ye can start makin' things hot for those gunners?" Sampson asked. His voice was tense, and he didn't sound amused anymore.

"Maybe half this distance, if you want me to have a good chance of hittin' 'em," Preacher replied.

"All right, just be ready when the time comes."

Preacher had the hammer drawn back on the rifle. He held it ready to lift to his shoulder and take aim. The *Calypso* continued racing over the water as the gunners on board the British ship scurried around preparing the cannon to fire again.

Soon they were close enough that Preacher saw sparks sputtering from the slow match a sailor held in readiness to touch off the powder charge in one of the cannon. Preacher raised the rifle to his shoulder, drew a bead, and squeezed the trigger. The rifle boomed and kicked against his shoulder as smoke gushed from the barrel.

A split second later, Sampson bellowed, "Hard a-port!" and once again the steersman leaned on the tiller and angled the sloop to the left. Only one of the cannon on the British ship had fired, and that ball went into the sea with a big splash, although it landed closer to the *Calypso* than the previous shots had.

Preacher lowered the rifle and looked at the man he had targeted, who was now reeling back and clutching the hand that had held the slow match. Preacher didn't know if his ball had struck the match or the hand itself, but he had stopped the man from touching off the cannon's charge without killing him, which had been his intention. At that range and firing from one ship to another, it had taken a near-miracle to make such a shot, and Preacher was well aware that he could have killed the British sailor.

But he hadn't, and as he reloaded, he picked out his next target, a man about to use a wet wad of cotton on the end of a pole to swab out the barrel of the other cannon and extinguish any lingering sparks from the previous shot.

"Come around, come around!" Sampson shouted. "Starboard gunners ready!"

Abner Rowland called back to him, "Starboard gunners ready, aye!"

Preacher was ready again, too. As the man on the British ship lifted the pole, Preacher fired. The ball hit the swab and knocked it out of the man's hands. He dived for cover, in case some other rifleman was drawing a bead on him.

"Fire!" Sampson roared.

CHAPTER 27

The *Calypso* had swung around so that it was broadside to the British merchant ship. The six cannon on its starboard side exploded in a ragged volley. The gunners had aimed them well. Preacher saw several of the shots strike the merchantman. Splinters flew as some of the balls crashed into the hull, while others ripped through the sails or skipped along the deck, wreaking bloody havoc among the British sailors.

Preacher's jaw tightened. Trenches appeared in his cheeks as a grim expression settled over his face. Men were dying over there, he knew, and even though it wasn't his doing, he felt like he should have stopped the attack somehow. Unfortunately, the odds stacked against him were too great to overcome—for now.

"Reload!" Sampson snapped at him. "Reload, blast it!" The captain's right hand gripped Preacher's shoulder while he pointed with his left. "See the fellow there on the bridge? That's the cap'n. Kill him!"

Preacher's muscles responded automatically. He rammed a powder charge and a round ball down the rifle's barrel and then primed the weapon. He lifted the rifle to his shoulder and aimed at the figure

Sampson had pointed out on the other ship. Instead of pressing the trigger right away, though, he waited a couple of seconds until the *Calypso* bobbed and fired then.

The British captain's black hat leaped into the air. The man crouched instinctively and looked around.

"Ye missed him!" Sampson yelled as he smacked a hand into the middle of Preacher's back. "Ye said ye were a good shot!"

The mountain man's first impulse was to turn and slam the rifle's butt into Sampson's face. He managed to control that, but it wasn't easy.

Actually, he had cut it closer than he'd intended. He had meant to miss the British commander entirely, instead of shooting his hat off his head.

"What in blazes do you expect?" Preacher demanded, not trying to keep the anger out of his voice. "I'm a good shot on dry land. I never tried to hit anything with a blasted ship's deck jumpin' around under me!"

That argument made sense. Sampson said grudgingly, "All right, all right. Just do your best."

At that moment, the cannon at the British ship's stern boomed again. One of the balls missed, but the other tore through the *Calypso*'s sails without striking the mast, which would have been disastrous.

"They're gettin' the range," Sampson said. "Reload and make the blasted limeys hop!"

"Aye, Cap'n," Preacher muttered under his breath, telling himself that he was already picking up the lingo. He didn't know if he liked that or not.

The *Calypso* swung the other direction, bringing the port-side guns to bear. The little sloop's maneuverability, in contrast to the larger ship's lumbering progress through the water, came in handy. Rowland dashed across the deck and ordered the gunners to fire. Once again, flame spurted and deadly cannon-balls pelted the merchantman. As far as Preacher could tell, none of the hits did any serious damage to the vessel, although he was sure some of the men on deck were killed or at least badly wounded.

While the echoes of that volley were still rolling across the waves, the lookout up in the crow's nest called down, "Sails ho! More sails, Cap'n!"

Sampson cursed and yanked out his spyglass again. He squinted through the lens and his curses grew more vehement and sulphurous. "A couple of British frigates headed in this direction," he said as he lowered the telescope. "They'll be here before we'd have time to take that prize. We'll have to break off the attack."

Preacher kept his face impassive. He didn't want Sampson to see how relieved he was by that news. The *Calypso*'s captain might order him to kill a few more British sailors, just out of spite.

That didn't appear to occur to Sampson. He shouted orders for his men to break off the attack. They adjusted the sails, the steersman leaned hard on the tiller, and the *Calypso* swung far to starboard, heading south away from the British merchant ship and the Royal Navy frigates.

"They'll never catch us," Sampson said confidently. "I doubt they'll even try. They'll stop and render aid to that merchantman instead. But we'll run south at full speed, just in case."

"That'll take us off our course for that island you were headed for, won't it?" Preacher asked.

"Aye, but there's no certain time we have to arrive

there, as long as we deliver ye where you're supposed to go." Sampson eyed the mountain man. "And speakin' of what's in store for ye, I believe somethin' was said about some lashes . . ."

"I just fought on your side," Preacher said grimly. "You're still gonna punish me for not wantin' to get down on my knees?"

"I appreciate your efforts," Sampson said, "even though ye didn't actually kill any of the rascals the way I told you to." His eyes narrowed as he looked at Preacher. "It couldn't be that ye were missin' on purpose, now could it? Nobody is *that* good a marksman, to come as close as ye did and still not send any Englishers to hell!"

"I told you, I'm used to shootin' on dry land."

Sampson stuck out his hand. "Well, I'll be havin' that rifle back now, regardless o' what just happened."

Preacher hesitated, then glanced toward the sailor with the pistol, who raised the weapon and aimed it at his head. With a shrug, he handed the rifle to Sampson.

"The powder and shot, too," the captain said.

Preacher had draped the rawhide thongs attached to the powder horn and shot pouch over his shoulder, as he normally would have. As he started to lift them over his head, he heard a soft footstep behind him. He started to turn, suddenly sensing a trap, but Abner Rowland moved too fast. The tattooed man swung some sort of bludgeon that cracked hard against Preacher's skull and drove the mountain man off his feet, into a black void.

* * *

Regaining consciousness after being knocked out for the second time that day was even more unpleasant than the first time, Preacher discovered as awareness began to seep back into his brain. Pain thundered through his head with every beat of his pulse.

Gradually, he realized that his wrists were tied again, but they had been jerked above his head rather than behind his back. He was upright, leaning against a smooth, thick wooden pole of some sort. The *Calypso*'s mast, he told himself as his brain started forming coherent thoughts again. His captors had strung him up, just as they'd threatened to do.

They had removed his buckskin shirt, too. He felt the mast pressing against his bare chest and belly. His wrists were tied to the mast, and a rope had been passed around his waist as well to keep him motionless.

He had found himself in the hands of enemies many times before in his adventurous life, and he had learned not to let them know that he was awake until he'd had a chance to take stock of the situation. For that reason, he kept his eyes closed and his breathing regular. Let the pirates continue to believe he was still out cold.

He heard them moving around the ship, heard men's voices calling out to each other. None of them sounded alarmed, so Preacher figured they had gotten away from the British frigates and were no longer in danger from the warships. He was about to open his eyes a tiny slit and take a look around when he heard heavy footsteps approaching him.

"I swear, I think ye hit him too hard with that belayin' pin, Abner." That gravelly growl belonged to Captain Jabez Sampson.

"Naw, he's still breathin', Cap'n," Rowland said. "Just look at him. You can see he's breathin'."

"Aye. Wake him up, then."

That was all the warning Preacher got before what felt like a bucketful of water was poured over his head. No point in pretending anymore. He jerked his head and sputtered and tried to shake the water out of his eyes. Moving around like that caused fresh explosions of pain inside his skull, but they subsided after a few moments.

He twisted his neck to look over his right shoulder as best he could, which wasn't easy considering the way he was tied to the mast. From the corner of his eye, though, he saw Sampson and Rowland standing there looking satisfied with themselves.

Elsewhere along the deck, other members of the *Calypso*'s crew stood watching, some of them with avid interest on their faces. However, a few others appeared uncomfortable, as if they weren't looking forward to what was about to happen. Preacher noticed the redheaded, freckle-faced youngster beside whom he had been working earlier. The young man shuffled his feet and looked away as if he couldn't bear to watch.

Sampson moved so that Preacher could see him easier and said, "I told ye, discipline must be maintained on board ship, and in order to do that, once ye've transgressed and a punishment has been levied, it has to be carried out, no matter what else happens in between. Accordin' to the law and traditions of the sea, ye'll now receive five lashes with the cat-o'-nine-tails."

"I still think a dozen would be better," Rowland said. "Maybe even twenty."

"'Tis not your decision to make, Mr. Rowland,"

Sampson snapped. "And if you continue to question my orders, it may well be you there on the mast before much longer."

Rowland grimaced but said, "I'm not questionin' your orders, Cap'n. I'm sure you're right."

"Very well, then. Ye requested that ye be allowed to carry out Preacher's punishment, and I'm agreeable to that." Sampson gestured with a pudgy hand. "Have to."

Then, as he stepped back, he bellowed, "Attention on deck! All hands! Discipline bein' carried out!"

He wanted everyone to see this, Preacher thought, so they would know what would happen to them if they failed to obey orders instantly and without question.

The bonds around his wrists and waist were brutally tight. Preacher might have been able to work his way loose from them, but it would take hours to do that and he was out of time. He set his jaw as he heard Rowland step behind him. Something swished through the air, and then strands of fire slashed across his back at an angle.

That was what it felt like, anyway. His reflexes would have forced him to jerk away from the agony, but tied to the mast as he was, he had no place to go. Despite the pain, his jaw didn't unclench, and he didn't make a sound.

Rowland brought the second stroke back from the other direction, angling it opposite to the first lash so as to scourge more of Preacher's back. Preacher drew in a sharp breath, but that was his only reaction.

The third stroke made his head tip back a little. He felt the cords in his neck standing out as he fought not to yell. Rowland grunted with effort as he brought the cat-o'-nine-tails across Preacher's back for the fourth time. Preacher's lips drew back from his teeth in a grimace, but still no sound escaped from them.

Rowland paused then and leaned closer to Preacher, who felt the man's hot breath on his neck as Rowland whispered, "This is just the beginnin', you . . ." He added several obscenities, then repeated, "Just the beginnin' of how you're gonna suffer."

"Get on with it," Sampson said. "One more."

"Aye," Rowland replied, straightening. Preacher couldn't see the tattooed man, but he could imagine Rowland drawing his arm back and setting himself to put as much force as he possibly could behind this last stroke. The cat-o'-nine-tails whistled through the air—

"Aaarrgghh—" The groan came from Preacher before he could choke it off.

Sampson and Rowland laughed, and he heard several other members of the crew chuckling, as well.

Then Sampson said, "Cut him down." A knife sawed at the bonds, and as they came loose, Preacher slumped to the deck, unable to stand. One of the sailors, following Sampson's command, sloshed a bucket of seawater over his back. The salt water made it feel as if all the skin was being peeled off his back.

"Somebody take care of him," Sampson said. "You there. Tyler. You're in charge of him. Try anything funny, and ye'll wind up on the mast, too."

"Aye, Cap'n," a reedy voice answered. A moment later, bony knees clad in ragged breeches hit the deck beside Preacher. Breathing hard, the mountain man turned his head enough to see the scrawny, redheaded youngster leaning over him.

"You'll be all right," Tyler said, but he sounded like he wasn't sure if he meant it.

"I . . . sure will . . . be," Preacher grated. He was completely sincere about it, too. He had even more of a score to settle with Jabez Sampson and Abner Rowland, and the hate blazing inside him would keep him alive until he did.

CHAPTER 28

Crew members on the *Calypso* slept on the deck or in hammocks strung from the mast to the railings. With his back in the shape it was, Preacher had to lie on his belly, so Tyler helped him stand up and then stagger over to a spot on the deck where they would be out of the way.

Once Preacher had stretched out again, Tyler said, "I'll get some grease from the cook and put it on your back. That'll help a little."

"Much obliged to you, son." Preacher's voice was strong again. His back still hurt quite a bit, but the pain had receded enough that he could ignore it, put it out of his head, and concentrate on speculating about his course of action. He wasn't going to allow himself to be exiled to a sugar plantation on some godforsaken island where he would no doubt die from overwork and the miserable climate, all because Simone LeCarde had agreed to protect a couple of cheap crooks like Edmund Cornelius and Lucy Tarleton.

Tyler's footsteps pattered off. Preacher lay there, listening to the waves splashing, the sails booming, and the sounds of men going about their jobs on the ship. He thought about the ones who had looked unhappy about the flogging they were forced to witness, and he wondered if he might find allies among them.

After a few minutes, Tyler returned and knelt beside Preacher. "This is liable to hurt, Mr. Preacher, but it'll help these cuts heal up faster."

"Just Preacher," the mountain man said, as he always did in such circumstances. "No *mister*."

"All right, Preacher. Grit your teeth."

"Just get it done, boy."

Preacher had to follow Tyler's advice and clench his teeth tighter together as the young man gently rubbed grease onto the injuries. The process took a few minutes. When it was done, Preacher lay there, breathing hard from the pain and letting it subside.

"I think I can find a clean shirt for you, once the bleeding stops," Tyler said. "Well, maybe not completely clean, but not too dirty. It's pretty late in the day, so Cap'n Sampson probably won't expect you to do any more work today, but first thing in the morning he'll want you to be on duty again."

"How'd a young fella like you wind up bein' part of a pirate crew?" Preacher asked, keeping his voice quiet enough so the conversation wouldn't be overheard among the usual hubbub of shipboard life. "No offense, but you don't seem like what I think of as a buccaneer."

"I'm not. Not really. When I signed on, I thought the *Calypso* was just a trading vessel. That's what she's supposed to be. From what I've heard, that Mr. LeCarde who owns her has several other trading ships that sail back and forth between New Orleans and the Caribbean." Tyler paused. "I didn't find out until later that we were going to be seizing other ships and stealing their cargoes and raiding towns on the islands and . . . and hurting people . . ." His voice choked off.

Preacher waited, and after a moment, Tyler went on. "I guess even if I'd known, I would have signed on anyway." His voice was dull with despair. "It's better being a pirate than starving to death, after all. That's what was going to happen if I stayed in New Orleans. I don't have any family, and the people who took me in after my folks died were no good. At least here on the ship, the food's decent, and as long as you work hard and do everything Cap'n Sampson says, you're not mistreated. I know you probably have a hard time believing that right now, but it's true. Nobody gets flogged as long as they do their work and obey orders."

"That's the part I've never been very good at," Preacher said. "Followin' orders."

"You'd learn if you stayed on this ship." Tyler shrugged. "But from what I heard the cap'n and Mr. Rowland saying, you won't be aboard all that long. We'll reach San Patricio in four or five days, and you'll be getting off there."

"And left at that sugar plantation," Preacher muttered. "Can't say as I like the sound of that."

"It's just a plantation. More hard work, more following orders. But nobody's firing cannonballs at you."

"Reckon it's got that to recommend it," Preacher said dryly. He was getting drowsy as the pain in his back eased, the sun baked him, and the hardships of the day took their toll. He didn't want to doze off just yet, though. He asked Tyler, "Are there more fellas in the crew who feel like you do, who don't much cotton to bein' here?"

"Sure. The cap'n . . . well, he's a pretty hard taskmaster. And don't tell anybody I said this . . ." Tyler lowered his voice even more. "He laughs and jokes all the time, but he's got a real mean streak. Most of us are a little afraid of him. Maybe more than a little. But you didn't hear that from me."

"I sure didn't," Preacher agreed. He was very interested in everything Tyler had to say, though. From the sound of it, the seeds of a mutiny had already been sown. All he had to do was nurture them.

Preacher slept right there on the deck that night, and his slumber was very restless. Every time he moved a little, fresh bursts of pain shot through him. He was exhausted, too, and that helped to a certain extent in overcoming the discomfort.

Tyler brought him coffee, a chunk of bread, and a piece of salt pork for breakfast the next morning. Preacher sat up and ate. Moving still hurt, but the bloody stripes across his back had crusted over and as long as he was careful, the pain wasn't too bad. The food and coffee made him feel better, too.

He was just finishing up the meal when Jabez Sampson came over. Tyler scurried off when the captain gave him a hard look.

Sampson put his hands on his hips and stared down at Preacher. "Are ye ready to get back to work?"

"Holystonin' the deck? That ain't my kind of chore."

"And what did that attitude gain ye yesterday, my proud lad? Have ye already forgotten?"

"Not hardly," Preacher said.

The look he gave Sampson made the captain frown and take a step back as if he'd realized that he had just stepped up to a grizzly bear and poked it with a sharp stick.

Sampson recovered quickly, though "I think your talents would be goin' to waste wieldin' a holystone. Maybe ye'd be better off as a rigger." He pointed up into the sails with a thumb.

Preacher thought about words he had overheard the sailors calling to each other and said, "I don't know a jib from a mizzen or any other blasted thing about sailin'. I can't very well follow orders if I don't have any idea what it is you're yellin' at me."

"Ye don't have to know anything except to climb the riggin', hold on, and pull on the ropes that another rigger tells ye to pull on. Steady on your feet, are ye?"

"Tolerable so," Preacher replied.

"Then head on up." Sampson looked at Tyler, who had stopped a few yards away and was hanging around with an uncomfortable look on his freckled face. "Ye go up with him, boy. You're still responsible for him."

"That ain't fair to the boy. I don't want him punished because of me not knowin' what I'm doin'."

"Then listen close to the other riggers and pay attention to what they're doin'." Sampson jerked his thumb toward the sails again. "Up ye go!"

Preacher climbed to his feet and pulled on the linsey-woolsey shirt Tyler had brought him. The young man looked apprehensive about what was facing them, but he wasn't about to argue with the captain. He told Preacher, "Follow me," and led the way over to the mast, where he told the mountain man, "You'd better take off those boots. You'll do better with bare feet."

Preacher leaned against the mast to remove the high-topped moccasins he always wore with his buckskins. He had gone barefoot enough as a youngster that the soles of his feet were permanently callused. The mast had pegs driven into it that served as hand- and foot-holds.

"You've worked in the riggin' before?" Preacher asked.

"Yes," Tyler replied, "and I don't like it. It's the most dangerous job on the ship. But if you're careful and don't move too quickly, you should be all right." He pointed to a man strolling back and forth on the deck and looking up into the sails. "That's the sailing master, Mr. Holland. He tells the riggers how to adjust the sails. Just listen to him. Well, listen to *me*, I suppose I should say. I'll tell you what he's talking about. Watch what I do and try to do the same."

"You'd better be careful up there, too. You fall, and I'll be plumb lost up yonder."

"We'll both be careful," Tyler said.

He began climbing the mast to join the other riggers already aloft. Preacher watched how he did it and followed his example. The climbing itself wasn't difficult, although every time he reached above his head for a new grip, his back twinged. The wind seemed to blow harder the higher he climbed, although he knew that might be his imagination.

Above the deck, though, it smelled fresher, and when he looked around, he got a real sense of the immensity of the sea. He was accustomed to being able to gaze across vast distances from the mountains that had become his home. That perspective always made him aware of just how puny humankind was, compared to the world on which they dwelled. The sensation up in the rigging was much the same, although the view was more monotonous. Just mile after endless mile of restless blue-green water under a sweeping blue sky broken up here and there by towering white clouds.

Some fellas were natural sailors, Preacher supposed, and responded to such sights. He was impressed by the vista—but the sea wasn't his home and never would be.

"We're high enough," Tyler called to him over the soughing of the wind. "See those ropes running out from the mast to your right?"

"Yeah."

"Hold on to the top one and put your feet on the bottom one and work your way out along them. Keep your body as straight as you can so the rope you're standing on won't swing back and forth and unbalance you."

Preacher took a deep breath, shifted one hand and foot onto the ropes, then the other hand and foot. Those ropes, narrow lifelines that they were, along with his own strength, were all that separated him from a likely fatal plunge to the deck.

Suddenly, facing a horde of bloodthirsty Blackfoot warriors didn't sound quite so bad.

CHAPTER 29

That morning was one of the longest of Preacher's life. By the time he and Tyler climbed back down at midday, Preacher's muscles were trembling from the exertion of holding himself aloft in the rigging and hauling on other lines to adjust the sails. The swaying, bobbing deck felt as good under his feet as solid ground would have.

The good news was that while the wounds on his back had seeped enough blood to stick to the shirt in places, he no longer felt much pain from the results of the flogging. His iron constitution was already working its usual wonders.

The sea air, always on the move, had swept the last of the cobwebs from his brain, too. He was able to think a lot more clearly—and that meant beginning to make plans for turning the tables on his captors.

A cup of water and another chunk of bread formed their midday meal.

As they sat cross-legged on the deck to eat, Tyler said, "Tonight there'll be lemons and oranges to ward off scurvy, beans and salt jowl, and a bit of rum. Better than what you can scrounge from the alleys of New Orleans, like I told you."

"Not as good as pan bread and an antelope steak seared over an open fire in the mountains, though," Preacher said.

Tyler shook his head. "I've never seen a mountain, except on some of the islands we've come across, and they're not really that big. I can't imagine an entire range of them stretching for hundreds of miles, like I've heard they have out on the frontier."

"More like thousands of miles, from up in Canada clear down across the border into Mexico." Preacher smiled. "And I've trekked over most of 'em at one time or another."

"Isn't it frightening, being out there all by yourself when you're surrounded by wild animals and blood-thirsty savages?"

"After climbin' around up there in that riggin', the frontier don't seem so bad." Preacher looked point-edly toward the rear deck where Captain Sampson stood with Abner Rowland. "Besides, I reckon the sea's got its share of wild animals and bloodthirsty savages, too."

"Well, I can't argue with you there," Tyler mut-tered. After a moment, he went on wistfully. "I guess I wouldn't mind seeing the frontier one of these days. Who knows? I might discover that I like it."

"You might," Preacher said. "Maybe if things work out right, I'll take you along with me sometime."

The young man gave him a pitying look. "I'm not sure that'll ever be possible. I think you're supposed to stay on the plantation from now on."

"I ain't never been good at doin' what I'm supposed

to. Of course, that gets me into a mite of trouble sometimes."

Abner Rowland came along the deck then and said, "You're finished eatin'. Get back up there, you monkeys."

"Aye, sir," Tyler answered without looking at the tattooed man. The youngster scrambled to his feet and took his empty tin cup back to the water barrel. Preacher stood up more deliberately and gazed coolly and defiantly at Rowland.

"You and me ain't done, are we?" Rowland said.

"Most likely not, I reckon," Preacher said as he straightened to his full height.

An ugly grin spread across Rowland's face. "Next time, I'll use that cat-o'-nine-tails to flay every inch of skin off of you."

"It's a lot easier when the man you're dealin' with is tied up and can't fight back, ain't it? That's the coward's way."

Rowland clenched his fists and took a step toward Preacher as he scowled. "You'll pay for that, you—"

"Preacher!" Jabez Sampson called from the rear deck. "Get back up in the riggin'! Now!"

"Reckon I'd best get to work," Preacher drawled. He swung around, turning his back contemptuously on Rowland, and ambled toward the mast to join Tyler in the rigging. He felt Rowland's hate-filled gaze boring into his back, but the tattooed man didn't say anything else.

Preacher felt a little more comfortable working with the sails that afternoon, but he still didn't like it, not one bit. He was glad when the long, grueling day was over. After supper—which wasn't bad, as Tyler had promised—he stretched out again on the deck and fell into a deep, dreamless sleep.

The next day was more of the same. The boredom and strain of the work was relieved only by the brief sight of a few small islands to the south.

"We should be off Cuba by tomorrow night," Tyler told him.

"Will we be stoppin' there?" Preacher asked.

"I don't know. From the way the cap'n was talking, we're supposed to head straight for San Patricio. We'll probably put in at Havana on our way back to New Orleans and take on some cargo then. But you won't be—"

The youngster stopped short, and Preacher realized Tyler had been about to say that he wouldn't be on the *Calypso* by then. He would be enduring his brutal exile on San Patricio.

They'd just see about that.

In the middle of Preacher's second afternoon aloft, the clouds began to thicken. A dark line appeared on the horizon to the southeast.

Tyler paused in what he was doing to peer toward it and muttered, "I don't like the looks of that."

Preacher heard his comment and asked, "Is that a storm of some sort?"

"Probably just a little squall, but some of them can get pretty bad." Tyler looked around. "There are no islands close by, no cove where Cap'n Sampson could put in for shelter. We'll have to ride it out."

"Have you been through storms before out here?"

"I have. I don't like them."

The wind began to swing around, and the sails had

to be adjusted so the ship could tack and continue to make headway. The onrushing clouds seemed to swallow the blue sky like a hungry beast. They thickened and darkened, and Preacher saw skeleton fingers of lightning clawing through them.

"Haul in!" the sailing master, Holland, called from below. The riggers began furling the sails so they wouldn't be damaged by the strong winds that were undoubtedly headed their way. Crewmen inserted oars in the oarlocks and settled in to keep the vessel moving. It was slow going. They had to strain against the wind and waves.

Preacher leaned one way and then the other as the ship swayed in the growing waves. He almost slipped a couple of times but managed to hang on. His heart pounded. If he ever made it back to dry land, it would be just fine with him if he never set foot on a ship again.

Then he realized that sentiment wasn't correct. Sooner or later, a ship would be required to take him back to New Orleans to finish the chore that had taken him there.

"We're finished!" Tyler called to him over the wind, which was fairly howling. "Let's get down from here!"

They worked their way back to the mast and began to descend with the other riggers. Preacher was glad to drop the last couple of feet to the deck. Tyler landed beside him.

The waves were high, and spray came over the sides. Preacher felt it against his face and asked Tyler, "What do we do now?"

"Find something to hang on to!"

The blue sky had disappeared completely. The heavens were a mixture of black and leaden gray.

The clouds looked to Preacher like giant fangs ready to reach down, snatch up the suddenly flimsy-seeming sloop, and chomp it to bits, along with every poor, luckless sailor on it.

"Is this one of them hurricanes I've heard about?"

Tyler shook his head. "No, this is just a little blow."

With no warning, the sea seemed to drop out from under the *Calypso*. The ship's bow tilted down and she dropped for a couple of seconds that seemed longer. Then with a bone-jarring jolt, the ship struck the bottom of the trough between waves that had climbed to what seemed to Preacher to be towering heights. With nothing to grab hold of on the open deck, the men lined the rails and clung to them. Preacher and Tyler took their places.

Preacher looked aft and saw Jabez Sampson still on the elevated deck. He had the tiller, although trying to steer the ship in the wild seas seemed a hopeless task.

If this was just a little blow, Preacher thought, he didn't want to experience a big one.

So far the storm had been just wind and waves, but then the rain struck, huge, slashing drops that pelted painfully against Preacher's skin, followed immediately by blinding flashes of lightning and thunder that rolled like the volley of a thousand cannon. In a matter of seconds, Preacher was soaked to the skin. When the rain hit his back, it felt like he was being flogged again. He bellowed a curse that the wind snatched away.

The rain fell in such heavy sheets that when he looked over, he could barely see Tyler clinging to the rail right beside him. He leaned over closer to the young man and shouted, "How long . . . does a storm like this . . . last?"

"Maybe . . . half an hour! Maybe . . . longer!"

With the pounding the waves were giving the *Calypso*, Preacher didn't see how the ship could hold together for even a quarter of an hour, let alone longer. But she had been sailing the Gulf of Mexico and the Caribbean since the days when Catamount Jack LeCarde was her captain, he reminded himself, so evidently the sloop was pretty sturdily built. In that time it must have come through dozens of storms like this one, maybe even worse.

Preacher had been able to tolerate the ship's motion without getting sick, but the constant, dramatic rising and falling, and the tilting back and forth was different. He felt his stomach begin to roil. For some unfathomable reason, it was important to him that he not look like a landlubber. He tried to suppress the sensation, but after a while it was impossible for him to do.

Almost before he knew what was happening, he hung his head over the railing and began unleashing the contents of his stomach. Everything he had eaten that day and, seemingly, for the past month or so went into the sea.

Sick as he was, and as hellishly loud as the storm was, he almost didn't hear Tyler cry, "Preacher, look out!"

His instincts took over and he twisted his body around fast enough that he saw a huge, bulky figure looming up in front of him. Powerful arms shot around Preacher's waist, lifting and heaving so his bare feet came off the deck and he felt himself going up and over the rail toward the angry sea below.

CHAPTER 30

Preacher flailed out with his right arm, and his hand slapped the railing. In desperation, he clamped his fingers around it as his attacker let go of him and he started to plummet toward the waves.

All his weight hit his arm, causing pain to shoot from his hand up to his shoulder and then into his back. But his grip held fast on the slick wood, and that was the only important thing. Preacher was a strong swimmer, but no one could survive a sea like the one raging below him. It would swallow him up and never spit him out.

The big man who had thrown him overboard loomed at the railing. Through the sluicing rain, Preacher caught a glimpse of him drawing his foot back. The man kicked at Preacher's right hand in an attempt to knock the precarious grasp loose and dump him into the sea. Preacher grabbed the railing with his left hand and let go with the right just in time to avoid getting his fingers smashed. At the same time, he kicked upward with his right leg and hooked his ankle over the rail.

Someone shouted, but Preacher couldn't make out

the words in the middle of all that infernal commotion. He saw the would-be murderer struggling with someone. The two figures swayed back and forth.

That had to be Tyler, Preacher thought. The young redhead was probably the only one on the whole ship who would even attempt to come to his aid.

The attacker—Preacher had no doubt in his mind it was Abner Rowland, seizing the chance to get rid of him—flung the smaller figure away after a moment. But Tyler had provided enough of a distraction to give Preacher time to pull himself up and roll over the railing onto the deck.

He was still lying there when Rowland tried to stomp his head in. Preacher got his hands up in time to grab the booted foot and stop it a few inches away from his face. With a grunt of effort, he heaved on Rowland's leg, putting all the strength he could muster into the effort.

On the rain-slick deck, Rowland couldn't maintain his balance as his legs shot out from under him. He crashed down onto the planks.

Preacher flipped over onto hands and knees and scrambled after Rowland. He always took a fight straight to an enemy if at all possible. While Rowland was still stunned by his fall, Preacher landed on top of him and rammed his knee into the tattooed man's belly.

Rowland grunted and swung a wild backhand that clipped Preacher on the side of the head and sent him sprawling. Even the glancing blow packed power. Preacher used the momentum to roll over and come up on his feet again. Rowland was slow recovering, but he tried to lumber upright, too.

If Preacher had been worried about fighting fair,

he would have waited until Rowland was standing again. But the blasted varmint had just tried to kill him. Preacher didn't feel like extending the former keelboater any consideration. He clubbed his hands together, swung both arms, and walloped the blazes out of Rowland as soon as the tattooed man reached his knees.

Rowland went over backward and didn't move again.

It would have been easy then, while Rowland was out cold, to drag him over to the railing, lift him, and tip him over. Mighty easy, Preacher thought. The sea would claim Rowland just as it had almost claimed Preacher.

The mountain man couldn't do that. He was a killer many times over, but always in battle with men who were trying to kill him or harm innocent folks. He wasn't a cold-blooded murderer, and that was what it would take to do such a thing.

He peered around through the rain and spotted a huddled shape lying on the deck a few yards away. He went over, dropped to his knees beside the figure, and rolled the young man onto his back. It was Tyler, all right. As the deluge struck him in the face, he started to sputter. Within a minute or two, he was awake and tried to sit up. Preacher put a hand on his shoulder to keep him lying down.

"Wha' . . . wha' happen?" Tyler managed to ask.

"Rowland tried to throw me overboard." Preacher looked at the other men clinging to the railing along that side of the ship. "And you were the only one who even tried to stop him."

"I . . . I didn't even think about it. I just saw some-body about to grab you, so I yelled, and then I thought you were a goner. How . . . how in the world did you manage to save yourself?"

"I had a whole heap of luck," Preacher said. "And thanks to you, I had a chance to get back on board before Rowland could knock me off again."

"He threw me aside like I . . . I was nothing," Tyler said. "I tried, but I couldn't even start to put up a real fight, Preacher."

The mountain man patted him on the shoulder. "You done good, son, and don't think for a minute that you didn't. I reckon I owe my life as much to you as anything, and I don't forget things like that."

The wind howled, and the rain still lashed at them as they talked. The waves tossed the *Calypso* this way and that, and sometimes the vessel tilted so much it was a wonder everyone on board didn't slide right off.

Rowland was starting to move around as his senses returned to him.

Preacher helped Tyler to his feet and said, "Let's go over to the mast and hang on there. That varmint won't sneak up on me again."

They staggered across the deck to the mast and sat down at its base. Preacher looked toward the rear deck but couldn't see Jabez Sampson anymore. The wild thought crossed his mind that maybe Sampson had been swept overboard, but he thought it was more likely the captain had sought shelter from the storm somewhere on board. He gave the impression of having been a sailor for a long time.

Preacher figured Sampson knew how to ride out a squall.

It was difficult to keep track of time in the midst of such chaos. To Preacher, the storm already seemed like it had been going on for hours. But eventually he realized the rain wasn't pelting them as hard as it had been, and the wind wasn't howling as loud, either. The sea was still very rough and choppy, but maybe not as bad as earlier.

The men stumbled away from the railings as they figured out that they were no longer in imminent danger of being washed overboard. It became easier to see through the rain, another indication that it had slowed down considerably. Preacher looked for Abner Rowland but didn't spot the tattooed man.

Jabez Sampson appeared from wherever he had ridden out the storm and started bellowing orders. "Get those sails unfurled, Mr. Holland!" he ordered the sailing master. "We've got a fair wind now, and we'd best make good use of it!"

"Aye, sir!" Holland responded, then began calling names of sailors and telling them to get aloft. Preacher was a little surprised he and Tyler weren't among the men being ordered into the rigging.

He said as much, and Tyler laughed hollowly.

"That's because you and I really aren't very good at handling the sails. I know what to do but I'm not strong enough to do it efficiently, and you're plenty strong but don't know what to do. Between the two of us, we added up to one fairly mediocre sailor."

That made Preacher laugh, too. He had never been accused of being mediocre at much of anything in his life—but he knew he wasn't cut out to be a sailor.

They wound up on one of the oars, once the long poles had been inserted in the oarlocks again. Above them, the riggers unrolled the sails and fastened them in position. A loud booming sounded as the canvas caught the wind and billowed out. The *Calypso*, which had been wallowing in still heavy seas, began to pick up speed and cut through the waves again, instead of being tossed around at the whims of nature.

The wind was strong enough that the oarsmen were ordered to bring the oars back in. Preacher and Tyler stowed the one they had been using with the others, down in the middle deck that Tyler called the orlop.

"Is there a name for that place up there on top of the cabin where the cap'n and the steersman stand?" Preacher asked.

"That's the poop deck," Tyler replied. He smiled. "You keep learning things and we'll make a sailor out of you anyway, Preacher."

"Not likely," the mountain man growled.

They went back up onto the main deck. Preacher's clothes were soaked and uncomfortable, but he didn't have anything else to change into and there wouldn't have been a point to it, even if he had.

They barely had time to step out onto the open deck, where Preacher noticed the late afternoon sun starting to break through the clouds here and there, when a loud, angry voice proclaimed, "There he is! The scum who tried to murder me!"

CHAPTER 31

Preacher turned toward what he had just learned was called the poop deck. Abner Rowland stood there with Captain Sampson.

Rowland pointed a finger at Preacher as he went on. "Tried to throw me overboard durin' that blasted storm, he did!"

"That's a lie!" Tyler exclaimed, then immediately looked shocked for speaking up defiantly. But then a determined expression appeared on his face, and he went on. "What really happened was just the opposite. Mr. Rowland tried to kill Preacher. He nearly did it, too!"

"What's wrong with you, boy?" Rowland growled. "You tired of livin'?"

"Hold on, hold on," Sampson said. "We'll get to the bottom o' this, I promise ye that." He beckoned to Preacher. "Come on up here. The two of ye should settle this face-to-face."

Preacher didn't think that would do any good. He didn't believe Sampson would ever accept his word over that of Rowland. Of course, Preacher had another witness on his side.

That thought made him look over at Tyler. Quietly, he said to the redhead, "You don't want to get mixed up in this. Rowland's likely carryin' around enough of a grudge against you already, just because you helped me before. If you stick up for me now, he'll wind up hatin' you almost as much as he does me."

"But what I said was the truth, Preacher," Tyler objected. "You know that."

"Yeah, but that ain't the only thing you got to worry about. One way or another, I ain't gonna be on this ship that much longer, and when I'm gone, you'll have to deal with Rowland by yourself." Preacher paused and gave the youngster an intent look. "Unless you think that some of the other crewmen might be willin' to stand up to Sampson and Rowland?"

"I . . . I don't know about that. Some of them might. There are quite a few of us who don't like what we've gotten mixed up in. I've been talking to them about that." Tyler shook his head. "But regardless of that, I'm not going to lie just to protect myself."

"I know the feelin', son. Bein' honest can be blasted inconvenient sometimes."

From the raised deck, Sampson said, "I told ye to get up here. The two o' ye have done enough jawin'."

Preacher and Tyler climbed the narrow flight of steps at the side of the deck. Sampson had turned the tiller back over to one of the sailors, who held the ship steady as the wind continued filling the sails. Sampson stood waiting with his hands on his hips, while Rowland was beside him, glowering.

"All right, Mr. Rowland," Sampson said when Preacher and Tyler were facing them. "Tell these two what ye told me a few minutes ago."

"It's simple," Rowland declared. "Durin' that storm,

Preacher slipped up on me from behind, like one of those red Injuns he lives with in the mountains, and tried to throw me overboard. I never would've made it if I'd gone into the drink." He crossed his brawny arms and sneered. "Luckily, I was able to fight him off, even when that one"—he nodded toward Tyler—"tried to help him."

"That's your story?" Sampson asked.

"Aye. And every word of it is true."

"Every word of it's a blasted lie," Preacher said. "I'm the one who nearly got throwed overboard, and Rowland's the one who tried to do the throwin'. All Tyler did was try to make him stop while I was clingin' to the rail. Rowland was doin' his best to kick my hands off it."

Tyler moved up alongside Preacher and said, "That's the truth, Cap'n. That's just the way it happened."

With his scrawny body, weak chin, and reedy voice, Tyler wasn't much of a candidate for heroics, but at that moment, Preacher was proud of the young man. Standing up for what was right and true was something that everybody had in them, no matter their size or shape or age or anything else. It was just a matter of whether they also had the courage to go with it.

The odds were against the two of them, however, and Preacher knew it.

"Did anybody else witness this incident?" Sampson asked.

Some of the other men along the railing must have seen *something*, but in the middle of that terrible storm, they honestly might not have known exactly what was going on.

Preacher had a hunch some of them did. "You'd have to ask the other fellas who were on deck."

"That's exactly what I intend to do," Sampson said. He raised his voice so it carried out over the main deck. "Did anyone see what happened between our guest and Mr. Rowland? Anyone at all?"

Guest, Preacher thought wryly. That was one way to refer to him, he supposed. Better than *prisoner destined for a short, miserable life as a slave on a sugar plantation.*

He and Tyler turned to look along the deck as they waited to see if anyone was going to speak up in support of what they had told Sampson. No one did, but several of the men looked down shamefacedly at the planks.

They wanted to say something but were afraid to, Preacher thought. Maybe a few of them would find the courage to make a stand, if they had somebody to lead them.

Sampson shook his head slowly and said, "It appears that what we have here is a case of two sides tellin' different stories. As the captain of this vessel, 'tis up to me to decide which side is tellin' the truth. Since Mr. Rowland is the boatswain, and as such an officer of this ship, I have to give him the benefit of the doubt."

"That don't come as any surprise," Preacher said.

"I imagine it don't. So, mister, ye stand accused and now convicted of tryin' to murder one of my officers—"

"Wait a minute. There was no trial."

Sampson snorted. "Indeed there was, just now, with me as the judge and jury."

"And executioner, I reckon," the mountain man said in a low, dangerous voice.

Sampson shook his head. "There'll be no execution,

although under other circumstances, the penalty for what ye did would be death. I'd keelhaul ye and be happy to do it." He sighed. "But 'tis not what the African said our mutual employer desires, so I'm forced to take other measures." The captain's voice hardened. "I thought I might get some work outta ye, but ye'll spend the rest o' the voyage in chains instead. *Take him!*"

Sampson barked that order at several sailors who had gathered at the foot of the steps while the conversation on the poop deck continued.

In response to the command, they swarmed up the steps and charged at Preacher, who whirled around to meet the attack. He had halfway expected Sampson to try something, so he wasn't surprised.

The men were armed with belaying pins, but as the one who was closest to Preacher drew back his weapon, the mountain man struck first. A knobby-knuckled fist lashed out, caught the sailor on the jaw, and threw him back against a couple of his companions. Their feet and legs tangled together. Two men fell, but three more continued the assault.

Tyler tried to get in the way of one of them, but the man poked him hard in the stomach with a belaying pin. Tyler doubled over and fell to his knees, gagging and retching.

Preacher ducked under a sweeping blow and lifted an uppercut of his own under his assailant's chin. The punch rocked the man's head back and buckled his knees. Preacher snatched the belaying pin out of his hand and used it to block a swipe from another sailor. He leaned aside and kicked the man in the belly, knocking him all the way off the poop deck.

The man crashed down onto the steps leading below to the captain's cabin.

The whirlwind of action continued as the men who had gotten tangled up and fallen down regained their feet and again joined the assault on the mountain man. Preacher twisted and turned, the belaying pin in his hand flashing back and forth as he blocked the blows aimed at him. A few years earlier, he'd had to defend himself in a sword fight, and this battle somewhat resembled that one—parry, thrust, and slash, only with a bludgeon instead of a blade.

Preacher heard a bone snap as he cracked the pin across a sailor's forearm. The man dropped his pin and staggered back, howling with pain.

Knowing Sampson and Rowland were behind him, Preacher expected a treacherous blow from one of them at any moment. They stayed out of the fight, though. Evidently they enjoyed watching him battle against overwhelming odds.

The problem was, where Preacher was concerned, five to one odds weren't necessarily overwhelming. As a matter of fact, he had already whittled them down to three to one. That became two to one as Tyler recovered enough to tackle one of the attackers around the knees and knock the man off his feet. At that same moment, Preacher smacked another man on the side of the head with his belaying pin and knocked him senseless to the deck. In a continuation of the same move, he hooked a foot behind the ankle of the remaining man and jerked his legs out from under him. Preacher raised the belaying pin, ready to rap the man on the head and put him out of action for a while.

A pistol boomed. The ball struck the belaying pin in Preacher's hand and knocked it out of his grip. The violent impact made the mountain man's hand go numb. He grimaced as he tried to shake some feeling back into his fingers and turned toward the sound of the shot.

Rowland had a pistol in each hand. Smoke curled from the barrel of the one in his right, which he lowered to his side. The gun in his left hand pointed at Preacher. From the looks of it, it was loaded, primed, and ready to fire.

So was Abner Rowland.

Preacher sensed that he was close to death, despite the fact that Simone had wanted him delivered alive to the sugar plantation.

Before Rowland could squeeze the trigger, Sampson said, "Hold your fire there, Mr. Rowland, unless that devil tries somethin' else. Then ye have my leave to shoot him."

"Give me a reason," Rowland said to Preacher in a low voice. "Please."

Preacher stood stock still.

Sampson reached under his coat and brought out a pistol as well. He cocked it and aimed it at Tyler, who had struggled back onto his knees.

"'Twas quite a brawl," Sampson said, "but 'tis over now. Unless ye'd like me to shoot this young friend o' yours."

"Leave him alone," Preacher said. "He's not part of this."

"This is twice now he's tried to help ye. I'd say he's made hisself a part of it." Sampson shook his head. "But I'm a merciful man. Everyone says that about

me. I'm willin' to overlook the lad's transgressions . . .
provided ye cooperate."

Tyler said, "Don't do it, Preacher. Not on my account."

Preacher ignored him and asked Sampson, "What
do you want?"

"Now, that's more like it," the captain said. "Mr.
Rowland, see to it that he's clapped in irons and tossed
back in the bilge."

"My pleasure," Rowland growled.

Preacher stood there while manacles were brought
to the poop deck. A couple of sailors roughly jerked
his arms behind his back, then another man snapped
the manacles in place around his wrists.

"Leave his legs free for now," Rowland ordered.
"We'll put the shackles on his ankles the last thing
before we drop him into the bilge." He gestured with
the loaded pistol he still held. "Get down those steps,
mister."

Preacher went, seething but knowing he had to
cooperate for the time being. If Sampson and Rowland ever completely lost patience, they would kill
him out of hand. Worse, they might easily do the same
to Tyler, and Preacher didn't want to be responsible
for that happening to the young man.

As the mountain man was prodded over to the
hatch leading down into the orlop, Tyler called from
the poop deck, "I'm sorry, Preacher."

"Not as sorry as you're gonna be, lad," Sampson said.

Preacher heard that and stopped short. With his
arms manacled behind him, he jerked around and
said, "You promised you wouldn't punish him!"

"I did no such thing," Sampson replied. "I said I
wouldn't kill him if ye cooperated, and I'll keep my

word on that. But for defyin' orders and tryin' to help ye murder Mr. Rowland, the lad must pay." He looked at a grinning Rowland. "Eight lashes, I'd say. To be carried out immediately."

Still on his knees, Tyler went pale with horror, making the freckles on his thin face stand out even more than usual.

"You son of a—" Preacher yelled at Sampson as he tried to lunge away from the hatch. The burly sailors flanking him grabbed his arms and threw him backward. Manacled the way he was, he couldn't catch his balance. He fell through the open hatchway and crashed down on his back into the orlop with stunning force.

CHAPTER 32

The fall knocked the air out of Preacher's lungs and paralyzed him long enough for men to leap down around him and tackle him when he tried to surge back up. Their weight pinned him to the deck. He couldn't use his arms to fight, but he kicked out at them the best he could. Men seized his legs, and a second later he felt the iron shackles closing around his bare ankles.

"Make 'em good and tight!" Rowland called down through the open hatch. "I want him to feel them!"

In irons, Preacher couldn't walk, so his captors picked him up and carried him over to the ladder leading down into the hold. Some of them descended and reached back up to take him as the others lowered him through the opening. If Preacher had been the type to yell and curse, he would have loosed a storm of invective on them, but he knew that wouldn't do any good and maintained a grim, stony silence instead. Again they carried him over to an open hatch. Below was the bilge. He heard the filthy water sloshing around down there.

They held him over the opening and dropped him.

Preacher grabbed a breath and held it, knowing that his head might go under before he could struggle back into a sitting position. The reeking, oily bilge-water splashed up around him as he landed, blinding him and getting in his nose. Snorting, he fought his way up out of it. He pressed his back against the hull, grimacing because it was still tender and sore from the flogging.

With all the hatches open, enough light penetrated for him to be able to look around. There was nothing to see except the planks of the hull and the water with greasy scum floating on top of it.

"Is he down there?" Rowland called from the main deck.

"Aye," one of the sailors answered. "Want us to close him up in the dark?"

"No, leave the hatches open for now," Rowland said. He laughed harshly. "I want him to hear what's gonna happen next."

That statement made Preacher's heart slug harder in his chest. He remembered what Jabez Sampson had said about Tyler being flogged. Eight lashes, the captain had decreed—three more than Preacher had received.

He knew how much he had suffered from those lashes, and Tyler wasn't nearly as hardy. That much agony might be enough to kill the boy. Preacher's teeth ground together as he strained against the iron bonds on his wrists and ankles.

He couldn't do a thing to ease their painful grip. They didn't budge.

A few minutes later, he heard Tyler scream.

The mountain man closed his eyes and took a deep

breath. After a brief pause, Tyler screamed again. Fury burned so fiercely inside Preacher that it threatened to consume him. He knew Tyler was probably trying to hold the screams in, but the youngster wasn't strong enough to do that. Again and again, the agonized shrieks drifted down to Preacher in the bilge, and his hate and resolve grew stronger each time.

Unfortunately, at the moment none of that did Tyler one blasted bit of good.

The screams seemed endless, but of course, they really weren't. Preacher didn't count them. As they went on, though, he heard other cries. Angry shouts, from the sound of them, and he wondered if some of the crew members were calling on Rowland and Sampson to lay off on the punishment. Tyler had told him that some discontent existed among the crew. Those sounds might be a demonstration of that.

If so, it didn't do any good. Tyler's cries continued, then abruptly fell silent. He might have passed out or the ordeal might have reached its end.

Or Tyler might have died.

Preacher tried not to consider that possibility. Tyler might not be a hardened frontiersman like himself, but he had worked as a member of the crew on the *Calypso* for a while and had to have toughened up some in that time. Before that, he had led a helter-skelter existence as an orphan in New Orleans, so he had to know something about survival.

The boy was going to be all right, Preacher told himself.

It had been late in the afternoon when the storm took place. Preacher figured evening was closing in. Darkness descended suddenly, as it did at sea, closing in around him even though the hatch above his head was still open. He sat there in the gloom, pondering on his next move.

He had only limited options. He had hoped to stir up a mutiny before the ship reached the end of its voyage at San Patricio. That seemed unlikely with him in chains, stuck down in the bilge. At the moment, he saw no way out of that plight. Down there, he had nothing to work with, no way to free himself.

That bleak realization didn't make him give up. That just wasn't in his nature. But for the moment, he couldn't do anything except wait for a better chance— and resolve to seize it as soon as he could.

A while later, flickering light spilled down through the hatch. Preacher heard several sets of footsteps approaching the opening. A man with a lantern held it over the hatch while Tyler was lowered into the bilge. The youngster wasn't chained or tied, but from the way his head lolled loosely on his shoulder, Preacher could tell he was unconscious. He wasn't dead, or they wouldn't have bothered taking him down there. When Tyler's body twisted in the grip of the men dangling him from his arms, Preacher saw the bloody stripes on his back where the cat-o'-nine-tails had shredded the flesh.

They dropped Tyler, and he splashed into the water. Preacher thought the shock would revive him, but it didn't appear to. As Tyler slid down, his face went under. Preacher cursed and stuck his legs out. The fetters around his ankles didn't prevent him from getting his feet under Tyler's shoulders and lifting his head out of the water. Tyler began to sputter and cough.

"Hang on, son," Preacher told him.

The sailors up in the hold laughed and spewed curses down on the two prisoners. They were loyal to Sampson and cut from the same brutal cloth as the captain, no doubt about that. Preacher knew he couldn't hope for any help from the likes of them. They weren't the only ones on board the *Calypso*, though.

After a minute or so, the men tired of the verbal abuse and left, taking the lantern with them. Darkness closed around Preacher and Tyler again.

Preacher held the youngster up so he wouldn't slip under again and drown, until finally Tyler groaned and muttered, "Wh . . . where . . ."

"You're down in the bilge with me," Preacher told him. "Can you sit up on your own?"

"I . . . I don't know . . ." Tyler moved around a little, and his weight lifted from Preacher's legs. "I think I'm . . . all right . . . Ohhhh." Pain filled the long moan.

Preacher said, "No, you ain't all right, but you will be. You're strong enough to make it through this."

"I never . . . I never hurt like that. I don't remember . . . Rowland stopping. He just whipped me . . . and whipped me . . . I must have . . . passed out."

"Probably a good thing that you did."

"My back . . . hurts."

"I saw it when they brought you down here," Preacher said. "I won't lie to you, son, it looked pretty bad. But it's nothin' you won't get over."

Unless the wounds festered from being dunked in

this bilgewater, he thought. He ran the same risk, since his back was far from fully healed. But there was nothing they could do about that except hope they wouldn't come down with a fever. In the tropics, such maladies were usually fatal.

"Sit up and keep your back out of the water as much as you can," Preacher went on.

"I don't know if I can. I'm so tired."

"You got to. If you lay down in this water, you'll drown, and I won't be able to help you."

"I . . . I'll try." A few moments passed in silence, then Tyler said, "I'm sorry, Preacher."

"Sorry? What in the world for? You've tried to help me more 'n once when nobody else on board this ship would."

"But if Cap'n Sampson hadn't threatened me, you wouldn't have had to surrender."

"And likely they would have killed me," Preacher pointed out. "I don't blame you for a thing, son, and you hadn't ought to blame yourself, neither. I'm just grateful to you." He paused. "No matter how this voyage turns out, I made a friend along the way."

Tyler made a little choking sound. Preacher thought the youngster was too moved to speak, but then he got to worrying that Tyler had gone under the water again and that sound had been him dying. He said sharply, "Tyler! You still there?"

To Preacher's great relief, the young man said, "Y-yeah. I'm here, Preacher." He took a deep breath, and what he said next put a grin on Preacher's face in the darkness. "We need to start thinking about how we're going to get out of here."

* * *

In the dark, Preacher and Tyler had no way of telling how much time had passed. No one bothered to bring them any food or water, so eventually hunger and thirst made it obvious that quite a few hours had gone by. Preacher kept them talking so Tyler would stay awake and not slip under the water. Unfortunately, they didn't come up with any workable escape plans.

A few shafts of light began to penetrate the tiny cracks in the deck above them. Preacher didn't know if that meant it was morning and all the hatches had been opened, or if someone had carried a lantern into the hold.

The latter case proved to be true. The hatch lifted and swung back, and a bearded face peered down into the bilge. The owner of the whiskers called, "Tyler? Are you alive down there, boy?"

"I'm here, Chimney," Tyler responded in a weak voice.

"If I drop a bundle to you, can you catch it?"

Tyler squinted up into the light. "I . . . I'll try."

"I got you some bread. Here you go."

A small bundle wrapped in sailcloth dropped through the hatch. Tyler caught it before it hit the water.

"There's a little jug of rum in there, too," the sailor called Chimney went on.

"You're a lifesaver, friend," Preacher told the bearded man.

"The cap'n don't want either of you fellers to starve down here," Chimney explained. "He still figures on gettin' work outta you, Tyler, and as for you, mister, he plans on deliverin' you to the plantation on San Patricio just like Balthazar Crowe told him to."

With shaky hands, Tyler opened the bundle and took out a chunk of bread. He tore a piece off it and leaned over to put it in Preacher's mouth. With his hands chained behind his back, the mountain man couldn't feed himself.

He'd been without food long enough that the bread tasted mighty good just then. He chewed and swallowed while Tyler ate a piece of bread, too. Being careful to keep the bundle above the filthy water sloshing around them, Tyler took out a small jug and pulled the stopper with his teeth. He held the neck of it to Preacher's mouth and tipped it up so Preacher was able to get a drink of the rum inside the jug. He immediately felt its bracing effects.

"Rum ain't normally what I drink for breakfast, but I'm sure obliged to you for it, Chimney."

"Well, the cap'n just tol' me to bring you boys somethin' to eat and didn't say nothin' 'bout no grog, but I figure what he don't know won't hurt me." Chimney laughed about that, then went on, more quietly. "Here's somethin' else for you. I'm gonna drop it in the water, and you can let it lie there until after I'm gone before fishin' it out."

Preacher caught a glimpse of something metallic as it fell through the lanternlight and landed in the bilge with a small splash.

Chimney went on. "Me and some o' the other boys been talkin', and we've had enough of bein' pirates. We're gonna take the boat, jus' like you said we oughter, Tyler boy. So you and that Preacher feller be ready when they come to get you later, and when you take 'em by surprise, so will we."

Preacher's heart pounded faster at those words. That was exactly the sort of trouble he'd been hoping to stir up when he'd planted the seeds of mutiny in Tyler's head. It looked like the effort had been successful—if this wasn't some sort of trick.

"Somebody comin'," Chimney exclaimed. "I got to go." The hatch cover dropped back into place, and darkness once more enveloped the prisoners. Chimney's rapid footsteps pattered away on the deck above them.

Preacher and Tyler sat in tense silence for a moment before Preacher asked, "Do you trust that fella?"

"Chimney Matthews? Yeah. Yeah, I do. He's been a good friend to me."

"Why's he called Chimney?"

Tyler chuckled in the darkness. "Because when he gets that pipe of his going, so much smoke billows out of it that he looks like a chimney." He sounded more like himself than he had ever since the flogging. The bread and rum had given him some strength—and the flicker of hope hadn't done any harm, either.

Preacher heard a faint stirring in the water and knew Tyler was looking for the second item Chimney had dropped. After a minute or so, he said, "I can't find . . . Wait! There it is! It . . . it's a key, Preacher."

Preacher had a pretty good idea that it would unlock the chains on his wrists and ankles. A savage grin pulled his lips back as he thought that when Sampson's men came to drag him out of this filthy bilge, they would have a surprise waiting for them.

CHAPTER 33

Working by feel in the darkness, Tyler unlocked the shackles from Preacher's ankles and removed them. He unlocked the manacle around Preacher's right wrist, too, but at the mountain man's suggestion, he left the one on the left wrist fastened, so that the foot-long length of chain and the other manacle dangled from it.

"That won't make a bad weapon," Preacher commented to explain his request. "When I go to swingin' it, along with those shackles you took off my legs, I should be able to mow down some of those varmints like a scythe goin' through wheat."

"I like the sound of that," Tyler admitted.

"They've got it comin'. Especially Rowland and Sampson."

The thought of settling the score with those two invigorated Preacher, despite everything he'd been through. The chance to do that couldn't come soon enough to suit him.

Unfortunately, the opportunity didn't seem to be in the offing any time soon. Time dragged by. The bilge lightened a trifle, and Preacher knew that meant the sun was up and high overhead. After a while, he said to Tyler, "You said we'd be off Cuba later today, didn't you?"

"That's right. I don't know if the captain plans to put in to port, but we'll be sailing near there, at least. Why do you ask?"

"I was thinkin' that might be a good place to put any survivors ashore, once we've taken over the ship."

"You don't plan to kill all of them?"

"Like I said before, I ain't no murderer. If any of that bunch surrenders, we'll find somethin' to do with 'em, even if it's just puttin' 'em in that little boat hangin' from the back of the ship and givin' 'em some food and water. At least that way, they'd have a chance to survive."

"I wasn't planning on taking any prisoners," Tyler muttered.

"I don't blame you for feelin' that way. And to be honest, it may not come to that. They may put up enough of a fight that we don't have any choice." Preacher chuckled. "For that matter, we don't know how many fellas are willin' to throw in with us. We may be the ones who wind up on the losin' end. But if that happens, we'll go down fightin', and that's always been the way I figured on crossin' the divide."

"Crossing the divide," Tyler repeated. "You mean . . ."

"Yep. Comes to all of us sooner or later. Worst thing about it is when you don't have any say in how it happens. As long as a man can go out on his own terms, I figure it ain't nothin' to fear."

"I'll try to remember that. But I'd just as soon not have to deal with that any time soon."

Preacher laughed. "I understand, boy. I plan on bein' around for a long time myself."

They sat there in the shallow, sloshing water and waited some more. Preacher was about to decide that Jabez Sampson intended to leave them down there until the *Calypso* reached San Patricio, but then heavy footsteps sounded above their heads.

Two men, Preacher judged.

A moment later someone opened the hatch and let it drop to the deck with a loud thud. One of the men lowered a ladder into the bilge.

A harsh order followed it. "Get on up here, Tyler. The cap'n says it's time for you to get back to work."

"I . . . I can't," Tyler responded. The shaky weakness in his voice wasn't completely an act. The youngster wasn't in good shape, but he and Preacher had decided earlier that if anyone came to get them, they would try to lure the men down into the bilge.

"You'd better be able to," the man snapped. "If you can't work, there ain't no reason for the cap'n to keep you alive, after what you done."

"I . . . I'll try," Tyler said, "but maybe . . . maybe one of you could help me up the ladder."

That brought bitter cursing from the men, but after a moment the one who had spoken said, "All right, but once you're up on deck, you're on your own. You either do what the cap'n says, or he'll have you tossed overboard." The man laughed. "I'd be glad to take care of that little chore for him, too." He descended the ladder, his back turned to Preacher and Tyler.

When he reached the bottom, he stepped down into the bilgewater and turned toward them. Preacher vaguely recognized him from seeing him on board the ship, but he didn't know what the man's name was.

Nor did he care. The varmint was an obstacle to be

overcome. To that end, Preacher surged to his feet, swinging the shackles he held in his right hand.

The heavy chain and circular cuff at the end of it crashed across the man's face, pulping and slashing flesh. Blood spurted as he reeled back. Preacher swung again and heard bone crunch in the man's skull. He fell, landing face-first in the shallow water.

By the time the man splashed down, Preacher was swarming up the ladder. The second man didn't appear to be armed, and evidently he didn't want to stay and fight with the mountain man, either. He turned and ran toward the ladder leading from the hold up into the orlop, yelling as he fled.

Preacher couldn't stop the man from giving the alarm, but as deep in the bowels of the ship as they were and as noisy as it could be on deck, maybe the shouts hadn't been heard. As he scrambled into the hold, Preacher flung the shackles after the man. The chain whirled through the air, the cuffs on each end acting as counterweights, and the chain wrapped around the man's legs and dumped him on the planks before he could reach the ladder.

Preacher was on him in an instant, swinging the manacles still attached to his left wrist. The loose cuff slammed into the back of the man's head and left a bloody gash. While the man was stunned, Preacher grabbed the chain, looped it around the man's neck from behind, and heaved upward, twisting as he did so. No longer able to yell because of the chain crushing his throat, all the man could manage was some feeble thrashing before he went limp.

Preacher let go. The way the man fell told the mountain man he was dead.

Hearing movement behind him, Preacher looked

around and saw Tyler emerging from the bilge. The young man was pale and unsteady, but he climbed out fairly agilely.

Not only that, he held a knife in his right hand. "I found this on Clark. Figured we could use it."

"Good thinkin'," Preacher agreed. He listened intently but didn't hear anything except the usual shipboard sounds of splashing and creaking. "This fella hollered a couple of times, but I ain't sure anybody heard him."

"We can hope not. What do we do now?"

"Your friend Chimney said him and some of the other crew members would be waitin' for us to make our move, didn't he?"

"That's right," Tyler said.

"When we do, I reckon they're plannin' to jump the ones who are loyal to Sampson. Will there be enough of them to turn the tide in our favor?"

Tyler shook his head. "I really don't know. There are about a dozen of us who hate what Sampson has made us become, and I'm pretty sure they'll all fight. Likewise, there are a dozen men, maybe a few more, who are completely loyal to him. All the others . . . it's a good question which way they'll jump. Probably to the side that looks like it's going to win."

That made sense, Preacher thought. Unfortunately, they wouldn't really know the answer until they tried to seize control of the ship. By then it would be too late to do anything except play out the hand and see what happened.

Quickly, Preacher checked for weapons on the body of the man he had just killed but didn't find any. Tyler offered him the knife, but he told the young man to keep it.

"I got these chains," he said. "I reckon I can do a goodly amount of damage with them."

They turned toward the ladder.

Tyler suggested, "Let me go up first and take a look around. Those men were supposed to fetch me, so maybe if anybody sees me, they won't realize right away that something's wrong. But everybody on board knows that *you're* not supposed to be free."

"That's smart thinkin', but are you sure you're all right, son? You look pretty peaked."

Tyler swallowed and nodded. "I think I'm running a fever, and I feel about as weak as a little kitten, but I'll be fine, as long as we can put an end to Sampson's tyranny on board this ship. He's run wild in the Gulf and the Caribbean for long enough."

"All right," Preacher said. "I'll be close behind you."

Tyler tucked the knife into the waistband of his canvas trousers and started up the ladder. Preacher got a good look at the young man's back and frowned at the damage Abner Rowland had done with that cat-o'-nine-tails. Blood had crusted thickly over the slashes, but red, puffy flesh surrounded them. Tyler's injuries needed actual medical attention, but they wouldn't get any as long as Jabez Sampson was captain of this vessel. Preacher knew that Sampson would let the youngster sicken and die and not give it a second thought.

Preacher kept a close eye on Tyler as he climbed the ladder into the orlop. No one shouted a warning that something was wrong. Tyler stepped off the ladder, looked around, and then motioned for Preacher to follow him. The mountain man supposed that everybody was up on deck.

Preacher went up the ladder quickly. The chains

clattered against it as he climbed. Even though his back was still sore and twinged whenever he moved the wrong way, he had recovered quite a bit from the lashing and was confident that he could handle himself all right in whatever battle broke out.

He stepped onto the orlop deck and looked around its gloomy confines. A few yards away, the hatch to the main deck stood open at the top of a flight of stairs. Bright light poured down through it.

A pair of bare feet appeared suddenly on the steps and started down them. Preacher looked around for a place to conceal himself and saw a stack of crates. He dropped behind it while Tyler stood in the open, waiting to see who was coming down from above.

A couple of seconds later, the young man exclaimed softly, "Chimney!" He looked over at Preacher and beckoned.

Preacher straightened from his crouch and came out from behind the crates. The bushy-bearded, mostly bald seaman known as Chimney stared at him.

"I knew the cap'n sent a couple o' bruisers down to fetch you, Tyler," Chimney said, "and I got curious what'd happened. I reckon those boys ain't comin' back?"

"They're not," Tyler confirmed grimly. "The men who are willing to mutiny . . . they're ready?"

"Aye. I passed the word that somethin' might happen today. The fellers are scared, I ain't gonna lie about that, but they've had enough o' Sampson. And it's been even worse since that varmint Rowland signed on. Him and Sampson is two peas in a pod when it comes to bein' mean and no-account, lemme tell you."

Chimney was babbling a little. Preacher held up a hand to halt the stream of words and said quietly, "Go back up on deck and let the fellas on our side know what's about to happen. Where are Sampson and Rowland?"

"Sampson's back at the helm, as usual. Last time I seen him, Rowland was wanderin' around up at the bow."

Preacher frowned. He would have preferred that his two main enemies were together. But as usual, he would have to deal with the situation the way it actually was, not the way he wished it could be.

Chimney looked at Tyler and asked anxiously, "Are you all right, boy? You look like you're just about ready to fall over."

"I'll be fine," Tyler said, "just as soon as Jabez Sampson isn't in command on this ship anymore."

Preacher said to Chimney, "Go back up and let the fellas on our side know it won't be much longer. When I come up out of here, I'm headin' for Rowland first. He's got to be put down. Somebody else will need to take care of Sampson."

"Aye, I'll see to it meself," Chimney said, nodding.

"Are you sure that's a good idea?" Tyler asked.

"Ol' Chimney can get close to him without him ever suspectin' a thing." Chimney pulled up his loose, billowy shirt to reveal the butt of a small flintlock pistol stuck in the waistband of his trousers. "And once I am, he'll do what I tell him or get his head blowed off."

Preacher hoped the old-timer was as sure of that as he sounded and that things worked out that way. But no matter what happened, nothing would be served by delaying the showdown any longer.

"I'm going on deck, too," Tyler declared. "Seeing me will distract Sampson, but he shouldn't be alarmed. He sent those men to get me out of the bilge, after all."

Preacher nodded. "Good luck to both of you. I'll give you a couple of minutes, and then we'll make our move."

CHAPTER 34

As Preacher counted down the seconds in his head, he listened to see if Tyler's appearance on deck caused any commotion. As far as he could tell, it didn't. As the young man had said, Sampson would be expecting to see him. When Preacher judged that enough time had passed, he started stealthily up the steps, pausing in a crouch near the top for a moment to listen intently again.

He heard Jabez Sampson's gravelly, rumbling tones and after a moment began to be able to make out some of the words. ". . . no mercy," the captain was saying, ". . . over the side."

Sampson was talking to Tyler, Preacher realized, laying down the law to the young sailor and telling him what he could expect if he crossed Sampson again.

That was about to happen a lot sooner than the captain figured it would.

Realizing the plan had just changed, Preacher drew in a deep breath and then charged the rest of the way up the steps and onto the deck. Sampson had just become his responsibility.

Someone yelled behind him. A quick glance showed

Chimney a short distance away. He realized Preacher was headed to the poop deck to take on Sampson and pointed to himself then to the bow indicating he would fight there.

Preacher understood. A couple of quick leaps took him to the narrow steps leading up to the raised deck where Sampson stood with Tyler and the steersman. The captain's eyes widened in shock, and he clawed at the butt of a pistol stuck behind his belt.

Tyler struck first, yanking the knife out of his pocket and slashing at Sampson's hand with it. Bright red blood flew. Sampson yelled in pain and batted Tyler away from him with his other hand. He got the gun out.

By that time, Preacher was there, swinging the shackles. The chain smashed against Sampson's arm, and the pistol dropped to the deck as his fingers opened involuntarily. Preacher struck with the manacles attached to his left wrist, but Sampson reacted with surprising speed for one of his bulk. He ducked under the swinging chain and launched himself forward in a bull rush that slammed into Preacher and drove the mountain man backward. Both men flew off the raised deck and landed near the steps leading down to the cabin.

At least they hadn't landed *on* those steps. Such a turn of events might have resulted in him breaking his back, Preacher knew. As it was, he felt blood running from the wounds left behind by the flogging. The fall had broken them open.

Losing a little blood was the least of Preacher's worries. He had his hands full battling Sampson as the two of them rolled across the deck. At close quarters, with no room to swing them, the chains weren't very good weapons. Preacher dropped the shackles and tried to get his hand on Sampson's thick throat.

Sampson ducked his head, hammered a short punch into Preacher's ribs, and tried to ram his knee into the mountain man's groin. Preacher twisted aside and jabbed a fist into Sampson's face.

Vaguely aware of the sounds of battle elsewhere on the ship, he heard yells, thudding, and the occasional gunshot, but he couldn't risk taking his attention off Sampson. It was a fight to the death, at least as far as the captain was concerned. Preacher was willing to spare Sampson's life, but only if the man was no longer a threat.

Sampson writhed away from Preacher and kicked out, landing the heel of his boot against the mountain man's shoulder. The impact drove Preacher to the edge of the steps. Sampson leaped at him and landed on top of him. That bent Preacher's head and shoulders down over the first step. The edge cut painfully into his flesh and made the wounds on the upper part of his back bleed even more. Sampson got his hands on Preacher's throat and clamped down. His thumbs dug brutally for Preacher's windpipe.

Preacher slung the manacle chain across the back of Sampson's neck, caught hold of the loose manacle, and wrapped the chain around Sampson's throat. Preacher tightened his grip and squeezed the chain around Sampson's neck, hanging on grimly as he kept increasing the pressure.

It was just a question of which man would pass out—or die—from being choked first.

Sampson's face quickly turned red, then began to take on a purple hue. His eyes opened wider and wider. Preacher was suffering, too, though. A reddish tinge spread over the whole world as if it had been dipped in blood . . .

The strength suddenly deserted Sampson's grip, and his hands fell away from Preacher's aching throat. He slumped forward, his dead weight pinning Preacher to the deck.

Preacher let go of the manacle, put his right hand against Sampson's left shoulder, and rolled the captain off of him. As Sampson flopped onto his back, Preacher saw his chest rising and falling. Sampson wasn't dead, just out cold. He had a raw, angry red mark around his throat where the chain had dug in.

Preacher pushed himself up and dragged in several deep breaths. The sea air felt wonderful flooding into his desperate lungs.

The blast of a shot made him look along the deck toward the bow.

Knots of fighting men were scattered the length of the *Calypso*. The sides appeared to be about even. Preacher looked for Abner Rowland but didn't see him. He thought he spotted the old sailor called Chimney lying on the deck near the bow, however. Chimney wasn't moving, which caused alarm to leap up inside Preacher. Clearly, his part in the bow fight hadn't turned out well.

That made Preacher think of Tyler. He swung around to look for the redhead, who he had last seen being knocked aside by Sampson.

Tyler was sprawled on the upper deck, as motionless as Chimney at the other end of the sloop. Preacher went up the steps in a couple of bounds and dropped to a knee beside his young friend, who was lying on his side. When Preacher rolled him onto his back, Tyler began turning his head from side to side, moaning and muttering incoherently. Preacher rested the back of his hand on Tyler's forehead. The boy was burning up with fever, all right, probably from those wounds on his back. Carefully, Preacher turned him over so he was lying on his belly.

That was all he had time for. The mutiny he had orchestrated was still going on.

He got to his feet and picked up the pistol Sampson had dropped. Hurrying down the stairs and then toward the battles, Preacher checked the weapon and saw that it was ready to fire. Again he searched for Abner Rowland, thinking that the tattooed man would make a good target, but Preacher didn't see Rowland anywhere, which was puzzling.

Preacher didn't have much time to ponder on that mystery, though. A moment later several men charged up through the hatch from the orlop, yelling and swinging cutlasses. Rowland was in the forefront of the attack. Preacher figured out instantly that after dealing with Chimney, Rowland had led some of his allies down below to retrieve the cutlasses that were stored there between attacks on other ships. The *Calypso*'s quartermaster only broke out the weapons when a fight was imminent.

Preacher would have preferred blowing a hole through Rowland, but when one of the men lunged at him, swinging a cutlass high so he could bring it swooping down and cleave Preacher's skull, the mountain man did the only thing he could do. He brought up the pistol and pulled the trigger. The lock snapped and the pistol boomed, and a good-sized chunk of the cutlass-wielder's skull flew into the air as the lead ball smashed into his brain.

Preacher darted out of the way as the dead man's

momentum carried him on a couple of steps farther, then he caught the cutlass out of the air as the man's suddenly nerveless fingers dropped it. Somewhere during the battle with Sampson, Preacher had lost the shackles, but now he had an even better weapon.

During the sword fight a few years earlier, Preacher had acquitted himself fairly well. He had survived, after all. But the heavy cutlass was more to his liking, more like fighting with a big hunting knife. He waded in, hacking and slashing with the blade while at the same time swinging the manacles attached to his left wrist and cutting down some of his enemies with that. Blood soon spattered the right sleeve of the linsey-woolsey shirt up to the elbow as he chopped down the men who'd been loyal to Sampson and Rowland. Bodies littered the deck, and it was slick with gore.

Preacher jumped between one of the pirates and a mutineer who was about to be cut down. He rammed cold steel into the man's belly, ripped it free, and shoved the collapsing corpse away.

The man whose life he had just saved shouted, "Look out!"

Preacher twisted around and saw a cutlass coming toward his head with blinding speed.

The mountain man's lightning reflexes were all that saved him as he darted aside. The blade caught his left sleeve and ripped it away instead of splitting his skull. A bitter curse followed the missed stroke. Preacher twisted his wrist, batted the other man's cutlass to the side, and stepped back quickly to give himself some room.

Then a grin split his rugged face as he said to the man he was facing, "I thought that was you."

"I'm gonna spill your guts all over this deck," Abner Rowland growled.

"Come on, then," Preacher said, and sparks flashed as the two men's cutlasses came together with a mighty clash of steel.

CHAPTER 35

Rowland was strong, but Preacher already knew that. The tattooed man's cutlass hammered against Preacher's blade with enough force and ferocity to make the mountain man give ground for a moment.

Then Preacher planted his feet and braced himself as he began a fierce counterattack. Rowland had more experience using a cutlass, but Preacher matched him force for force and was slightly quicker. The advantage swung to him as Rowland backed up a couple of steps.

That retreat was short-lived, just as Preacher's had been. Rowland parried one of Preacher's strokes and suddenly slashed at the mountain man's legs. Preacher started to drop his cutlass to block that attack but realized at the last second that it was a feint. The tip of the cutlass in Rowland's hand darted upward at an angle that would bury the blade in Preacher's throat.

Preacher jerked his head back and got his own cutlass in the way just enough to make Rowland's blade slide a little to one side as more sparks flew. Preacher felt the keen edge nick his chin, as if he had cut himself shaving.

Rowland had drawn first blood.

Since Rowland's cutlass was high, Preacher tried to go low. He slashed at the man's belly, but Rowland jumped back in time to avoid the blade, which left a long rip in his shirt. Preacher saw a few drops of crimson appear on the shirt, and knew he had sliced into skin a little.

Rowland growled a curse and bored in again, hewing so swiftly with his cutlass that Preacher had to jerk his own blade back and forth as fast as he could to parry the attacks.

While he was concentrating on that, Rowland tried another trick, hooking a foot between Preacher's ankles and jerking his right leg out from under him. Preacher went over backward, and Rowland pounced, springing forward and chopping downward with the cutlass in his hand.

Preacher rolled out of the way, but the blade came so close he felt as much as heard it whisper past his ear before it struck the deck with a *thunk!*

Rowland's strength backfired on him then. The cutlass's edge penetrated far enough into the wood to get stuck. As he tried to wrench it free, Preacher kicked him in the belly.

Rowland grunted and doubled over, bringing his chin in range of Preacher's other foot, which he used to land a kick on Rowland's jaw that sent the tattooed man flying backward. Rowland hung on to the cutlass, though, and the added impetus of the kick was enough to pull the blade free from where it had lodged in the deck.

Rowland landed hard on the planks and slid several feet. Preacher scrambled up and went after him. He had time for a split-second glance around the ship and saw that the fighting seemed to have ended except for the battle between him and Rowland. He wasn't sure which side had emerged victorious, and before he could figure it out, Rowland, still lying on the deck, pushed up on an elbow, lunged at him, and tried to cut his legs out from under him.

Preacher leaped in the air and let the cutlass pass underneath his feet. As he came down, he swung his own cutlass. He wasn't trying to spare Rowland's life, but it happened to be the flat of the blade that smacked against the side of the tattooed man's head. The blow seemed to stun him. The hand holding the cutlass sagged.

Preacher kicked him in the jaw again. That stretched Rowland out on the deck. When he tried to lift the cutlass, Preacher's foot came down hard on the wrist of that hand. Rowland yelled in pain and rage as Preacher pinned the hand to the deck. The cry was cut short as Preacher rested the tip of his cutlass against Rowland's Adam's apple.

"I'm mighty tempted to give this pigsticker a push," Preacher told him.

"Go ahead," Rowland grated, then added a couple of colorful curses.

"But I've said it before, and I'll say it again—I ain't a murderer." Preacher bent over and took the cutlass out of Rowland's grip. He tossed it away, saw it slide across the deck and come to a stop at the feet of another man. Preacher was a little surprised to realize that man was Chimney Matthews.

The old-timer picked up Rowland's cutlass. "You sure you don't want to go ahead and kill the varmint?" Chimney asked. He had a swollen welt on his forehead where someone, probably Rowland, had walloped him. "I don't reckon there's a soul in the world that'd miss him."

Preacher ignored that and looked around. He didn't know the members of the *Calypso*'s crew well enough to be sure who was on his side and who wasn't, but the fact that Chimney seemed to be satisfied with the way things had turned out indicated that the mutineers had won.

Numerous bodies sprawled on the deck. A group of men huddled together near the bow while others surrounded them, holding pistols and cutlasses. The handful of prisoners backed against the railing must have been the only ones remaining who had been loyal to Captain Sampson.

The captain himself sat on the steps leading down to his cabin while a man stood near him holding a cutlass. Sampson had his head in his hands and seemed utterly defeated. Preacher wasn't completely convinced of that. He told the man guarding Sampson, "Keep a close eye on him."

"I plan to," the sailor replied grimly.

Chimney came up to Preacher and tugged on his sleeve. "Where's the boy?" the old-timer asked.

"You mean Tyler?" Preacher nodded toward the raised deck. "Up there, the last time I saw him."

Both of them hurried up to check on the young man. Tyler still lay where Preacher had left him, only half conscious. He muttered and raved, causing Chimney to peer down anxiously at him and say, "He's in pretty bad shape, ain't he?"

"Those wounds on his back have festered," Preacher said. "They're causin' him to run a fever. They need to be cleaned out and doctored. Do you have a ship's surgeon on board?"

"We did have, but he got drunk, fell overboard on our last voyage, and drowned. The cap'n ain't got around to replacin' him yet."

"Tyler needs a real doctor." Preacher rubbed his chin and frowned in thought. "Closest one is probably in Cuba. We ain't far from there, are we?"

"We could get there in a few hours, I reckon," Chimney said.

"Do you or one of these other fellas know how to navigate?"

Chimney snorted disgustedly. "Shoot, I was *born* knowin' how to navigate. I can get us there, don't you worry 'bout that. The question is"—he looked at Sampson and then at the other prisoners—"what do we do about these fellers? Every blamed one of 'em oughter walk the plank!"

Preacher looked at the small boat hanging from ropes and poles at the stern. "They'll be pretty crowded in that, but I reckon that's better than . . . What do you seagoin' fellas call it? Windin' up in Davy Jones's Locker?"

Chimney laughed, then grew serious as he asked, "You really mean to let 'em go?"

"That's right. We'll give 'em a little food and water, enough for 'em to get by for a while."

"They'll head for Cuba, too, you know. Havana's the closest port."

Preacher thought about that for a moment. Then he went over to Sampson and said, "Get up."

Without raising his head, Sampson replied obscenely what Preacher could do.

Preacher put the tip of the cutlass under Sampson's chin and used it to tip his head back. "I ain't gonna kill you in cold blood right now, but I'll give you this warnin'. If I ever see you again, as soon as I lay eyes on you, I *will* kill you. I don't intend to say a blasted thing or ask you what you're doin'. I'm just gonna kill you. Same goes for Rowland, so you tell him that once he comes to."

"Ye best go ahead an' take that cutlass and lop my head off right now, mister," Sampson said. "Because I *will* see you again, and when I do, I'll be the one doin' the killin'."

"I've been threatened by a lot of folks, and I'm still here," Preacher pointed out. He turned to Chimney. "You and your friends see to gettin' the prisoners in that boat." He thought for a moment. "Don't give 'em any oars. The current'll take 'em ashore sooner or later, but it'll be a while."

"Aye, that's a good idea," Chimney agreed, bobbing his head. "I'll see to it, Cap'n."

"Hold on there!" Preacher said as he stared at the old-timer. "What'd you just call me?"

"Cap'n," Chimney repeated. "You're the one who defeated Sampson and Rowland both. None o' this would've happened without you and Tyler helpin' me and these other fellers find enough courage to fight back. If anybody's got a right to call hisself the cap'n of the *Calypso*, it's you, Preacher."

That idea struck Preacher as ridiculous. He didn't know a thing in the world about how to be the captain of a sailing ship. But a lot of being in command of anything was just common sense, he supposed, and as long as he had fellas who *did* know what they were doing to help him out, there was a good chance they could get where they wanted to go.

"All right," he said, "but you're first mate. I want

Sampson, Rowland, and the rest of the varmints who sided with them off this ship as quick as possible."

Chimney gave him a whiskery grin and a rough salute. "Aye, aye, sir!"

The steersman must have deserted his post to join in the battle, because the tiller was unattended and the sloop was going wherever the wind and waves took it. With the cutlass in one hand, Preacher strode over to the tiller to loop his other arm over it and steady it.

As he felt the *Calypso* respond to his touch, he sleeved some blood away from the cut on his chin, shook his head in amazement, and said, "Cap'n Preacher. If that don't beat all."

CHAPTER 36

It didn't take long to drop the small boat into the sea and then prod the prisoners to jump into the water after it. Abner Rowland was still unconscious when a couple of men dragged him to the rail and pushed him over, but he came to when he hit the water, flailing and thrashing and gulping until he got control of himself and realized what was going on. Sampson, who had already dragged himself into the small boat, called to him and got his attention. Rowland swam over to the craft, where Sampson and the others pulled him in.

As Chimney leaned on the railing and watched what was going on below, he said to Preacher, "You know, there are sharks in these waters. That's why those fellers scrambled into the boat as fast as they did."

"You didn't tell me about the sharks before those men went overboard," Preacher said.

"Who am I to deny a poor shark the chance for a good meal?" Chimney asked with a grin. "Anyway, they're all in the boat now, and none of 'em got et."

One of the men left on the sloop rounded up a bundle of supplies that included some bread and salt pork and several earthenware jugs of fresh water. He tied it to a rope and lowered it to the men in the small boat.

Once that was done, Preacher told Chimney to get the *Calypso* started toward Cuba. He wanted to reach the island nation as quickly as possible so Tyler could receive some actual medical attention. He had several men carry Tyler into the cabin and place him on the bunk as gently as possible. Preacher used a rag soaked with rum to clean the young man's wounds, but the job needed a more expert hand to do it properly.

He needed to start thinking about his own plans, too, he reminded himself. He hadn't forgotten about Edmund Cornelius and Lucy Tarleton. And he had a score to settle with Simone LeCarde, too. Beautiful she might be, but she had condemned Preacher to either an early death on the ship or a short, miserable life as a slave on the sugar plantation, and he wasn't going to forget that.

Chimney issued orders for how the sails were to be set and chose one of the men to take over handling the tiller. Then he and Preacher conferred on their destination.

"Havana's the biggest port, but there's another town up the coast called Verdugo where we've put in sometimes in the past," Chimney explained. "We've got friends there, and there's a sawbones, too. An English feller who came to the islands for his health."

"From what I hear, it ain't all that healthy in this part of the world. Lots of fever in the tropics."

Chimney scratched at his beard. "Yeah, but this feller had neck problems. As in, the law was gonna stretch it for him if they caught him. Since Cuba's under Spanish rule, he finds it a mite more hospitable."

"I don't care about any of that," Preacher said, "as long as he can take care of Tyler."

"I reckon he can do that. You want me to set course for Verdugo?"

Preacher nodded. "Yep. Just get us there as soon as you can."

With the wind filling its sails, the *Calypso* seemed to skim over the water. By midafternoon, a low dark line appeared on the southern horizon. As the ship drew closer, the line grew larger and took on a green hue from vegetation. They were approaching land at last.

Chimney stood on the raised deck with Preacher. Using the spyglass he had taken away from Jabez Sampson, Chimney studied the distant island. After a few minutes, he handed the telescope to Preacher and said, "Aye, that's Verdugo, all right. You can see it there at the base of a ridge that looks like a hog's back."

Preacher peered through the glass, moving it slightly until he spotted the cluster of buildings next to a small cove with a sandy beach. Topped with trees waving gently in the breeze off the water, the ridge Chimney had mentioned rose behind the settlement. Verdugo was far from being a city, but it appeared to be a good-sized town.

Preacher saw the bell tower of the local mission, as well as two tall, stone towers, one at the end of each spit of land enclosing the cove. "What are those towers?" he asked Chimney. "Anything we have to worry about?"

"Naw. The Spaniards built them fortifications back in the days when they was fightin' with the English all the time, not to mention pirates like Blackbeard and Flint and privateers like Cap'n Shark who roamed the Caribbean. 'Tis more peaceful in these waters now, so there ain't no Spanish garrison in Verdugo, and we didn't ever raid the town, so folks there are friendly toward us. When we show up, we spend money, instead of stealin' it, so they're always glad to see us."

The *Calypso* sped on toward its destination. The sloop sailed between the two towers. Chimney had assured Preacher there was nothing to worry about, but he eyed the fortifications warily anyway. He could see cannon poking their snouts over the walls at the top of the towers, but no one seemed to be moving around. As Chimney had said, the forts weren't manned anymore. They were impressive sights to behold, anyway, even if they had fallen into disuse.

People ashore spotted the ship approaching and went down to the docks to welcome it. A crowd of a couple of dozen figures waited there. Even though the *Calypso* had a much smaller crew than usual, the sailors did a good job of bringing the sloop alongside one of the piers, using the vessel's momentum after the sails were struck to guide it into place. Several men jumped to the dock with ropes and made the sloop fast.

Preacher had found his buckskin shirt and trousers and high-topped moccasins in Sampson's cabin and donned them. He felt more like himself as he waited to go ashore. Tyler had continued drifting in and out of consciousness without ever really becoming coherent. Preacher wanted to get him some actual medical attention as soon as possible.

Beckoning for Chimney to follow him, Preacher jumped easily from the sloop to the dock. He had a couple of pistols tucked behind his belt, but he'd left the cutlass aboard and he had long since unlocked the manacle from his left wrist. He said to the old-timer,

"You probably speak these folks' lingo a lot better than I do, so make sure they know we don't mean anybody any harm."

"They know that. Here comes the *jefe* now. He's the boss around here."

A rotund, well-dressed figure with an impressive, sweeping mustache strode along the dock toward them. As he came to a stop, he asked mostly in English, "Where is *Capitan* Sampson?"

"Not cap'n anymore," Chimney replied. "This here is Cap'n Preacher. He's in command of the *Calypso* now. Cap'n, meet Señor Alphonso."

The man bowed slightly and said, "Alphonso Gonzalez y Bustamente Rodriguez, *alcalde de* Verdugo." He chattered some more in Spanish. Preacher knew a lot of the words but the speech was too rapid for him to comprehend the order in which they were arranged.

"He says it's an honor to meet you, Cap'n," Chimney translated, "and says that however the good people of Verdugo can serve their *norteamericano* visitors, they'll be plumb happy to do so."

"Tell him what we really need right now is a doctor for Tyler," Preacher said.

Chimney conveyed the request and got another spate of Spanish in return. Then Gonzalez motioned several men forward and they went aboard the *Calypso* by using the gangplank that had been put in place while the conversation was going on. Another man ran off into the town and came back a few minutes later with a wide board that he took onto the ship. He and the others used it as a stretcher to carry Tyler onto the dock. They started off with him, trailed by Preacher, Chimney, and Gonzalez.

"They're taking him to Dr. Flynn's house," Chimney explained. "He's the feller I told you about."

"The one who was gonna wind up on the gallows if he stayed in England."

"Yeah, but a lot of fellers have been hanged who weren't such bad sorts if you just got to know 'em."

The doctor turned out to be a wiry, middle-aged man who had graying hair and a narrow mustache. He came out of an adobe house with a wildly profuse flower garden in front of it. After speaking with Gonzalez and Chimney, he motioned for the men carrying Tyler to take him on inside.

While they were doing that, he extended his hand to Preacher and said, "I'm Roger Flynn." He still had a bit of an English accent, but life in the tropics had softened it. "What happened to the young gentleman?"

"He was flogged," Preacher replied bluntly. "And now he's runnin' a fever, seems out of his head most of the time."

Flynn nodded. "The wounds are probably infected. I'll clean them out and give him something that should help him."

Chimney gestured toward Preacher and said, "The cap'n got a whippin', too, before he was the cap'n."

"Really? Would you allow me to take a look?"

"I'm fine—"

"It won't take but a minute."

"Well, all right, but it's Tyler you really need to be tendin' to."

"My nurse will begin preparing him for my examination. Now, if you'd just raise your shirt . . ."

Preacher lifted the buckskin shirt without pulling it all the way off. That was enough for Flynn to get a look at the wounds the cat-o'-nine-tails had left on his back.

The doctor murmured an oath and said, "Some of these wounds have been bleeding recently."

"Yeah, earlier today," Preacher admitted. "I tussled with a couple of varmints."

"Whoever did this is an absolute brute!"

"Yeah, I can't argue with that. He was one of the fellas I was tusslin' with. And he beat that boy inside."

"These injuries seem to be healing well. You must have the constitution of an ox, sir. But it would be better if they were cleaned, as well. My nurse can do that and then spread some salve on them that will help them even more. You'll have numerous scars, however."

"They won't be the first ones," Preacher said.

CHAPTER 37

Preacher told Chimney to go back to the docks and see that everything was squared away on the *Calypso*. Then he followed the doctor into the house, which, with its thick adobe walls, was shady and cool inside.

Flynn told him, "Take off your shirt."

Preacher shook his head. "See to Tyler first. I can wait."

Flynn shrugged. He had none of the typical briskness about him that Preacher associated with Englishmen. Life in the tropics had worked its magic—or its curse, depending on how you looked at it—on Roger Flynn, leaving him with a languid, unhurried attitude.

Preacher followed the doctor into another room where Tyler had been placed facedown on a narrow bed with a corn-husk mattress. Preacher heard the husks crackling and rustling as the young woman who perched on the edge of the bed shifted a little while she cleaned dried blood away from the wounds on Tyler's back.

She glanced around as Preacher and Flynn came into the room. The mountain man saw a pretty, heart-shaped face with skin just a shade darker than honey, surrounded by thick hair blacker than midnight. Dark eyes flashed as she frowned at Preacher for a second, then she went back to work. He could tell how gently her fingers moved as she stroked the wet cloth over the young man's skin.

"*Muchas gracias*, Estellita," Flynn said. "Let me see how this looks."

The girl stood up and moved aside so he could study the wounds. He bent over Tyler for a few moments, then turned to a small table beside the bed and picked up a sharp-bladed instrument he used to probe at the deep gashes. A stink came into the air in the room as the blade uncovered the putrefaction beneath the injuries.

"A clean cloth," he told Estellita. "And a basin of hot water, *por favor*."

She hurried past Preacher, who stepped aside to give her room to get through the doorway. As she did, she cast another glance at him and shied away as if he were some sort of wild animal she didn't want to approach too closely.

Flynn must have caught that reaction on the girl's part. He chuckled and said quietly, "You frighten her, Captain."

"She's got no reason to be scared of me," the mountain man said. "And you don't have to call me Cap'n, neither. Preacher will do just fine."

"But you have a great deal of blood on your hands, isn't that true?"

Preacher shrugged. "I've run into more than my share of trouble over the years, I reckon."

"Estellita is a very sensitive girl. She can tell that about you, just by being in the same room with you.

I've seen the reaction before. Jabez Sampson came here from time to time. She always hid from him."

"Smart girl."

"What happened to Sampson? Is he dead?"

"Not as far as I know."

"But he's no longer the master of the *Calypso*. He wouldn't give that up willingly."

"He didn't have any choice in the matter," Preacher admitted. "We put him and the other men who stayed loyal to him in a boat and set them adrift."

"Isn't that the same as condemning them to death?"

"We gave 'em food and water. They'll have to take their chances from there. The *Calypso*'s done with bein' a pirate ship, though."

"Well, I wish you luck, whatever your plans are," Flynn said as he turned back to Tyler. Without looking around, he added, "You probably should have killed Sampson when you had the chance, though."

"That's what folks keep tellin' me," Preacher said.

Flynn and Estellita worked together over Tyler for quite a while, draining the infected wounds and washing them with hot water. Without ever fully regaining consciousness, Tyler shifted around and made pained noises while Flynn and Estellita were tending to him, but by the time they'd finished, the young man appeared to have fallen into a deep sleep.

Flynn covered the wounds with clean cloths and straightened from the task. The doctor stepped back from the bed and wiped his hands with a clean cloth.

"When I was back in England," Flynn said, "I read papers by all sorts of learned men speculating on what causes wounded flesh to decay the way it does, and most of them never even mentioned the fact that if kept clean, such wounds stand a much greater chance of healing properly. They blame an imbalance in the bodily fluids for disease and putrefaction, or in some cases, nebulous humors in the very air! What never seems to occur to any of them is that the typical hospital or surgery is a veritable pesthole, an ugly death just waiting to happen. There is a great deal of truth to the old saying about how cleanliness is next to godliness, my friend. But it took me coming here and experimenting on my own to confirm that truth."

"Is that why you came to the islands, Doctor?" Preacher asked dryly, knowing the search for knowledge hadn't been Flynn's only reason for leaving England—if, in fact, it had entered into the decision at all.

"Well . . . no," Flynn admitted. "Through no fault of my own . . . well, perhaps a *bit* of fault . . . I made some powerful enemies who arranged for me to appear to be a criminal. Unable to convince the authorities otherwise, I was forced to flee. At least for the present, this island is out of reach of English law, and Verdugo is isolated enough that it's unlikely I'll ever be found."

Preacher didn't know if there was any truth to Flynn's story or if the doctor actually was a criminal, and as far as he could see, it didn't matter one blasted bit to him, one way or the other. The important thing was that Flynn was tending to Tyler's injuries and seemed to be doing a good job of it.

"We'll let him rest for the time being," Flynn went on. "Now if you'll take your shirt off and go into the other room, you can sit at the table while Estellita sees to your injuries."

The girl didn't look too happy about that, but she didn't argue. Preacher did as Flynn said and sat there while Estellita used clean cloths and hot water to wipe away the blood.

Flynn studied the wounds and frowned. "How long ago did this flogging take place?"

"A couple of days," Preacher replied.

"And you've exhibited this much healing already? My word, man, you must be some sort of freak of nature. You should have been laid up for a week or more!"

"Fresh air and clean livin'," Preacher said with a grin. "Besides, I had things to do, like gettin' even with the fellas responsible for this."

"I don't believe I'd want to have you bearing a grudge against me," Flynn murmured. "Estellita will apply some salve to these wounds, but other than that, I don't think any treatment will be necessary as long as you keep them clean and don't abuse them. And I don't believe it would hurt for you to take it easy for a few days, if you can manage that."

"I'll see what I can do," Preacher said.

Flynn nodded and went back into the room where Tyler was resting. Estellita took a jar from a shelf and approached Preacher. When he looked over his shoulder at her, he saw the wary expression on her face, as if she might bolt at any moment.

"Don't worry," he told her, not knowing if she understood English. "I don't bite."

"I am not worried, señor," she said. She fingered the little gold cross that hung at her throat. "*El Señor Dios* protects me from *demonios*."

Preacher laughed. "I'm no devil, girl, just a man."

"Yes," she said softly as she began spreading the salve from the jar on his wounds with a gentle touch. "I can tell that you are very much a man."

He heard something in her voice warring with the apprehension she felt in his presence. He was considerably older than her and much too rugged-looking to be considered handsome, but most women responded to him and found him attractive. That seemed to be true of Estellita as well, even though he frightened her at the same time. There was a good chance the air of danger about him drew her to him that much more.

He hadn't come to Verdugo looking for romance, just medical attention for Tyler and maybe a place to pick up some supplies before sailing back to New Orleans. He had already decided that was what he was going to do, and he thought Chimney and the other remaining members of the *Calypso's* crew would be willing to go along with that course of action.

He had no desire to remain in Cuba or to become a pirate. The mountains were still waiting for him; once he had settled up with his enemies, recovered as much of Charlie's money as he could, and gone back to St. Louis to check on his young friend and deliver that money.

Still, he didn't want to leave until he knew that Tyler was going to be all right, and since he was going to be there for at least a few days, he supposed there was nothing wrong with finding a pleasant way to pass the time.

"Muchas gracias, señorita," he said when Estellita had finished putting salve on his wounds. He was able to manage that much Spanish.

"Is there anything else I can do for you?" she asked. Her tone was carefully neutral, but again he thought he heard a slight catch in her voice.

"Well, I could do with somethin' to eat, and maybe if you've got somethin' to drink handy—"

She shook her head, peered into his eyes, and said, "Not here. But if you would like to come with me to *mi casa*, I will prepare supper for you."

She left unspoken what else she might do for him, but there was enough promise in her gaze for Preacher to smile, nod, and tell her, "I reckon I'd like that."

CHAPTER 38

A fella could get used to living like this, Preacher thought as the hammock in which he was stretched out swayed slightly in the breeze. The trees to which the hammock was tied cast cooling shade over him, and that soothing breeze made him even more comfortable.

His eyes were closed and he was only about half awake as he listened to the sound of waves washing up gently on the sand about fifty yards away on the other side of the beach. But when he heard footsteps approaching him, he instantly became alert, and his hand drifted closer to the butt of the pistol tucked behind his belt.

"I have brought rum," Estellita said, and Preacher relaxed. He opened his eyes, sat up, and swung his legs out of the hammock, but he didn't get to his feet yet. He paused to look at Estellita.

She wore a low-cut white blouse that left her honey-brown shoulders and the upper slopes of her breasts bare, as well as a colorfully embroidered skirt that revealed her calves and sandal-shod feet. She wasn't a classic beauty like Simone LeCarde, but she was still one of the most attractive women Preacher had seen in a long time, and spending several long, lazy days with her had made her seem even more so to him. They had talked enough for him to know that she was intelligent, too, and had been learning about medicine from Roger Flynn.

"He will not be here in Verdugo forever," she had explained, "and when he is gone, someone should know how to care for my people. So he teaches me as much as he can."

"I reckon you bein' as pretty as you are don't have anything to do with him wantin' to teach you," Preacher had said.

That prompted Estellita to wave a hand dismissively. "Señor Flynn does not care about women in that way." She added hastily, "Do not misunderstand. He is not the sort that cares for men, either. His only interest is in knowledge."

Preacher didn't believe that for a second. He had never encountered a man who was *that* immune to the pleasures of the world and the flesh, in whatever form they took. But it was none of his business so he hadn't pressed Estellita for any more information. All he really cared about was that he and Tyler were both recovering from their injuries.

In Preacher's case, that recuperation was coming along fine. His back was still a little stiff and sore but gave him no real trouble. Tyler had been pretty sick for a couple of days before his fever finally broke. He was weak but slowly gaining strength, and his mind was clear again. Preacher and Chimney had explained to him where they were and how they had gotten there. Preacher had thanked him, as well, for helping him escape from almost certain death.

Estellita blushed under Preacher's scrutiny and held out the earthenware cup she was holding. "Here. Drink your rum. Señor Flynn says it is good for you, that it balances the body and the spirit."

"Can't argue with that," Preacher said as he took the cup and sipped the rich, dark rum. One thing he could say for this island, the folks sure could brew some fine liquor.

"The old bearded one is here to see you, as well," Estellita added.

"Chimney?"

"*Sí.*"

"That's fine," Preacher said. "Send him on around." He stood up and continued sipping from the cup.

A minute later, Chimney Matthews appeared, smoke billowing from the curved pipe clenched between his square yellow teeth.

The old-timer walked up, took the pipe from his mouth, and grinned. "I been by the doctor's house just now to see the boy. Seems to be doin' fine." He looked over at Estellita, who had followed him out to the trees at the edge of the beach. "He asked if I was comin' over here and said somethin' about how he ain't seen you today, señorita. I'd say he's a mite smitten with you. Can't blame him. Most fellas would feel that way if they woke up with a pretty gal like you takin' care of them. When he was ravin' with that fever, he prob'ly thought you was an angel who'd come down from heaven to claim him."

"Tyler is a nice young man," Estellita said stiffly. "I hope he recovers fully from his injuries."

"Well, I told him I'd pass along his greetin's and let you know he's lookin' forward to seein' you again, and I done that." Chimney turned back to Preacher and went on. "The boys have started talkin' about where we go and what we do from here, Cap'n. They'd like to know what you're thinkin'."

Preacher took another drink of the rum and then said, "We're goin' back to New Orleans."

Chimney made a face. "I figgered that's what you'd say. I got to tell you, though, Cap'n, some of the fellers 'd be just as happy to stay here from now on. They've decided they sorta like the way things are goin' here."

"I can't really blame 'em, I reckon," Preacher replied with a shrug. "And I ain't gonna force 'em to leave. Do you think enough of 'em are willin' to go back that we can handle the ship?"

"Oh, aye, I expect so. We'd be shorthanded, but if everybody's willin' to work hard, we can make it. And there's a chance I might be able to recruit some boys here in Verdugo who'd be willin' to sign on with us for a chance to go to New Orleans." Chimney puffed hard on the pipe a couple of times and frowned. "There's somethin' ye should know, though, Cap'n."

Preacher had given up on getting the old-timer to stop calling him captain. "What is it, Chimney?"

"A lad I trust here in the village was headin' to Havana yesterday to deliver a load of bananas. I asked him to have a look around the harbor and maybe ask, quietlike, you know, if a small boat with some men in it had drifted in. He brought back some news with him."

Preacher's jaw tightened. "I don't much like the sound of this."

"I don't blame ye. Jabez Sampson is known in Havana. There's a rumor that he showed up a couple of days ago, along with a big feller with a tattooed head and some other men . . . but they weren't in no small boat. They was on a schooner flyin' the French flag."

Preacher's forehead creased. "How in the world did they wind up on a ship like that?"

"Onliest thing I can think of is that the schooner come along and found Sampson and the others driftin' in that boat we put 'em in. The Frenchies must've took the lot aboard, thinkin' they was rescuin' 'em . . . and then Sampson and the rest massacred the Frenchies."

Preacher muttered an oath under his breath. He didn't doubt for a second that Jabez Sampson, with Abner Rowland to help him, would be treacherous and ruthless enough to commit such an atrocity.

"They sailed on into Havana to pick up supplies," Chimney continued, "and then they left again."

"You think they're comin' here to look for us?" Preacher asked.

"I might've. Sampson's put in to port here often enough to figger it might occur to us, too. But they would've been here by now. The boy I sent asked around in the waterfront taverns, and he found out that Sampson and Rowland were talkin' about headin' back to New Orleans." Chimney raked a fingernail along his whiskery jaw. "That goes along with somethin' else I overheard the two of 'em sayin' once on board the *Calypso*, afore we mutinied against 'em. They was drinkin' and schemin' in Sampson's cabin with the door ajar a mite, and I was right outside. I heard 'em sayin' that after this voyage, there'd be nothin' stoppin' 'em from goin' back and takin' over the whole operation. The cap'n said he'd been waitin' for the right man to come along and give him a hand with that, and he was convinced Rowland was just the feller to do it."

Preacher stood there mulling over what the old-timer had just told him. The rest of the rum in his cup was forgotten.

If anyone had asked him, he would have guessed that Jabez Sampson was so filled with hate that he'd be eager to settle the score with the men who had taken his ship away from him. But from the sound of the information Chimney had received, greed had won out over vengeance, and when fate had presented Sampson with a means of returning to New Orleans and carrying out an audacious plan, he had seized it.

Sampson meant to overthrow Simone LeCarde, just as he had been overthrown on the *Calypso*. If he could take over all of Simone's criminal enterprises, he would have plenty of time and money to hunt down Preacher and get his revenge. Preacher nodded slowly as those thoughts arranged themselves in his mind. He could believe that Jabez Sampson had come to the same conclusion.

"You reckon it means what I think it does?" Chimney asked.

"It means Sampson is willin' to put off torturin' all of us to death if he's got a chance to get rich first," Preacher said.

"So him and Rowland are goin' after that LeCarde feller?"

"That's the way I see it." Preacher didn't correct him about Simone's true identity, although after everything that had happened, he had no reason to keep it a secret anymore.

"Well," Chimney said with a note of hope in his voice, "better him than us, right?"

Preacher shook his head. "That ain't the way it works. Sampson and Rowland may fail. We don't know about that. But if they take over like they plan to, they'll be worse and more powerful enemies than ever. With money and an organization like the one LeCarde has at their command, they'll find you and me and everybody else involved in that mutiny. In the long run, none of us will be safe" Preacher glanced at Estellita, who was standing to the side with a puzzled expression on her face that said she comprehended only some of what she was hearing. "Neither will any of the folks who helped us. Sampson will take his revenge on them, too."

"So what in blazes do we do?"

"Only one thing I can think of," Preacher said. He glanced at Estellita, and a pang of regret went through him. His decision meant leaving her and the other friends he had made in Verdugo. It meant leaving Tyler behind. The young man still hadn't recovered enough for what would be facing them.

And it would mean helping Simone LeCarde, the woman who had condemned him to death. She was a lesser threat than the other one facing him, and despite everything that had happened, he still remembered the times they had shared.

"We've got to get back to New Orleans as fast as we can and stop Sampson and Rowland," Preacher said.

CHAPTER 39

There was no time to waste. Preacher told Chimney to gather the crew—as many of them as were willing to return to New Orleans, anyway—and start getting the *Calypso* ready to put to sea again. Preacher had found a stash of gold coins in Sampson's cabin, and they could be used as an inducement to get the sailors to agree, as well as signing on some new crewmen if possible.

"How soon can we leave?" the mountain man asked.

Chimney scratched at his beard and frowned in thought. "We oughter be able to weigh anchor later today."

"And how many days to get back to New Orleans?"

"Four or five, if we've got a fair wind."

Sampson and Rowland had roughly a two-day start on them, Preacher thought. A lot could happen in two days. But they couldn't get back any sooner than was humanly possible, so he just had to hope those two varmints wouldn't have eliminated Simone and taken control of the town's criminal underworld by then.

He wasn't sure how he would feel if they killed Simone. Under the circumstances, he had no real reason to feel any sympathy for her, but he reminded himself that she hadn't had him killed outright when she had the opportunity. She had given him a chance to save his life, however slim it might have been. Whether or not that counted for anything, Preacher just didn't know.

When Chimney had hurried off to begin the preparations, Estellita looked at Preacher with a mournful expression and asked, "Do you have to leave?"

"If Sampson and Rowland are successful in what they're fixin' to try, it means that sooner or later, hell's gonna come callin' here in Verdugo," he explained. "They're pirates, just like in the old days. I wouldn't put it past 'em to raid the town and put the whole place to the torch, once they found out the folks here helped us."

"The days of pirates are not so old," she mused. "I remember hearing stories of Jean Lafitte and Dominique You when I was a little girl. The difference is, those men had at least some shred of honor left in them. From what I have seen of Sampson and know of this man Rowland, I believe they do not."

"They sure don't," Preacher agreed. "So you see, me leavin' and tryin' to put a stop to their plans is the only thing I can do to protect you and Dr. Flynn and everybody else in Verdugo."

"Then do what you must, Preacher," she said as she put her arms around him and held him close, pressing her body to his. "And perhaps someday fate will bring you here again."

"Could be," Preacher said, although he considered the possibility that he would ever sail across the seas again to be a mighty slim one.

* * *

Later, he went by Roger Flynn's house to see how Tyler was doing and explain to the young man what was going on. He arrived to find Tyler struggling to get dressed, while Flynn stood by with an exasperated look on his face.

"What in blazes do you think you're doin'?" Preacher asked.

"Getting ready to go on the *Calypso* with you, of course," Tyler replied. "You didn't think you could just sail off and leave me here, did you, Preacher? That's what Chimney said."

"That's durned sure what I did think." Preacher looked at Flynn. "He ain't in no shape to go gallivantin' off like this, is he?"

The physician shrugged. "It would be much better if he remained here and rested for another week or so. The fever is gone and his wounds are beginning to heal, but he's hardly back to normal."

"It'll take several days to reach New Orleans," Tyler argued. "What if I promise to take it easy on board the ship until then?"

Flynn inclined his head and admitted, "That would at least provide more time for recovery. I still feel like it's a bad idea, though."

"You heard what the doctor said," Preacher told the young man. An idea occurred to him. "And another thing, if you stay here, Estellita can keep on lookin' after you. You're her prize patient, after all."

Tyler had been trying to pull on a shirt. He paused in the effort and frowned, obviously intrigued by the idea of having Estellita to himself after Preacher sailed off. If he was going to have any chance with her, it would be much more likely after the mountain man was gone.

But then resolve came over his face again, and he shook his head. "I always tried to be loyal to my captain, even when he was a brutal animal. You're my captain now, Preacher."

Preacher let his own exasperation show. "Blast it, I never asked for the job!"

"But it appears to be yours, nonetheless," Flynn said. "If Tyler wishes to accompany you, I give him my medical blessing . . . reluctantly."

Preacher could see that he wasn't going to get anywhere arguing. He glared at Tyler for a second, then jerked his head in a curt nod. "Better be on board when we're ready to cast off," he warned. "That's what they call it, ain't it? Anyway, we won't be waitin' for you."

"I'll be there," Tyler said. Then he looked worried. "I'll have a chance to thank Estellita and say good-bye to her, won't I?"

"I'll tell her to come by here and see you," Preacher said.

Days earlier, a crowd had turned out to welcome the *Calypso* to Verdugo, and the people of the town gathered again at the docks to bid the vessel and its crew farewell. Alcalde Gonzalez made a speech. Estellita put on a brave face, but a tiny tear trickled from the corner of her right eye. Roger Flynn saw that and patted her consolingly on the shoulder.

Tyler stood at the railing next to Preacher and Chimney. "I'm going to come back here," he said as he looked at Estellita. "As soon as we're finished with our business in New Orleans, I'm going to sign on with a real trading ship and get back here. I promised Estellita."

Preacher didn't know what else was said between the two young people when they met briefly before the *Calypso* was ready to sail, and he didn't want to know. But he hoped Estellita had realized it would be better to turn her attention to someone who might actually return to her, rather than a fella like him who likely never would. Tyler had the makings of a fine man, and the two of them would be good for each other.

Chimney said, "I might just come back here with you, lad. A nice, peaceful place with friendly folks. I can't think of nowhere better to live out my days."

"But you have a lot of years left, Chimney," Tyler said. "I can't imagine an old sea dog like you ever staying on dry land for very long."

"I know what you mean, but even when it's somethin' in your blood, somethin' you love doin' no matter what it is, sooner or later a feller gets tired and wants to just sit in the shade and put his feet up and watch the beauty of the world go by." Chimney puffed in his pipe and sent a cloud of smoke into the air. "I'm gettin' to that time in my life, and like I said, I can't think of no better place to do it than here."

"Worry about all that later," Preacher advised the old-timer. "Right now, we still got work to do."

He lifted a hand in farewell to Estellita, Flynn, Gonzalez, and the rest of the *Cubanos* gathered on the dock. Then he went up the steps to the rear deck, strode over to the tiller, and called the order to cast off.

Funny how this business of being a captain sort

of rubbed off on a man, he mused as the oarsmen maneuvered the sloop away from the dock and into the open water of the cove.

Tyler remained at the rail, watching Verdugo dwindle in the distance. Chimney, acting as sailing master, ordered the sails unfurled.

As the big sweeps of canvas filled with wind and popped against the lines holding them in place, Preacher called to Tyler, "Come on up here and take over the tiller."

The youngster needed a job to do, to take his mind off what he was leaving behind.

Tyler sighed and turned away from the railing. He climbed to the rear deck and told Preacher, "I was never the steersman before."

"Think you can handle the job?"

"I know what to do, if that's what you mean."

"Good, because you're still recoverin' and you don't need to be climbin' around in the sails like a monkey or holystonin' the deck. Not that it needs it right now. The fellas cleaned it up pretty good while we were in port."

Tyler took the tiller and said, "I appreciate the trust you're putting in me, Preacher."

"You've earned it."

The next four days passed without any trouble. Now that the crewmen weren't being bullied and mistreated all the time, as they had been under Jabez Sampson's command, they worked eagerly, without complaint. The *Calypso* didn't encounter any storms on the voyage, and Preacher was grateful for that stroke of good fortune. In the waterfront taverns of Verdugo, Chimney had been able to recruit a few more men for the crew, but they were still short-handed and a big blow might have been too much for them to handle.

The only thing that didn't go exactly as Preacher might have wished was the fact that the wind was inconsistent. They were never becalmed, but from time to time their progress slowed, and that delay chafed at him. He ordered the oars brought out and the men put their backs into it willingly enough, but he would have preferred to be moving along at a better clip.

By the evening of the fourth day at sea, Chimney came to him and said, "We ought to be in sight of the mainland by midday tomorrow, Cap'n. Do you plan on us sailin' into N' Orleans, bold as brass?"

"What else can we do?" Preacher asked.

"Well"—a sly look came over Chimney's bewhiskered face—"I ain't sayin' that I have firsthand knowledge o' such things, mind you, but down below there, along the delta, there be a number of places where the old-time pirates used to lie up. Jean Lafitte was fond of a place called Barataria Bay and even had a settlement there. There are others like that. We could put into one of those little coves, get our hands on some horses, and ride into town. Sampson and Rowland might not be as likely to see us comin' that-a-way."

Preacher thought about the suggestion and nodded slowly. It was a shrewd plan and had a good chance of working.

"We can leave a few men on the *Calypso*," Chimney continued. "The ones who signed on in Verdugo ain't got no personal grudge agin those two varmints, but the fellers who served under 'em sure do. Most of 'em, maybe the whole bunch, will want to come with you for the showdown."

"And I'll be glad to have 'em," Preacher said with a nod. All the men who had come back to New Orleans with Sampson and Rowland might not have joined in their scheme to overthrow Simone LeCarde and take over the city's underworld, but most probably had, and Sampson and Rowland wouldn't have had any trouble recruiting others from among the dregs of the waterfront.

As Chimney had predicted, the low, dark line that represented the Louisiana mainland came into view late the next morning. It didn't change much as they approached it. Unlike Cuba with its wooded hills, the Mississippi River delta was flat as it could be. Stretches of open water twisted between low, grassy hummocks. Here and there a larger piece of dry land could be found, some dotted with scrubby trees. The landscape reminded Preacher a little of that found around the Platte River, which men sometimes said was a mile wide and an inch deep. These winding waterways were a lot deeper than that and also were wider than a mile, starting out, although the channels narrowed as the sloop penetrated farther into the delta.

Preacher saw men fishing from small, flat-bottomed boats, and shanties made of scrap wood daubed together with mud began to appear on the shores. Smoke curled into the sky from cooking fires.

Chimney took over the tiller. The sloop had a fairly shallow draft, but even so, the delta country could be tricky, according to the old-timer. Despite what he'd said about not having firsthand knowledge of the old pirate lairs, he steered the *Calypso* with an expert touch and finally took the vessel into a channel that ran past a small settlement with a dock sticking out into the water. As Preacher and Tyler watched with admiration from the bow, Chimney put the *Calypso* alongside the dock and men leaped ashore to tie it up.

Preacher felt good to be stepping on American soil again. At last he could get on with the long-delayed quest that had brought him from his home in the mountains.

CHAPTER 40

The settlement was called Abelard. The money Preacher had left from what he'd found in Sampson's cabin paid for the loan of half a dozen saddle horses, as well as a wagon and a team of mules to pull it. The rest of the men who were going with Preacher would ride to New Orleans in the wagon.

The city was far enough away that it would be night before Preacher and his companions reached it, but that was all right. It was easier to move around in the dark.

Preacher hoped that they weren't already too late. If his enemies had overthrown Simone, possibly even killed her, getting his revenge on Sampson and Rowland and finding Edmund Cornelius and Lucy Tarleton would be that much more difficult.

Even if things turned out that way, he still didn't intend to let it stop him.

Preacher tried to talk Tyler into staying with the men who would remain aboard the *Calypso*, but as he expected, the young man was having none of that.

"I haven't come this far and suffered as much as I have, only to miss out on justice being done," he insisted. "I have a score to settle with those two as well, you know."

"All right, just be careful," Preacher told him.

"Do *you* intend on being careful?"

The mountain man's grin was the only answer he gave.

After all that time at sea, it felt mighty good to have a horse and saddle underneath him again instead of a ship's deck. Chimney was just the opposite, though. He bounced and complained all the way into New Orleans as he guided the group through the delta, but Preacher was glad to have the old-timer along. Despite his own uncanny sense of direction, Preacher had a hunch he would have gotten hopelessly lost trying to find his way through the marshland.

As evening set in, the lights of the city became visible. Preacher's pulse quickened as he saw their destination spread out before them. And he picked up the pace they were traveling, as well.

As they moved through the outskirts of town, he began to recognize some of the buildings and have a general idea where they were and where they were going. Full dark had almost fallen when he saw the livery stable and blacksmith shop belonging to Jean Paul Dufresne. He led the other riders and the wagon to the pair of adjoining stone buildings where a lantern still burned in the blacksmith shop. Inside, hammer rang against anvil.

Preacher reined his mount to a halt. Beside him, Chimney did likewise and the other riders and the wagon came to a stop behind them. They were still a short distance from the French Quarter and the Catamount's Den, but more than likely Simone had spying eyes scattered all throughout New Orleans. If

Dufresne agreed, they would wait at the livery until the darkness was thicker before approaching the tavern.

The blacksmith looked up from the anvil when Preacher walked in. Recognition made his eyes widen. "Preacher!" he exclaimed. "I thought it likely I would never see you again."

"It came mighty close to that a few times," the mountain man said, "but I'm back now and ready to take up where I left off. You haven't had any more trouble around here, have you?"

A grim smile tugged at Dufresne's mouth. "You mean since I came in to find bodies littering my shop that morning? No, it has been quiet."

"How about over in the French Quarter?"

Dufresne cocked his head to the side and said, "Ah, now, that has not been so tranquil. A big disturbance occurred there last night. The authorities called it a riot, but from what I hear, it was more like a war."

Preacher's heart slugged in his chest. That was exactly what he had hoped not to hear. There could be lots of explanations for trouble in the French Quarter, he supposed—but the most logical one was that Sampson and Rowland had made their move against Simone.

There was one way to find out. He would have to go to the Catamount's Den.

"I've got about a dozen friends outside," he said. "You reckon them and their horses could stay here for a while?"

"Of course," Dufresne replied with a nod. "Do you want the horses stabled?"

Preacher thought about it and shook his head.

"Not yet. We might have to move fast, so they'd better stay saddled."

Dufresne laid his hammer aside. "Let me go next door and open the barn for them."

It didn't take long to get men, horses, and wagon inside the livery barn, although it was a bit crowded in there when they did. Preacher explained the situation to the men, then said, "I'm goin' around to the tavern to have a look and see if I can tell what happened."

"I'm coming with you," Tyler said immediately. He insisted that he was recovered from the flogging he had received, but Preacher knew that wasn't completely true. Tyler still hadn't regained his full strength. He had ridden in the wagon from Abelard to New Orleans.

"No, you stay here," Preacher told him. "I'll take Chimney along, and you'll be in charge of the rest of the bunch. Reckon you can handle that?"

"Of course I can," Tyler replied without any hesitation. "You'll come back here and get us when you've found out if Sampson and Rowland are there?"

"I sure will," Preacher said. He motioned with his head to Chimney, and the two of them walked out of the livery stable into the night.

"Pretty smart, what you did with the boy just then," Chimney commented quietly.

"Puttin' him in charge, you mean?"

"Yeah. Otherwise, he'd 've kept on arguin' with you. Say, that blacksmith is a brawny lad, ain't he?"

"He is, and I sure wouldn't mind havin' him on my side in a fight. He needs to stay out of it, though. He's got a wife and young'un dependin' on him, and I already almost got him in trouble by leavin' a few carcasses in his place after some varmints jumped me there."

"Yeah, I noticed how he mentioned that." Chimney chuckled. "You just sorta leave carcasses behind you wherever you go, don't you, Preacher?"

The mountain man sighed. "Yeah, and I ain't sure how come it always seems to work out that way. I'm a peaceable man, after all."

"Ain't we all, son. Ain't we all."

There might have been a small war in the French Quarter the previous night, but the area seemed to be back to its normal raucous self. The taverns, whore-houses, cafés, and gambling dens were doing good business. A lot of people were on the streets.

The Catamount's Den, though, was dark. No one was going in or out as Preacher and Chimney studied it from the mouth of an alley diagonally across the cobblestone street. A frown creased the mountain man's forehead.

"That the place?" Chimney asked in a half-whisper, although it seemed unlikely anyone would overhear them with the noise from nearby businesses and the hubbub of pedestrians.

"That's it," Preacher said.

"Don't look like nobody's there. Why do you reckon it's closed? If Sampson and Rowland already took it over, wouldn't they have it open?"

"You'd think so." In the darkness, Preacher rubbed his chin. "I'm gonna get in there and take a look around." To forestall the inevitable question, he went on. "You stay here, but if you hear any commotion in there, come a-runnin'."

"I'll sure do it," Chimney said as he closed his hand around the butt of the pistol stuck in his trousers.

Preacher was armed with two pistols and a knife. He wished he had his tomahawk, too, as he cat-footed through the shadows and circled around to approach the tavern's side entrance through another alley. That tomahawk was a fine weapon for close work, but he had no idea what had happened to it. It was gone when he'd woken up from being drugged by Balthazar Crowe.

The gloom was so thick that Preacher had to find the side door by feeling along the stone wall until he came to it. He tried the latch. It was fastened, but when he worked the knife's heavy blade between the door and jamb, he was able to pry the catch loose. He opened the door carefully so the hinges wouldn't squeal, then eased the door closed behind him.

It was even darker inside. He shifted the knife to his left hand and pulled one of the pistols from his belt. He didn't cock the weapon but looped his thumb over the hammer so he was ready to ear it back and fire at a second's notice.

Staying close to the wall to minimize any creaking from the stairs, he started up toward the second floor. He felt certain that if Simone was there, she would be in her quarters. If she wasn't . . . Well, he would deal with that when he knew more.

When he reached the landing at the top of the stairs, he paused to listen intently. He didn't hear any sounds from inside the building. The Catamount's Den was as quiet as the grave—which was a disconcerting thought.

Preacher sheathed the knife and felt for the knob of the door into Simone's quarters. After a few seconds of fumbling around, he found it. Unlike the alley door below, this one wasn't locked. The knob turned easily in his fingers.

He slipped inside the darkened room and started to call Simone's name, then stopped himself. There was no reason anybody would be lurking, waiting to ambush him. Nobody in New Orleans even knew he was still alive except Jabez Sampson and Abner Rowland. Despite that, he didn't want to announce his presence just yet. So far, he had moved with the same sort of stealth that had allowed him to slip in and out of numerous Blackfoot camps and acquire the name Ghost Killer among his enemies. No reason to change that, he decided.

He had come to find out what had happened, he reminded himself, and couldn't do that by standing around in the dark. Since he had flint and steel, he could strike a spark if the fireplace had any tinder. A small fire would give him enough light to look around the sitting room, and maybe that would give him a clue where Simone was.

He had just knelt down in front of the fireplace when the door whispered open behind him, making just enough noise to alert him. As he turned, light spilled into the room, and he squinted against the sudden glare of a lantern.

The twin barrels of the shotgun pointing at him looked like a pair of cannon.

CHAPTER 41

The dwarf called Long Sam held the upraised lantern in his left hand, the shotgun in his right. A bandage was wrapped around his head, forming a band of white above his eyes. Preacher could tell that he was about a second away from pulling the shotgun's triggers.

"If you fire that scattergun one-handed like that, it'll break your arm," he warned. "Not to mention, it's liable to kick you all the way down the stairs."

"Yeah, but your mangy hide will be full of buckshot," Long Sam said. "I reckon the trade might be worth it."

"Take it easy. I'm not here lookin' for trouble."

Actually, that was a lie. Trouble was *exactly* what Preacher was looking for in the Catamount's Den. And now he'd found it, although not quite what he'd expected.

"What are you doing back here? What are you even doing alive? You're supposed to be a prisoner at that sugar plantation on San Patricio."

"Well, those plans got changed a mite," Preacher said dryly.

"Those double-crossers." Long Sam added a few colorful obscenities in a flat, hard voice. "Are you working with them?"

"You mean Sampson and Rowland?" Preacher laughed, but no humor lurked in the sound. "Not hardly. I want those two varmints dead just as much as I reckon you do. They're the reason you've got that rag tied around your head, ain't they?"

Preacher could tell by the way Long Sam's expression changed a little that his shrewd guess had been correct.

Long Sam let the shotgun barrels sag toward the floor. "They raided us last night," he rasped. "I know Sampson by sight, but he didn't come in at first. Some big fellow with tattoos on his head did, though."

"That's Abner Rowland," Preacher said. "Pure snake-blooded scoundrel."

"Yeah. And he had some other men with him I didn't know. But they knocked the right way, so I figured they were all right. I'm sure Sampson told them what to do. They came in, drank a little, and then pretended to start a fight. While I was dealing with that, Sampson and the rest of the bunch burst in through the front door and started shooting. That's when Rowland and the others dropped the pretense and attacked me and the rest of mam'selle's men. That's when I got this knock on the head. It put me out of the fight, and when I came to . . . it was all over." Long Sam shook his head. "They must've thought I was dead already, or they might've cut my throat."

"Wouldn't put it past 'em." Preacher asked the question that loomed uppermost in his mind. "Where's Simone? Did they get her?"

"That's the only good thing about this whole affair.

She and Balthazar weren't even here. They'd gone up to Colonel Osborne's plantation for a visit."

The surge of relief that went through Preacher at that news surprised him with its strength. "Then she's all right?"

"As far as I know. But it doesn't end there. After the fight was over, Sampson got hold of one of the bartenders and tortured him. He told Sampson where mam'selle and Balthazar had gone. The fellow admitted as much to me before he died from what Sampson and Rowland did to him." Long Sam took a deep breath, then with a look of despair on his face, he said, "They took their gang and headed up there."

"To the plantation, you mean?"

"That's right. They don't know that mam'selle is, well, mam'selle, but they want to kill Simon LeCarde because they know that's the only way they can really take over." Long Sam sighed. "I sent a man to warn her, but Sampson and the others were ahead of him. I . . . I don't know if he even got there all right, let alone whether he made it in time."

Preacher felt grim resolve settling over his face and into his bones. "How come you didn't go yourself?"

"Because I was too dizzy from this knock on the head to stay on a horse," Long Sam snapped back at him. "Don't you think I wanted to go? But I knew the best chance of getting word to her in time was to send a rider on a fast horse, so that's what I did. It's taken me until tonight to be able to stand up without falling down!"

The wheels of Preacher's brain turned over swiftly. "Do you know where this plantation of Osborne's is?"

"Of course I do. It's about sixty miles northwest of

here. I've never been there, but I know how to find it, if that's what you're getting at."

"It sure is," Preacher said. "I've got some men with me. We're headin' up there right away to find out what's happened."

"You'll have to take me with you."

That bold declaration didn't surprise Preacher. He nodded and said, "I figured as much. I've got a wagon. You can ride in it."

"A wagon will slow us down. We need to move a lot faster than that. I can ride now. Don't think for a minute that I can't. And you need me to know where you're going."

Preacher couldn't argue with that logic. Maybe Jean Paul Dufresne could help them come up with more saddle mounts. Even if he had to leave some of the men behind, Preacher knew he couldn't afford to wait. Long Sam was right about the need for swiftness.

"Let's go, then. The sooner we get on the trail, the better, if you can find your way in the dark."

"I can," Long Sam said. "Along the way, you can tell me what in the world you're doing still alive."

As they started out of Simone's sitting room, the dwarf added, "There's one more thing, Preacher. Mam'selle and Balthazar took Cornelius and the Tarleton woman with them."

"Why in blazes did they do that?"

"Because the colonel insisted. He knows that they probably intended to bilk him when they first met him, but he's still smitten with the woman."

That was a stroke of luck for Preacher. If he could save Simone from being murdered by Sampson and Rowland, she might think twice about her arrangement to protect Cornelius and Lucy.

And since Preacher still wanted to settle the score with those two . . . maybe fate was about to present him with the opportunity to take care of all of it at the same time.

Preacher had told Chimney about Long Sam, so the old-timer wasn't completely shocked to see a shotgun-toting dwarf accompanying the mountain man. But since Long Sam had been part of the treachery intended to exile Preacher to the hell of the sugar plantation on San Patricio, Chimney hadn't expected the little man to turn out to be an ally.

Knowing such twists of fate happened sometimes, Chimney accepted it quickly. Once he learned what was going on, he said, "We'd best move fast, then. If we ride all night, we can get to the colonel's plantation sometime tomorrow mornin'."

Preacher asked Long Sam, "Do you know how many men Sampson and Rowland had with them?"

"Somewhere between fifteen and twenty in the whole bunch, I'd say."

"Would there be enough men on the colonel's plantation to put up a fight and hold them off?"

"How in blazes would I know?" Long Sam snapped. "Balthazar's there, and he's worth three or four regular fighting men. Plus Osborne's overseers . . ." Long Sam shrugged. "They could hold out for a while, I imagine. That's what we're counting on, isn't it?"

"And if we can take that bunch of varmints by surprise," Preacher said, "that ought to be enough to tip the scales in our favor."

The plan might work, but first they had to get

there. Preacher, Chimney, and Long Sam hurried back to Jean Paul Dufresne's livery barn.

Dufresne had enough horses in his stable that, combined with the mounts Preacher and the others had brought from Abelard, everyone could ride except for a couple of men.

Before Preacher could even say anything, Tyler frowned at him and said, "Don't even try to stop me this time, Preacher."

"All right," the mountain man replied, "but you got to keep up. We're gonna be movin' pretty fast."

"I'll keep up. Don't worry about that."

Within half an hour, the force of a dozen men had left New Orleans and was heading northwest toward Colonel Osborne's plantation. The hard-packed dirt road they followed for the first part of the trip was wide and easy to see, even by light of the stars and a half-moon. Later, though, Long Sam warned them, the way would get trickier.

"The plantation backs up to a swamp. I've heard the colonel talk about it. Men have gone in there and never come out again, so we want to avoid it."

Maybe, Preacher thought. But maybe there was something in Long Sam's warning that might be useful.

They stopped now and then to rest the horses but mostly just pushed on at a fast clip throughout the night.

During one of those brief halts, Preacher asked Tyler, "How are you holdin' up?"

"I'm fine," the young man replied, but his voice revealed the strain he was feeling. "A little tired, that's all."

"You can stay here, rest a while longer, and follow us later."

"And by the time I get there, it'll be all over." Tyler shook his head. "No thanks, Preacher. I'm in this to the end."

"All right. If that's the way you feel. You get to where you can't go on, though, we won't be able to wait for you."

"I know that. I wouldn't have it any other way."

As Long Sam had said, the path became harder to follow once they branched off the main road. That meant they had to go slower. Trees with moss growing thickly over their branches crowded in on both sides of the trail, and the dangling vegetation cast dense shadows. Finally, Long Sam said, "We have to stop until it starts to get light, or we risk losing our way completely."

Preacher didn't like it, but he knew Long Sam was right. He told the men to dismount. "As soon as we can see well enough, we'll be on our way again."

Although none of them said it, not even Tyler, he could tell the men were grateful for the chance to rest. He had been pushing them hard for quite a while. It was still a few hours until dawn, he estimated. That would give his companions a chance to recover a little.

As for himself, he could have pushed himself until he dropped—and that would take a mighty long time.

"Don't wander off," Long Sam advised the men. "I'm not saying for sure you'd step on a snake or trip over an alligator . . . but it might happen."

"Don't you worry, son," Chimney told him. "I figure on stayin' right here where I am."

After everyone had rested for a while, Preacher said to Long Sam, "I ain't forgot that you had a hand in what happened to me. I reckon you helpin' us like this will go a ways toward squarin' that up."

"I did what I thought best for my boss," Long Sam said. "If you're waiting for an apology—"

"I ain't. Just don't ever try to double-cross me again. That's all I'm sayin'." As he spoke, Preacher noticed that the sky had taken on a slightly gray hue. Dawn was approaching. Soon they would be able to resume their journey to Colonel Osborne's plantation. "How much farther is it?" he asked Long Sam.

"Not far. A couple of miles, maybe—"

As Long Sam abruptly fell silent, Preacher stiffened. He thought the dwarf must have heard the same thing he had—a faint popping in the distance that he recognized as gunfire.

CHAPTER 42

Long Sam recovered from his surprise and cursed. "Those shots have to be coming from the plantation!"

"And it sounds like they're fightin' a war," Preacher said. "We can't wait around for it to get any lighter."

"I know. We can see well enough." Long Sam grabbed his horse's reins. "Somebody give me a hand, blast it!"

One of the men lifted Long Sam so he could scramble into the saddle. The rest of them swung up onto their mounts. With Long Sam leading the way, they galloped off toward the sound of the guns.

The sky continued to brighten as the shots grew louder. By the time Preacher and his companions were close to the Osborne plantation, a few streaks of gold had begun to appear in the heavens to the east. The sun would rise in another half hour.

In the meantime, there was enough light for the men to see Preacher when he held up a hand and signaled for them to stop. He said, "Sounds like we're within a quarter mile or so. I'm gonna scout ahead on foot with Chimney and Long Sam. The rest of you fellas stay here. Tyler, you're in charge again."

"All right, Preacher," Tyler replied with a nod. His face was haggard. Maybe it was just the gray light that made it look like that, but Preacher didn't think so. The youngster needed to hang on for a little while longer, and then, with any luck, this whole affair would be over.

Chimney started to help Long Sam down from his horse, but the dwarf swung a leg over the saddle and dropped to the ground, staggering a little as he landed. "I can manage that part of it," he snapped.

"Don't get touchy," Chimney told him. "I was just tryin' to help. Didn't mean no offense."

"Come on, you two," Preacher said, impatient to have a look at the situation. Guns were still going off. That was good, the mountain man told himself, because it meant the forces led by Jabez Sampson and Abner Rowland hadn't taken over the plantation yet. If they had, the early morning air would be quiet.

Other than maybe some screaming as those two varmints indulged their taste for torture.

Preacher, Chimney, and Long Sam stole forward through the shadows that still clustered beneath moss-draped cypresses. They came to a lane that turned off and ran between two rows of pine trees. At the far end of it, three hundred yards away, the plantation house with its white-columned portico was dimly visible.

Flashes of muzzle flame spurted from several of the house's windows and were answered by shots from the trees and other places of concealment around the front of the house. From where Preacher was, he couldn't tell if the house was completely surrounded, but from what he could see, that seemed possible.

"That swamp you talked about," he said to Long Sam, "how close does it come to the house?"

"It's maybe five hundred yards away, around on the other side. The bayou that runs through it comes even closer, though. It runs right behind the house." A note of excitement came into Long Sam's voice. "Are you thinking we could sneak up on them that way?"

"Not all of us. But I reckon I could. If you fellas gave me time to get into the house, I could have Simone's men ready to charge out and counterattack that bunch at the same time as you're hittin' from behind. We'd have 'em caught between us."

"That could work, all right. But Sampson's liable to have men behind the house, too."

"I'd have to deal with 'em," Preacher said.

Chimney put in, "That could wind up bein' pretty bad odds."

"I've had the odds stacked against me before. I'm willin' to risk it."

Long Sam asked, "How are you going to find your way through the swamp?"

"One wilderness is pretty much like another, I reckon. I'll just steer toward the shootin' and try not to step on a gator."

Preacher, Chimney, and Long Sam returned to the others, and Preacher explained the plan to them.

"You shouldn't be going alone," Tyler objected.

"I've had a lot of experience at slippin' up on fellas." Preacher didn't take the time to tell them about all his deadly nocturnal visits to various Blackfoot camps.

"I'm gonna have to move fast and quiet, and I can do that best by myself."

"How long you reckon it'll take you to get in position?" Chimney asked.

Preacher considered the question. "Give me until half an hour after sunup. I ought to have made it into the house by then."

Long Sam gave him some rough directions to follow, but the dwarf couldn't be too specific. He didn't know the terrain all that well, either. Just had a general idea of the lay of the land. Preacher would have to rely a great deal on his instincts, but they had never let him down so far and he didn't expect them to now.

He checked the loads in his pistols, then said his farewells and loped away, leaving his horse with the others. He would circle through the swamp and make his approach to the plantation house on foot. For a moment, he wished that Dog was with him. The big cur was an invaluable ally in a fight. Dog was back in St. Louis, though, safe at Patterson's livery stable.

Preacher followed the trail back the way they had come, and after a while, he cut off through the trees to his right. The shadows instantly closed in around him. Strands of moss hanging from the branches over his head brushed against his face as he moved along.

After a few minutes of making his way through the trees, a particularly thick and heavy strand of the moss came loose and fell onto his shoulder. At least, that was what he thought at first. But then it continued to writhe around, and Preacher realized with a surge of horror that a snake had dropped from a tree limb as he passed under it. He doubted if it was a deliberate move on the snake's part, but that didn't really matter.

He jerked his shoulder, reached across his body with his other hand, and caught hold of the scaly body. In the dim light, he saw the snake's mouth open wide with fangs ready to embed themselves in his flesh. A vicious rattling sound told him the snake was deadly.

By a stroke of luck, he had caught hold of the snake only a short distance behind its head. It couldn't whip its body around and bite him on the arm. He pulled his knife with his other hand and with a swift stroke of the blade beheaded the blasted thing. The jaws were still trying to bite as the head fell to the ground at his feet. With a grimace of revulsion, he kicked it away. The rattles at the other end of the part he still held buzzed faintly and then fell silent. Preacher flung the snake's body away.

Preacher didn't really hate any of the Good Lord's creatures, but if he was going to, snakes would be high on his list.

The mountain man wiped the snake's blood off on his trousers, sheathed the knife, and moved on. He was more careful as he brushed the moss aside, and he watched where he put his feet, too, remembering what Long Sam had said about tripping over an alligator.

The trees, which crowded close together alongside the trail, began to spread out more, and the ground became softer under Preacher's feet. The rank smell of rotting vegetation grew stronger. Preacher hadn't spent much time in swamps, but he knew that smell and didn't care for it. One of his feet sank into water and mud. He withdrew it carefully and searched for more solid ground for his next step.

Having to search for a good path slowed him down.

The light around him grew brighter, telling him that the sun was up, but it had a green, unearthly tinge because of the trees. He circled around pools of water that were a sickly black in the strange illumination.

He saw other snakes but avoided them. Insects buzzed around his face and came right back no matter how often he batted them away. Even early in the day, heat hung in the air like a physical thing. He missed the cool, clean air of the mountains.

After traveling through the swamp for what seemed like a longer time than it really was, he came to the edge of a stream that flowed sluggishly from his left to right. That was the bayou Long Sam had told him about, the one that ran behind Colonel Osborne's plantation house. As Preacher stood on the bank, he listened to the gunshots coming from that direction. They were more sporadic as the siege entered another lull.

He hoped that Simone was all right. For one thing, he wanted to see her face when she first laid eyes on him again. She probably wouldn't know who to be more scared of, him or Sampson and Rowland. He didn't intend to hurt her, but she wouldn't know that.

Preacher looked closely at the water in the bayou, searching for any suspicious "logs." He had heard that sometimes alligators would plunge right out of a stream if they spotted potential prey on the bank, and the critters moved a lot faster than most people gave them credit for. Not seeing anything that appeared dangerous, he started along the bank to his right.

Something black wiggled through the water. A cottonmouth snake, Preacher decided. They would chase a fella, too, but this one stayed in the bayou. He heard a splash, and when he looked, he saw a turtle swimming. Birds flitted around in the trees. Swamps might smell like they were full of death—and in many ways, they were—but they were full of life, too, right down to huge, colorful flowers that began to open as the light grew stronger and a new day began.

Preacher heard a rustling ahead of him and paused again. A man stepped out from behind a tree fifteen feet away. He had a rifle tucked under his left arm and was tying a rope belt around his waist, giving Preacher a pretty good idea what he'd been doing behind that tree.

The man came to a sudden stop when he spotted the mountain man and exclaimed, "Who in blazes are you?"

Preacher thought fast. He stepped forward and thrust his jaw out belligerently. "Who in blazes are *you*? You ain't one of Cap'n Sampson's men. I'd recognize you if you were one of us!"

He knew the man hadn't been on the *Calypso*. Preacher figured he was one Sampson and Rowland had recruited when they got back to New Orleans.

Tall and rawboned, with a thatch of yellow hair under a pushed-back hat, the man finished tying the rope belt and said, "I am so workin' for Sampson."

Preacher strode forward, squinting. "Let me take a better look at you. It's hard to see in this light. It's so blamed murky."

The man, who obviously wasn't too bright, wasn't suspicious. As soon as Preacher was within reach, he launched a right-hand punch that crashed into the stranger's jaw. The blow landed cleanly with enough power to jerk the man's head to the side and buckle his knees. Preacher caught the rifle as the man dropped it and collapsed.

The man wound up lying facedown. Preacher took the rope belt off him and cut it in half, using one length to tie the man's hands together behind his back, the other to bind his ankles. Spotting a bandana tucked into the man's pocket, Preacher pulled it out and crammed it into his mouth. Satisfied that the man wouldn't be a problem for a while, Preacher left him there.

He hoped some snake wouldn't come along and sink its fangs into the fellow—but when you signed on with murderous, no-good varmints like Sampson and Rowland, you sort of deserved whatever happened to you.

Preacher hurried along the bank, taking the man's rifle with him. The increase of light in the swamp was so gradual that it was impossible for him to tell how high the sun was. Enough time had gone by that it seemed like Chimney, Long Sam, Tyler, and the others would be making their move against the enemy soon, and Preacher had to be ready to take advantage of it.

That was what he was thinking when the water suddenly stirred to his left, ripples spreading, and then exploded with no more warning than that. He caught a glimpse of a rough, scaly hide and long, gaping jaws filled with teeth as he dropped the rifle and leaped for his very life.

CHAPTER 43

After battling the gator and killing the beast, Preacher found himself looking up into the ugly, grinning face of Abner Rowland. Keeping the pistol trained on Preacher he said, "It's a good thing I came back here to check on Fitzgerald. Otherwise you might've been able to sneak up on us. What in the world are you doin' here?"

Preacher shook his head to get his wet hair out of his eyes. "Figured you'd know that. I came to kill you."

"And help Simon LeCarde? He tried to send you away to your death, you fool!" Rowland toyed with the pistol's trigger. "Of course, you're fixin' to die anyway, 'cause I'm gonna blow your brains out—"

"Not if that gator eats you first, you won't," Preacher said.

Rowland frowned. "You don't think you can fool me with an old trick like that, do you? I watched you kill that gator. I was sort of hoping he'd rip you to pieces, but then I wouldn't have the pleasure of shootin' you, so I suppose it worked out all right."

"Well, I don't know that much about gators," Preacher drawled with astounding self-possession for a man with a gun stuck in his face, "but I reckon they must travel in pairs, because there's sure enough one comin' up behind you right now."

Rowland's grin disappeared as he snarled, "I'm tired of this. Time for you to die, you—"

The alligator behind him opened its mouth wide and let out a loud, throaty, bloodcurdling bellow as it lunged forward.

Rowland yelled in sudden terror and leaped into the air, twisting so he could look back over his shoulder and see the giant reptile charging at him. As he landed, he brought the pistol around and fired. Preacher didn't know if the ball struck the gator, but the boom and the gush of powder smoke must have disoriented the beast. It slewed to a stop a few yards short of Rowland and thrashed its tail.

Preacher surged up on hands and knees and then powered to his feet. He rammed his shoulder into Rowland from behind and drove the tattooed man forward. Taken by surprise, Rowland couldn't keep his balance. He tripped and fell—right on top of the gator.

Howling, Rowland flailed and flopped and fought desperately to get away from the predator. The alligator twisted its head around and the gaping jaws flashed toward Rowland's leg. He jerked it out of the way just in time. The gator's teeth snapped together on empty air. Rowland rolled across the muddy grass with the gator in pursuit.

Standing nearby, watching the battle between man and beast, Preacher thought about leaving Rowland to deal with the gator, but that would mean having a deadly enemy at his back if Rowland somehow survived. Preacher didn't want that. He might have been tempted to pull out his pistols and shoot both of them, but he knew the weapons wouldn't fire after that dunk in the bayou. They would have to be cleaned, dried, and reloaded before they were any use again.

Rowland ran toward the nearest cypress tree. He leaped up, caught hold of a mossy branch, and lifted his feet just as the alligator snapped at him again. He tried to kick his legs high enough to get them over the branch so he could pull himself higher, but he was too burly and awkward for that. All he could do was hang for dear life and keep jerking his feet and legs out of the creature's reach as it snapped at him.

Preacher figured it was only a matter of time before the gator tired of the game and started looking around for different prey—namely, him. He still didn't want to leave Rowland alive and thought about throwing his knife at the man, but as he'd said on the *Calypso*, he wasn't a cold-blooded killer.

Of course, if he threw some branches at Rowland and caused him to lose his grip and fall, it would be the gator who did the actual killing, not him.

Muttering a curse, Preacher turned and ran along the bank toward the plantation house. Rowland would just have to take his chances. Preacher figured the odds favored the gator.

Behind him, Rowland roared curses. After a minute or so, the obscenities stopped abruptly. Preacher didn't know what that meant, but he didn't slow down or look back.

The ground firmed up underneath him as the bayou reached the edge of the swamp and emerged into a broad, open grassy stretch dotted with pine trees. Two men with rifles were behind those trees, one to his right, the other to his left. The man to his left was drawing a bead on the house and getting ready to fire again. The one on the right was reloading.

The man concentrated so much on his task that he didn't lift his head to look at Preacher, thinking he was either Rowland or Fitzgerald returning from the swamp. Realizing his mistake too late, the man brought his rifle up as Preacher charged toward him, knife in hand.

The man didn't have a chance. Preacher drove the knife into his chest, penetrating all the way to the heart. The man's eyes opened wide with pain and shock. His face only inches away, Preacher recognized him as one of the crewmen from the *Calypso* who had been loyal to Jabez Sampson.

As the man died, Preacher grabbed the freshly loaded rifle.

The other attacker had noticed what was going on and yelled, "Hey!" Preacher spun toward him as the man dropped his empty rifle and clawed at a pistol in his waistband.

Smoothly, Preacher lifted the first man's rifle to his shoulders, cocked it, and fired without ever seeming to pause to aim. The heavy ball smashed into the man's chest and knocked him back against the rough-barked trunk of the pine behind him. He hung there for a second, then pitched forward and didn't move.

Preacher tossed the rifle aside. He took pistols from both men he'd killed and headed for the plantation house at a fast lope. He hoped somebody in there would recognize him. Otherwise the defenders were liable to shoot him, thinking he was one of Sampson's men.

Before he could reach the big white house, a fresh wave of gunfire came from the front. Too many guns were going off for it to be just Sampson's bunch firing. Long Sam, Chimney, Tyler, and the others had launched their attack—and Preacher, having been slowed down by his battles with the first alligator and then Abner Rowland, was too late to rally the defenders and mount his part of the assault.

He veered to his right and headed for the front of the house. He could still take Sampson and the rest of the attackers by surprise, even though he was just one man.

He wouldn't be the only counterattacker, though. As he rounded the house, he saw Balthazar Crowe emerge from the house and charge toward the trees along the lane. He had a huge pistol in each hand. Spotting Preacher from the corner of his eye, he slowed abruptly and swung those pocket blunderbusses toward the mountain man.

"Hold your fire!" Preacher yelled. "I'm on your side, blast it!"

Both men came to a stop facing each other. Crowe's face wore a look of open astonishment. "Preacher!" he exclaimed, then glanced at the trees where a battle was raging and added, "Then who—"

"Jabez Sampson and some of his pirate crew," Preacher explained. "He's double-crossing Simone and trying to take over. I found out about it and came back to stop him."

Crowe frowned and rumbled, "You'd help her, after what she did?"

"I got a score to settle with her, but a bigger one with Sampson. Those are friends of mine tusslin' with that no-good bunch right now, along with Long Sam. He'll vouch for me once this is over."

With guns roaring nearby, Crowe couldn't take long to ponder the situation. The fact that a rifle ball suddenly hummed wickedly through the air between them hurried his decision. He whirled toward the trees and brandished the pistols. "Come on!"

Side by side, Preacher and Crowe charged into the fracas. Rifle and pistol balls whined through the branches and thudded into tree trunks. One of Sampson's men loomed in front of them, grimacing as he tried to bring a pistol to bear. Preacher would have shot him, but Balthazar Crowe was quicker. The giant's left-hand gun blasted, and Sampson's man flew backward as the ball smashed into his chest.

An instant later, Preacher fired, too, but his shot passed close by Crowe's head. Crowe glared at him in surprise, then saw a rifleman's body tumbling out of the brush where he'd been drawing a bead on the huge black man. Preacher had spotted him just in time to save Crowe's life. Realizing that, Crowe jerked his head in a curt nod of gratitude.

They forged on, into a madhouse of noise and powder smoke, trying to root out the rest of the attackers.

The melee continued for several minutes. Preacher and Crowe each gunned down another of the attackers. The man Preacher shot had a cutlass shoved behind his belt. Preacher didn't know where he'd gotten it—the man hadn't had it when he'd been set adrift from the *Calypso* with Sampson and the others—but he took it from the corpse and grinned as he hefted it.

"I sort of like these big pigstickers," he commented.

He got to use it as another of Sampson's men charged out of the brush at him, rifle lifted to strike at him with the butt. Preacher whirled and thrust with the cutlass, which went into the man's gut with surprising ease. The entrails spilled out as Preacher ripped the blade loose.

"Balthazar! Balthazar!"

The anxious shout made Preacher and Crowe wheel around. Long Sam panted up to them. His face and the bandage around his head were grimy from powder smoke, but he didn't appear to be any the worse for wear since the last time Preacher had seen him.

"Long Sam!" Crowe rumbled. "What happened? Are you all right?"

"Yeah, I'm fine. Sampson's bunch raided the Catamount's Den and then headed out here when they found out where mam'selle was. Is she all right?"

"She was when I left the house," Crowe said.

Chimney, Tyler, and the rest of the men came up behind Long Sam. Echoes from the gunfire still lingered, but no fresh shots rang out, telling Preacher the battle was over. Some of the men sported scrapes and bloodstains from minor wounds, but he was relieved to see that all of them had made it through the battle.

Then Tyler asked, "Where's Sampson? Have you seen him?"

"You fellas didn't get him?"

"We never laid eyes on the varmint," Chimney said. "We was hopin' you put him down like the mad dog he is, Preacher."

A bad feeling welled up inside the mountain man.

He had just started to shake his head when more shots blasted, coming from the direction of the plantation house.

Every instinct in Preacher's body told him that was where Jabez Sampson was. Abner Rowland might be there, too, if he had escaped from that alligator.

And that was where Simone LeCarde was, as well.

CHAPTER 44

Preacher and Balthazar Crowe led the charge back toward the house, bounding right over the pair of steps leading from the portico to the entrance. Crowe flung the heavy wooden doors open as if they weighed next to nothing but then abruptly skidded to a halt on the marble floor. Preacher came to a stop alongside him.

On the other side of the large entrance hall, Jabez Sampson stood with his left arm around Simone's waist, holding her tightly against him while his right hand pressed a pistol against her ribs. His captain's cap was gone, and blood trickled down his cheek from a gash on his forehead, but he didn't appear to be badly hurt.

He grinned. "I figured you boys would be right along, if my men didn't manage to wipe ye out."

Preacher's gaze darted around the entrance hall, quickly taking in the rest of the scene. Over near the marble staircase that curved up to the second floor, Colonel August Osborne stood with Abner Rowland pointing a pistol at him. Nearby, on the steps themselves, Edmund Cornelius lay crumpled, his head supported on Lucy Tarleton's lap as she sat with him.

A large, dark bloodstain was visible on Cornelius's white shirt. He had been shot or knifed in the belly but was still alive, wide-eyed and gasping in pain.

"I see you got away from that gator," Preacher said to Rowland.

"No thanks to you," the tattooed man snarled. His hat was gone, so the inked patterns on his bald head were more visible than ever.

"Likely you would've made him sick to his stomach anyway."

Sampson snapped, "That's enough banter. I want this business settled—now! Where's Simon LeCarde?"

Simone began to laugh. "You fool! Haven't you figured it out by now? There is no Simon LeCarde! I have no brother. There's only me, and I run this gang!"

Sampson frowned at her. Preacher saw the surprise in the burly pirate's eyes.

Sampson muttered, "I knew old Catamount Jack had a daughter, too, but I never thought—"

"That's right. You didn't," Simone broke in. "Because you're an idiot. All of you were. You took the orders from 'Simon' that Balthazar relayed to you and never dreamed they were coming from me."

Sampson tightened the arm around her waist enough to make her wince. "It don't matter," he declared. "Simon or Simone, your days of runnin' things around here are over. I'm the boss now, and Abner there is my second in command. 'Tis time for us to get rich."

"That will never happen," Simone declared confidently. "My organization will never follow you."

"They'll follow whoever brings them the most loot, and ye know it."

Preacher suspected that Sampson was right about that. He'd heard the old saying about honor among thieves, but he'd never seen much evidence of such a thing in real life.

He saw the way Simone kept glancing at him from time to time. She was astounded to see him back in Louisiana when she expected him to be exiled on San Patricio. But there was no time to worry about any of that. The menace of Sampson and Rowland was much more pressing.

"Now, here's the way things are gonna go," Sampson continued. "All of ye are gonna leave here except for you, Crowe. Ye'll saddle two horses, and then Abner and me are ridin' away from here with the lady. Ye can find her later at the Catamount's Den, where she'll hold a meetin' of all her lieutenants and inform them that she's turnin' the business over to us."

"That will never happen," Simone told him coldly.

"'Tis the best deal ye'll ever get, lass. Otherwise we kill ye here and now."

"If you do, you'll never walk out of here alive."

"Then I reckon nobody'll get the business, but ye'll still be dead, won't ye?"

Simone looked at Crowe and said, "Don't do it, Balthazar. That's an order. Listen to me. You, too, Long Sam. And Preacher. Preacher, I have no right to ask anything of you, but please, all of you . . . don't allow these animals to get away with what they're trying to do."

Rowland said, "That's some high-and-mighty talk for a woman. Why don't you just go ahead and shoot her, Cap'n? I'm willin' to take my chances."

"No, lad. They're gonna give in," Sampson said. "They've no choice, no matter what this strumpet says." He added a particularly foul oath describing Simone.

Preacher expected the standoff to break one way or another, but when it did, the break came from an unlikely source.

In response to Sampson's obscenity, Colonel Osborne shouted, "Sir, I can stand no more!" and rushed Rowland.

Instead of firing, the tattooed man lashed out with the gun in his hand and slammed it against Osborne's head, sending the old man spinning off his feet. Sampson's eyes turned involuntarily in that direction

Sensing that his attention was diverted for a split second, Simone grabbed the barrel of his pistol and shoved it down. The gun went off with a roar, counterpointed by her cry of pain.

At the same time, Balthazar Crowe flung himself forward. Crossing the entrance hall in two bounds, he crashed into Sampson and jolted the pirate captain away from Simone, who crumpled to the floor as she clutched at her wounded leg.

Rowland swung the pistol toward Preacher, who drew back his arm and threw the cutlass. Rowland pulled the trigger and the pistol boomed as the cutlass buried itself in his chest with a solid *thunk!* The shot went high and wild, shattering a crystal chandelier hanging in the entrance hall.

As the broken crystal showered down, Rowland staggered to the side, dropped the empty pistol, and pawed at the cutlass. Blood poured from the wound as he pulled the blade free. He fell to his knees, and the cutlass clattered on the marble in front of him.

Preacher scooped it up again and rested the point against Rowland's bloody chest.

Rowland glared up at him and rasped, "You never did . . . beat me . . . hand to hand . . . in a fair fight."

Preacher said, "As long as you're dead, you sorry varmint, I don't much care how you got that way."

Then, as Rowland's eyes rolled up in their sockets and his final breath rattled in his throat, Preacher pushed him over backward with the cutlass. Rowland sprawled on the marble floor, limp in death.

Preacher turned to see Balthazar Crowe rising from a huddled shape that had been Jabez Sampson, whose head sat at a grotesquely unnatural angle on his shoulders. Preacher figured Crowe had come close to twisting it off before Sampson died.

Long Sam had already rushed to Simone's side. He knelt beside her and supported her head and shoulders as he cried, "Mam'selle! Mam'selle!"

"I . . . I'm all right, Long Sam," she told him. She was pale and shaken but composed. Her dress was bloody but not excessively so. "That shot . . . just grazed my leg. I'll be fine."

"Balthazar!" Long Sam called. "Come help me with the mam'selle!"

Knowing that Simone was in good hands for the moment, Preacher went over to Colonel Osborne and helped the old man to his feet.

Osborne had a bloody lump on his head from being clouted with Rowland's gun, but he said, "I'm all right, sir. I must help tend to Mademoiselle LeCarde."

Preacher let him do that and turned toward the stairs where Edmund Cornelius still lay gasping with Lucy Tarleton beside him. She glared defiantly at

Preacher, who stood over them still holding the bloody cutlass.

Cornelius was the one who spoke, though. "Go ahead . . . kill me. Avenge . . . your friend. Isn't that . . . what you want to do?"

"The thought crossed my mind," Preacher admitted. "But I've seen plenty of men gut-hurt like that, and not many of 'em survived. So I reckon you're done for, anyway, Cornelius. What I want to know is how you got shot."

Lucy answered that angrily. "He was trying to defend Mademoiselle LeCarde. He tried to fight off those horrible men when they came bursting in. Doesn't that count for anything?"

"He knifed my friend and left him for dead," Preacher said. "Doin' one good thing don't square up a lifetime of bein' a thief and a killer." The mountain man shrugged. "But I reckon it's that much on the other side of the scale. Don't really matter now anyway."

Lucy looked down at Cornelius's face and cried out. The life had gone out of the man's eyes.

"Preacher."

He heard Simone call his name and turned to see that Crowe had picked her up in his massive arms and was cradling her like a child.

"Preacher, I want to tell you . . . I regretted what I'd done, once you were gone. In my zeal to keep my secret, I . . . I went too far. I'm glad to see that you're alive. We have much to talk about, you and I, once all this"—wearily, she waved a hand at the carnage around them—"once all this is cleaned up."

Preacher just nodded. He didn't say anything as Crowe turned and carried Simone up the stairs, followed by Long Sam and Colonel Osborne.

Let her think what she wanted, he mused, but as far as he could see, the two of them didn't have a whole lot to say to each other.

St. Louis, ten days later

"Are you sure I can't convince you to come with me?" Charlie Todd asked. "Just for a visit? I'm sure my family would like to meet you."

Preacher smiled and shook his head. "No, if I'm gonna make it back to the mountains 'fore it gets too late in the season, I'd best get a move on."

"The next time you see Hawk, give him my best wishes."

"I sure will," Preacher promised.

Charlie looked a little gaunt. He had lost quite a bit of weight while he was recuperating from his injury, but his face was starting to fill out again and he had gotten some of his color back. By the time he reached his home in Virginia, he probably wouldn't be completely recovered, but he would be a lot closer.

The two of them stood on the dock next to where a riverboat was tied up. Soon, that boat would be heading downriver to New Orleans, and Charlie would be on it. Once he was there, he would board a ship that would take him through the Gulf of Mexico, around Florida, and eventually to Virginia.

Preacher hoped the vessel wouldn't run into any pirates along the way. Simone had promised him she would spread the word that whatever ship Charlie wound up taking was under her protection. Preacher figured that was the least she could do.

She had done more, though. The money in Charlie's poke came from her. She had paid it out of her own coffers, refusing to make Lucy Tarleton turn over what was left of the money she and Cornelius had stolen from Charlie.

Preacher thought back to their last conversation.

"She'll have a hard enough life from here on out, now that Cornelius is gone," Simone insisted. *"Girls like her always need some man to tell them what to do."*

"Just the opposite of you, eh?" Preacher asked as he sat with Simone in her quarters, sharing dinner with her.

"Are you worried that if you stay, I'll try to tell you what to do?" She laughed. *"Don't be, Preacher. That would never happen."*

"Whether it would or wouldn't don't make any difference. I'm a mountain man, and that's where I'm headed."

He told her everything that had happened on the Calypso *and in Cuba.*

She told him Chimney Matthews was the new captain of the sloop, but only until he took it back to Verdugo, where he and Tyler would remain, Chimney to live out the rest of his life in peace as he had dreamed of, Tyler to see if there truly was anything between himself and Estellita.

"I wish them both well," Preacher said.

Simone made the argument that she needed someone like him to make sure no one else in her organization ever tried to double-cross her again, but as far as he was concerned, that was her worry, not his.

"You have two very loyal and capable lieutenants in Balthazar Crowe and Long Sam," Preacher pointed out. *"There aren't many problems those two can't handle."*

Simone smiled at him over the glass of wine in her hand and asked, "Is there nothing I can do to make you change your mind? I can be very persuasive when I want to."

"Yeah, I recollect that," Preacher said as he got to his feet. "But it's time for me to go."

She stood up and came around the table to him, limping slightly on her wounded leg. She put her arms around him and murmured, "Take my memory with you when you go, then."

Watching Charlie board the riverboat, Preacher stood to wave good-bye to his young friend as the boat pulled away from the dock and its paddle wheel churned the waters of the Mississippi. He waited until it had gone out of sight before he turned and smiled at the sight of Horse and Dog waiting for him at the end of the dock.

He had taken Simone's memory with him, all right, along with the memory of the cat-o'-nine-tails biting into his flesh, the stink of the swamp, the gut-clenching revulsion of feeling a rattlesnake writhing on his shoulder, the terror of those gaping alligator jaws coming at him, and the sheer evil of Jabez Sampson and Abner Rowland. Preacher had found treachery and brutality in Louisiana and at sea, balanced somewhat by the friendship of Tyler, Chimney, Jean Paul Dufresne, Roger Flynn, and Estellita. No matter where a man went, he would find good and bad, and the best he could do was hope that in the end, the good would outweigh the bad.

One thing was for sure, he thought as he walked toward his four-legged trail partners and friends, getting back to the high country, seeing those snow-capped peaks, and breathing that clean mountain air would help.

*Keep reading for a special preview of the new
Smoke Jensen western epic!*

National Bestselling Authors
WILLIAM W. JOHNSTONE
and J. A. JOHNSTONE
BLOODY TRAIL OF THE MOUNTAIN MAN

If there's one thing Smoke Jensen hates, it's a man
who fights dirty. And no one fights dirtier than a
politician. Especially a lying, cheating, no-good
grifter like Senator Rex Underhill. Luckily, with
another election coming up, this senatorial snake
in the grass has some serious competition: Smoke's
old friend, Sheriff Monte Carson. Carson's an
honest man, and he's got Smoke's full support.
But Underhill's got support, too: a squad of
hired guns ready to hit the campaign trail—
and stain it red with blood . . .

Swapping bullets for ballots, Underhill's henchman
make it all too clear that Sheriff Carson is not just
a candidate on the rise, he's a target on the run. But
with Smoke's grassroots support—and lightning-
fast trigger—he manages to stay alive in the race.
That is, until Carson's righteous campaign takes a
near-fatal turn when the Senator Underhill tricks
his opponents, traps them in a mine, and literally
buries the sheriff's political ambitions. When the
going gets tough, Smoke gets even. When this
game turns deadly, it's winner kills all . . .

Look for **BLOODY TRAIL OF THE MOUNTAIN MAN,**
available where ever books are sold.

CHAPTER 1

Big Rock, Colorado

It had rained earlier in the day, and though the rain had stopped, the sky still hung heavy with clouds, as if heaven itself was in mourning. Phil Clinton, editor of the *Big Rock Journal,* made the observation that this was the largest number of citizens ever to turn out for a funeral in Big Rock, Colorado. The Garden of Memories cemetery was so full that the mourners spilled out of the grounds and onto Center and Ranney streets. The service had been held in the First Baptist Church, which shared the cemetery with St. Paul's Episcopal. And because of Sheriff Monte Carson's popularity, memorial rites were held in St. Paul's even as the funeral was being conducted in the Big Rock Baptist Church.

Father Pyron stood with the mourners, but it was the Reverend E. D. Owen who was conducting the burial service. Monte Carson, dressed in black, and with his head bowed, stood alongside the coffin of Ina Claire, his wife of the last fifteen years.

Sheriff Carson had invited Smoke and Sally Jensen, Pearlie Fontaine, and Cal Wood, all of whom were also wearing black, to stand with him next to the open grave. That was because the four represented the closest thing Monte had to a family.

It was quiet and still and Reverend Owen stood there for just a moment as if gathering his thoughts. In the distance a crow cawed, and closer yet, a mockingbird trilled.

The pastor began to speak.

"We have gathered here to praise God and to bear witness to our faith as we celebrate the life of Ina Claire Carson. We come together in grief, acknowledging our human loss. May God grant us grace, that in pain we may find comfort, in sorrow, hope, and in death, resurrection.

"Monte, we say to you in the midst of your sorrow and loss that we are grateful that your love for Ina Claire was such that we are all able to share in her quiet gentleness and firm resolve to live her life for you, and others. We take joy and relief in knowing that her suffering has ended, and now into the everlasting arms of an all-merciful God, we commit the soul of our beloved Ina Claire. Amen."

Reverend Owen nodded, and six of the leading citizens of Big Rock: Louis Longmont, Tim Murchison, Ed McKnight, Elmer Keaton, Mike Kennedy, and Joel Montgomery, using ropes, lowered Ina Claire into the grave. When the coffin reached the bottom, the ropes were withdrawn, then the six men stepped away. Reverend Owen nodded toward Monte, who stepped up to the open grave and dropped a handful of dirt, which, in the silence, could be heard falling upon the coffin.

"Ashes to ashes, dust to dust, in the sure and certain hope of eternal life," Reverend Owen said.

When Reverend Owen turned and walked away from the graveside, Sally stepped up to embrace Monte.

"We will miss her so," Sally said.

"Thank you, Sally," Monte replied, his voice thick with sorrow.

The funeral reception was held in the ballroom of the Dunn Hotel. Ina Claire had been an orphan and was without any family. She had been married and divorced before she met Monte, but her former husband had died several years ago. The funeral reception was organized by Sally and some of the other ladies in town.

"It's too bad none of Sheriff Carson's family could have been here," Mrs. Carmichael said.

"He doesn't have any family," Mrs. Owen said. "That's why Ina Claire's death is so sad. It has left him all alone."

"But I hear she was suffering terribly with something they call the cancer over the last month," Mrs. Carmichael said.

"Yes, she was. And now, mercifully, her suffering is over. In a way, Monte's suffering is over as well, as he suffered with her."

Smoke and Pearlie had been standing with Monte, but because Smoke thought that their standing together might prevent others from coming up to offer the sheriff their condolences, he put his hand on Monte's shoulder and squeezed.

"In case you need us for anything, Monte, we'll be right over here," Smoke said.

Monte nodded as Smoke and Pearlie walked away.

Smoke had poured himself a cup of coffee and was perusing a table strewn with various pastries when Phil Clinton, the editor of the local paper, stepped over to speak to him.

"You and the sheriff seem to be close friends," Clinton said.

"We are."

"You two have been friends for as long as I have been here. I'm curious. How did you two meet?"

Smoke chuckled as he chose a cinnamon bun. "He was hired to kill me," Smoke said, easily.

"What?" Clinton gasped.

"Once, there was a fella in these parts by the name of Tilden Franklin. He was a man of some importance who had plans to take over the county and he planned on using Pearlie and Monte Carson to help him.

"Then, when I came along and started my ranch, Franklin figured I was in the way. He told Monte and Pearlie that he wanted me killed. Neither one of them would go along with that, and the result was a battle between a lot of Franklin's men, Monte, Pearlie, and me.

"When it was over I offered Monte the job of sheriff here in Big Rock, hired Pearlie on as foreman of Sugarloaf, and those two, onetime enemies, have been my best friends ever since."

Smoke waited until he saw Monte and Sally standing together, then he walked over to join them.

"How are you holding up?"

"I've already been through this once before, Smoke,

when I lost my first wife. It isn't fair that I would have to go through it again."

"I can't argue with that, Monte."

"I know everyone is saying that Ina Claire is in a better place," Monte said. "And I know that she is, especially since she was in so much pain toward the end. The laudanum helped with the pain, but to be honest, it sort of took her away from me even before she died, if you know what I mean."

"I know," Smoke said. "And, Monte, I can fully relate to the pain you're going through now."

"Yes, you lost a wife and a child."

Smoke nodded. "Nicole and Arthur. Murdered." For just a moment the hurt Smoke was sharing with Monte became his own, as he recalled returning home to find his family dead. Smoke went on the blood trail, tracking down and killing the men who had so destroyed his life.

After that, Smoke didn't think he would ever be able to love again. But he met a beautiful and spirited young schoolteacher who changed his mind.

"I got over it once before," Monte said. "I can get over it this time as well."

"You will get over it, but don't force the memories of Ina Claire away too quickly," Sally said. Sally had been standing with the two men, listening to their conversation. "I know that there is a place in Smoke's heart where Nicole still lives. I'm not jealous of that, I love him for it, because it tells me how deeply Smoke can love. In fact, even though I never met Nichole, I can't help but think of her as my sister."

"It's funny you would say that, because Ina Claire once said that she thought of Rosemary as a sister. But you don't have to worry that I'll ever forget her,"

Monte said. He smiled. "I believe, with all my heart, that the thunderstorm we had earlier this morning was just her talking to me. Lord, that woman did love thunderstorms for some ungodly reason."

Sally laughed. "I remember that a thunderstorm came up during yours and Ina Claire's wedding reception. We had it out at Sugarloaf and I told her I was sorry that the reception might be spoiled by the storm, but she said, *'No, I love it! It's just God applauding the fact that Monte and I were married.'* For a long time I thought she had just said that so I wouldn't feel bad about the storm."

Monte chuckled as well. "No, she actually believed that. She told me the same thing."

Sally embraced Monte. "Anytime you feel the need for company, you are always welcome at Sugarloaf."

"Thank you, Sally. With friends like Smoke, you, Pearlie, and Cal, I'll get through this."

The obituary in *the Big Rock Journal* the next day was accorded the honor of appearing on the front page of the paper.

INA CLAIRE CARSON

INA CLAIRE CARSON, 36, wife of Sheriff Monte J. Carson, died yesterday after a long battle with the terrible disease of cancer.

Mrs. Carson was raised in the Baptist Orphanage in Jackson, Mississippi. Because she was left there as an infant by persons unknown, she was without family, save her husband, Sheriff Carson.

Although Mrs. Carson was without family, she certainly wasn't without friends. Kirby Jensen, better known to his friends as Smoke Jensen, was there with his lovely wife, Sally. Smoke, Sally, and Smoke's two longtime friends and employees, Wes (Pearlie) Fontaine and Cal Wood, were accorded family positions at both the church and graveside funeral services.

Mrs. Carson was well known and well loved by all the citizens of Big Rock. She was especially renowned for her oatmeal cookies, which she graciously baked for all the prisoners in the Big Rock jail.

Although the atmosphere in Longmont's Saloon was never boisterous, it was generally happy and upbeat. Not so today, as even the patrons who had not attended the funeral on the day before, were quiet and respectful. That was because Monte was in the saloon, as were Smoke, Cal, and Pearlie. Louis Longmont, who owned the saloon, had just read the obituary.

"This is a very nice article about Ina Claire," Louis said. "You and she have been such a wonderful part of our community. I know it will be hard for you, but I also know that you will carry on, providing the steadying influence that will keep Big Rock the fine town it is."

"I have no doubt about it," Mark Worley said. For some time Worley had been Monte's deputy, but six months ago the town of Wheeler was in need of a city marshal, and they sent a delegation to talk to Monte about Mark. Monte gave him the glowing recommendation that got him hired. So far, Monte had not taken on a new deputy. Mark had come to town for the funeral and had stayed an extra day.

"How are you liking it over in Wheeler?" Pearlie asked.

"It's been great," Mark replied. "Oh, I miss all my friends over here, but I've made new friends, and I really like being in charge. Not that I minded deputing for Monte, you understand, but it is good to be the top dog."

Pearlie laughed. "Yeah, well, just don't let it go to your head. You always did think a lot of yourself."

Pearlie was teasing. Actually, he and Mark were good friends.

"I should get another deputy, I suppose," Monte said. "But to be honest, searching for another deputy hasn't been the most important thing in my mind for the last few months."

"Take your time in looking for one," Smoke said. "It isn't like you can't make an instant deputy if there is a sudden need for one."

Monte nodded. "Yeah, that's the way I see it. You, Pearlie, and Cal have helped me out more than once. And I appreciate that, because it means I can afford to be choosy."

"Speaking of deputies, and sheriffs, and all that, I'd better get back to Wheeler and my never-ending battle of fighting crime and/or evil," Mark said with a laugh.

"Thanks for coming over, Mark. I appreciate that," Monte said.

"Smoke, we should get going, too," Pearlie said. "We've got a lot of calves we have to gather."

For a while Sugarloaf had abandoned cattle and

raised horses only. But when Smoke's friend Duff MacCallister had introduced him to Black Angus cattle, Smoke had gone back into the cattle business. Angus were a little more difficult to raise than long-horns, but they were many times more profitable.

"What did you say?" Smoke asked.

"I said we needed to get back to the ranch. We have work to do."

Smoke looked at the others and smiled. "Would you listen to this man, telling me *we* have work to do?

"Pearlie, maybe you don't understand, you are the foreman of Sugarloaf, but I am the owner. Do I need to tell you who is in charge?"

Although Smoke spoke the words harshly, he ended his sentence with a laugh to show that he was teasing.

"We need to get back to the ranch, we have work to do," Smoke added.

"The boss man is right," Pearlie said to the others. "We need to go."

Shortly after Mark, Smoke, and Pearlie left, Monte told Louis good-bye, and walked down to his office. There was nobody in jail at the moment, and because he was without a deputy, he was all alone.

He was unable to hold back the tears.

CHAPTER 2

Capitol Hill, Denver, Colorado

State Senator Rex Underhill's house sat but a few blocks from where the new capitol building was to be built. His Victorian house was large with wings and bay windows and gingerbread decorating features. He built the eight-bedroom house in the most elegant part of Denver merely for show. It was a gaudy display of ostentation, especially since, except for his servants, he lived alone in the house.

After Senator Underhill finished reading the obituary of Ina Claire Carson in the Denver newspaper, he laid it beside his now-empty breakfast plate.

He thought of the names he had just read; Monte Carson, Smoke Jensen, Pearlie Fontaine, Cal Woods. It was too bad that the obituary was not for one of them. It would be even better, if it could be for all of them.

"Another cup of coffee, Señor Underhill?" The question snapped Underhill out of his reverie.

"Frederica, I have told you to call me *Senator* Underhill."

"*Sí, señor*, uh, *sí*, Senator. Sometimes I forget," Frederica said.

"You are forgetting too many times, and if you don't start remembering, I'll let you and Ramon go and hire some new domestics, perhaps Americans who understand the language so I won't have to keep repeating things."

"I will not forget again, Señor Senator."

Frederica was a plump woman whose dark hair was now liberally laced with gray. Her husband, Ramon, took care of the lawn, and his hair was all white.

"Are you going to stand there gabbing, or are you going to pour me another cup of coffee?" Underhill asked.

"Coffee, *sí*," Frederica said as she poured a dark, aromatic stream of liquid into the cup.

Senator Underhill eased his harsh admonition with a smile. "What would I do if I let you go, Frederica? Where else would I find someone who could make coffee as good as yours?"

"*Sí*, Señor Senator, nowhere else will you find coffee this good," Frederica said with a relieved smile.

Underhill took his coffee out onto the front porch and sat in a rocking chair to watch the vehicles roll by. Here, in Capitol Hill, nearly all the vehicles were elegant coaches, fine carriages, or attractive surreys, for only the wealthy lived in this part of town.

Rex Underhill hadn't always been wealthy. His father had been a sharecropper barely scratching out a living in Arkansas, and even that was gone after the war. When Underhill left home nobody tried to talk him into staying, because his departure just meant one less mouth to feed.

Underhill survived by a few nighttime burglaries here and there, then he graduated to armed robberies. He robbed a stagecoach in Kansas, killing the driver, the shotgun guard, and a passenger. Because he left not a single witness, he was never regarded as a suspect for the crime. He got twelve thousand dollars from that holdup, and he moved on to Colorado, where he became the secret partner of a couple of men—Deekus Templeton and Lucien Garneau—in a scheme to take over most of the ranch land in Eagle County. It was a plan that, on the surface, had failed, miserably.

Underhill glanced at the paper again. He had read the obituary because it was about the wife of Monte Carson. Carson was the sheriff of Eagle County. Eagle County was also the locale of the Sugarloaf Ranch and Smoke Jensen. Smoke Jensen was the biggest reason for the failure of the grand plan to own all of Eagle County.

Underhill was fortunate, however. The principals in the attempt to take over Eagle County were all killed. Underhill survived the plan because nobody knew that he had been involved. Also, he had not only been Deekus Templeton's and Lucien Garneau's secret partner, he had also been their banker, providing some operating funds in the beginning, but holding on to the money from a couple of bank robberies that neither Templeton nor Garneau could afford to deposit in a bank. When the two men died, Underhill profited from their deaths, immediately becoming over forty thousand dollars richer.

That was the money he had used to begin his political campaign. He was a state senator now, an office that put him in a position to take advantage of the many opportunities for enrichment that came his way.

Lately, Rex Underhill had been contemplating another political move, one that would greatly increase his chances to capitalize on his political position. He sold influence now as a state solon. How much more valuable would be the influence of a United States senator?

Rock Creek, near Big Rock

Just under one hundred miles west of where Rex Underhill was having his breakfast, six men were staring into a campfire, having just finished their own. They were camped on Rock Creek at the foot of Red and White Butte, about five miles north of Big Rock.

A little earlier that morning the leader of the group, Myron Petro, had proposed a job he thought they should do.

"It'll be like takin' money from a baby," Myron said. The men to whom he was pitching his idea were his brother Frank, Muley Dobbs, Ethan Reese, Wally Peach, and Leo Beaujuex. All of the men were experienced outlaws except for Beaujuex, who was the youngest of the lot.

"I don't know how you ever got the idea that robbin' a bank in Big Rock is goin' to be easy," Wally Peach said. "There ain't no way it's goin' to be easy on account of Monte Carson is the sheriff there, 'n he sure ain't easy. Hell, he's one of the toughest sheriffs there is anywhere."

Myron grinned. "Sheriff Carson ain't goin' to be no problem at all 'cause, case you don't know nothin' about it, his wife just died. That means he's so all broke up about it that he can't hardly do his job no more."

"I ain't never seen this Sheriff Carson feller but I've sure heard of 'im," Muley Dobbs said. "'N what I've heard is the same thing what Wally just said. Sheriff Carson's s'posed to be one tough son of a bitch. So, how is it that you know his wife died?"

"I heard talk of it yesterday when I was in Red Cliff."

"Yeah, well, I wish they was some way we could be sure," Muley said.

"All right, s'pose you 'n Beajuex go into town 'n have a look around?" Myron suggested. "You could maybe scout the bank whilst you was there, too."

"Nah, don't send the kid," Frank said. "He wouldn't have no idea what the hell he would be lookin' for. I'll go."

"All right, tomorrow you 'n Muley go into Big Rock, have a look around town, then come back 'n tell me what you've found out. We'll hit the bank day after tomorrow."

That night, as the six men bedded down around the dying campfire that had cooked their supper, they talked excitedly about the money they would soon have.

Leo Beajuex listened, but didn't join the conversation. He had never done anything like this before and he was very apprehensive about it. He wasn't going to run out on them—these men were the closest thing to a family he had. He had met them six months earlier, when he was supporting himself as a cowboy on the Bar S Ranch down in Bexar County, Texas.

Actually, saying that he was a cowboy would be a considerable overstatement of his real position. Ron Stacy, owner of the Bar S was a tyrannical boss, especially to someone who was a menial laborer, as Leo was. Whereas the cowboys got thirty dollars a month and found, Leo was paid fifteen dollars. He got the worst jobs on the ranch, and Stacy wasn't averse to physical abuse.

It all came to a head one day when Stacy took a leather strap to Leo because he hadn't cleaned a stall. As it turned out, he had cleaned it, the mess was from a horse that had just been moved into the stall.

Deciding that he had had enough, it was Leo's plan to steal a couple of cows and sell them for just enough money to help him get away. However, while he was in the act of cutting them out, he saw the Petro brothers and the other three men doing the same thing but on a larger scale.

"Boy, if you got 'ny idea of tellin' anyone what we're a-doin' here, we'll shoot you dead," Myron Petro warned.

"Why would I want to tell anyone?" Leo replied. "I'd rather join you."

They rustled forty-nine cows and sold them for twenty-five dollars apiece. That gave them a little over two hundred dollars each, which, for Leo, was more than a year's wages.

There had been a few other, small jobs. They got a hundred and fifty dollars from a stagecoach holdup, and eight hundred dollars from some stolen mules.

So far, at least since Leo had been with them, there had been no shooting. But when the subject came up this afternoon, Frank said that if they had to, they would kill anyone in the bank, as well as anyone on the street who tried to stop them.

Although Leo had come close, he had never killed

anyone, and he hoped that nobody would be killed as a result of the job they were planning now.

As the campfire burned down, a little bubble of gas, trapped in one of the burning pieces of wood, made a loud pop and emitted a little flurry of sparks. Leo watched the golden specks as they rode the rising shaft of heated air into the night sky, there to join with the wide spread of stars.

He wondered what would happen in two more days.

Big Rock

The next day Frank Petro and Muley Dobbs rode into town. Even at an easy pace, the ride into town took less than an hour.

"Lookee there," Frank said, pointing to some of the shops and businesses they were passing. "All them buildings has black ribbons on 'em, so that means for sure that somebody died."

"Yeah, but it don't mean for sure that it was the sheriff's wife what died, without we hear someone say it," Muley said. "'N the best place to hear it said is in a saloon, just like this one."

They were just passing the saloon as Muley pointed it out.

"Longmont's," Frank said, reading the sign. "I don't know, it looks a bit fancy for the likes of us."

"The fancier it is, the easier it is to find out information. Besides I'm a mite thirsty, aren't you?"

"A beer would be good," Frank agreed."

"No, I don't know, Muley, I've seen you play poker before. More times than not, somethin' gets your dander up, then you go off half-cocked 'n wind up in trouble. We most especial don't want no trouble today, that's for damn sure."

"You don't worry none 'bout me playin' poker. That's a good place to find things out. You just stand up there at the bar, drink your beer, 'n keep your eyes 'n ears open," Muley said. "If you hear somethin' that don't sound right, let me know."

The two men stepped inside, then looked around.

"Whooee, I sure ain't never seen no saloon this fancy before," Frank said.

The long bar that ran down the left side of the saloon was more than just gleaming mahogany. The front of the bar was intricately carved to show a bas-relief of cowboys herding cattle. The hanging overhead lights weren't wagon wheels and coal oil lanterns as was often the case, but cut crystal chandeliers.

"There's a card game," Muley said, pointing to a table where a game was in progress.

"Muley, be careful. Don't go gettin' yourself into no trouble," Frank cautioned.

With a nod as his only response, Muley walked over to the table. "You fellers willin' to take on a fifth player?"

"No need for five players, you can have my seat," one of the players said. "I need to be gettin' along anyhow."

"The name is Muley," the big scruffy-looking man said as he took the chair just vacated.

A short while after Frank and Muley rode into Big Rock, Smoke and Sally came into town. Sally could ride as well as any man, but they came in a buckboard because Sally wanted to do some shopping and it would be easier to take the purchases back in a buckboard than on horseback. They drove in from the west, following Sugarloaf Road until they passed the depot and Western Union, at which place Sugarloaf Road turned into Front Street. As had Frank and Muley before them, Smoke and Sally noticed that many of the buildings on Front Street had a black ribbon on the door.

"That's nice of them to honor Monte in such a way," Sally said.

"You aren't surprised, are you, Sally? Monte is a popular sheriff and Ina Claire was well liked," Smoke said.

"*Well loved* is a better description."

"I'll go along with that," Smoke said as he parked the buckboard in front of the Big Rock Mercantile.

"I'll be in Longmont's when you're ready to go back home," Smoke said as he tied off the team.

"Really? And here I thought I might find you in the library," Sally teased.

"Sally, has anyone ever told you that sarcasm doesn't become you?" Smoke asked with a little chuckle.

"You mean besides my mother and father and all four of my grandparents? Oh yes, you have as well."

Sally kissed Smoke on the cheek, then started toward the store, as Smoke crossed the street to get to the saloon.

Owner and proprietor of the saloon was Louis Longmont, a Frenchman from New Orleans, who was quick to point out that he was truly French and not Cajun. The difference, he explained to those who questioned him, was that his parents moved to Louisiana directly from France, and not from Acadia.

Longmont's was one of two saloons in Big Rock, the other saloon being the Brown Dirt Cowboy Saloon.

The Brown Dirt Cowboy tended to cater more to cowboys and workingmen than it did to professional men, storekeepers, and ranch owners. The Brown Dirt Cowboy provided not only alcoholic beverages and a limited menu, but also bar girls who did more than just provide friendly conversational company for the drinking man.

Longmont's, on the other hand, was more like a club in which ladies were not only allowed, they were made to feel welcome, and assured there would be no stigma to their frequenting the establishment. It also had a menu that could compete with the menu offered by Delmonico's Restaurant, which was just down the street from Longmont's.

Like the other business establishments along Front Street, Longmont's had a black ribbon on the door.

Stepping into the saloon Smoke stood just inside the door for a moment to peruse the patrons.

There were seven men standing at the bar, only one of whom he had never seen before. Three of the tables had customers, and two of the girls were standing near two of the tables, having a smiling conversation with the drinkers. Smoke knew both Becky and Julie and he exchanged a nod with them. He also knew the seated drinkers. There was a poker game going on at the third table, and here Smoke recognized three of the men. Two were cowboys from a nearby ranch, and the third was Mike Kennedy. He didn't know who the fourth man was, but there was something about him that gave Smoke a sense of unease.

In addition to those three tables, there was a fourth table. This was Louis Longmont's special table, so designated because nobody but Louis ever sat there unless they were personally invited by Louis.

The pianist was playing, not one of the typical saloon ballads, but a piece by the Polish composer Frédéric Chopin. This kind of music would never be allowed in most other saloons, but it had become a signature for Longmont's.

Tim Murchison, owner of Murchison's Leather Goods, was sitting at the table with Louis, and Smoke, without being invited because Louis had once told him that his invitation was permanent, joined them.